Praise for *The Whaler*

MW01615571

"The author uses his unique un current plight of the Northwest Coastal Indians to create a novel depicting the clash and ultimate acceptance of two societies trying to subsist in one environment. His vast knowledge of the geography of the region makes the sea and the islands active characters in the narrative.

"The tension between Alana, the white lawyer, researching a 40-year-old disappearance and Quanah, the half-breed whaling captain, trying to reconcile his 'Indian-ness' comes to a compelling and satisfying completion as the two cultures mesh in a thought-provoking climax." —Virgina Walters, Columnist, *Peninsula Clarion*, Kenai Alaska

"Mahlon Kriebel's work is sensitive to Native people's struggles and culture, is as close to historical fact as possible, and yet has the creativity of an artist writer to make it an interesting addition for all readers.

"The author has had the patience and humbleness to endear himself to the Native communities with whom he interacts." —Scott Tyler, MD, Makah Tribal member

"I am not a fan of killing whales, but Kriebel (and Quanah) put the Makah practice into meaningful cultural context. And the description of the process of the hunt reflects the depth of the research done by Kriebel (thus, by Quanah). Apparently, such research was not done by even some modern Makah Indians, as their most recent actual whale hunt was bungled by relying on a 50 caliber rifle rather than a harpoon.

"Kriebel gives a meaningful explanation of the 'circle of life' - not as musical as in Disney's Lion King, but much deeper and more spiritual. He gives us an insightful look into the parallelism (and differences) between cultures; not only generally White vs. Indian, but also quite specifically (and perhaps unexpected) German vs. Indian.

"Kriebel's book is meticulously researched and well written; it offers a very pleasurable read and a rewarding learning experience." — Oliver Brown, Ph.D

"We found *The Whaler and the Girl in the Deadfall* to be a fine blending of environmental Indian knowledge, conflicting White man's laws and subtle romance." —Bruce and Judith Billings, two avid readers

i

"The village of Neah Bay is covered by tumbling, heavy clouds, bursting with moisture. Quanah watches sheet lightning release a downpour, closing the harbor from the Strait of Juan de Fuca. He ignores these ominous signs....

"So begins the first of numerous encounters in the Pacific Northwest and beyond that transport readers into mysterious worlds where water meets land amidst tensions past and present. The characters inhabiting Mahlon Kriebel's novel bring into focus the dramatic contrast between 21st century federal law and wider societal norms with the ancient whale hunting traditions of the native coastal Makah people. Environmental lawyer-activist Alana Svoboda takes up the case of the young Makah whaler, Quanah, and his crew in an adventure that affirms the abiding values of friendship, commitment, and tradition." — Richard D. Scheuerman, Ph.D. Author with C. E. Trafzer of *Renegade Tribe* and with M. O. Finley, *Finding Chief Kamiakin*

"*The Whaler And The Girl In The Deadfall* is a well written and thoroughly researched tale of cultural history, loss and contemporary issues. Mr. Kriebel's characters are complex and believable. This book underscores how tragic cultural loss can be to Tribal identity. The cultural clashes are factual in the presentation of differing perspectives. I highly recommend this book for anyone who desires to look further into the dynamics of cultural practices and preservation."
—Jayne Singleton, Director, Spokane Valley Heritage Museum

"The Native Americans' experience was and still is, although to a lesser extent, miserable. The author's presentation of their attitudes towards the white man is convincing and informative.

"The discussions of brain function, self-awareness, and consciousness are perhaps a bit much for the lay reader. However, it's okay that a lot of the issues are not yet resolved. And it is socially useful to inform the reader that along with the progress, there remains uncertainty and ambiguity." —Michael V. L. Bennett, D. Phil. Distinguished Professor of Neuroscience, Albert Einstein College of Medicine.

"A wise and passionate homage to traditional whaling and its importance to Native American cultural identity. Beautifully written, strikingly illustrated, and deeply researched, Kriebel's novel provides an enlightened perspective on conquest and assimilation, bringing ancient practices alive with dramatic storytelling and a keen eye for natural history. Impressive in scope, the book is an artful melding of the past, present, and the uncertain future of a proud people clinging tenuously to their land, their language, and their way of life." —Buddy Levy, bestselling author of *Labyrinth of Ice: The Triumphant and Tragic Greely Expedition*

"The author's dedication to careful research and vast knowledge shine through in this tale of cultural reconciliation. As an outsider in Quanah's world of the Makah Indian, it is Kriebel's painstaking investigation and attention to detail, which immediately win the reader's trust. Although compelling as a work of fiction, his devotion to objectivity, along with the precise, direct language, creates a novel that reads like some of the best nonfiction and literary journalism of our time." —Larry N. Mayer, author of *"Who Will Say Kaddish?: a Search for Jewish Identity in Contemporary Poland"* (Syracuse University Press)

"In sum, a powerful story of coastal Indian heritage, of hardships and prejudice, of whales and the sea, of resilience and determination, of outreach and hope for the future. An important story that will stand the test of time." —Alex McGregor, Ph.D, author of *Counting Sheep*

THE WHALER AND THE GIRL IN THE DEADFALL

a novel

Mahlon E. Kriebel

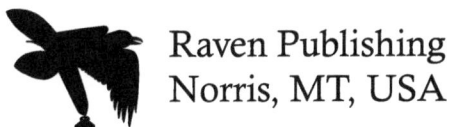

Raven Publishing
Norris, MT, USA

THE WHALER AND THE GIRL IN THE DEADFALL
ISBN: 978-1-937849-56-6
Copyright © 2019 by Mahlon E. Kriebel
Cover art: copyright © 2019 by Amrita Stützle

Published by Raven Publishing, Inc. P.O. Box 2866, Norris, MT
www.ravenpublishing.net

Library of Congress Cataloging-in-Publication Data

Names: Kriebel, Mahlon E., author.
Title: The whaler and the girl in the deadfall : a novel / Mahlon Kriebel.
Description: Norris, MT : Raven Publishing, 2019. | Includes bibliographical references and index.
Identifiers: LCCN 2019018266 (print) | LCCN 2019019071 (ebook) | ISBN 9781937849573 (ebook) | ISBN 9781937849566 (trade paper : alk. paper)
Subjects: LCSH: Indians of North America--Washington (State)--Fiction. | Whaling--Fiction. | Whales--Fiction. | Missing persons--Fiction. | GSAFD:
Suspense fiction
Classification: LCC PS3611.R495 (ebook) | LCC PS3611.R495 W53 2019 (print) |
DDC 813/.6--dc23
LC record available at https://lccn.loc.gov/2019018266

Author's Note

I began following Makah whaling in 1998 and, even though a hunter, I was initially appalled by the act of shooting a whale in 1999.

Revulsion was my reaction because I knew so little about the Makah Indian culture. According to news media, the whalers shot the whale with a .50 caliber rifle, and Native Americans celebrated by dancing on the whale carcass which did not present Indian culture in a positive light. During visits to the Makah cultural museum in Neah Bay—which houses artifacts found in a village preserved in a mud slide 500 years ago—I learned the Indian viewpoint. Their relationship to nature is based on the concept that all things, living and inanimate, are incorporated into a circle of life and that Makah don't kill the spirit of an animal that they 'take.' By contrast people of Euro based religions attempt to subjugate nature and believe that only man has a soul. I learned that the US Federal-Makah treaty of 1855 guarantees that the Makah can whale in perpetuity and the 1834 Supreme Court Rulings of Chief Justice John Marshall explain that treaties must be upheld by the United States Government. These judgments and the Boldt decision of 1974, handed down in Tacoma, which gives half the salmon catch to Indians, are some of the reasons for present day cultural conflicts.

The reader will notice that there are many images, and, might ask why so many? The Makah culture and history as well as that of all coastal Indians are extremely rich. My novel plays in the shadow of history. The shadow is pervasive and even suffocating. I hope the images capture the ephemeral space from which my modern characters and themes emerge. Tourist totem poles, cigar Indians, drums, masks and items exhibited on dusty museum shelves, I think, present an incorrect vision of the modern Indian because Indian cultures are not extinct. David Treuer in *The Heartbeat of Wounded Knee* writes that the Native American has survived and is flourishing! The Indian has not disappeared as Dee Brown predicted in

Bury My Heart at Wounded Knee fifty years ago. However, conflicts between Indians and whites are still present, and each tribe has its own set of problems. Most whites believe the Indian tribes are rich beyond imagination from casino gold and that Native Americans pay no income tax. There is also the pervasive white notion that the federal government hands out enormous sums of guilt money and that the Indian should be content to have received large tracts of United States of America land for their reservations, when, in fact, the Indians signed away most of their land by treaties with the hope of retaining a small piece in the form of a reservation. In this novel, I focus on one tribe with one very contentious problem which ignites vitriolic debate. The Makah tribe wishes to take Whale as their ancestors hunted Whale because Whale is central in their culture.

In regards to the Makah Indians, the photographs of Edward and Ashmel Curtis, made in the early 1900s, present an in depth view of Makah Indian culture based on Whale. Curtis images of the distribution of Whale demonstrate the importance of Whale to the Makah. Edward Curtis also took photos and made a movie of the Kwakwaka'wakw (Kwakiutl) band living at Alert Bay, Vancouver Island, B.C. The movie was released in 1913 with the title *In the Land of the Head Hunters* (silent) and was re-released in 1972 with the title *In the Land of the War Canoes* (voice overlay). This movie was written, acted by, costumes designed and made by the Kwakiutl tribe. A Kwakiutl directed the action and Curtis operated the camera.

The characters in this novel as well as the three court scenes are fiction. However, places, history, judges, congressional personages, court rulings, and natural history are real. As a white man, it is impossible to put myself into the Indian persona. I can only imagine the pain of defeat while defending one's homeland which presses into the soul of a human being. Father Joset wrote to his superior—after the Plateau Indian Battles of 1858—that he knows the Coeur d'Alene language, knows much of their culture, works with Indians to plant fields of wheat, they built the mission (now named Cataldo, Idaho) to embrace Catholicism (half the tribe), he tends to issues of heart but does not know the soul of his congregation. Today, much that I have read about Father Joset applies to me and humbles me. I am on a learning curve. I ask that my Indian friends accept my apologies for not portraying their hurts, despair, and rage as only an Indian can express. The scope of genocide—forced marches of removal from ancestor lands to foreign lands, child theft, broken treaties, starvation, slaughtering entire villages by state militias and federal armies—paints a vivid holocaust that most whites and the United States Government have neither accepted nor acknowledged.

THE WHALER AND THE GIRL IN THE DEADFALL
Table of Contents

For my wife, Moni

CHAPTER 1

Neah Bay - Western Tip of Continental United States

The village of Neah Bay is covered by tumbling, heavy clouds, bursting with moisture. Quanah watches sheet lightning release a downpour, closing the harbor from the Strait of Juan de Fuca. He ignores these ominous signs thinking, *I need to motor to Tatoosh Island before I drive back to Seattle for midterm exams. The gray whale migration has started. This is my one chance to document their route around the cape.* He pulls on his pants and the blue sweater he tore yesterday. He quietly pulls his door shut.

Stooping in front of the hall mirror to retie his blond hair into a warrior bun, he remembers his father using the same mirror without the need to stoop. *Dad was short like grandfather, but really strong.* Wishing he looked more like them with their stocky build and small noses, he sighs and takes his shoes from the hallway shoe rack to put on in the porch. He hears his mother rustling around in the kitchen.

She calls when she hears the door to the porch open, "Quanah, don't leave, I've started breakfast. Why are you up so early?"

As Quanah enters the small, tidy kitchen, he answers, "Good morning, Mom. I thought I'd take Dad's boat out, and I want to get an early start."

As Monika takes eggs from the refrigerator, she addresses her son with a worried look, "Please take your sweater off. I'll make breakfast. Are you going in the strait or staying in the harbor?"

"I had the engine running yesterday, and if it starts, I'll run out to Tatoosh Island," Quanah replies with a reassuring voice.

As Monika breaks eggs, she looks toward her son. "I wish you wouldn't go. Tatoosh is where your uncle Micah disappeared. You know that! I watched from the tribal trail winding around the Cape, and your dad motored around the Island for days looking for his boat. We found no sign of your uncle or his boat."

Noticing worry lines around his mom's pale blue eyes, Quanah softly replies, "I know the channel. It's easy to navigate."

Intent on not burning the bacon, Monika brushes a few strands of graying blond hair from her forehead and sighs, "It worried me sick when your dad took you out. I never interfered because I trusted him. And, he let me run the household. That's why we got along. Nevertheless, the ocean worries me. What if the engine quits? I know your dad wasn't able to get it repaired because there were not many salmon the last few years." Frowning, Monika softly adds, "He didn't even make gas money."

"Mom, don't worry."

"I can't help it. I know the boat isn't coast-guard certified," she says, shaking her head to toss the errant wisps of hair back into place.

"Mom, I'm working on the boat, not using it commercially. The guard doesn't care."

"Well, I care," Monika says in a stern voice. "I thought you needed to relax a few days. Are you satisfied with your courses at the marine laboratories?"

"Yeah."

2

Placing a frittata on the table, Monika rests her hand on her son's shoulder and teases, "Are you staying away from girls?"

"Come on, Mom, be serious," Quanah says and laughs. His eyes sparkle remembering how his mom chided him in high school about girls.

Taking the blue sweater from Quanah's lap Monika says, "I am serious. This sweater matches your eyes, but it has a hole. You can't wear it until I mend it."

Returning from her kitchen work table, she places a sweater around her son's shoulders commanding, "Wear this gray one."

"Mom, at the docks no one cares."

"Well, I care how you look. No son of mine is going to wear torn or dirty clothing."

"OK, Mom, I'll change, but then I'll attract girls."

"Haha," Monika scoffs.

She looks out toward the harbor. "Please don't take the boat out of the harbor. The forecast is terrible. High winds and rain. Why is it so important to go out today?" She demands.

"If Tatoosh Island is socked in, I promise to turn back."

"You didn't answer my question." After a pause she continues, "Why is Tatoosh Island so important?"

Finishing his frittata Quanah gets up from the table and hugs his mother, "Mom, you sure know how to prepare eggs and bacon. And, your blackberry jam on biscuits is terrific."

"Flattery will not help. Why go to the Island today?"

"Gray whales are migrating from Baja to the Bering Sea. I need to study them. The migration will be over in a couple of months."

"Quanah, I thought you were studying killer whales?"

"I am. Killer whales are following pods of gray whales. The interactions between gray and killer whales are part of my study."

Hugging her son and realizing she can't dissuade him, Monika relents, "When your mind is made up, you're just like your dad. Greg was so proud when the tribe harvested a gray whale a few years back. He wanted to take part, but was too old."

"Dad told me his grandfather whaled. He was a chief. That

made Dad a chief."

"It makes you a chief too." Monika eyes him suspiciously and asks, "Are you planning to whale?"

"Mom, what makes you think that?"

"Charlene at the museum told me you asked to see the harpoons and other whaling stuff kept in storage. She saw you take measurements of the whaling canoe and whale skeleton. She also said you were looking at archival photos of whaling scenes." After a pause Monika continues, "You are planning to whale. You don't have tribal permission, do you?"

Using his newly acquired academic voice, Quanah lectures, "I know the gray whale isn't endangered anymore. I want to whale to honor our ancestors. They harvested many whales, rendered fat, and traded trane oil with coastal and plains Indians."

Monika sternly replies, "Quanah, you know it's illegal to hunt whales. The crew that killed a whale a couple years ago without permits landed in jail. You will be arrested and will lose your scholarship at the university."

"Mom, I know the arguments against whaling. The federal government hasn't lived up to our treaty rights. The treaty states we can catch the whale forever. Our ancestors did not fight the United States army. They signed over most of our land to prevent bloodshed. The government promised to provide medical care and other support. The Feds are the bad guys because they have always failed to keep their end of the treaty."

Monika signs, "I know the history. Your dad lived in the past."

Her son continues to lecture, "What is our future? The salmon have disappeared, so we have little commercial and sports fishing. We have no casino. Tourism for whale watching hasn't happened. Even though six *dentalium* tooth shells were worth a slave a hundred years ago, we have forgotten how to catch the shells."

Monika replies, "Shells, haha, Whiteman's beads ruined the shell trade." Monika rubs her son's cheek saying, "I love your humor, use more of it."

Quanah grimaces and pulls away, "Mom, don't laugh, this is

serious. You know our culture is based on whaling. We need to re-instate whaling for our identity."

Monika moves toward her son, sternly addressing him, "Qua-nah, I know this position. Whaling today isn't relevant. Think about your future. Please, stay in the harbor."

"You know I grew up on Dad's boat. I know all the channels. Dad taught me all the rock formations that make eddies which tum-ble bait fish about to be easy prey for ling cod. You know he showed me how to fish the ling. Ling cod are a favorite at Pikes Fish Market in Seattle. Maybe I can bring one home today."

Pinching her son's check, Monika whispers in his ear, "Just bring yourself home."

As Quanah leaves the house, his mother presses a lunch into his hand. He walks the half mile to the tribal dock and climbs aboard his dad's boat. He presses the starter button. Reluctantly, the engine turns over, and sputters, only to refuse his plaintive, "Ah, come on."

Rummaging through stuff tossed atop the dash board and piled into cabin cubby holes Quanah mutters, "I knew Dad would have a can of starter fluid." He tilts the motor cover from the inboard, pulls the air filter, and directs a spray into the carburetor. He replaces the filter and hits the starter. There is an immediate belch, and the engine springs to life—a wonder, as the battery is essentially dead. Swinging the cover back, he admonishes himself, "I should've cleaned the carburetor yesterday and connected the trickle charger to the battery."

Quanah slides the lines from the dock cleats, pushes off, and engages the clutch. It is eight in the morning. Heavy fog tumbles over Bahakas Peak from the west and billowing upward over Neah Bay smacks against an opposing air stream, leaving the harbor clear. The young man motors past the United States Coast Guard Station that anchors the south shore to the harbor entrance, where a small-craft warning flag is whipping its tether.

"I should turn back," he mutters to his boat, "But, I know these waters." Like his dad, he ignores the warning flag. His tribe had not asked the United States Government to occupy this piece of land for a guard station. Quanah's dad, Greg, often groused when passing the guard station, "We have survived since the beginning of time without government intervention."

Leaving the harbor, Quanah turns westerly into the Strait of Juan de Fuca, which separates Washington State from Vancouver Island, Canada. There is a low ceiling, but the strait is clear. "OK, Mom, I can see Vancouver Island, so I'm going to Tatoosh." He knows that visibility can change instantly, but the purring engine and the three-quarters full gas tank override all caution. He says to his boat, "The battery will be charged by the time I reach Tatoosh Island."

Quanah throttles back to buck wind and waves. Even though the small boat is wallowing between waves, he maintains a bearing. His dad taught him well. He powers back when the propeller lifts out of water and adds power on top of waves to maintain bearing and not get caught sideways or take a wave head on. Quanah reminds himself, "Uncle Micah must have run against a forty-foot rogue to roll his forty-eight-foot fishing boat."

A turbulent sea off Cape Flattery is not an alarming condition but usual because of the Olympic Mountains which split prevailing winds. The northern air stream flows through the Strait of Juan de Fuca, and the southern air stream spreads over the southwestern part of Washington State. Winds climbing over the Olympic Mountains drop moisture as rain or snow and a drizzle in Seattle, but create a rain shadow along the eastern slopes.

Today, early spring, the sky is overcast as Quanah turns from the Strait into the channel between Cape Flattery and Tatoosh Island. He scans the horizon, just like his ancestors. His dad christened the boat Thunderbird, telling him that Thunderbird used Lightening Sea Serpent as a harpoon to teach their ancestors how to catch Whale. Consequently, Thunderbird carries Whale for the Makah tribal emblem. Dad also told him, with a chuckle, "Whale, Thunderbird, and Lightning Sea Serpent are the holy trinity for our ancestral religion."

Within minutes, Quanah is off Flattery Rocks. Ocean currents streaming from Alaska are cold. A man would survive only minutes if overboard. Watching breaking waves, he shouts, "Thunderbird, are you telling me to turn back?" Passing Bodelteh Islands, he sees spouts on the horizon, "Ha, whales are Thunderbird's answer. OK, Mom, the sea is clear so I can continue."

CHAPTER 2

*2,900 miles east of the pounding surf
against the Olympic Peninsula
2,800 miles east of Seattle drizzle
Syracuse, New York*

Alana Svoboda is always the first to arrive at the law office. As the youngest, most recent member of the law firm, she thinks it prudent to meticulously review her client's history. The upcoming trial is her first at the plaintiff's table. Alana paces back and forth, wringing her hands. She sits down to look over the cases only to spring back up, thinking, *I have researched the effects of lead on the fetus for the last two years and have interviewed scientists from Syracuse University and Syracuse Medical Center. They will testify as expert witnesses.* She continues to pace back and forth, reminding herself, *I will sit with senior members of the team to provide immediate access to my research.* Returning to her chair she asks herself, *Why am I so nervous? I shouldn't be nervous. I have cross referenced each client's history to scientific findings.* She pauses in her pacing for a moment, as her thoughts run on. *I know I'm compulsive. But a trial lawyer has to be prepared, and that requires practicing in front of a mirror.* Her boss had cautioned, "Alana, the average juror will reject testimony from expert witnesses. It's your job to make science understandable."

Alana looks about the conference room. She recalls jibes from senior members who said, "Alana, your argument is academic flim-flam" and "You're flummoxing us with theory."

The senior members have not yet arrived, and Alana thinks about her start in law. Even with very good undergraduate grades she hadn't landed an environmental job, so she applied to law school. She was accepted and found a niche where her undergraduate courses in genetics and embryology were relevant. After graduation, the law firm of Armstrong, Payne, Silber, and Samuels hired

9

her to research the effects of lead poisoning on human fetal development.

Alana, the newly minted lawyer, stares at the table and concedes, *Theory is over, now I need to face our clients. We will not bring their children into court, of course, but it is imperative that we understand the challenges these parents face.*

Five lawyers rise as Mr. and Mrs. Cyrus Muller are ushered into the conference room by the law firm's secretary. Rising from his chair, Mr. Armstrong, the firm's founder, makes the introductions, "Mr. and Mrs. Muller, this is Ms. Alana Svoboda who researched effects of lead on the developing fetus. Mr. James Payne is our legal expert for class action suits. Mr. Jeffery Silber and Mr. Mitch Samuels will argue our case in the Syracuse District Federal Court."

As Mrs. Muller tugs her four-year-old child to the table she explains, "We think it necessary to introduce our child. He is autistic. This is Alex. Alex, say hello."

The child doesn't answer. He pulls into his mother. Alex is beautiful. The child looks away as Alana attempts to make eye contact. Smiling, she addresses the boy with a soft, "Hello, Alex, I'm very pleased to meet you."

Mrs. Muller, tightly holding Alex and glancing at the other lawyers who obviously don't know how to interact with this child, calmly remarks, "Please, don't be surprised or embarrassed. Autistic children ignore strangers. They appear not to listen. Their world isn't our world, and science hasn't yet figured out what defines their world."

Alana can't help a wave of pity rising in her voice as she addresses the mother, "Yes, we understand the condition. Our job is to convince the jury that negligence on the part of the Environmental Protection Agency, the City of Syracuse, and the coal power plants is responsible for your son's condition. Your son will likely require attention and supervision his entire life, as I'm sure you know. There may be many causes for autism. It's been proposed that lead ions prevent fetal brains from developing normally. Unfortunately, the prognosis of severely challenged children to recover from this condition is not encouraging."

Alana thinks, *Darn, that assessment was cold; where is my empathy?*

Mr. Armstrong leans forward and gently addresses Mrs. Muller, "We don't want to alarm you, but Alex's blood has a lead level one hundred times that permitted by federal government safe levels. The lead in your drinking water is twenty times the allowable level."

"Where does the lead come from?" asks Mrs. Muller. "Don't they test for it?"

"We believe that the city water, which is acidic from acid rain, leaches lead from your house water pipes," Alana explains.

"Mrs. Muller, did either the Environmental Protection Agency or the City of Syracuse inform you of acidic city water?" Mr. Armstrong asks.

As Mrs. Muller pulls her son tightly to her side, she softly answers, "No."

Mr. Armstrong shows Mr. and Mrs. Muller out and returns with Mr. and Mrs. May. They are accompanied by their son Steven. Steven is eight, has a contagious smile, and is very engaging. His shirt sags around his torso. He doesn't have a shoulder girdle and hence is armless.

Alana knows his condition is phocomelia syndrome, which was seen in the 1950s when the antidepressant, Thalidomide, was widely prescribed to pregnant women. Lead in drinking water can also prevent fetal limb buds to grow. The men on Alana's legal team are too shocked and embarrassed to respond, so Alana picks up the slack, rises, and walks to the boy. "Hi Steven. My name's Alana. What's your favorite hobby?"

Extending his right foot to shake Alana's hand Alex replies, "I love soccer, I don't need arms to be an attack kicker."

After a short interview, the Mullers leave, and Armstrong returns with the third family. A single mother with twins. The girls smile widely. Their long, wavy black hair is folded upwards to hide their condition. They have very tiny heads. They have a developmental condition termed microcephaly which is Latin for 'small head.' This condition gained widespread news coverage a few years ago with infections caused by Zika virus spread by mosquitoes. Lead ions also cause microcephaly.

Mr. Armstrong asks Mrs. Ruby, "As a single mom, how do you raise these children?"

Mrs. Ruby bursts into tears. "It's really difficult and social services cut my SSI. I have no idea how I'll manage. My husband left me. I don't know where he is."

Alana rises, sits beside Mrs. Ruby, and embracing her, exclaims, "Please don't fret, we have a strong case."

After Mrs. Ruby is shown out, James quips, "Several generations ago, people with afflictions made a good living working in the circus as freaks. The girls were called 'pin heads' and the boy would have been billed as the 'shoulderless man.'"

"If we project this callous attitude, we will lose the jury. Why make such a pejorative statement, James?" Asks Armstrong.

"The world has always had afflicted people. I'm not saying that's how it should be. I'm only playing the Devil's Advocate," James explains in a defensive tone.

Alana responds quietly, "Statistically, today, there are more children with afflictions."

"Alana, that is why we have you at the plaintiff table, to make statistics understandable," Armstrong says.

"I understand. And, yes, each case is supported by science. But I fear that science is too difficult and too removed from ordinary experience. I know how difficult it will be to link these cases together with a common thread based on embryology. These poor children don't deserve their lot in life." Alana sighs.

Armstrong stands and lectures. "Alana, it is very important to control emotions during a trial. A good trial lawyer never loses control of the jury. Common sense will tell the jury that acid city water should not be dangerous because our stomach is acid. The connection between acid rain and lead in household water is not obvious. We will depend on your expert witnesses to convince the jury."

Eingang der Meerenge von Juan de Fuca.

CHAPTER 3

Cape Flattery, Washington State

While Alana battles her emotions, preparing for the court case linking acid rain and lead in household water to fetal developmental problems, 2,900 miles to the west, a young man caught in a rough sea quietly tells himself, "I'm losing power!" Remaining calm in the face of death is in his genes. His ancestors were selected for survival along this unforgiving shore of thundering surf.

As a child, Quanah watched his dad confront seemingly hopeless predicaments with unflinching resolve. Once when hunting elk in the Sol Duc Valley and after loading the quartered carcass, they slid off a logging road into a mud hole. Quanah's dad, Greg, hooked a double-pulley winch to the bumper and to a tree. As Greg tugged on the rope, he yelled for his nine-year-old son to start the engine in gear. The pickup churned onto the road. The boy turned the motor off and pushed the brake, thankful he didn't run over his dad. They didn't encounter a game warden either. On reservations, Indians battle the elements with battered pickups and boats that are not Coast Guard certified.

Years ago, while fishing for ling cod off the shelves of Koitlan Point, the inboard started to run rough just as a storm was barreling into the Strait of Juan de Fuca. Lightning struck Bahokus Peak overlooking the village of Neah Bay and the break water to Waadah Island. As Greg and his son drifted toward Koitlan rocks, Greg pulled kelp bulbs into the boat and instructed his son to tie them with a piece of rope for a make-shift mooring. Greg removed the carburetor gas bowl, poured gas over the filter and blew out the gas line. A lesson in Indian ingenuity, a trait which has been honed by the necessity for survival during decades of federal neglect and programs designed to wipe out Indian culture. As Greg and Quanah rounded Waadah Island to motor into Neah Bay the downpour closed around them to obliterate the shore line. Greg motored along the kelp floats into the Bay, past the Coast Guard Station, until they reached the docks.

Today, as his boat is tossed by waves, Quanah talks to his boat just as his dad would have done, "It must be your carburetor or moisture in your gas line. No way can I clear the gas line in this rough water. I need to run onto the beach."

The wind blows mist skyward, revealing the rocky shoreline of Cape Alava. As the underpowered boat crests on waves, Quanah struggles to maintain a southern bearing. Just inland is the ancient village of Ozette which yielded the artifacts displayed in the tribal museum. Quanah thinks, *A canoe towing Whale back to the village of Ozette would be more stable than Dad's boat.*

He skirts Cape Alava and turns toward shore. Just as Quanah mutters, "I'm going to make it," a breaker pushes his boat sideways, rolls it, and slams it against the sandy beach. Quanah hangs onto the wheel as surf tosses the boat like flotsam. The boat rights, and the spring flood carries it over the jumble of bleached tree trunks to deposit it right side up against the bank. Shaking, Quanah climbs out and pats the boat. "Thank you, Thunderbird, I knew you would protect me."

Quanah clambers over driftwood to the Coast Trail and heads

north several miles to Ozette, a popular trail to Cape Alava. He doesn't notice the drizzle and walks only three miles on the Ozette Lake Road toward Neah Bay when a Subaru with two bikes strapped to the roof top pulls alongside. "Can we give you a lift?" Asks the driver.

Surprised by the friendly voice, Quanah answers, "Sure, thanks."

"I'm Brian, and my wife's name is Karla. Where you headed?"

"Neah Bay."

Karla, a trim fifty with frizzled short hair jumps out the front door exclaiming, "You're taller than I am, so please take the front seat. We're on our way to visit the Makah Cultural and Research Center and then a drive to Cape Flattery to watch the sunset."

Quanah folds into the seat and sits stiffly looking straight ahead. Brian smiles at his passenger. "You can slide the seat back."

Karla asks, "Please excuse me for prying, but I can't help notice that your clothing is wet. Would you like a blanket?"

The woman's unexpected concern surprises Quanah, and he manages a soft, "Yes."

Karla wraps a blanket around the young man's shoulders. "Here, pull this forward around your chest. What happened?"

"My boat swamped."

That brings a sympathetic grunt from Brian and a gasp from Karla. She reaches forward to adjust the blanket and says, "Please bend forward so I can push the blanket between you and the seat."

Quanah complies and mutters, "Thank you."

Karla asks, "I see your jacket has an eagle embroidered on the back. It's similar to some I've seen Native Americans wear."

"Yes. I'm Makah. The bird is Thunderbird," Quanah says.

"Really! I didn't know there are Native Americans like you. I mean, I've never seen a blond Native American." Karla sits back into the seat, and continues, "Pardon me, I didn't mean to be rude. Is Thunderbird carrying a fish?"

"A whale," Quanah says stiffly, staring straight ahead.

"We love whales. We have watched them while kayaking in the San Juan Islands. Last year we followed gray whales in the Strait of

Juan de Fuca from Port Angeles to Port Townsend." Karla stops for a breath, and continues. "We know how treacherous these waters can be. I think you're lucky to be alive."

"Thunderbird protected me."

"Yes, I believe so." After a pause Karla continues, "The Olympic Peninsula is so lovely. And such a variety of special animals such as the Roosevelt Elk and hoary marmot. You are lucky to live here."

Quanah nods weakly. He thinks, *Whites seem to say what they think. They aren't reserved. I guess the reason tribal elders caution us not to talk with Whites is because conversations end up in papers.* But he mutters, "Yes."

Karla questions, "Do you hunt?"

Quanah slouches and grunts another, "Yes."

Noting a stiffening of Quanah's shoulders Karla apologizes, "Oh, I'm sorry. I didn't mean to ask personal questions. We seldom have a chance to talk with a Native American."

"I understand."

"Do you live in Neah Bay?" Karla continues to question.

"No."

"Oh, there I go again asking personal questions. Please forgive me."

"It's OK."

"In Seattle?" She continues.

"No." After a silence Quanah figures he should be polite, after all, they are giving him a ride to Neah Bay, so he explains, "My mother is White. She came from Germany. I'm a student at Friday Harbor."

"Oh, that's fantastic. We know the University of Washington Laboratories on San Juan Island." After another pause Karla continues, "What are you studying?"

"Whales."

Karla gushes, "We love whales and contribute to Green Peace but Paul Watson of Sea Shepard and his tactics of ramming whaling ships are too violent for us to support."

After another period of silence Karla continues, "We read that

Makah elders have decided not to hunt the gray whale. We applaud this position. What do you think?"

Quanah nods toward Brian and points, "Here we are. Turn left into the parking lot."

"We can drop you in town," says Brian.

"This is fine." Handing the blanket back to Karla, Quanah suggests, "Be sure to look at the whaling canoe and the gray whale skeleton hanging from the ceiling. Thanks for the lift."

As Quanah turns to leave, he hears Karla ask her husband, "Are tall, blond Native Americans very common?"

CHAPTER 4

Syracuse, New York
Federal Court

A world apart from Neah Bay, Syracuse residents are assembling in federal court. Alana is the first to enter the courtroom. She sits at the plaintiff table and surveys the quiet room. Two women enter the court room from a side door. They walk to their places between the jury box and judge's desk and plunk down their stenographic machines. One, wearing a wool dress, is pregnant. She complains, "Can't they get the temperature right. It must be ninety degrees in here, and we froze yesterday."

When the gallery fills to standing room only, the bailiff enters the courtroom. He is an enormous man. His necktie knot is lost under heavy jowls, and sweat glistens on his forehead. His handlebar mustache droops. Reading the court docket, he bellows:

"Court of Judge Weichselbaum, 10:00 a.m.,
United States District Court, Northern District of New York.
The Honorable Judge Weichselbaum presiding
Court in session: Muller vs Wolff
Plaintiffs: Mr. and Mrs. Cyrus Muller
Class action plaintiffs with autistic children,
premature babies, children with deformities and
women who suffered trimester abortions
v
Defendants: Dr. Wolff, Deputy Director of EPA,
Michigan Electric Power, and the State of New York.

The Bailiff catches his breath and continues, "Please rise for the Honorable Judge Weichselbaum."

Judge Weichselbaum, dressed in a flowing robe and sporting cropped, gray hair enters from his chambers and takes his place behind a walnut desk that rests atop a walnut parapet, ensconced by walnut paneling. He sits bolt upright, appearing tense and ready to spring coyote-like. He barks, "Bailiff, please seat the jury."

From the security of her chair, Alana feels adrift on an ocean without horizon. Yet, her mind races to organize questions. Her law firm's clients claim that lead in city water prevented normal fetal development. Alana makes eye contact with the fourteen jurors, a plumber, a carpenter, a mailman, secretary, and a salesperson, all working people, honest folks who have experienced the hard knocks of life. Alana hopes they will be sympathetic.

She knows that the Flint, Michigan, debacle concerning lead contaminated water affecting children's ability to learn, failed to affect any change in government policy. Otherwise, the EPA would not have granted permits to coal burning plants with no restrictions on emissions.

The American and New York flags sag and disappear as specks against the vast, gray walls. The room is stifling as radiators whistle.

Yesterday, Judge Weichselbaum denied plaintiff objections against expert witness testimony for the defense. Consequently, last night Alana's law firm determined it imperative to change the lead and decided Alana Svoboda, the most junior member, should cross examine. Alana's boss explained, "This is a risky move, but Mitch floundered. Alana presents a fresh face."

Alana has butterflies as she realizes she will question the deputy director of the EPA, the distinguished Dr. Quinton Jeffery Wolff. Yesterday, he impressed the jury, claiming that acid rain and global warming are academic hoaxes. Good grief, Dr. Wolff holds several university positions and is editor of two scientific journals. He has published books on acid rain and climate change, giving him an enormous following on conservative talk shows.

Alana wipes her brow, takes a sip of water, and looks over the audience. Her mother, Judy, returns a thumbs up. Alana is jarred into action when the stenographer recalls Professor Wolff for her to question.

"Professor Wolff," Alana begins, "Thank you for your time. As a deputy director of the EPA you have enormous social responsibilities, so I'll get right to it. Is the study of acid rain on biological systems new?"

Prof. Wolff, with an air of superiority answers, "Understanding acid rain began in the 1960s."

Alana presses on, "Scholars have written that the Roman Empire fell because of lead poisoning in the homes of the rich. Would you comment?"

The defense attorney objects. "This trial is not about history."

"Sustained," the judge says. "Ms. Svoboda, keep your questions relevant."

Alana nods. "Professor Wolff, could you describe acid rain chemistry at my level of understanding?"

"Certainly. Acid rain is only slightly acidic and never approaches that in your stomach."

Alana asks, "Do lead ions impart a taste to tap water?"

The defense makes another objection which the judge sustains. She sees how this is going to go and is relieved when the judge adjourns for lunch.

By the end of the day, her confidence had taken a blow, yet her boss insists she continue.

On Day 6 of the trial, after consultation with her team, she says, "We recall our first witness from day one, Dr. Oliver Powers."

Mr. Rosen, the lead defense attorney whines, "We protest, Your Honor, you rejected his testimony on day one."

Alana said, "Your Honor, before you rule, may we approach the bench?"

As she approaches the bench Alana lectures herself, *Yesterday afternoon you lost all the judge's rulings. You are behind for the second half of the game.* Noticing Mr. Rosen's diminutive form, she straightens her shoulders, tells herself she can do this, and takes a position, directly in front of the judge. Just like in high school basketball, she sets a screen, blocking Rosen from the judge.

She addresses the judge, "Yesterday, Professor Wolff discussed acid rain. The effects of acid on lead pipes are pertinent to our case, and Professor Powers is an expert."

Craning his neck, Rosen says, "Your Honor, this trial is only about acid rain and not lead pipes."

Judge Weichselbaum says, "The jury should know about the connection between acid rain and lead pipes."

With Dr. Powers in the witness seat, Alana asks, "Dr. Powers, is your field of research on the effects of lead on embryonic brain development?"

Rosen objects, "Your Honor, this trial is about acid rain and not embryology."

The judge says, "Noted. But the jury will want to know if the fetal brain is altered by lead. Dr. Powers, my wife has Parkinson's disease, could lead cause Parkinsons?"

Dr. Powers answers, "Perhaps. The poisonous effects of lead ions can be catastrophic in the adult brain."

"Dr. Powers," Alana continues, "Professor Wolff stated that acid water would not affect the fetal brain. Is that true?"

"Yes," he answers, "because the mother's blood would neutralize acid from a glass of water."

Alana presses. "Dr. Powers, what is the chemistry of acid rain on fetal development?"

"The acid dissolves lead from lead pipes which connect some older homes to city water mains. When an expectant mother drinks tap water, lead ions enter her blood stream. The placenta does not isolate the fetus from lead ions in the mother's blood."

"Dr. Powers, what is the effect of lead ions on the fetus?"

The witness explains, "When pregnant rats were fed diets laced with lead ions, their young were deformed, small and incapable of learning a maze."

When it's Rosen's turn to question the witness, he asks. "Professor Powers, are you a real doctor?"

"If you mean do I have a medical degree, no, I am not a physician. I have a Ph.D. in biophysics. I am chair of the Neuroscience Department, and I determine what a physician should know about ions and acid."

Rosen demands, "Dr. Powers, rats aren't humans, are they?"

"No."

"So, the rat studies aren't relevant to humans," Rosen says. "Correct?"

"No, you are not correct. Rats and humans share 95% of the genetic material. Man and rats have the same developmental processes and ..."

Rosen interrupts, "Thank you. That's all I need to know."

But the judge is interested and says, "No, go on Dr. Powers, I'm sure the jury will want to know."

Rosen protests, "But the defense council is satisfied."

"Continue Dr. Powers," Judge Weichselbaum says.

Dr. Powers nods and goes on. "During human fetal development, cells come together to make tissues for liver, gut, muscle, and brain. The tissues organize into organs such as the brain and heart. Cellular movements in embryonic tissues are sensitive to lead ions."

Rosen bellows, "Your Honor, I ask that the answer to your question be stricken from the record. Your question is irregular, we ask for a mistrial?"

Judge Weichselbaum: "Your objection is recorded. However, I believe that the question is relevant and the jury may evaluate Dr. Power's answer. Chief Justice Roberts of the Supreme Court believes that judges should ask expert witnesses pertinent questions. Moreover, members of the Supreme Court have set a precedent by asking questions to both defense and plaintiff councils. Dr. Powers, how do lead ions affect fetal brains?"

Alana smiles as Dr. Powers answers: "The organization of cells and tissues into the fetus brain depends on small electrical currents that cross cell membranes. These currents are carried by sodium and chloride ions, as in table salt. Calcium ions, which the fetus gets from mothers' blood, regulate sodium currents. Lead ions interfere with calcium ionic currents resulting in developmental errors."

Judge Weichselbaum: "Thank you."

Court begins the next day with the defense recalling Dr. Wolff.

Once the witness is reminded that he's still under oath, Defense Attorney Rosen begins, "Dr. Wolff, is the chemistry presented yesterday relevant to the plaintiff's case?"

Dr. Wolff answers, "No. We have examined the birth records in Syracuse and find that the percentage of still births and premature babies is that of the United States. Therefore, the plaintiff has no statistical basis for their case."

"Thank you, Dr. Wolff," Rosen says, with a smirk. "Ms. Svoboda, your witness."

Alana is ready. "Our clients live in neighborhoods with homes valued over $300,000. Can we group these homes as a subclass?"

Dr. Wolff: "Uh, let me think...."

"Dr. Wolff, answer with a 'yes' or 'no.'"

Rosen says, "Your Honor, Ms. Svoboda is badgering the witness."

Alana clarifies, "Birth defects in our group are twenty times the US. Are our statistics correct?"

Dr. Wolff: "I'm not sure."

Judge Weichselbaum says, "Don't attempt to flummox us. Answer the question."

Dr. Wolff stalls. "What was the question?"

"We selected neighborhoods of at least fifty contiguous homes," Alana tells him. "Is there a problem with this class definition for statistics?"

"Well, ah, no," Doctor Wolff answers.

Alana says, "No more questions but I reserve the right to recall."

The defense recalls Dr. Powers. When the witness is seated, Rosen asks, "Dr. Powers, can you explain your statistics?"

Dr. Powers: "Yes, the expensive homes in our subclass were built before 1936 and have a long setback from the city water main. The water pipes are made of lead, and acid water leaches lead ions from pipes."

And so the questioning continues, buttressing Alana's arguments, much to Mr. Rosen's discomfort. In the end, the jury ruled in favor of the prosecution. After the emotional toll of the trial, even though victory is tentatively won, Alana makes a life-changing decision. Now she just has to tell her mom.

Her chance comes later when she sits across from her mother, sipping coffee. Her mother, Judy, smiles, and her eyes sparkle as she addresses her daughter, "Alana, you won your first big case, I'm so proud."

"Mom, I was only part of the litigating team. And, the most junior member. In fact, I'm not so sure we convinced the jury. They were swayed by emotion." Alana sighs.

Judy, looks into her daughter's eyes, "You can't fool me although you eventually charmed the judge. I was there."

Alana half listens as her mom recounts the trial and makes critical remarks about Alana's appearance and demeanor, comparing her attire to that of TV sit-com attorneys.

"Mom! I hate it when you tell me what to wear." Alana rolls her eyes.

But her mom goes on. Finally, Alana points out the obvious. "Mom, we did win. I need to be focused as a trial lawyer, not pandering to the camera."

Seeing her daughter's determination, Judy changes the conversation. "What are the settlements?"

"The final amounts will be determined as to the severity of each child's disability. The dispensation will range from seven to twenty-one million per child."

"My goodness, Alana, your firm represented over thirty clients, that's a huge amount."

"Unfortunately, the verdict will probably be reversed by the appeals court."

"Oh, Alana, why?"

"Our firm believes the appellate judges will rule that Judge Weichselbaum didn't instruct the jury to disregard his comments, which were prejudicial."

"Well, I'm sure it'll go better with the next case your firm has coming up."

Alana says, "No, Mom, I found that representing people with

personal and tragic problems is emotionally gut wrenching. Our firm has decided to litigate cases of malformed babies and conjoined twins caused by ultrasound," answers Alana as she leans forward rubbing her forehead.

Judy reaches across the table placing her hand on Alana's, "Alana, honey, what are you saying?"

"I don't think I can handle any more of these morally difficult cases. Jury decisions can be capricious and many times punitive awards are mean." Alana's eyes tear up. Blinking, she continues, "Juries are unpredictable, and higher courts seem uncaring."

"I know, but you're making good money. Someone must represent these parents."

"Mom, I know our clients. They are elated that we won. They will be devastated when the court of appeals overturns the verdict."

Judy gets up, and walks behind her daughter, and gently strokes her hair. "I suppose you're right."

Alana leans back, feeling the tension leave her body as she grabs her mom's hand. "Mom, thanks for believing in me. I liked environmental law courses. Several years ago, I attended a sit-in to preserve old growth trees in the Adirondacks. Did you know that the environment needs good lawyers?"

Judy returns to her chair. "But, Alana, can you make a living as an environmental lawyer?"

"Yes, I think so. My moot court team won the Native American litigation competition in Tucson. I like the notion of helping Native Americans."

Alana gazes into her mom's eyes, softly saying, "Mom, I'm joining a firm specializing in Native American and environmental law—in Seattle."

"Oh, no, honey, are you sure? Why didn't you tell me?"

"Until this case, I wasn't sure. Mom, you grew up in Seattle, so you'll enjoy visiting me."

"Well, I'm not so sure. Remember my daddy disappeared near Seattle when I was only seven. I hardly remember him."

"I know that. It must have been really terrible. You said your dad disappeared in the San Juan Islands. Maybe I can visit that area and find out something. Wish me luck." Alana remembers something else and adds, "And didn't you tell me your family farm is in eastern Washington?"

"Yes, in the region called the Palouse."

"Come visit, and maybe we can find it together."

"I'll miss you, but I know you'll do well. You'll love Seattle." As Judy embraces her daughter she whispers, "When you feel trapped, you can always come home."

CHAPTER 5

Early Morning, May 11, Neah Bay
Olympic Peninsula, Washington State

One hundred miles to the west of Seattle, ten Indians meet at 4:00 a.m. at the old Makah tribal dock in Neah Bay, silently load their gear into the war canoe and cast off. They paddle past the moldering fishing fleet and into the bay leaving a luminous wake of diffused moonlight. The seawall forces incoming fog skyward, leaving the harbor clear and the Indians exposed. The villagers of Neah Bay sleep, unaware that their lives are about to be disrupted, turned upside down, relentlessly analyzed, and criticized by news people, coast guard, police, federal agents and lawyers. The small tribe of Makah Indians which resides at the western extremity of the continental United States will again come under international scrutiny. The canoe with ten Indians is exposed for the mile paddle to the Bay entrance. For now, the fishing village is quiet, at this hour even dogs are asleep.

The war canoe slips through the fog curtain, draped from Koitla Point to Waada Island, as men pull hard against paddles. The night guard at the United States Coast Guard Station sees the canoe but no cause to sound an alarm. The small-craft warning flag sags against its pole. There is little wind. Within minutes, the pullers are hidden in heavy mist and know they can't be stopped by Indian Harbor Police.

Escaping apprehension into the fog bank, the Indians must contend with the task of navigation. Quanah, the whaling chief, maintains a westerly bearing with a compass. Nevertheless, without land markers, dead reckoning will be demanding. Of course, the compass was not traditional in ancient times but was used a few generations ago to help Indians navigate the treacherous waters of the Strait of Juan de Fuca. Mist settles through the blanket of fog to smother the usual chop into gentle swells. Quanah strains for a glimpse of shore against the foreshortened, gray horizon and watches for a change in wave patterns. He scans for beach flotsam which would signal the immediate danger of the shore. The canoe continues against the current parallel to the coast, but how far out from the rocky shoreline, Quanah can only estimate, based on currents observed during earlier trips. It is spring, so kelp bed fronds have not grown to float on the surface. Quanah sees no eddies to indicate the submerged shelves of Kydikabbit Point. There is the danger of straying into the shipping lane where a freighter could steam over the canoe. Few Indians can swim, not that swimming in ice-cold waters would help one survive.

Quanah has resisted bringing a GPS device. Of course, no one has an iPhone. This hunt is to be traditional, and Quanah wants to connect with his great-great-grandfather, who was a whaler chief four generations ago. Quanah's crew paddles in silence. There is nothing to discuss.

Quanah's crew had been practicing this course for a year while training for "The War Canoe Regatta," which will visit Indian villages to demonstrate Canadian First Nation and United States Indian solidarity. All Indians are Americans. Native Americans and First Nation Peoples had no say in drawing the boundary which dips below the 49th parallel to encompass all of Vancouver Island into Canada. Caucasian governments drew boundaries for Indian reservations with little regard for traditional Indian hunting and fishing grounds. The Washington Territorial Governor Isaac Stevens forced "standard" federal treaties onto coastal tribes in the 1850s. To this day, Indians feel the impact of treaties, and the hurt is as raw as if treaties had been signed only yesterday. The bitterness of coerced treaties 150 years ago has been kept alive in Indian culture by seven generations of oral tradition. Most Whitemen don't know and don't care about treaties and government policies designed to crush Indian culture and tradition. The White notion of making this red race of men into White men has not succeeded.

Initially, the Makah Tribe of Neah Bay and their brothers, the Nuu-chah-nulth (Nootka) who live to the north along the west coast of Vancouver Island had planned to invite only members of their linguistic group. If the US and Canadian border had been placed across Vancouver Island at the 49th parallel, many of the Nuu-chah-nulth bands would reside in Washington State. On the other hand, Oregon and Washington Territories could have ended up as part of British Columbia, based on the Doctrine of Discovery and the 1811 shared occupancy between Britain and the United States.

The planned canoe regatta morphed into "The Largest Ever Canoe Regatta!" A really "Big Do" with dancing, potlatches, and canoe races. The "Big Do" spread through the Internet like a giant smoke signal. The Salish-Chilkoot, Kwakwaka'wakw (Kwakiutl), Bella Coola, Tsimshian, Tlingit, and other tribes scattered along the Coast of British Columbia and Alaska and tribes of Puget Sound were invited.

Before the Caucasian invasion, it was the canoe that linked Indian villages for trade and war. Coastal land travel was prevented by the tree covered mountains which plunge into the Pacific Ocean from Puget Sound to Alaska. During the last ice age, the Puyallup Glacier gouged out the maze of inlets, bays, fjords, and channels leaving innumerable islands. Rugged coastlines of the Inland Passage between the continent and Vancouver Island and off-shore islands provide shelter against the pounding waters of the Pacific Ocean. The inhospitable coastal mountains and the jagged coastline made ideal conditions for migratory salmon. Salmon nurtured the rich diversity of coastal Indian Tribes, each with a unique language and customs.

The canoe regatta will start at Neah Bay and be joined by tribes as the flotilla paddles north through the Inland Passage to the Kawakwaka'waka (Kwakiutl) village at Alert Bay, British Columbia, on Vancouver Island. Northern tribes such as the Tsimshian of Prince Rupert, British Columbia, will paddle south to Alert Bay.

Today, David, a Tsimshian from Prince Rupert, paddling in the middle of Quanah's canoe is conflicted. One moment he is pleased, the next, he is sure that he has made a disastrous decision. Quanah had instructed his crew to follow Makah whaling traditions. No sex for four weeks before the hunt. No gossip. Refer to canoe trips as training for the regatta. Bathe in rivers or under cold showers. Dry with cedar boughs.

When young, David witnessed medicinal powers of plants which sparked his interest in chemistry at the University of British Columbia. With respect for his uncle who is a shaman, he kept silent on customs contrary to science. As the hunt drew near, his wife accused him of having an affair. This hunt could cost him his license, his lively-hood, his ability to help his people, and his marriage.

Participating as a crew member gives David a sense of adventure not experienced since childhood. This whale hunt is illegal, and it is not sanctioned by the Makah tribe. David has sometimes thought he has become too White, but joining this crew gives meaning to being Indian. Watching Quanah's figure cutting through fog David wonders, *Why is this man, an Indian, so driven, what is he seeking?*

For the canoe regatta, the official Makah schedule stipulated that David's tribe would paddle south to join the powwow at the Kwakwaka'wakw village at Alert Bay. City officials of Port Mc-Neil, across the channel from Alert Bay, declined to participate. The Kwakwaka'wakw had hosted an intertribal potlatch in 1950 to celebrate the newly enacted Canadian First Nation laws permitting potlatches after a half-century prohibition. They honored the memory of Chief James Sewid and commemorated the Edward Curtis film *In the Land of the Head Hunters*. The Curtis silent movie was filmed in 1913, and canoes were central to the love story enacted by the Kwakwaka'wakw People. The canoe trip from Neah Bay to Alert Bay is 300 miles.

Even though the Salish Indians of Puget Sound had not been seafaring tribes, they were invited because of inter-tribal marriages and potlatches. The Nisqually Tribe of Puget Sound hosted Chief Seattle Days one hundred years ago.

The Haida of the Queen Charlotte Islands had historically been feared up and down the coast for raiding parties who pillaged and carried off hapless victims as slaves. For the Makah regatta, the Haida would leave Skidegate on the Queen Charlotte Islands and paddle 125 miles to St. James, the most southern point of the Queen Charlotte Islands, and sail open sea for 100 miles to the Northern tip of Vancouver Island. The Haida people are still the Norseman of the Americas. Quanah wanted a Haida for his navigator during the whale hunt.

Today, using an extra-large paddle as a rudder, Sam, a Haida, maintains a westerly course. He fashioned the paddle from yellow cedar and carved an eagle, his family crest, into the blade. He feels a strong connection to his forefathers who would have plied these same waters after raiding villages in Puget Sound. Sam has mixed feelings because, in 1856, one hundred Haida warriors battled the U.S. Navy at Port Gamble, just east of Neah Bay. Those were his ancestors, and their defeat still reverberates after seven generations.

Sam, feeling both the rage of defeat suffered by his ancestors and pride that he had been selected as navigator for the whaling party, thinks of his forefathers who would be transporting bound captives to be enslaved whereas he is guiding nine men from different villages. They have been pulling for an hour into sea mist. The dip of paddles is monotonous, but Sam diligently watches for a change in wave patterns which would signal shore. The success of the hunt depends on Sam's ability to "read" the water. Sam admires Quanah's resolve to continue into the fog bank and wonders if his Haida ancestors would have turned back.

While planning the regatta, Makah elders hoped that a hundred canoes would gain worldwide awareness and heal raw feelings between Whites and Indians. They invited the press to film events. The elders didn't know of Quanah's plan for an illegal hunt. If they had known, they would have prevented it. Reconciliation between the Indian and the Whiteman is important with two recent Supreme Court appointments which will change the court to the right. Lawyers caution it is important to be friendly to the press. It is time to acknowledge the past and move forward. The date for war canoes to arrive at the Kwakwaka'wakw (Kwakiutl) Village in Alert Bay, B.C., is set for September.

Today, in early spring, the war canoe continues on a westerly bearing through the Strait of Juan de Fuca. Every half hour, David throws a piece of bark onto the glassy water so Sam can "read" the course from the angle between the canoe's wake and bark. The crew puts their fate in Sam's ability to navigate. Sam and Quanah nod in agreement. No words are passed. The pace is grueling, but no one complains.

Quanah knows his hunt will unleash bitter conflict between Indians and animal activists. *The Whites don't care about Indians, but the Japanese will buy whales. Those Makah's who behave like Whites with no backbone are putting on a mask for the world community. Those apples will come around,* he thinks.

Last summer during practice, Quanah felt solidarity between crew members. They lodged with families at Neah Bay and in motels. Training began with four-mile jogs. Within a month they climbed Waatch Peak, a run through ancient tribal lands. At the end of fall training, they climbed Cheeka Peak. Tribes hosted potlatches with salmon bakes, drumming, and dancing. There were so few sockeye salmon in the Makah waters that the Nuu-chah-nulth of Canada contributed 200 fish for each event. Merle, the Coeur d'Alene representative of Plateau Tribes, learned how to paddle in the war canoe.

Merle had not maintained conditioning over the winter. He feels blisters forming on his hands and with back and elbows aching wonders why he consented to this madness. An accountant, he carefully thinks about all aspects of life and plays by rules. Merle thinks *We are breaking federal law, ignoring international law, and God knows how many Indian regulations. I come from a tribe that rode horses and fished salmon from rivers.* He'd consented because his wife, Louise, is a Makah.

Merle is not a hunter, not a fisherman, not an outdoorsman.

34

Merle is Catholic, a "Good Injun" and not of the warrior class referred to by Jesuits as "Bad Injuns." He sits at a desk. Training had been strenuous because the first leg of the canoe regatta will cross the Strait of Juan de Fuca to Vancouver Island. Initial canoe trips were confined to Neah Bay where they 'pulled' to Waadah Island at the end of the sea wall. As training progressed, they ventured into open ocean to conquer enormous swells generated by Japanese Currents colliding with Cape Flattery. Merle dreamed he would drown. He can't swim.

Now, blistered and fatigued, Merle is surprised he is keeping pace. During training, his wife watched from shore and cheered him on. He didn't want to embarrass her in front of Quanah, her childhood friend. Merle wonders, *Why am I trusting Quanah and this Haida Indian, Sam? Coeur d'Alene Indians have a tradition not to trust any tribe.*

The war canoe, with its contoured hull and sculpted bowsprit, has little drag, as its long, raised prow slices through the sea to deflect the spray and minimize pitch. Merle is mesmerized, and like the Indian in front of him, he can only paddle.

When the second hour passes, Merle doesn't know where they are. Their goal is Tatoosh Island, thirty-six miles from Neah Bay. Looking at Quanah bracing against wind-bearing mist, with rivulets running from blond hair, Merle blurts, "I'm a Plateau Indian, not a friggin' Viking."

Last summer, between Tatoosh Island and Cape Flattery the Indians experienced a surging tide creating ten-foot standing waves. Quanah's crew had felt exhilaration as their canoe angled up, over, and slid down waves. When wind and tide are opposed, currents churn with unpredictable, chaotic swells and whirlpools. Sam determines their course, and the crew has learned to accept his split-second orders.

Today as the canoe reaches the open sea, mist is interspersed with downpours. Quanah feels overwhelmed with pride. His men are now warriors and don't change cadence when penetrating walls of rain. He reckons they need another hour to reach Tatoosh Island before the tides change.

Last summer, past the Light House on Tatoosh Island, Quanah's crew spotted gray whales for the first time. Plumes of vapor were followed by reports like rifle shots from blowing whales. Adrenalin surged as the crew gained on the pod. The whales sounded. Suddenly a whale blew forty yards to port. A seventy-foot behemoth surfaced near the canoe. An eye as large as a grapefruit appeared. Then they looked into its blow-hole. The whale dived, lifting its broad fluke high as if saying, "Don't mess with me, this is my ocean."

At that moment, Quanah told his crew that the whale hunt would be conducted with traditional equipment. He had selected each man for a particular talent. It was their destiny to present a role model for Indian youth. Indian life is not as simple as Coyote and Raven tales. Indian languages evolved with complexities required to intimately describe nature and hunting. Indian schools destroyed Indigenous Peoples' heritage and language. Bent on "killing the Indian to save the man," the Whiteman's oppression emasculated Indian men—no, it effectively castrated Indian warriors.

Quanah's ancestors made their living selling whale oil and meat to other tribes. *Whaling is my Indian right,* Quanah thinks.

Three hours have passed, and they are still lost in sea fog covering the Strait of Juan de Fuca. The canoe maintains its westerly course. It passes north of points jutting into the Strait. Sam is maintaining a safe bearing as the canoe glides over gentle, expansive swells. There is no conversation. The swoosh of paddles is damped by rain settling through the mist. There is no horizon, only a canoe filled with ten men. Thomas, the Kwakwaka'wakw artist from Alert Bay, Canada, breaks into a canoe song, each vocal uttered with a paddle stroke. Thomas' song is eerie, swallowed by fog,

"Aw, ha ya ha ya hä
Ha ya he ya ä
He ya ha ya ä
A, ha ya ha ya hä
Aw, ha ya he ya hä

He ya ha ya hei
Ya hä
Ha ha wo wo wo."

Others join for a couple minutes, and Thomas continues alone, keeping cadence,

"Why, Why, Why, Why, Ya Hä
Ya ä Kill, Kill, Kill
He ya ha ya ä
Yë hei Yë hei yë hei
Great Spirit he ha ya
Noble Whales He ya
Ya hä
Ha ya ha ya ä
Artists in motion
Ha ha wo wo wo."

Thomas is not brave and certainly not foolhardy. He reflects on Bill Reid's masterpiece sculpture 'The Spirit of Haida Gwaii' in the Vancouver airport and in front of the Canadian Embassy in Washington DC. The bronze canoe carries mythical creatures, a chief, and one Indian puller, all crammed into a twenty-foot canoe. Reid called the human puller, wrapped in a cedar bark cape, "The Ancient Reluctant Conscript" in reference to a Carl Sandburg poem. Thomas relates to the Ancient Reluctant Conscript, who looks like Bill Reid. Reid playfully referred to his work as "a ship of fools.'" Thomas, an artist, is greatly impressed how Reid wove raven, bear, eagle, frog, beaver, dogfish women, wolf, mouse women,

37

and bad cub, good cub with human mother into a fabric of reality. The chief, anchored in the middle of the canoe, standing tall with wide, woven hat, robe, and talking stick that is topped by a killer whale, expresses a resolute countenance. Even though the chief's charges are arguing and bickering, he knows where he is taking his crew.

Thomas wonders, *Does Quanah know where he's going? We are not squabbling, does this mean Quanah is a good chief? Will he abort this hunt or continue into the fog? Why is this blue-eyed Indian so driven?*

Suddenly, mist cleaves as Thunderbird thrusts the blue lance of Sea Serpent between the worlds of sky and horizon. The black ocean turns blue. Tatoosh Island rises with ribbons of mist entangled in Douglas Firs. Quanah signals a change of course to the southwest. Thomas feels the tightness that gripped his shoulders relax, his questions go unanswered. He laments, *This is no place for an artist who loves animals. I am Bill Reid's 'Reluctant Ancient Conscript' and my steersman, the Haida, Sam, is Reid's Raven.*

Last summer Quanah practiced harpooning techniques. At the end of fall, the men returned to their homes and built more canoes. The cold grip of winter on Coastal Indian Villages subsided, spring came, and the men returned to Neah Bay.

Quanah's canoe is now between Tatoosh Island and Cape Flattery. Quanah knows these waters; he is comfortable. The westerly winds have swept fog from the sea revealing rugged cliffs and pounding surf. The tide is running against a westerly wind. The jagged coastline conspires with the tide to form treacherous standing waves and force huge eddies behind submerged boulders the size of houses. The observation deck at The Hole-in-the-Wall at the end of Cape Flattery Trail is shrouded in mist. There are no hikers. The canoe is making four knots running with the tide but against the wind. Tatoosh Island is a quarter mile from the mainland where two granite giants cut the channel into thirds, the widest channel of a couple hundred yards is near the Island. The canoe rushes past the Island and is out to sea within seconds.

The crew spots the blows of a cow and yearling. Usually, the grays travel in pods, but this cow and calf are traveling alone. The Indians are in luck, they don't have to paddle another ten miles to Cape Alava where some members of the Makah had illegally killed a whale in 2006. Those Indians landed in jail, had to pay a fine and perform community work. Quanah speaks into the wind, "Whale meat and trane oil will unite our tribes. The world will be impressed. Pull hard," he commands, "The whales are only one mile away!"

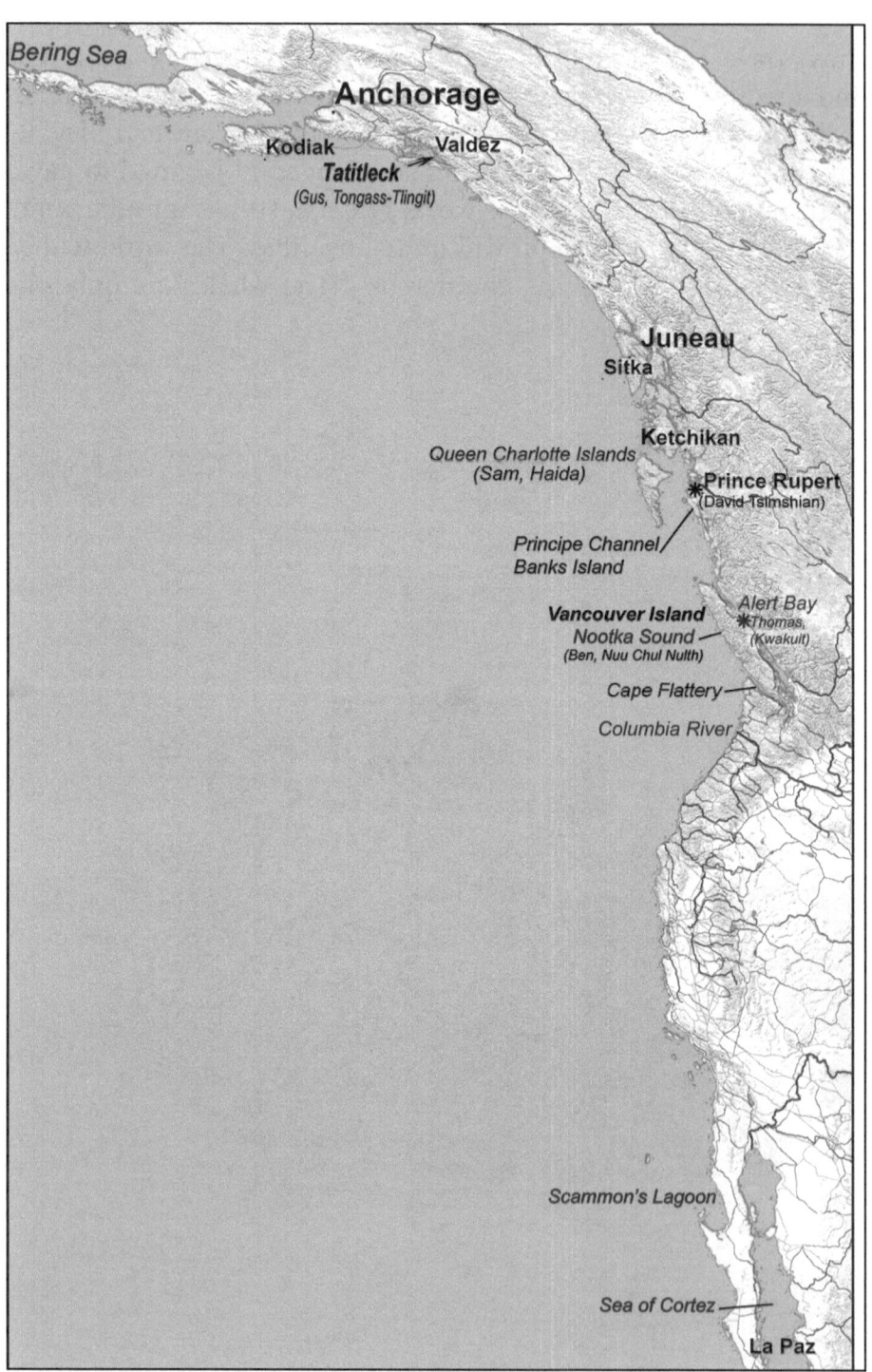

Bering Sea

Anchorage

Kodiak Valdez

Tatitleck
(Gus, Tongass-Tlingit)

Juneau
Sitka

Ketchikan

Queen Charlotte Islands
(Sam, Haida)
＊Prince Rupert
(David-Tsimshian)

Principe Channel
Banks Island

Alert Bay
Vancouver Island ＊*Thomas,*
(Kwakult)
Nootka Sound
(Ben, Nuu Chul Nulth)

Cape Flattery

Columbia River

Scammon's Lagoon

Sea of Cortez
La Paz

CHAPTER 6

Whales off Tatoosh Island

Mia, the gray whale cow, and her yearling spent the night making deep sounds (dives) five miles from the rugged coastline of Washington State to evade a pack of killer whales. Yesterday, the cow and yearling along with members of her pod were ambushed by the top predators, killer whales, just south of Tatoosh Island. This morning, the cow deemed it safer to navigate near land than to swim to the west where the killers would be patrolling.

The gray whales are twenty days into their yearly migration north, and up to yesterday have avoided killers since leaving Scammon's Lagoon, Baja Peninsula, in February. Twenty nights ago, the sheltered Baja Lagoon was peaceful. It was neap tide with humid air and longer nights, signaling the change of seasons. Whale watchers had motored from Scammon's Lagoon leaving rafts of sea birds mewing and squealing with dozing whales, a symphony of bassoons and flutes. The Milky Way spread diagonally across the sky like a giant compass needle.

All winter, whales had foraged in the tranquil waters surrounding Baja Peninsula. Mia and other gray whales, fed on dense clam beds in the Sea of Cortez and Baja lagoons during the winter months. To the delight of whale watchers, she would rise from the sea, forcing sand and water through baleen plates to leave clams, sand shrimp, and sea worms to be swallowed whole. At this time of year, invertebrates are plump and ready to spawn, after which, they will lose much of their nutrient value. It was time for the whales to leave. During ebb tide, Mia led her pod from the lagoon, over the shoal into the Pacific Ocean to start their four-thousand-mile odyssey to the Arctic Ocean.

Over the winter, the whales laid a foot of blubber under their skin to fuel the long swim to the Arctic, where they will feed on the summer krill bloom and herring balls. After a season of gluttony, with the onset of fall, gray whales will return to Baja, a migratory route established after the last ice age.

Baja Peninsula supports a thriving whale-watching industry. The downside is that Mia and other whales must dodge the myriad of boats and skiffs full of tourists anxious to pet a whale. Nevertheless, Mia's yearling loved the attention and was particularly fond of a man with a straw hat and melodious voice who captained a yellow Panda skiff. The tour guide christened the yearling, José and his mother, Mia. Both mother and yearling would swim to the boat when the man called by splashing with a paddle or knocking against the gunwale with his knuckles.

Mia and José had arrived in the waters of Baja in December with eight relatives from the Bering Strait. José was a year old when the pod of females and young swam into *Ojo de Liebre* Lagoon. On arrival, José's aunt gave birth. José had come to expect complete devotion from his mother and was surprised when she ignored him while attending her sister's birthing. Mia pushed the newborn's head above water so he could fill his lungs and breathe. Midwife help is imperative because fetal lungs are collapsed which means that a twelve-foot-long, 1000-pound newborn would sink like a stone without the first breath of life to provide oxygen and buoyancy.

Baby whales grow exceptionally fast. Calves reach a length of sixteen feet and weigh three thousand pounds by the end of the first winter. Gaining an astonishing forty pounds a day from milk, they store fat, a source of energy for the epic journey a few months after birth.

After assisting her sister, Mia, responding to hormones, sought the attention of several large males wintering offshore near Laguna San Ignacio. She frolicked with the males and ignored José. He was jealous and bewildered when his mother permitted the big bulls to roughly push him aside. José was confused because, during his first year, which included one Arctic migration, his mother never let him out of her sight. Whenever he strayed more than a few yards, he was scolded with a series of "clicks."

Now, his mother swam between two bulls alternately rolling to one side for face-to-face embraces. Even though her genitalia are swollen and the male's penis is eight feet long, mating is difficult, because the sea doesn't offer resistance against which to push. A successful union requires one male to press against Mia's back so that the second male can copulate. Belly to belly copulation is facilitated as a bull can move his inflated penis, something like a human tongue, to locate the vaginal opening. Unlike most mammals, whales do not have an os penis (penial bone), and penial erection is a function of blood pressure. Whale watchers were embarrassed as bulls rolled to thrust enormous pink penises skyward showing their virility. Mia picked bulls with the most tumescence because this signals good blood pressure and overall excellent health. In this aspect of animal behavior, cows may select mates similarly as did females of the human kind early in human evolution. After two weeks of carousing, Mia again turned her attention to José and showed him how to scoop mouthfuls of mud from the sea floor for clams.

The lagoon, today, is pastoral with humans and whales in harmony. By contrast, in the year of 1848, the protected waters of *Ojo de Liebre* were turned into slaughtering pens with the demand for whale oil to light the fine homes of the human species and to lubricate the machinery of the Industrial Age. Cultured ladies with hats decorated with egret plumes wore corsets made from whale baleen to mold dainty wasp waists. Captain Charles M. Scammon discovered the entrance to *Ojo de Liebra* which now bears his name. Fast and agile whale-boats were lowered from mother brigs. They were rowed by four oarsmen and steered by a tillerman. A marksman shot a bomb lance from a bow-mounted Greener's Harpoon Gun, point blank into the guts or lungs of yearling whales. Attempting to protect their offspring, mothers would attack their tormentors only to die by explosive warheads. Whaling crews were surprised when behemoths rammed their whale-boats. Gray whales learned to avoid age-old migratory routes and shallow lagoons, but the whalers always discovered new birthing locations.

The Leviathan Holocaust occurred because humankind believed that whales were non-thinking fish, put into the oceans for men to render into twenty barrels of oil. Whalers saved only the layer of fat and baleen plates while discarding meat and bones. By the early 1900s, finding the few remaining individuals of the depleted whale population became too costly, and humans learned to distill crude oil into kerosene, oils, and grease, thus saving whales from extinction. Synthetic plastic replaced baleen splats. The brutality of whaling administered by the humans faded from the collective memory of the gray whale.

With spring's approach, Mia felt the pull to migrate north as she had learned from her grandmother. It was time to retrace the swim to the Arctic Ocean and Bering Strait as her kind has done for millennia. In Scammon's Lagoon, it was high tide when Mia led her pod into the Pacific Ocean. José had lagged behind as the man with the pleasant voice called. Whales have been conditioned to swim to tourist boats. Perhaps mothers teach their babies how to use sonar around boats. Women lavished attention on José and affectionately called him Pépé. Impatiently, Mia splashed her fluke, until José dutifully followed.

The trip takes about one hundred days as whales follow the North American coast to the Arctic Ocean. The route is long and arduous, and the entire migration is completed without feeding. There is the risk of losing bearings and stranding onto a beach. But the greatest danger is to be ambushed by killer whales. Adult grays can out-swim these top predators, but young whales are vulnerable to vicious attacks, where the hunters rip fins and flukes, rendering young whales immobile. The calves suffer an excruciating death while orcas rip their tongues out. Killer whale packs kill thirty young grays every year. Adults swim in tight formation to provide an escort for yearlings and newborns, but orca packs know how to disrupt the convoy. Nevertheless, migration is necessary for pod survival because Baja seas don't support enough marine life during the summer months for foraging whales.

Mia's pod swam to Cape Flattery, Washington without incident. Swimming on the surface, they used landforms on the horizon and their sonar to avoid running aground. However, as the family approached the Cape a westerly wind and opposing rip tide created a vicious, chaotic chop which tossed them about like flotsam and disrupted their protective formation. The family was ambushed by a pack of killer whales who focused on a young cow and her calf. Mia, the lead cow, with her son, turned south-west to gain deep water where they evaded the hunting party by sounding. They remained offshore for a day before retracing their swim toward Tatoosh Island. From past migrations, the cow knows she will cross the Strait of Juan de Fuca and swim north along the western coast of Vancouver Island to regroup by using sonar.

CHAPTER 7

The Taking of Whale

The war canoe shoots through the narrows between Tatoosh Island and the mainland as if from a cannon. Sunlight penetrates here and there making a spotted patchwork of blue and black ocean. There is a horizon!

Spotting whales, the men pull harder and stroke longer. The long paddles permit the use of leg and back muscles. Most crew members had participated in coastal canoe races as youths. For coastal tribes, canoe races are like rodeos for White people and Plateau and Plains Indians. During the summer, rodeos move from town to town with the same cowboys, Brahma bulls, steers, calves, and bucking horses. Canoe races are held at coastal Indian villages in Washington State and British Columbia. Two- and four-man racing canoes are transported on top of reservation cars. The eleven man, 60-foot canoes are trailered. Canoe races are a magnet, holding clans together for potlatches, salmon bakes, craft shows, and gossip.

Sam picks up the cadence with vocals,

"Ha wo
Ha wa
Ha wo
Ha wa"

With increased speed, the prow raises from water exposing the lower jaw and front claws of the sea monster, Wasgo, painted on each side. The Wasgo painting transmogrifies the war canoe into a hunting sea serpent gliding on the horizon. Sam, at the tiller, had hewn the canoe from a single giant red cedar found on the Haida homeland of Graham Island, one of the Queen Charlotte Islands. Thomas, who sits in front of Sam, is the artist who painted Wasgo on the prow. Both Sam and Thomas are proud as their canoe is a worthy equal to an ancient war canoe.

Giant red cedar trees have been hewn into war canoes for count-less generations of Haida Indians and traded with southern Chilkoot Indians for robes and with Makah for whale oil. Surprisingly, the Haida don't have a whaling tradition even though they raided as far south as southern California.

The thirty-foot canoe, hewn by Sam, is relatively light as the walls are only two inches thick. Sam "hardened" the outer surface with flame and smoothed it to a silky finish with the dried skin of dogfish. After using a chainsaw to hollow out most of the log, he finished with an arm adze, leaving adze marks. Friends helped fill the hollowed canoe with water and hot stones to soften the sides. They widened the hollowed trunk with seat spacers—six two-inch diameter rods, covered with woven cedar pads. Sam capped the gunnels with strips of alder and fashioned the bowsprit and stern from blocks of alder which protects the relatively soft cedar.

Sam and Thomas knew from oral tradition that the bow figure of Sea Serpent (Wasgo) would strike terror in the mind of Whale and would impart strength to the warriors. Thomas wanted to use Wasgo for the bow figure because the sea monster is a powerful crest for many coastal Indians. Wasgo (Sgan for Haida and Sisiutl, the double-headed serpent for other tribes), wasn't a popular idea with Haida elders at the Skidegate Tribal Center on Gram Island because the feared "master of the sea" sometimes brings danger to Haida Indians. Nevertheless, Sam argued that Wasgo was appro-priate for this war canoe. He tactfully explained that the inspiration was the great Chief Kitkun whose back supported a Wasgo tattoo. This could only mean that if embraced by Indians, Wasgo would bring the crew luck and protection. The whale canoe is not only lovely and seaworthy but also embodies the Spirit of Wasgo who lives in the Underworld of Sea and hunts the Horizon.

The world Horizon, which is the inter-phase between the worlds Sky and Ocean, is the arena of Life and Death.

The days of training, the attention to details, and rituals per-formed for the hunt are now tested. Quanah steadies himself on the gunnel and forward seat with the harpoon point nestled into a notch

bored into the alder bowsprit. He braces against the 18-foot harpoon to look into the cold depths. He wears the traditional grizzly bear pelt, for which he had traded eight seal skins with a Blackfoot at a powwow at Fort Hall, Idaho.

Generations of canoe builders developed a hull of low drag dynamics and with stability in unforgiving chop. The sharp, high prow slices through the water leaving small wakes spaced ten feet apart. Aaron, the Seattle puller, commented that the prow reminded him of the front fender of the classic 1930 Jaguar car. The canoe and men are an object of grace and a deadly killer at the same time.

Quanah signals the intersecting course, and Sam swings the canoe toward a collision with Whale. The Chief Whaler removes the protective sheath from the harpoon point. They approach at forty degrees to port of the yearling and cow. The whales don't seem to notice the closing canoe and don't veer off course. The sharp points of paddles and canoe knife through the surface. Neither produces an alarming signal to alert Whale. Light rain dimples the oily surface. The whales are blowing every few hundred yards. Suddenly, they blow in synchrony twenty feet from the canoe. The right pullers pull strongly whereas pullers on the left back-paddle to change course and bring the canoe alongside the yearling. For a moment, canoe and Whale slide side by side. Quickly, the left front pullers pull hard while the right back pullers hold their paddles deep. The front right pullers backpaddle, and the left rear pullers hold their paddles deep. This complicated maneuver spins the bow and Quanah over Young Whale.

Quanah strokes the talisman hanging from a neck strap depicting a whaler carved into Whale made of a walrus tooth. The Alaskan Aleut had sent it with a prayer for Whale. Quanah steadies himself on the gunnels, raises the harpoon. Strangely, the yearling rolls to his side and raises his flipper to offer himself. All pullers hold their paddles deep. Quanah thrusts the eighteen-pound har-

poon two feet behind the flipper and eighteen inches below the backbone. A perfect aim as the harpoon misses the flipper and the large triangular shoulder blade. Quanah puts his body behind the harpoon. The elk antler point, gilded with razor-sharp muscle shells, slices through skin and blubber. It slows as it penetrates dense pectoral muscles. Quanah's forward momentum momentarily stops as the point hits a rib. As the point slides between round ribs, Quanah falls forward, and the harpoon plunges deep into the chest cavity to strike the opposite wall. The crew maintains position. The shaft of yew bends but does not break as it absorbs Quanah's 180-pounds. Had Quanah's aim been a few inches dorsal, toward the backbone, the point would have wedged between ribs where they are flat and spaced close together, and Whale would have pulled free.

In an instant, Quanah recovers, bracing against the gunnels, he pulls back on the shaft which separates from the point leaving it and rope buried deep within Whale. A jet of blood follows the harpoon as

Quanah pulls it from Whale. The harpoon pierced the heart. The rear pullers on both sides hold their paddles deep, and the front right pullers pull hard while the front left pullers back paddle so that the canoe pivots to swing the bow and Quanah away from Whale and the expected thrash of Whale's fluke. Whale does not sound. Gus plays rope into the water and throws the first float overboard. Picking a coil of the cedar bark rope from the rope basket, Gus casts the rope into the bow notch and pulls back. The rope tightens against the barb, ripping a hole in the heart and tearing the pericardium before snubbing against the inner wall of the thoracic cavity. The wild cherry bark holds the rope to the point as it wedges between ribs. Gus knows that a poorly cast coil and a sounding whale would entangle him and the whaler. Managing the rope is a dangerous part of taking a whale, but this 8,000-pound yearling doesn't flinch. Whale had not felt the harpoon penetrate his body.

This harpooning took only two seconds!

Whale must wonder what is happening. He rolls onto his side, lifts his flipper. He looks at the boat with men and the man with the long stick. Quanah raises the lance, thrusts it between flipper and back. The aim is perfect. The lance misses the shoulder blade, slices through neck muscles and slips between ribs to plunge into the thoracic cavity to rip through the aorta. The following short thrust severs massive pectoral and latissimus dorsi muscles that power the flipper. It penetrates deep to sever the brachial artery. Mercifully, Whale loses consciousness within seconds. Quanah thrusts again, a bit forward, and the lance hits the lungs, cutting pulmonary arteries. Blood and regurgitated bile, emulsified with surfactant from lungs, shrouds the canoe in a red-green aerosol. Frothy mist penetrates the eyes, nose, and lungs of the warriors.

The three lance thrusts took only six seconds!

The forty-pound heart, with the force of a four-horsepower engine, beats two more times, a beat every six seconds, each beat pushing ten quarts of blood out tears in the ventricle and aorta. The whale did not react, didn't raise a flipper, or change course—as if it felt nothing. Even though the physiological responses of bradycardia, a slowing of the heartbeat, were activated to restrict blood flow to the body, blood failed to reach Whale's brain. Quanah sees himself in Whale's huge eye. The eye rotates in its socket as extraocular muscles relax. Whale pupils dilate. Whale eyes slack and turn to glass, seeing nothing.

The cow stops, circling back to her yearling. She can't understand why he doesn't respond to her clicks. The yearling doesn't sound or thrash about. Quanah had made a clean kill, a rapid and humane kill. Not like the hunt in 2006 where the hunters had depended on a .50 caliber rifle to dispatch a harpooned whale. That whale had sounded and pulled the boat for 30 minutes. Finally, when the whale did surface, the Indians needed six shots before a slug penetrated its skull. Quanah, to assure he would do nothing that would cause the whale undue suffering, had thoroughly studied whale anatomy. He memorized the skeleton of a young gray whale at the Whale Museum in Friday Harbor and that of an adult which hangs in the tribal museum in Neah Bay. Quanah's knowledge of whale anatomy and behavior has paid off.

He thinks of the time his dad shot an elk which stood looking at them until it collapsed. Now he had harvested a whale. *Dad, I know you are proud.*

The men were outwardly tempered, but emotions roared within. They had learned from elders that prayer is important after taking an animal. The prayer would purify their souls making peace with nature. The Soul of Whale would understand. Spirituality gives meaning to the hunt as Whale Spirit knows his body will feed Indian villages. The men, not especially religious, but with mothers who baptized their babies into Whiteman's religion, realize the importance of Indian prayer, connecting to nature and their heritage. The warriors enter the Circle of Life.

Quanah is mute. He can't remember the Aleut prayer for Whale.

Ben, for most of his life, has been an angry person. Even striking out at those who loved him. He hadn't learned to speak his tribal tongue, even though his grandmother only talked in Nuu-chah-nulth. Ben had rehearsed the prayer, but the Indian words escaped him. Ben resorts to English:

"Thank you, O Chief from above for giving us Whale.
Thank you, Mother Whale for giving birth to Whale.
Thank you, Whale for swimming to us.
Thank you, Whale for accepting harpoon.
Thank you, Whale for feeding us.
Now, Whale Spirit, you are free."

The chant had sounded better in Nuu-chah-nulth. Ben's prayer surprises the Indians, as Ben has not interacted with any of the crew. He didn't want to socialize, thinking he did not belong with this group of educated Indians.

A great calm shrouds the canoe. The warriors are carved as in sculpture.

Whale body floats, rising and falling with swells. Still. Glass-eyed like in a Whiteman's mounted elk head. Whale and canoe drift as one on the horizon. Whale Spirit passes among the warriors.

The splash of Ben breaks the silence. Ben, with knife and rope, swims to Whale's head. Ben, the Nuu-chah-nulth (Nootka), had been picked by Quanah for this dangerous job because Ben is a powerful swimmer, a commercial fisherman, and scuba diver. He understands water and is fearless. Ben performs this part of the hunt traditionally, which requires him to dive into the water naked. Ben is deft with a knife. He needs only three dives to cut slits into the lips, thread the rope to tie the lips shut. Sewing Whale's lips together keeps lungs from completely collapsing, so the remaining air prevents Whale from sinking. It's freezing. Swimming to the fluke, he passes the tow rope around it. Ben's powerful legs turn to cold Jell-O. Surfacing, he gasps for breath, but he can't yell. He manages to hold his hand up before slipping beneath the oily surface. The men watch in horror as Ben disappears under Whale.

Aaron catches the others off guard as he rips his shirt off, shucks his shoes and pants in one fluid movement, and arches into the water. Within seconds, he surfaces with Ben. The men paddle to Aaron and haul them into the canoe. Ben shakes uncontrollably. His stout body, covered with a sheet of fat, which had protected him from the cold during the first couple of minutes is now sucking heat from his core. Ben collapses onto the cedar mats. He convulses twice, his jaw slacks, his eyes roll back, and he passes out.

David quickly slips his clothing off, lies down, and pulls Ben tightly against his body. Quanah covers both with his bearskin robe. Mats are thrown over the naked men. Ben lapses into a state of hypothermia, and all the bearskins in the world, if used alone, will not save him. His core temperature is so low that shivering has stopped. His body is not generating heat. His heart rate, dangerously low and irregular, could fibrillate any second, and Ben would die. David knows this. Using a fetal position, he presses as much of his surface against Ben as possible.

After a few minutes, David yells, "I'm freezing." Disengaging from Ben and standing, David says, "Next."

The wind has reversed and pushes the canoe north of Tatoosh Island. They paddle hard toward the island as there are dangerous rocks farther out. They take turns transferring heat to Ben. With Whale in tow, they are making only a half mile per hour.

Ben rouses himself after ten minutes, yelling at Merle who is pressed tightly against him, "Hey, man, what the hell you doing?" Slumping against the gunnel, in a halting voice, Ben continues, "Shit, I saw many ghost faces. Bodies shrouded. They opened their mouths, but nothing came out. I asked, 'Where am I'? They held their arms out and motioned me to join them. Then I saw you guys."

Thomas, grabbing Ben's shoulder, exclaims, "Ben, you saw Pokmus, a guardian of spirits, and the ghosts of drowned whalers."

Ben returns to his usual stoic countenance. Pulling on his clothing and grumbling to himself, he glares at David. "You should have let me die."

David says nothing but wraps Quanah's bear robe tightly around the now violently shivering Ben. He picks up his paddle.

The cow follows her dead yearling. She can't understand. In the calving grounds, she was always surrounded by boats. People loved to stroke their flippers, rub their skin and lips. The boats never rammed them. She follows her dead yearling as the last of his 150 gallons of blood drains from his body making a fifteen-mile-long chum slick.

Back in Neah Bay, residents prepare coffee. The crew has been missed. Louise, Merle's wife, is seven months pregnant and worried. She guessed that Quanah, her childhood classmate, would paddle too far for the crew's first outing after the winter lay off. Quanah was always talking about Cape Alava, a destination that would test his crew's mettle. Louise noticed, years ago, that Quanah was driven compared to other Indian boys and was fighting all the time. They called him Hitler because his mother is German. In grade school, he could whip any three. In high school, he proved himself in football and basketball, always trying to show his Indianness. During the penetrating dampness of spring and fall frost, Quanah went about town shirtless and hatless.

By afternoon, fog remains over the village of Neah Bay. Wind is picking up, and the Coast Guard issues small craft warnings. Louise can't control her anxiety and calls the coast guard. The Indians have an on-off relationship with the Coast Guard, but they can always count on the Guard when a Makah fishing boat is in trouble. Moreover, the Coast Guard enjoys showing off a response boat during the annual fall Makah Day Parade. This event makes the Guard part of the community.

It's evening when the pullers pass Tatoosh Island with Whale in tow. The canoe is now running with tide and wind. As they turn south-east into the Strait of Juan de Fuca, a coast guard helicopter emerges from the fog bank. A few minutes later a coast guard cutter breaks the horizon into sunlight. The cutter keeps its distance. The bone-tired Indians know they're on radar. They paddle in silence through the night. Fog closes about them. They're more than happy to follow the cutter through the Strait of Juan de Fuca as the horizon is lost to fog.

CHAPTER 8

At the eastern end of the Strait of Juan de Fuca, one hundred twenty miles from Neah Bay, Alana is the figurehead for the ferry, Yakima. She stands on the upper passenger deck overlooking the bow as the ferry pushes from the slip at Shaw Island to continue through the San Juan Archipelago.

Even though she's been in Seattle for a short time, she takes the ferry from Anacortes, just north of Seattle, into the San Juan Archipelago to visit Friday Harbor Laboratories where her grandfather studied forty years ago. Fog is heavy against the tree-covered walls of the channel between Shaw and Orcas Islands muffling the engine knock. The engines and generators come in and out of phase sending chaotic shivers through the hull. Her fingers tingle as she holds fast to the railing. Alana sees faint silhouettes of shrouded islands against the setting sun on the western horizon. She looks forward to walking miles of sunny beaches heaped with windrows of bleached detritus of drowned trees swept south from the Inland Passage.

Bracing against the wet wind sweeping over the forward observation deck, Alana silently addresses the bow wave as if it were a jury, *My grandfather disappeared somewhere near here, forty years ago. Even though this cluster of islands is remote, I don't believe that someone could vanish without leaving a clue. These lonely beaches and fiords hold answers to his disappearance.*

Walking back into the lounge, Alana retrieves Bernard Edward's letter from her backpack. Edwards resigned at Syracuse Law School to accept the newly created Ralph Johnson Chair in Native American Law at the University of Washington. Edwards also joined a Seattle law firm specializing in Native American law. Alana unfolds Edwards's letter:

Law Firm of Schneider, Lamb, and Moore
Native American Law Since 1963
Fishing and hunting, salmon and halibut allotments
River and stream water rights
Treaty Law, Tribal Law, State and Federal Law
24th Floor, Purcell Building, Seattle, WA
www.schneiderlambmoore.com
Phone: 206-118-2223

Dear Alana,
I offer you an instructor position in my department at the University of Washington and a junior position in our law firm in Seattle. I remember how much you enjoyed learning about the Oneida Tribe litigation against the State of New York.

Alana remembered it well—a history full of intrigue, avarice, and greed. Even though the Oneida Tribe had sided with the Americans during the War of Independence, the State of New York cheated them out of thousands of square miles of historic tribal lands with illegal 1880 treaties. The Oneida Tribal land case reached the Supreme Court in the 1970s. The Warren Court upheld the lower court ruling in favor of the Oneida claim which rested on the assertion that the State of New York violated the Trade and Intercourse Act of 1870. In this law, Congress prevented States from making treaties with Native Americans and determined that treaties could only be ratified by Congress. The Supreme Court ruled that New York State would have to either give back a huge tract of land or compensate the Oneida Indians with hard cash. The exact nature of reparations has yet to be decided. Anyway, this landmark decision spread throughout American Indian reservations. For example, the State of Idaho decided not to challenge the Coeur d'Alene Tribe when it reclaimed National Forest land for shore and water rights on Coeur d'Alene Lake. The Tribe based their claim on tribal history and the 1858 treaty forced onto the Tribe by Col. George Wright after the

Battles of Four Lakes and Spokane Plains.

Alana returns her eyes to the letter, which is wilting in the damp air.

We were impressed with your moot court briefs presented in Tuc-
son a couple of years ago regarding salmon rights of Washington
State coastal Indians. For these reasons, I believe this position will
be of interest to you and that your acceptance will prove an asset
to our firm.

I look forward to your reply,
Sincerely yours,
Bernard Edwards

Alana puts the letter back, fishes out a map from her backpack, and follows the ferry route winding through Wasp Channel between Shaw and Crane Islands to where it emerges into San Juan Channel to turn south toward San Juan Island. A dense fog settles over the Islands obliterating the horizon to force early darkness.

After accepting Dr. Edwards' offer, Alana did her homework regarding Coastal Indian hunting and fishing rights guaranteed by federal government treaties. As her professor, Dr. Edwards was fond of saying, "Students, it's the banal, the uninteresting facts, history, and dull reports written by federal agencies that win litigation. An astute trial lawyer will find the information necessary to sway a key juror."

As she mulls over history, the complexity boggles Alana's mind. Future court decisions will involve not only fishing rights but the preservation of salmon stocks judged to be on the brink of extinction. In salmon fishing litigation, water rights are paramount. Without water, there are no salmon. Alana recalls that the fate of four dams on the Snake River in eastern Washington State will be determined in court. Years ago, the Snake River twisted and tumbled as it sliced through the Columbia Plateau from Lewiston, Idaho, to the Tri-Cities in Washington where it meets the once-mighty Columbia River. Now the Washington State part of the Snake River is tamed into a chain of four reservoirs. The Columbia River has also been dammed for water power and transportation. Dam builders, the U.S. Corp of Engineers, had not thought about salmon during dam construction, and Native Americans had little clout when the dams were built from the 1930s to the 60s. Today, indigenous people's rights to salmon conflict with power plants, transportation, and agriculture.

Alana's mom receives a small income from the family farm. Alana hopes the farm doesn't lie in the Coeur d'Alene Tribal Reservation. *Mom doesn't know it, but she has a stake in Native American litigation because her wheat, although a small amount at 5000 bushels a year, is sent to Portland markets by barge. Dams providing irrigation water have decimated many salmon stocks.*

Alana smiles as she continues her train of thought. The legal interests of Native Americans are linked to salmon which in turn are dependent on water flow to the Pacific. Fishing and water rights are the legal issues of the future.

She sighs. *I can help save the environment and secure reparations for indigenous peoples of the United States. After all, Native Americans are the original environmentalists.*

The sun disappears without a sunset. There is no indication of the San Juan Archipelago against the western horizon. The ferry slows as it enters the harbor of San Juan Island. The Friday Harbor village lights are dimmed to yellow by heavy air.

Yes, I made the right decision moving to Seattle, she thinks.

The engine vibrations are mesmerizing, yet relaxing to the point that her mind drifts. *Why am I here?* She asks the fog bank, *Have I moved because of law? Or because of my grandfather who disappeared forty years ago?*

Lost in thoughts, she doesn't notice the oncoming ferry slip. The fore and aft screws churn frothy cauldrons against dock pilings. The 400-foot-long Yakima, capable of carrying 5000 linear feet, that's a mile of cars and trucks, slides into its berth. Alana braces against the handrail as the ship shudders to a stop. Within seconds, the deckhands secure hawsers around capstans and the ramp is lowered to the ferry deck. The foot passengers disembark, many pushing bicycles. With backpacks, most look like college students returning to the laboratory to study marine biology and physiology. Alana swings her pack over her shoulder and falls into line. After the bikers push to the sidewalk, the crew directs cars to drive off the side decks. The incline is steep because of low tide. Pickups follow cars. They are old and rusty with beds full of rotting fishing nets, bleached pink floats that at one time had been fluorescent red, yellow scraps of rain gear, and aging boat equipment like rusty generators that look like they haven't worked for years. The smell of gasoline hangs in the air as a rusting hulk grinds its way up the ramp.

Three tractor-trailers parked in the middle bay are last to drive off. Alana stops to watch an eighteen-wheeler with pony-trailer laden with concrete blocks. It's an old Freightliner with battered fenders. It stalls, leaving the pony-trailer on the ferry—obviously not an unusual occurrence because a dock tug is soon coming down the street.

The mist turns to drops. On a Tuesday evening with few if any visitors, Alana thinks she may have the Island and, for that matter, the whole archipelago to herself. Stalled trucks probably furnish the only excitement during the fall and winter. *One of the fishermen will undoubtedly jump at the chance to make a few bucks driving me around.*

The Lottia B&B, located on Harrison Street, is hosted by retired professors who once taught invertebrate and ecology courses at the labs. Over the phone, they seemed nice. Alana didn't tell them of her reason for the visit. She hopes they knew her granddad. She also plans to visit places she researched when contemplating her move to Washington: Fairyland sites like False Bay, The British Barracks, and The American Camp of The Pig War, Garrison Bay, and Roche Harbor with its lime kilns which had been worked by Chinese and Native Americans in the late 1800s.

The pea soup creates small islands of light surrounding street lamps. Alana walks straight from the dock past the ferry lanes to the intersection. In the yellow light, she makes out the Harrison Street sign. She turns left and proceeds up a steep incline as per directions. One hundred yards up the hill, on her left in the yard, she spies the Lottia B&B sign. Alana had looked up the name to find that Lottia is the genetic name of the common limpet. She guessed that the Applegates, with whom she'd made the reservation, had studied limpets, so the name is symbolic for a secure place. The B&B, Lottia, solidly adheres to a granite outcropping.

Alana muses, *Yes indeed, this house with its triangular profile is a cone-shaped limpet sticking onto a rock.* She follows the walk, winding over terraces to the front door. The knocker is a brass crab.

"Hello," says a tiny Chinese lady as she opens the door.

Behind her stands a thin, tall, academic-looking man with brass-rimmed glasses and a shock of white hair. Smiling the Chinese lady pushes the storm door open, "Do come in. You must be Alana. We've been expecting you and are pleased to have a visitor this time of year. My name is Megan, and my husband is Charlie. We took the liberty to set a bowl for you. There isn't much open tonight except for bars. Charlie, show the young lady to her room."

Charlie leads the way up the squeaking stairs which open into a wide hall with several doors, saying, "We think you would like the room overlooking the harbor and Brown's Island. You'll be able to see the biology laboratory buildings across the harbor in the morning. We don't expect other guests. Please come down after you freshen up."

Dropping her pack onto the luggage rack, Alana surveys the room. It has an enormous Victorian bed with a headboard that's a good two feet taller than her five-foot ten-inch, athletic frame. There is a make-up dresser with triptych mirrors, a nightstand with wash basin and pitcher, a dresser, and a roll-top desk. The furniture has marble tops. Alana hangs a few things in the walk-in closet, washes her face and hands, and goes downstairs. Megan and Charlie Applegate are waiting in the parlor.

Looking about the tastefully arranged setting, Alana marvels, "What a lovely room."

Mrs. Applegate replies, "We purchased the house in the late 1960s from an old couple who wanted to move into the newly completed retirement home. At that time, no one wanted Victorians with furniture. This house is more English than American, but that's another story for later. You'll see some outlandish American opulent homes. They don't fit the island. Well, let's go into the kitchen for a bowl of chowder."

Alana asks, "Are you sure it's not an imposition, Mrs. Applegate?"

"Yes, dear, and please call me Meg." The petite woman smiles and continues, "The chowder is ideal for a bone-chilling evening. To the stock of potato and onion soup I added cooked pieces of rockfish, steamed bent-nose and soft-shelled clams. Charlie, who volunteers at the labs, brought a squid which I diced along with shrimp he netted from the laboratory dock pilings. Charlie made the bread."

While ladling soup, Meg inquires, "Well dear, are you a student, a postdoctoral fellow, or a professor looking over the lab facilities for future studies?"

"None of the above. My grandfather was a student here in the 1960s. I hope to find out something about him. My mother was seven when he disappeared, presumed drowned."

Mrs. Applegate responds, "I'm so sorry dear. Perhaps we knew him, since we were also students in the sixties. What was his name?"

Alana says, "Erich Svoboda."

"Well, of course we knew him. What a tragedy! Your grandfather was well liked," Meg says.

"Could you tell me about him?"

Charlie smiles and begins, "Well let's see. Forty years ago. My, my! I took Arnold Kepler's class on Invertebrate Physiology, and Erich was the lab assistant. He collected the animals and organized equipment for experiments. Hmm... Let's see, I do remember one exercise where we studied the effects of drugs and ions on the clam heart. Its heartbeat is more sensitive than a mass spectrometer to biologically active chemicals. We used the very clam that you are eating in the chowder."

Alana looks at the bite-sized lump of grayish tissue filling her spoon and wonders if it's the whole clam.

Charlie continues, "Hmm…it's coming back to me now. I don't remember that much about your grandfather, but some things come to mind in regards to Arnold Kepler. It was in 1962 that the Zoology Department hosted a symposium at Friday Harbor. About neurotransmitters. These chemicals are released by neurons at synapses to stimulate adjacent neurons. Kepler had just discovered gamma amino butyric acid, GABA for short. GABA is an amino acid. Dr. Halpen, the zoology chair, was convinced that Kepler would win a Nobel Prize because GABA was found to be an inhibitory neurotransmitter in the mammalian brain. Drug therapy for depression is based on GABA. Even commercials talk about GABA."

Smiling, Meg interjects, "And to think it all started here, at Friday Harbor with shellfish."

Alana hopes there are no more clams in the soup.

Charlie continues, "The whole department turned around Kepler. Symposium participants flew in from Seattle on float planes. They stayed in university housing, so graduate students were relegated to tents for a week. The university hired cooks from The Seattle Hotel to create three-star menus. There were big hitters, Nobel Laureates, Sir Bernard and Sir John, were in attendance. No, wait, only John Eccles came and made a point that Kepler's GABA research was fundamental. The symposium was published in a book, giving Kepler more space and university money."

Mrs. Applegate interrupts, "Charlie, you are prattling. Alana, the shrimp in the soup are related to crabs. Both are arthropods. I remember your grandfather and Kepler were measuring the heartbeat of the red rock crab, *Cancer*. It was unusual physiology because they were rowing about the harbor with a portable oscilloscope. A wire connected the oscilloscope to a crab which wandered about the seafloor. Who could forget that? However, I don't remember your Grandfather's dissertation. Oh dear, now I'm the one boring you. You can find your grandfather's dissertation in the Lab Library."

Alana finds the stories interesting but wonders what the Applegate's remember about the accident. *Maybe they don't want to talk about it,* she thinks.

Meg Applegate breaks the silence. "If you go to the lab tomorrow, you can visit Bob Black. He's retired and volunteers at the Lab aquarium in the afternoons. He was a contemporary to your grandfather."

Smiling at Meg and Charlie, Alana says, "It was so kind of you to invite me for this wonderful chowder. Especially considering the weather." As she pushes from the table, she continues, "Thank you for the stories. I hadn't heard them. Mom was too young."

Meg and Charlie also stand, and Meg embraces Alana. "My dear girl, we are so pleased that you're here. We expect you for breakfast. Good night."

CHAPTER 9

Morning, Friday Harbor – May 12

Alana is up at six, after a restful night. No sounds drift from the village of Friday Harbor. She has no idea of the commotion at Neah Bay 120 miles to the West which will change her life. She pulls on jeans and shirt, grabs her pull-over, and descends the stairs. They squeak. She gently turns the doorknob attempting to sneak out.

"Good morning, Alana. We have scones, Friday Harbor honey, and wild rose-hip jam. Will you join us?" Asks Meg.

Alana jumps. "I'm sorry, I didn't think you'd be up. Would you mind terribly if I ran first?"

"Of course not. Don't hurry."

Fog envelops the village. No sunrise to see. No Cascade Range on the eastern horizon. No color, only shades of gray. Just out of town Alana passes several joggers, nay, serious runners. They have smart phones, and if she had been a white rhino, they wouldn't have seen her. She wonders if they are biologists.

She jogs another mile to the campus, turns around, and starts back. A runner races by without acknowledgment. She is back at the Lottia by 9:30. The fog hasn't lifted.

At the breakfast table, Alana remarks, "These scones are so light they don't need butter. Mmm. Delicious with this jam."

Meg brightens, "We made both the butter and the jam."

As Alana finishes, Meg asks. "Can we give you a lift to the labs?"

"No, but thank you. I can use the exercise."

Alana walks to the northern end of the village, past the restaurant filling with locals, toward the labs. She notes a sign in front of an old building and makes a mental note to visit in the afternoon. The sign says, **Whale Museum. Open daily 10:00 a.m. to 5:00 p.m.**

Entering the Friday Harbor Laboratory office, Alana taps lightly on the glass door.

The secretary looks up, and with a gruff voice, says "Please come in. May I help you?"

"Hi, I'm Alana Svoboda, and I'm in town for a few days. Would it be possible to use the library? Also, I heard from the Applegates that Dr. Bob Black has a desk in the reading room. Do you expect him today?"

"Dr. Black usually comes in about ten and works to four. You'll recognize him as he takes care of the sea tank under the stair-well," the receptionist replies in a noncommittal tone.

"Thank you. Could you direct me to the dissertation shelves?"

"First aisle on your left, arranged by name. Are you looking for anyone in particular?"

"Yes, Erich Svoboda's dissertation written in the 1960s."

The receptionist, with a changed demeanor, inquires, "We like to know who uses our library. Not to be nosy, but may I ask why you're looking for that dissertation?"

"He was my grandfather."

"Oh, I see. That was before my time, so I don't know him."

Alana traces her finger along the row of black binders and pulls two: Erich E. Svoboda, Master's Thesis, The Tunicate Heart, and, Erich E. Svoboda, Ph.D. Dissertation. Electrophysiology of the Tunicate Heart. Turning on the desk lamp, she sags into a chair muttering, "Wow, the dissertation is heavy." Thumbing through figures, she continues her conversation with herself, "All these equations, graphs, and tables with words are what one would usually find in physics books: resistivity, wavefronts, impedance, and electrical circuits. This is a far cry from following a crab, clambering over the sea floor as Mrs. Applegate described."

Engrossed in her grandfather's work, Alana hardly notices the passing of time. Looking out the library door, she sees a short man, bald and portly, poking about in the sea water tank below the stair-well.

"Good morning.…Dr. Black?" Alana inquires, looking down on

the man lifting a huge clamshell, dripping green slime, from the muck and dropping it into a bucket.

"My God, what a stench. These geoducks just don't last in our tanks. *Panope generosa*, yes, they are generous in size and smell!" The man looks up as green slime drips from his hand to the floor. "Young lady, what can I do for you?"

Alana, stopped by stench and thinking of clam chowder manages to say, "Excuse me, what?"

"What can I do for you?" The man replies.

Alana watches the man ladling the slimy mess into a bucket without gloves. She asks, "Did you know Erich Svoboda?"

The old man stops mucking about, swishes his hands under the faucet of running sea water. "Erich, my goodness, haven't heard his name for years. Why do you ask?"

"He was my grandfather. The Applegate's thought you probably knew him."

"Of course, I knew him. Let's have a cup of coffee."

There are two coffee dispensers and a box of donuts on a table in front of the office. Dr. Black draws a cup with caffeine and asks, "green or red?"

"Decaf, please," Alana replies as she sits down. With the stench of decaying clam still emanating in her nose, Alana wonders, *How can one eat what can stink so badly?*

"What do you want to know about your grandfather?" Black inquires, as he lowers himself into a chair.

The putrid smell remains, overpowering the coffee, so she is slow to respond. "Everything you can tell me about Erich Svoboda."

"We shared an office in Seattle and graduate labs here at Friday Harbor."

"Start in Seattle," Alana enthusiastically replies.

Dr. Black gazes out onto the harbor and slowly says, "We were graduate students. In those days it was required to get a master's degree before a doctorate. We had to pass five out of six qualifying exams in comparative anatomy, invertebrate zoology, embryology, physiology, ecology, and genetics. We were also required to read scientific papers in German and French. We sweat blood. We had some excellent professors, and most took teaching seriously. I remember Dr. Dixie Lee Ray who taught invertebrate zoology. Never married. Her parents were killed in a car wreck, and she raised four younger siblings while going to graduate school. What a bundle of energy!

"She was appointed Secretary of Energy by the Carter Administration. Can you believe it? She lived in a trailer, in Washington DC! She worked to abolish the position, and she did. She always drove around Friday Harbor in a Jaguar convertible with a wolfhound and a little mutt. We called her Dragon Lady. To beat all, she became governor of Washington. Dr. Ray was a practical biologist who saw both sides of ecological issues. She wrote a book about common sense ecology. Oh, I'm sorry. I seldom have a chance to talk about the good old days."

"No, please go on, I know so little about my grandfather. What happened?"

"Erich turned in a good dissertation. Doesn't seem fair. You know, the accident. Just a few months after he defended." Dr. Black turns to Alana. "We fished together off the pump dock along the shore where the bluffs drop into San Juan Channel. The dock isn't there anymore. We had a friendly competition for the largest ling cod. My best was forty pounds.

"He was alone the evening he disappeared. I know he didn't do anything stupid. The tide was past ebb running north from the harbor. We used small skiffs in which we could buck the tide to row back to the lab. No one could figure out what happened. Three days later, the San Juan Sheriff found the boat on Waldron Island northeast of Orcas Island. It must have been a freak accident. Your grandfather's body was never found." Dr. Black sighs as if a weight lifted from his chest.

After lunch at the wharf Café, Alana walks to the whale museum. The door to the Directors Office opens, and a well-groomed man approaches the receptionist.

The woman shrieks, "How could Quanah do this? I thought he was different! He's a student of yours, isn't he?"

The well-groomed man and agitated woman walk into the museum reception area. The man says, "I'm not surprised. If the fog lifts, I'll fly to Neah Bay this afternoon."

The woman rages on, "After all you did for Quanah! You gave him permission to take measurements of the whale skeleton. I saw him measuring the rib cage when the shoulder blade detached, and the whole flipper crashed to the floor. Someone could have been killed."

The man smiles. "Now I know why Quanah was so interested in the skeleton and why he asked me where the heart would be located in the rib cage. It seems that the anatomy lesson was effective. He did kill a whale."

Alana walks over to the woman who is now sitting behind the receptionist desk explaining, "I didn't mean to eavesdrop, but I couldn't help but overhear that the whale skeleton fell from the ceiling. Is that true?"

"Just one of the flippers," replies the woman, sharply.

"The skeleton looks OK to me. Were any bones broken?"

"No, our director, Dr. Dennis Farmington, remounted them. I would have thrown Quanah out with instructions never to return. Dennis is too forgiving. Now he's flying to Neah Bay to offer his help. Nothing good comes from helping those Indians."

Alana asks, "Where's Neah Bay, and what happened there?"

The woman's demeanor changes, and in a happier tone, answers, "Neah Bay is as far west in Washington as you can go. It belongs to some Indians. The town of Neah Bay is in the reservation. Quanah, a student here at the labs, killed a whale yesterday. He's in big trouble. He didn't have a permit."

After listening to the woman for a while, Alana changes the subject. "Is there a Native American village in the San Juan Islands?"

"Not now, but a hundred years ago there was. Recent archeological digs at English Camp found Indian graves. Indians came from all directions, and the locals weren't happy. Oh, I shouldn't complain. I'm just a bitter old woman."

"I don't mind. By the way, my name is Alana, and I'm staying with the Applegates. You probably know them."

The secretary grins as she replies, "Of course, we were graduate students together. In the Zoology Department."

Alana asks, "Did you know Erich Svoboda?"

"Certainly, we were students together under Ernst Kepler. Why do you ask?"

"Erich was my grandfather."

After a long pause, the secretary clears her throat. "Erich was Ernst's favorite graduate student."

Detecting what might be resentment, Alana changes the subject, "I met Dr. Bob Black this morning. How is it that all of you students ended up here?"

"When we were grad students, property was cheap, and, though we couldn't afford it, we bought land. Not beach property mind you. However, many professors purchased lots with beaches, and today they are worth millions."

CHAPTER 10

West entrance of Strait of Juan de Fuca
Late Morning - 12 May

By morning, the whale hunters are joined by a flotilla of official crafts, tribal fishing boats, and motor boats of all descriptions and sizes. There is one Coast Guard helicopter and three commercial helicopters—with photographers hanging outdoors—swarming overhead like hungry horse flies. Two additional Coast Guard cutters join the mêlée. One cutter steams alongside the war canoe to keep animal activists from ramming the canoe.

The boatswain yells through a bull horn, "Stay clear of the canoe and whale."

After fourteen hours of towing the dead whale, the Indians reach the seawall protecting Neah Bay. The fog has lifted. The Olympic Mountains loom high to the east and to the north, on the horizon, the mountains of Vancouver Island hover over the Strait of Juan de Fuca. As the Indians approach Waadah Island, they are met by Tribal Harbor Police.

Tribal Officer Richard, a former classmate of Quanah's, brings his boat alongside Quanah's canoe and shouts, "The Coast Guard, federal agents, and State Police are crowding the dock. The town is packed. The governor has called. Quanah, what are your plans?"

73

Quanah replies, "The crowds aren't my problem."

Glaring, Richard pleads, "There is a rumor that a Sea Shepherd ship is coming from Seattle and that Paul Watson will fly in to tow the whale out to sea. That guy looks forward to confrontation. He will probably try to sink your canoe. Let me tow you to shore."

Quanah waves Richard away, but Richard keeps his boat against the canoe. "I have to arrest you, damn it, Quanah. Why did you go kill this whale?" Tribal Officer Richard grabs the canoe gunnel. "Tribal elders are ready to skin you alive."

Quanah was always at odds with Richard, a dark-skinned, short, barrel-chested Indian. Richard was an exceedingly strong classmate of Quanah's. Richard was the Red Devils' running back when their high school took the 1B division in State. Quanah played end, and the two competed for yards. They are still competing.

As Richard ties a rope around the canoe bow, Quanah asserts, "Our Bill of Rights in the Makah Constitution gives me the economic right to hunt whales. In regards to animal activists, many are bigoted Whitemen who eat meat but are against hunting. I'm not afraid of them."

Looking over the canoe, Richard demands, "Who are the Indians with you?"

Quanah yells at Richard. "If you knew our tribal constitution, you would know that they have every right to be with me. Our civil liberties ensure that I have the freedom to associate with whomever I choose."

Officer Richard's eyes narrow. "Just because you go to the university doesn't mean you know shit, you *Go-Ge-We-H*!"

Quanah softly answers, "Hey, have respect for Whale. His Spirit is still with us."

"What do you mean?" Richard asks.

"Ask your elders."

Quanah and Richard would walk away from each other like in a football scrimmage if they could. Richard knows he needs to tow the canoe to the tribal dock. Knowing most Indians would not resist, Richard sees Quanah's resistance as acting White. The two

Indians are saved from each other as the Coast Guard cutter approaches, and a Zodiac edges between the war canoe and the tribal police Bayliner.

With a bullhorn, Boatswain Breugger shouts from the cutter, "Makah police, release your line to the canoe and standoff. The Coast Guard has federal jurisdiction here. Crew of canoe, grab the line from Zodiac, and let them tow you to the cutter."

On the bow of the cutter, a sailor stands at the ready with an M16.

Richard motors off, and Quanah doesn't respond. Boatswain Breugger again bellows, "If you don't grab the Zodiac line, we'll cut the whale free."

Quanah grabs the line.

When the crew of the Zodiac tows the war canoe to the cutter, a sailor drops a ladder into the canoe as Boatswain Breugger orders, "Climb aboard."

The Indians are dead tired, and it seems that the Coast Guard is a better choice than the tribal police launch, so they clamber aboard. There is little space in the cabin, and the Indians are jammed together like salmon in a purse seine.

Boatswain Breugger, as he handcuffs Quanah, says, "I'm sorry to do this. But it's regulation when we make an arrest for a federal offense. I will transfer you to the Coast Guard dock where you'll be flown by helicopter to the Federal Prison at the SeaTac airport."

The Indians are bone tired and collapse into chairs and onto the floor. A sailor remarks with awe in his voice, "You guys look beat. How did you kill that whale?"

CHAPTER 11

Wahoo sails to Neah Bay - noon - May 12

As Quanah and Richard are exchanging insults at the western reach of Juan de Fuca Strait, Commander Albert Sorenson is sailing west toward Neah Bay. Sorenson set sail with the Coast Guard Cutter, Wahoo, from Port Angeles at four A.M. His orders are to seize a whale being towed by Indians and maintain order between Indians and animal activist groups known for belligerent, aggressive tactics against whaling interests. A few years ago, a young woman in a powerboat rammed a Coast Guard cutter protecting an Indian canoe towing a whale. She sustained injuries and sued the Coast Guard for careless and reckless behavior.

With the gravity of the situation and as commanding officer of Homeland Security of Sector Field Office for the Eastern reach of San Juan Strait, Sorenson decided he should be in Neah Bay to oversee the operation and not assign a boatswain to the task.

This time of year, the Strait of Juan de Fuca is under blankets of fog which require instrument navigation, and Sorenson posted four sailors to watch for fishermen in small boats, which aren't always picked up on radar. The spring salmon run has started, and fishermen are out in twenty-foot outboards, which keeps the Coast Guard busy plucking uneducated sailors from capsized boats. Even though the Guard saves the landlubbers, the sailors take abuse because the Guard doesn't put bumpers between rescued boats. By contrast, Albert has a better relationship with Indians during search and rescue operations. As a young boatswain at Neah Bay, he helped many Makah who don't always keep their boats and equipment in good shape. Nevertheless, the Coast Guard cuts Indians slack, as they are cheerful and thankful when rescued.

The sail to Neah Bay is boring, giving Sorenson plenty of time to think about his relationship to the Indians. He watched Indian canoes all summer during patrols around Cape Flattery. Sailors had not been impressed in 2006 when a motorboat towed a canoe and whale during an illegal hunt. Those whalers used a .50 caliber rifle to kill the whale, and the gruesome killing was shown live on TV.

Albert remembers a conversation he once had with his brother, who is normally opposed to whaling. Albert got him to admit, "I wouldn't mind if Indians killed a whale with traditional harpoons and used a canoe. Using a motorboat and a .50 caliber rifle is bull-shit!"

Most of Albert's family were against whaling and didn't care that he was obligated to protect Indians after arresting them. Even Captain Sorenson's wife sided against the Makah. To Albert, the activists were the trouble makers.

Looking into the fog bank, Sorenson addresses his boatswain at the wheel, "Sailor, what do you think about our task today?"

"Sir, I haven't really thought about it."

"Son, it's acceptable to give me your opinion. Feel free to express yourself."

"I think Indians should be allowed to hunt if they use ancestral methods. Killing whales with harpoons is OK."

Nodding, the Commander says, "I agree. The .50 caliber rifle which propels a bullet with enough energy to penetrate an engine block gives the wrong impression. I believe a hunt can be spiritual and fulfill ancestral customs with traditional methods."

Looking at the sonar screen CDR Sorensen continues, "Today's hunt is different from the one in '96 because there is only one canoe with a whale in tow. There was no announcement of intention from the Makah Tribal office. Nevertheless, this is an illegal hunt. We'll have to arrest the Indians."

After a pause, Sorenson asks, "Do you remember the Indian canoes we saw a few months ago off Cape Flattery?"

"Yeah."

"Thinking of that, I guess I'm not surprised that they simply went out and killed a whale."

Albert Sorensen knows the waters of the Strait and Puget Sound like the back of his hand. He was born and raised overlooking Lake Union in Seattle. His family, Swedes, are fishermen and keep boats in Lake Union. He is the third generation. His uncle's fishing boat was rigged for longlining, and Albert helped as a deckhand while in high school. Longliners troll six to ten spoons behind two booms. Lines are fastened to the booms with a clothespin which snaps free when a salmon strikes. This method lacks sportsmanship as the crew simply drags salmon into the boat which doesn't slow down. These salmon fetch the best price because they're not cut or bruised as those purse-seined or caught in gill nets stretched across rivers.

It was apparent years ago that the salmon industry was doomed with the decreasing number of salmon. The Whiteman blamed the Indian, and the Indian blamed the White fisherman for the decrease in salmon numbers. The time bomb exploded in the 1970s with confrontations between the Nisqually Indians and White fisherman on the Nisqually River near Tacoma, Washington. Many Indians, as well as actor Marlon Brando, were arrested for netting fish illegally. The case went to the Federal Court where Judge Boldt ruled that Indians are entitled to half the fish allotment. White fishermen believed Judge Boldt's decision was wrong because there are ten times more white fishermen than Indians.

The Boldt decision split families, including Sorenson's. His brother was furious, yelling at Albert, "Goddammit, Al, you don't have to take the Indian position. The feds should keep their nose out of Washington State and my business. I'll need to convert to halibut and snow crab and move my boat to Alaska. Puget Sound salmon fishing is ruined because Indians can use gill nets. They let fish rot for days."

The sailor interrupts the commander's reflections, "Sir, how do you feel about protecting the Indians?"

"Son, it's our duty."

This question led Commander Sorenson to ask himself, *Why am I here?* After high school, Albert went to Coast Guard school at Woods Hole on Cape Cod. He had a fifteen-foot skiff which was barely large enough to fish The Hole during a strong ebb tide. Most of his training was rescuing members of the New York Yacht Club who thought they could sail through The Hole regardless of wind or tide. Albert muses, *Hell, the tide could run at four knots! And given winds of 15 knots, those folks were always running onto rocks. Some advantaged elite New Yorkers didn't know the difference between a 'can' and a 'nun.' Now, I'm rescuing farmers with more money than caution, who think they're safe with outboard boats designed for lakes."*

Sailor, "Sir, we are four miles offshore and 20 miles from Neah Bay. There are several small boats to port. There is no problem."

Albert's thoughts drift back to Massachusetts where the Cape offers tremendous striped bass and bluefish fishing.

After basic training, he attended officer school in Yorktown, VA. Yearning for the northwest he jumped at the chance to take a position at Neah Bay. After a couple years he moved his wife and three kids to Port Angeles.

Albert loves salmon fishing, but now as a sport. He is also an avid deer and elk hunter. As with fish, there is contention between Whites and Indians on the Olympic Peninsula. The Washington State Game Department manages the big game herds. There are so many White hunters that the Game Department must limit White hunters by lottery. Albert has applied for the last three years for an elk permit in a game management area in the Olympic National Forest. No luck so far. Chances are slim because the game department gives only twelve permits a year. There is little hunting land because most of the Olympic Peninsula is in the Olympic National Park. Indians have the right, under treaty, to hunt where and whenever they want in Federal National Forests, providing they hunt in historic locations.

White hunters grouse about Indian pickups full of elk capes with huge racks, driving from the Sol Doc Hot Springs and leaving carcasses to rot. The veracity of these stories is doubtful, but nevertheless, they irritate White hunters. The White hunter, if lucky to draw a permit, can only shoot spike elk. Moreover, Albert's Makah friend said it would be contrary to their religion to sell antlers to the Whiteman, and parts of the elk not used must be burned or buried.

Albert mumbles to the sailor, "Hunters and Indians should be on the same side of the hunting issue..." but didn't finish his thought as the Sailor interrupts, "Sir, I see our cutter standing off Neah Bay."

Sorenson orders, "Come to the port side of the cutter. Get Boatswain Breugger on the line."

Boatswain Breugger on the 44 Cutter calmly reports, "Commander, I have the whale in tow. The Indians are in custody. They don't have rifles. They killed the whale with a harpoon."

Commander Sorenson replies, "I am pleased there is no confrontation."

Boatswain Breugger, "Sir, no Green Peace and no Sea Shepherd ships are in the area."

Sorenson replies, "That's good news, Breugger. Under no circumstance allow tribal police to tow the whale into Neah Bay. Deliver the Indians to the helicopter crews at the station."

Sorenson explains to his helmsman, "In 1999, we protected the Indians and kept Whites from the whale. Today, our operation will become dangerous if a Sea Shepherd vessel arrives. Keep a sharp eye on the horizon."

Sorenson calls for quarter throttle to tow the whale four miles offshore. Helicopters arrive at the Neah Bay Guard Station from Port Angeles, Bellingham, and Tacoma. In 30 minutes, the Indians are whisked to the federal holding facility at SeaTac, Seattle.

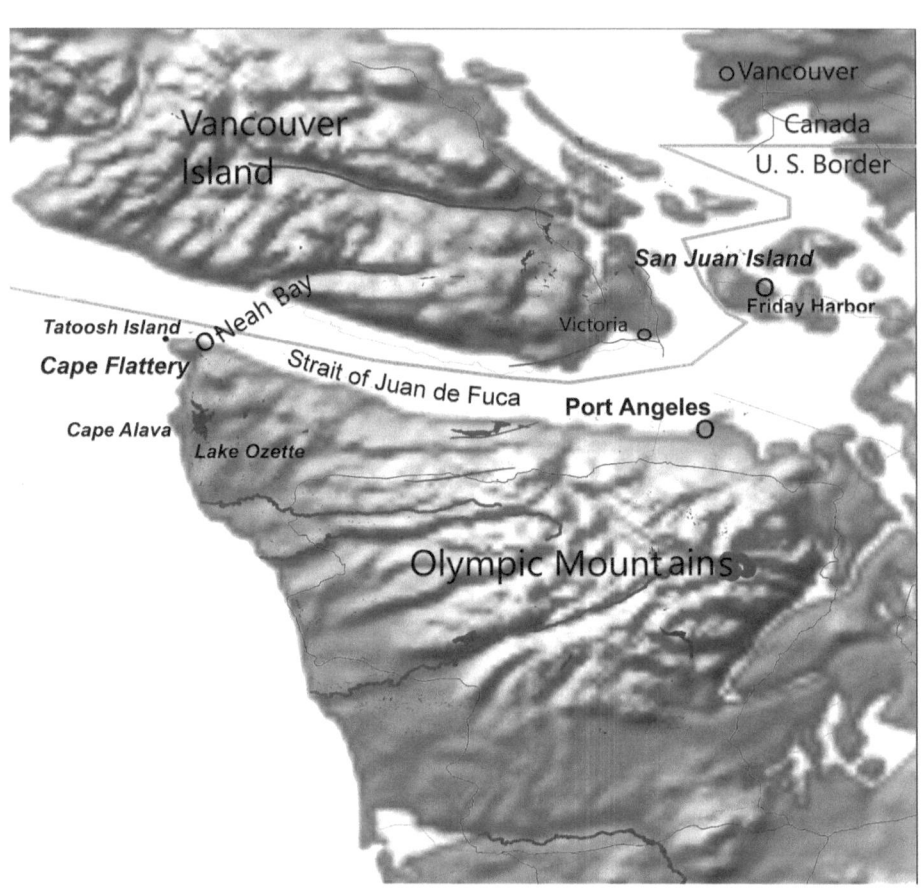

CHAPTER 12

Flight from Friday Harbor to Neah Bay
May 12, noon, Whale Museum

After hearing the news of the illegal whale hunt in Neah Bay from his receptionist at the whale museum, Dennis initially thought he should stay out of his student's private affairs. His student, Quanah, would have discussed the hunt if he had thought Dennis needed to know. Moreover, Native Americans are private. After a couple hours fretting, Dennis decides he needs to know what happened. *Maybe I can be of some assistance to the Makah Tribe.*

Dennis keeps a Cessna 180 with floats at his ramp at the Friday Harbor Marina and at the University of Washington marina. He loves flying, which makes his double appointment at the oceanographic department in Seattle and the Whaling Museum possible. Dennis's dad taught him to fly with a V-Tail Beechcraft Bonanza. The Bonanza, known unkindly as a Doctor Killer, is a high-performance plane that can hit 250 knots. Because of the speed, the pilot must think ahead, or he will fly into a mountain. His father warned, "It's easy to get behind." Doctor Killer seemed a fitting name, because his dad, a neurosurgeon, tended to fly by the seat of his pants. His dad quipped, "Neurosurgeons are like truck drivers when they suddenly come to a fork in the road. When we have an aneurysm burst during surgery, there's no time for a committee meeting."

For vacations, Dennis and his dad flew into remote lakes with a bush pilot in Alaska. These experiences provided the basis for Dennis's common-sense approach to flying. Dennis inherited his father's quick reflexes, which are useful in following whales when the ceiling is under 2000 feet. The Cessna serves him well. For example, during a reconnaissance trip along the western shore of Vancouver Island, he followed a pod of humpbacks as far as his tanks allowed him. On the return, some 125 miles out, he spotted a pod of nine orcas. Photos verified that these were a new pod of off-shore killer whales.

On seeing the photos, Quanah had remarked, "It's hard to believe that off-shore killer whale pods have escaped attention until now, at least for the Whiteman!"

Dennis quickly replied, "No, not unexpected. This is a good example that science can lag behind common knowledge. The study of these groups will be very important. A good dissertation project."

"Why?" Quanah had asked.

"Off-shore killer whales have different behavioral characteristics than those of transient and resident pods. Transient orcas hunt in packs, silently, and prey on seals and sea lions. It is a frightening experience to witness a five-ton orca heaving its body onto a beach to pluck a seal scrambling for his life. The resident San Juan Island orcas, by contrast, are noisy, 'talking' much of the time as they hunt and feed on salmon and ling cod. Opportunistic off-shores feed on salmon, seals, sea lions and have complex vocalizations quite different from the other whales. Off-shores talk except during a hunt. Most of what I've told you is hearsay and not verified with professional notes or reported in scientific journals."

Quanah agreed to the dissertation topic after witnessing a pod of off-shore orcas kill a gray whale by ripping its tongue out. The gray whale bled to death, but the killers did not eat the gray whale. Quanah remarked, "These orcas kill for sport, for the thrill, like Whiteman big-game hunters." This comment introduced Dennis to the Indian resentment of the Whiteman.

Dennis makes a call to the FAA flight center at SeaTac to file an instrument flight plan (IFR) from Friday Harbor to Neah Bay. This isn't required, but he considers it prudent. He will fly through Canadian air space south of Vancouver Island, but since he isn't going to land in Canada, he's not required to file with the Canadians. He will take a southwest by south bearing across the Strait of Juan de Fuca to the Olympic Peninsula and follow the coastline west to the Bay, roughly an hour and a half trip. He notes his destination is 120 nautical miles. He has fuel for 300 miles. The flight center calls back in ten minutes with clearance.

Dennis pulls the plane off the ramp and taxis into the harbor. No fishing or pleasure boats are in sight. With no supplies or passengers, the little Cessna is airborne before he enters San Juan Strait.

He's not surprised that the ring leader was Quanah who always wanted firsthand experience. In the plane, out of his office, Dennis has time to think about his new graduate student. Quanah never missed a field trip on the Friday Harbor Centennial research boat. He wasn't squeamish about mucking through a dredging up to his elbows in ooze. Quanah's professors liked him, as he performed well in marine biology and oceanography courses.

Dennis is about halfway to Neah Bay when he reminds himself that Quanah has some negative qualities that reflect his Native American heritage. *I shouldn't be surprised he killed a whale. After all, Quanah was arrested a couple years ago for digging clams out of season and without a license. He dug with a traditional digging stick. Nevertheless, the game warden wrote him a ticket. Quanah claimed that Whiteman game laws didn't apply, because his ancestors dug clams in the Olympic National Park long before there was a United States of America. The Dean of Indian Studies at the University got a phone call from the game department in Tacoma. We persuaded Quanah to write an apology. After the clamming incident, Quanah received his undergraduate degree in ethnology with a minor in anthropology. He accepted a graduate student fellowship offered by the Zoology department.*

Dennis knew Quanah was helping organize inter-tribal canoe trips. Smiling, he realizes what Quanah had been up to all along.

Approaching Neah Bay, Dennis sets the plane down on the inside of the breaker and taxies to the tribal dock. There is a commotion. As it turns out, Quanah and the rest of the Indians are already in a federal holding facility at SeaTac. Nevertheless, Dennis walks to the Cultural Center to visit with Makah elders. They are pleased to see him but decline help, as expected.

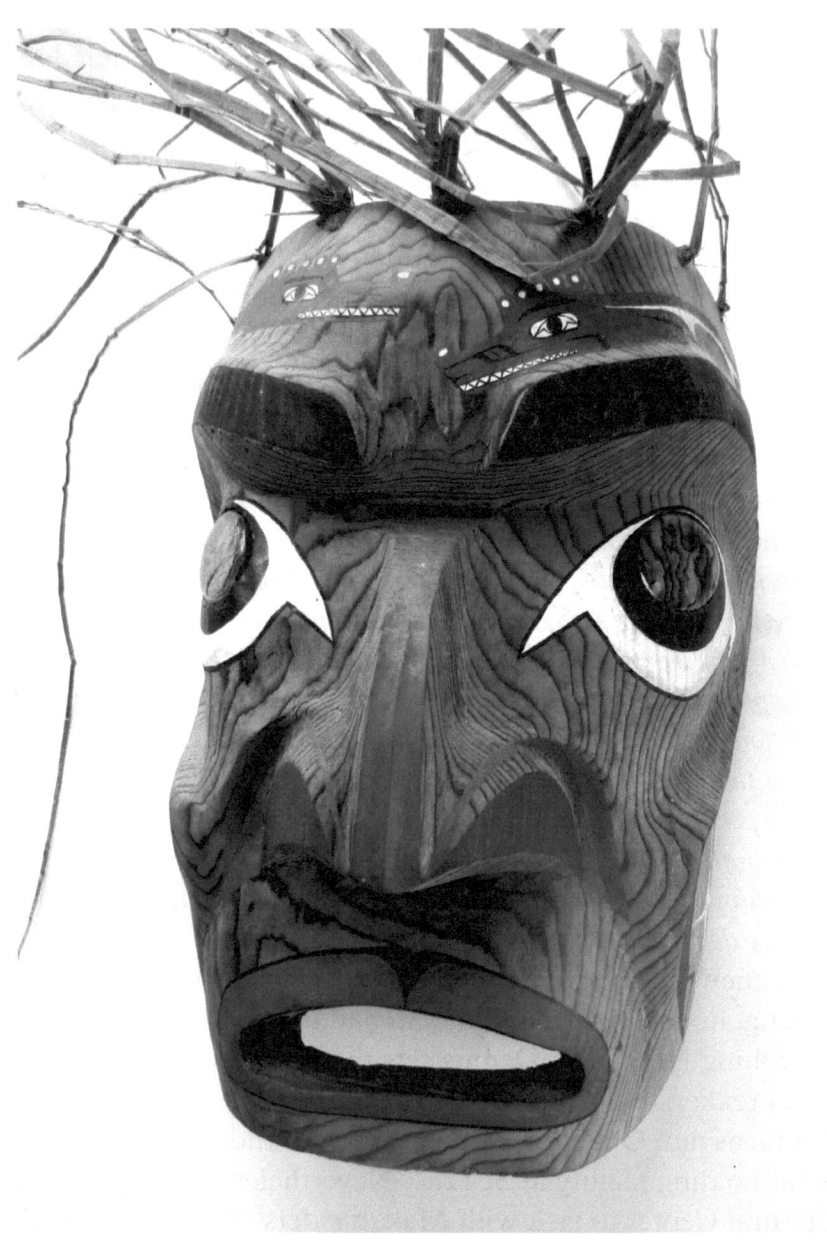

CHAPTER 13

Seattle Law Office of Bernard Edwards
May 13, 7:00 A.M.

Alana, sleepily answers her phone, "Good morning Bernie, why so early?"

Bernard Edwards, Alana's new boss, answers tersely, "You mean hectic morning! Makah Elders called this morning at 5:00 in an absolute panic. One of their enrolled members has been arrested and is now held in the Seattle-Tacoma federal jail. He and nine other Indians will be arraigned in federal court tomorrow."

"If I seem dopey, I am," Alana grumbles. "The last ferry from Friday Harbor arrived in Anacortes at ten. Traffic on I-5 was impossible."

Bernie ignores her explanation. "The Native Americans killed a gray whale yesterday and were arrested by the Coast Guard this morning as they were paddling into Neah Bay. First Nation Canadian Indians were also arrested. Thus, we have an international incident. The elders had no knowledge of the hunt. Thus, they had not granted permission to the whaling chief to hunt."

Alana says, "I heard about the whale incident in Friday Harbor yesterday afternoon. I was in the Whaling Museum and overheard the director talking about it. The Native American is his graduate student. Can you believe it?"

Bernie explains, "Seattle is large, but the academic community is small." After a pause he continues with an irritated edge to his voice, "I'm pissed. Just when we're ready to petition the Supreme Court for a *writ of certiorari* to hear our appeal of the ninth circuit court ruling which overturned the Burgess salmon allotment ruling, we have this problem. Killing a gray whale will cause public outrage."

"What's our plan? What can I do?"

After a long second, Bernie continues, "The elders are certain that Quanah didn't know of the Supreme Court appeal. I understand that the whalers acted in secrecy. Even though the Makah's are divided over the whaling issue, the elders decided they must defend Quanah and the other Indians. They believe, and I support this notion, that it's important to present a united front."

"But I like whales. It's wrong to kill such a beautiful animal!" Alana laments.

Bernie, taking a deep breath, replies, "You can't let personal feelings interfere with the practice of law."

"Yes, but ..."

Bernie cuts her off. "You will learn to defend the Native American. Powerful medicine is at play with this litigation because Indians believe the whale spirit stays with the body until the whale is blessed and the meat divided. Tribal elders informed me that if they don't perform sacred rituals immediately, the meat will spoil and the whale spirit will haunt the village for seven generations."

After a pause, Alana sighs, "Not much warning, but OK," she says. She thinks *You don't give me much time to adjust. I'm here only a couple months, and I'm right in the thick of things.* Standing up and stretching, she asks, "Will this have international coverage?"

"Yes, of course," Bernie answers, "TV coverage will be global. Judge Krieger called at 6:00 this morning to inform me that the State Attorney General filed criminal charges against the Indians. Animal activist groups are filing a civil complaint against the defendants. Our defense will depend on salmon and fishing opinions written in the 1970s. I think that Judge Krieger will be fair because he will have to reach the standards of the late Judge Boldt in regards to fishing rights. The Makah elders have asked us to answer and plead their case. We have to submit our positions by noon today, and Judge Krieger will send us the charges submitted by the prosecution and friend of the court who are the animal activist groups."

"What about bail? Will the charges be argued by the Federal prosecuting attorney or a plaintiff attorney?" Alana asks.

Bernie brusquely answers, "Because federal law has been broken,

Judge Krieger decided that the alleged violation is a misdemeanor. He has the right to opinion a civil judgment at the same time because both criminal and civil complaints refer to the same Indians and the same whale. Bail should be modest if he finds cause."

"Wow!"

Bernie continues, "Judge Krieger will hear our pleadings tomorrow at 8:00 am. We'll try to get the case dismissed."

"Who'll we be up against?"

"I think that the top dog will prosecute because of the high profile. We'll get their briefs by noon today to draft our answers or pleadings. My God, the courtroom seats only fifty, it'll be packed to the rafters."

"This is exciting." Alana is fully awake, now.

"I suspect that the prosecuting attorney will team up with plaintiff lawyers hired by animal activist groups. The animal groups have brought cases to the Ninth Circuit Court of Appeals before, and they have lots of money and citizen support. The real question is Judge Krieger's jurisprudence."

"What do you mean? Personal feelings and public opinion should have no relevance."

"Dear girl, judges are people. I wish that Judge Burgess were still alive and sitting. Nevertheless, I think Krieger will be fair based on his State Supreme Court rulings. And, we will be in the Burgess Courtroom in Tacoma."

"So?"

"Many judges are inspired, probably subconsciously, to continue the tenor of the judge they have replaced. I think of Judge Boldt, who, in spite of being nominated by President Eisenhower and confirmed by a Republican Congress, ruled for the Indians in regards to fishing rights."

"Will there be a jury?"

"No, I, in behalf of the Makah and other Indian defendants, have agreed to waive a jury trial. Judge Krieger informed me that this will be a bench hearing and that the timeline of discovery must be filed by six o'clock tonight. We'll have overnight to prepare our case against the district attorney arguments. Which, by the way, is all the time that the prosecution will have for their preparations. Krieger informed us that there will be no sidebar, no retreat into judge's chambers, and no closing arguments."

"It seems to me that Judge Krieger may be on the side of the Indians by ruling for an immediate trial," Alana reasons.

"Don't make assumptions. In regards to the prosecution, they have plenty of experience. Moreover, with two Ninth Circuit Court of Appeals opinions on their side, as well as animal protection lawyers with money and public support, they will have the upper hand. Dead whales have no meaning to white people, and white people don't believe that animals have souls."

"Then we're playing against a stacked deck, right?"

"No. We have constitutional law on our side." Bernie answers. "Treaties are protected by our constitution. Since the Indian Civil Rights Act of 1968 and the return of Congressional support to protect Indian self-governance, to promote Native American legal traditions, and to protect hunting and fishing rights, we can argue that the Indians have every right to whale without obtaining any more permits. The 1960s and '70s, when federal power over Indians was limitless, are over! Yet, the prosecution will argue that the Indians have broken federal statutes and law."

After a pause, Alana concludes, "So, we have four hours to prepare our answers for the defense and to state our case. Will we use briefs that we've been working on for the Supreme Court?"

"Yes. In this respect, we will have the advantage of time. Let's get to work. By the way, you're arguing the case."

"What! Why?" Alana gasps.

"The prosecuting law firm knows me and our litigation history. We reviewed your moot court case presented at the University of Arizona a couple years ago. Your presentation of the salmon issues in Washington State was thorough. You introduced Supreme-Court rulings. You even found 1854 correspondence written by Washington Territorial Governor Stevens and the Territorial Indian Agent concerning Washington State Indians. You showed excellent trial lawyer ability during the acid rain case in Syracuse. Here in Seattle, the plaintiffs and court do not know you. Thus, we decided this case should be presented by a new face, a pretty one at that."

"That's chauvinistic! Are you kidding?"

"No. Wear a light gray suit."

"Bernie, I can't believe that you said that."

"Welcome to the real world. Remember that Marsha Clark in the O.J. Simpson trial wore a red suit which worked for the audience but was like waving a red flag in front of the judge and jury."

CHAPTER 14

After the unsettling conversation with her new boss, Alana, calls her mother, "Hi Mom, everything OK in Syracuse?"

"Of course. Why are you calling so early, honey? You usually call me too late."

"I just wanted to touch base."

"What's troubling you? You don't like your new job?"

"Nothing is troubling me. I met the Applegates in Friday Harbor. Do you remember them?"

"No, should I?"

"They remember you, but you were only seven when your dad was studying at the Friday Harbor Laboratories. The Applegates are really nice people. They said good things about granddad."

"Alana, you didn't call to talk about your granddad. What's troubling you? You're not happy?"

"Mom, of course I'm happy. Bernie Edwards is really smart. I'm learning lots about Native American Law. And, I love where I live. The running trails wind through a wild area, and my apartment is only a few miles from downtown Seattle."

"Alana, are you sure it's safe where you live? I remember the Green River Murderer."

"That was years ago, Mom, and fifty miles east of Seattle." When her mother says nothing, Alana adds, "I guess the traffic gets to me."

"Traffic's not the problem, is it?"

"Well, I like the office staff and the fact that there's lots of action and, I mean Bernie is going to be in the middle of important Native American litigation. We may even plead before the Supreme Court next year."

"That's good news. Do you like Friday Harbor?"

"Yes, Mom, what do you remember of your dad's disappearance?"

After a long silence her mom says, "Why call me about that? It was forty years ago."

"Everybody remembers your dad as a nice guy. They can't imagine how he disappeared. Do you think he simply drowned?"

"Alana! I was only seven. I was crushed and really didn't understand what was going on. I'm sorry, we'll talk about your granddad another time."

Finally, Alana blurts, "Mom, I love whales! Tomorrow, I'm in court to defend some Native Americans who killed a gray whale. I moved out here to save salmon, tear down dams on the Snake River, work for the environment, and be a protector of sea life. I want to help Native Americans, but I didn't know they killed whales. Everybody in Seattle is against the Native Americans."

"I love whales too. I hope you lose." After only a moment, she adds, "Honey, I'm only kidding. I'll still love you after you win."

"Mom, I love you too. Everything is moving so fast. My law firm agreed to a rapid bench trial. Litigation usually takes months, even years. Yet, my firm expects me to plead this case."

With a laugh Alana's mother proudly states, "Alana, honey, you have always been ready. Quickness is your strong point. Remember to be courteous to the opposing lawyers. And, be sympathetic to the Native American cause. Call me after court."

CHAPTER 15

Court in session – 14 May, 8:00 A.M.

Case: preliminary hearing - 615 F3d 2018
United States v. Makah Indian Whale Hunters and NOAA
United States Federal Court in Tacoma
Judge Quinton Geoffrey Krieger, presiding

Prosecution: Federal District Attorney Russell Murkovitch
Defendants: Makah Tribe Whale Hunters of Neah Bay, US & NOAA, Quanah Tatoosh, Makah Tribe, Captain (Chief) of canoe, Neah Bay, Washington, Merle Blackhorse, Coeur d'Alene Tribe, Spokane, Washington, Aaron Dullknife, Tulalip (Salish) Tribe, Seattle, Washington, Gus _____, Tongass/Tlingit Tribe,_____, Alaska, Darrell Leschi Ross, Chinook (Salish) Tribe and Nisqually, Washington. Canadian First Nation Peoples: Thomas Sewid, Kwakiutl Band, Alert Bay, British Columbia, Canada, Ben Maquenna, Nootka Band, Kyuquat, British Columbia, Canada, George Alex George, Cowichan Bay, British Columbia, Canada, Sam Two Fish Charles, Haida Band, Masset, British Columbia, Canada, David Sharpknife, Tsimshian Tribe, Port Edward, British Columbia, Canada
Counsel for prosecution: Dilbert Ferguson; Protectors of all animals; World Organization for Animal Rights; Kayakers and Bikers for Open Waters and Forests; Citizens for Wolves and Killer Whales; Alliance for Breaching Dams
Second counsel for prosecution: Chuck Morlwey, lead Counsel for Sea Shepherd
Counsels for defense: Law Firm of Schneider, Lamb and Moore, Seattle, Washington, and NOAA
   A shortened, unofficial transcript follows:
Bailiff: Court stenographer, Ms. Clark, and Counsels, please rise for Judge Krieger.

Judge Quinton Geoffrey Krieger: Good morning. This is a bench trial. There will be no postponement. The prosecution claims the Indians killed a gray whale in violation of the Marine Mammal Protection Act (MMPA). The defendants argue that the treaty of 1855 between the Makah Indians and the United States Government guarantees the right to whale.

I thank prosecution and defendant counsels for briefs and counter arguments. I am holding an immediate trial because, as we know from history, retribution can come swiftly. For example, in 1858 the United States Army tried Palouse Indians within minutes after suspects surrendered to Col. George Wright near Spokane, Washington. After Indians admitted to fighting in the Battle of To Hots Nim Me, they were immediately hung (see 35th Congress, 2nd Session; SENATE; EX. Doc. No.32 Report of The Secretary of War). Another reason to follow the 1858 example for this case of modern federal-Indian interaction so that the Coast Guard does not have to dispose of a dead whale.

I expect lawyers to use language that adheres to Supreme Court Justice John Marshall's rulings in the 1800s that treaties must be interpreted as Indians would understand English. I will close this hearing by 11:00 A.M. Do not object or request to approach the bench. I will present my ruling at 2:00 PM tomorrow. I will hear arguments for the prosecution and defense.

Russell Murkovitch, Counsel for Prosecution: Native Americans and Canadian First Nation People have broken United States Federal laws pursuant to the Marine Mammal Protection Act (MMPA) by killing a whale. The defendants failed to file National Environmental Policy Act (NEPA) statements, have not prepared Environmental Assessment (EA) and Environmental Impact Statement (EIS) papers. We refer to Metcalf v. Daley in 2000 and, Anderson v. Evans in 2002 in the United States Court of Appeals for the Ninth Circuit. Their rulings require the Makah Tribe to file documents in order for NOAA to grant a permit to whale.

The EIS, in compliance with NOAA and NMFS, drafted seven methods for the Makah Nation to whale. The Native Americans did not follow one method.

Alana Svoboda, Counsel for Defense: The EIS report with seven options for whaling techniques is 900 pages. The defendant, Quanah, followed many suggestions. A nine-hundred-word regulation is ridiculous, because state hunting regulations require only a couple of pages for each animal. The EIS report is contrary to Federal law as outlined by Chief Justice Marshall in 1835.

We apply the 1974 findings of Judge Boldt to show that the Makah Indians have a right to take whales. Judge Boldt's ruling was upheld by the Supreme Court in 1977 where Indians have the right to take fish and whales guaranteed by the Treaty of 1855 drafted by Territorial Gov. Isaac Stevens and ratified by Congress in 1856. Judge Boldt ruled that Indians have the right to one half of the salmon. The Treaty of 1855 reads:

> "Articles of agreement and convention, made and concluded at Neah Bay, in the territory of Washington, the thirty-first day of January, in the year eighteen hundred and fifty-five by Isaac I. Stevens, Governor and Superintendent of Indian affairs for the said Territory, on the part of the United Sates and the undersigned chiefs, head-men and delegates of the several villages of the Makah tribe of Indians, viz: Neah Waatch, Tsoo-Yess, and Ozett, occupying the country around Cape Classett (Flattery), on behalf of the said tribe and duly authorized by the same."

Article 4 reads:

> "The right of taking fish and of whaling or sealing at usual and accustomed grounds and stations is further secured to said Indians in common with all citizens of the United States …"

Article 4 guarantees the right to whale in all traditional waters

TREATY WITH THE MAKAH, 1855

Jan. 31, 1855. / 12 Stat., 939/Ratified Mar. 8, 1859./ Proclaimed Apr. 18, 1859

Articles of agreement and convention, made and concluded at Neah Bay, in the Territory of Washington, this thirty-first day of January, in the year eighteen hundred and fifty-five, by Isaac I. Stevens, governor and superintendent of Indian affairs for the said Territory, on the part of the United States, and the undersigned chiefs, head-men, and delegates of the several villages of the Makah tribe of Indians, viz: Neah Waatch, Tsoo-Yess, and Osett, occupying the country aroundCape Classett or Flattery, on behalf of the said tribe and duly authorized by the same.

ARTICLE 4.

The right of taking fish and of whaling or sealing at usual and accustomed grounds and stations is further secured to said Indians in common with all citizens of the United States, and of erecting temporary houses for the purpose of curing, together with the privilege of hunting and gathering roots and berries on open and unclaimed lands. Provided, however, That they shall not take shell-fish from any beds staked or cultivated by citizens.

without government restraints. Quanah Tatoosh resides on the Makah reservation in Ozette. Quanah Tatoosh is a direct decedent of chief whalers dating back to the treaty. Judge Boldt's rulings are applicable to whaling because in 1855 whales were considered fish.

Prosecution argued by Marsha Waterman: The opinions of the Ninth Circuit Court of Appeals written by Stephen S. Trott in 2000 and Berzon in 2002 state that the phrase in treaty article 4, "in common with all citizens of the United States," means that Indians are to be held to the same laws as all Americans and should not receive special treatment.

Alana Svoboda: The Ninth Court of Appeals opinion was not unanimous. Judge Andrew J. Kleinfield wrote a blistering dissent. Makah ancestors would not have agreed to limit whaling rights. Gov. Stevens could not speak Makah, and the Makah didn't know English. Consequently, the treaty was translated into Chinook Jargon. We present four arguments against the veracity of Chinook Jargon.

First argument: By 1830 Chinook Jargon had evolved into a language with syntax but was not adopted by the Makah. Nootka/ Makah language contributed only forty words to the Chinook vocabulary that initially had 400 words, which was adequate, accompanied with sign language, for trade, but not for a treaty between nations.

John R. Jewitt published *White Slaves of Maquenna,* documenting his experiences as a slave of the Nootka Chief Maquenna in 1802. Jewitt conversed about sophisticated, cultural ideas in Nootka language. In 1778 Captain Cook translated 2000 Nootka/Makah words into English. Their cultural complexity is demonstrated with: *Tuttayin* - to lament; *Ta-ta-put-hi* - to consider; *queel-ha* - to pray; *pooh-pootsah* - to dream; *Payh-eyk* - to praise; *Kouts-mah* - the soul; *Chay-her* - a place for spirits. Gov. Stevens ignored the Makah wish to speak in Makah. We have translated Article 4 of the 1855 Stevens/Makah treaty into Chinook Jargon and back to English.

I enter as evidence *document number one*: English to Chinook Jargon. Then the translation back to English. English is in bold font, Chinook in italics, translated Chinook back to English is in normal font. The three versions are projected onto the court screens:

The right of taking fish and of whaling or sealing at usual and accustomed grounds and stations is further secured to said Indians in common with all citizens of the United States.

O'koke / na-wit'ka / kopa/ is'-kum / pish / pee / hul-o-i-ma/ is'kam / kwahnice/pe ten'as le bal / ol'-hi-yu / ko'-pa / hy-iu' / pee / yuk'-wa / kum'-tuks / il'-la-nie /pee ma'ht-wil-lie/ pee/ma'ht-wlin-nie/win'-a-pie/kwutl / kwa'h-ne-sam/ ko'pa / pot'-patchsi- wash / ko'-pa/ kon'-a-way/til-i-kum /al'-kie / o' koke / al'-kie/ lo'-lo / boston ahah

That to say certainly to take fish and other to get whaling or shoot seals at much and here know grounds and in shore and off shore by and by fasten forever to give Indians with all citizens presently that of whole American tribes.

Alana Svoboda: This translation demonstrates that the Makah could not have understood the Stevens treaty.

Our Second Argument is the interpretation of line 3 of article 4. To wit: "The privilege of hunting...on open and unclaimed lands." Thus, the Makah would have assumed they would hunt whales in the ocean. Therefore, the Indians are guaranteed by treaty to hunt within the twelve-mile US Territorial Waters. In 1853 (Exec Doc. 2nd ses, 33d Cong. Vol 1 pt 1) Gov. Stevens, referencing Makah Chief Flattery Jack, wrote:

"Indians venture well out to sea in their canoes, and even attack and kill the whale ... in 1853, 30,000 gals of oil was purchased by vessels. The Indians take sea otter skins to sell in Victoria... [in] the subject of the right of fisheries ... [it was] never [the] intention of congress that Indians should be excluded from their ancient fisheries."

Chief Flattery Jack is a whaling ancestor of defendant Quanah Tatoosh. From Gov. Stevens' quote we contend that the word "fisheries" included whaling because in 1855 a whale was a fish. Arguments against Makah whaling based on the National Marine Sanctuaries Act of 1994 or the Cape Flattery Rocks National Wildlife Refuge are irrelevant because the archeological digs at Ozette, near Cape Alava, prove the Makah hunted whales for 500 years.

Our Third Argument is that Gov. Stevens was also the Superintendent of Indian Affairs which would have created a conflict of interest.

Our Fourth Argument is that B. F. Shaw, a trader on the Columbia River who knew Chinook Jargon and was the interpreter was biased against Indians. One year after the treaty, B. F. Shaw, leading the Washington State Militia, attacked a band of peaceful Umatilla and Cayuse Indians digging camas roots along the Grande Ronde River near present day Elgin, Oregon. In four hours, Shaw's volunteers slaughtered over 40 unarmed old men, women, and children. In addition, Col. Shaw and Gov. Stevens marched into the Columbia Plateau Indian lands against the policy of Col. Geo. Wright. Your Honor, the Col. Wright that I refer to is the same Col. Wright that you referenced in granting a rapid hearing. Shaw and Stevens were surrounded and faced certain death had it not been for Col. Steptoe who rescued Stevens' and Shaw's militia.

Marsha Waterman for the prosecution: Article 13 of the 1855 treaty states:

"The said tribe finally agrees not to trade at Vancouver's Island or elsewhere out of the domains of the United States, nor shall foreign Indians be permitted to reside in the reservation without consent of the superintendent or agent."

Thus, the Makah who permitted Canadian Indians to live on the Makah reservation have broken treaty law. We have no documentation of Col. B.F. Shaw's persuasion toward Indians. In fact, Shaw had an Indian wife. Gov. Col. Stevens was not a racist because he gave his life fighting against slavery in the Civil War. That the dual responsibilities of Governor and Indian Agent created a conflict of interest in Steven's judgment is speculative. To translate the treaty into Chinook Jargon is meaningless because the defense used English syntax.

Svoboda: The final argument of the prosecution is precisely our point. The translation from English into Chinook Jargon would not carry the proper syntax, and that is exactly why the Makah did not understand the 1855 treaty.

The Makah treaty signers would not have signed had they understood that their decedents would not be able to trade in Victoria and visit their relatives, the Nuu-chah-nulth (Nootka) on Vancouver Island. We base our position on the following briefs:

Brief 1: The treaty of 1855 was signed by 42 Makah. There were only 150 living Makah out of 550 after a measles outbreak (tallied by Gov. Stevens). The Makah would not have abrogated trading rights because they had a lucrative trade in whale oil, sea otter skins, halibut, and salmon with the Hudson's Bay Company of Victoria and tribes of Puget Sound.

Brief 2: The Makah Indians had Canadian Nootka spouses and vice versa. Both tribes spoke the Nootka language and did not recognize the border between Canada and United States. They would not have accepted a treaty where they needed Indian agent permission for marriages and potlatches.

Brief 3: The screen shows Article 13 of the treaty in bold font, Chinook Jargon in italics, and translation back to English in normal font. *Document piece number two:*

The said tribe finally agrees not to trade at Vancouver's Island or elsewhere out of the domains of the United States.

O'-Koke / pot'-latch si-wash win'-a-pie wake / ma'k-kook / wau'wau/ huy-huy/ ik'-tah / Klat'-a-wa / King Chautsh klat'-a-wa / sia'h / Ma'h-kook/pee/ huy-huy // win'-a'pie/ sia'h Il-la-hie toh-pelh al'-kie boston/ ahha

That give Indians by and by no barter, talk, trade, merchandise to go King George house / Store to go far barter by and by far Earth and ocean of American tribes.

Judge Krieger: Let's adjourn for a thirty-minute recess. When we return defense should explain the syntax issue that the prosecution referred to.

After recess

Alana Svoboda: Every language has its own usage of words which is termed syntax. To substitute words of one language for words of a written text of a second language is not speaking in the second language. Neither B. Shaw nor Gov. Stevens knew Makah language and the Makah did not know Chinook Jargon. Therefore, the treaty must be interpreted in the broadest of terms. I will continue with our submitted briefs.

> **Brief 4:** Gov. Stevens graduated number one in his class of 1839 at West Point. Stevens knew precisely what he intended to convey to congress as Governor and Superintendent of Indian Affairs where he reported in Executive Documents 2nd Sess. 33d Cong. Vol 1 pt 1 1854-55. page 449, to wit:
>
> *"Makaws (sic) have superior courage [and] as [to] their treachery, make them more difficult of management."*

Steven's usage of 'management' is not the same as agreement as applied in treaty terminology and Steven's word 'treachery' demonstrates prejudice.

Brief 5: In the early 1800s, the Makah sold 30,000 gallons of whale oil to the Hudson's Bay Company in Victoria each year and traded for blankets, buttons, fish hooks, muskets and powder. Indian agent M.T. Simmons wrote to Col. J.W. Nesmith in the *Washington Territorial Reports of 1856* that the Makah wanted a physician to vaccinate their people and requested a rapid treaty ratification by congress. Simmons wrote that the Makah catch many whales and sell the oil at high prices in Victoria. The Makah asserted the Tatoosh Island lighthouse keeps whales away. Makah killed twenty whales for 30,000 gallons of oil, killed two to five whales for tribal use, and another five or six for trade with Puget Sound Indians.

Brief 6: The Makah signed 14 treaties with England which were transferred to The United States of America in 1846 when the boundary was set at the 49th parallel. The transference was upheld by the Supreme Court in 1831. G.W. Manypenny, commissioner of Indian Affairs, wrote in Washington Territory Government Reports of 1853-1858 that Stevens was to permit the Makah to trade with Hudson's Bay. Stevens reported on Makah whaling and selling oil to Hudson's Bay in exec doc 1854, part 5. Indian agent M.T. Simmons wrote to Col. J.W. Nesmith that the Makah are most independent but are eager for a ratified treaty because half [of the tribe] had already died of small pox. Simmons continued, "These Indians catch many whales" and they ship the oil by canoe to sell to Victorian traders. The Superintendent of Indian Affairs in Washington and Oregon Territories, Col. J.W. Nesmith, also wrote of the commercial importance of whaling to the Makah Indians. R. McClelland, Secretary of the Interior in President Franklin Pierce's cabinet, wrote in 1854:

> *'The Hudson's Bay rights given to Indians contained in 14 treaties must be upheld by Gov. Stevens.'*

Sec. McClelland directed Gov. Stevens to preserve ocean waters to give clear and just rights to the Indians.

Brief 7: Whaling is central to Makah culture and religion. Gov. Stevens reported, "Their marriages are said to have some peculiar ceremonies such as going through the performance of taking the whale, manning a canoe, and throwing a harpoon into brides house."

Now what could be more important than marriage?

Jewett, author of *White Slave of Maquenna,* describes the importance of whaling to the Nootka. One of the defendants, Ben Maquenna, is a descendant of Chief Maquenna. Before the treaty of 1855 whaling formed the basis of Makah/Nootka sustenance. Gov. Stevens continued in his report to congress:

"The subject of the right of fisheries .... [was] never [the] intention of congress that Indians should be excluded from their ancient fisheries."

Applying word usage of 1855, "ancient fisheries" would include whaling, as whales were fish. The intention of the US Government in 1855 was to promote Makah whale hunting and to sell whale products on the world Market.

Judge: Prosecution, your turn.

Marsha Waterman: The defense's briefs are not relevant for the following reasons:

Brief 1: Since the treaty was signed by 46 Makah, it was clearly articulated and understood.

Brief 2: It would not have been a burden of the Makah defendant, Quanah Tatoosh, to inform the Indian Agent of visiting First Nation Peoples of Canada.

Brief 3: It is conjecture that B. F. Shaw would have misrepresented the treaty article, forbidding trade with Victoria.

Brief 4: We have no idea as to what Gov. Stevens meant with the word "treachery" as used to describe the Makah.

Brief 5: The two Ninth Circuit Court of Appeals opinions state that there is to be no whaling without satisfying the NEPA, MMPA and NOAA regulations.

Brief 6: The trade restriction with Victoria was clearly stated by the treaty. The Makah were anxious for the treaty to be ratified so they could be vaccinated.

Brief 7: The right of commercial fishing is not sustenance. Sustenance means food necessary to meet basic needs.
Your Honor, the prosecution has answered the defense briefs.

Judge Krieger: Defense, your rebuttal.

Alana Svoboda: The Department of Interior was aware of animosity between white settlers and Indians in 1855. There were numerous Indian Battles in the Puget Sound area. The United States Army attempted to maintain peace but the Oregon and Washington Territorial Militias agitated for war. Wide spread racism was reported in editorials in the Oregon Statesman concerning the massacre of 35 Takelma Native Americans by the Oregon Volunteers led by Major James Lupton at the Kiota Camp on Butte Creek on the 8th Oct. 1855. George Lawson entered in the Oregon State Legislature in 1868 that the 1855 volunteers were 'lawless parties of men...' and were out 'to exterminate the race' The legislative quote:
> "It being the opinion of this legislature that a negro, Chinaman or Indian has no right that a whiteman is bound to respect, and that a whiteman may murder, rob, rape, shoot, stab and cut any of those worthless and vagabond

106

races, without being called to account therefore – provided he shall do the said acts of bravery and chivalry when no whiteman be troubled by seeing the same."

Marsha Waterman: These comments made in an Oregon newspaper are not relevant to Washington Territory, and they were published ten years after the 1855 treaty.

Judge Krieger: Ms. Svoboda do you have further comments?

Alana Svoboda: We offer Makah Oral Tradition concerning the 1855 treaty since Native Americans relied on Oral Tradition and not the written word. We show on the monitor a paragraph translated from 1920 Oral Makah to written English:

"We, the Makah Indians, understand that the United States promises to let us fish and hunt seals and kill whales as our forefathers, and that this right is passed to our children forever. The United States will forever protect us from White people. We, the Makah Indians, can kill whales in ocean. We can beach whales in Neah bay and make meat and trane oil. We can sell oil to other Indians and King George at Hudson's Bay Company."

Marsha Waterman: Your Honor, these oral traditions have changed over the last 150 years.

Alana Svoboda: Native American oral tradition speaks to seven generations. Seven generations is one unit of time for Native Americans. Thus, from 1855 to the present is only one unit of time. The art and execution of oral tradition is accurate. Written word usage changes with time. Oral tradition is a cultural talent. Linguists proposed that the United States Government initiate a priesthood employing oral tradition to ensure that the danger of buried nuclear waste at Yucca Flats would survive 10,000 years because written languages would change.

Marsha Waterman: The Makah have not considered conservation policies relevant to the gray whale sub-population that summers in the Strait of Juan de Fuca. In Anderson v. Evans, experts testified that the resident gray whale population is vulnerable. The Supreme Court citing United States v. Oregon in the Fryberg case found that federal rules must apply to Tribal People. In Washington v. Washington Commercial Passenger Fishing Vessel Association case, the court ruled that the phrase 'in common with' means co-tenancy and Indians warrant no special rights.

Alana Svoboda: In regards to the local population of summer gray whales, it has not been proven that whales residing in the Strait of Juan de Fuca constitute a sub race. This notion can only be verified by DNA analysis and this study hasn't been reported. There is an exchange of 30% of the individuals making up the Puget Sound population every summer with the whales that migrate to Alaskan waters. This exchange would preclude the establishment of a sub-species. Moreover, in the waters of Baja California, female gray whales seek males from outside their pod with whom to mate. Biologists conclude Washington State waters can only support 200 to 300 summer residents. In Anderson v. Evans, experts didn't discuss Professor Robert May's rules that govern populations. Professor May published that population numbers are not fixed but fluctuate according to non-linear dynamics which is also known as chaos theory. This dynamic explains our heart beat, respiration, foot traffic, highway traffic, cloud patterns, wave action, weather, climate and fluctuations in animal populations. Chaos theory indicates that Puget Sound gray whale numbers would fluctuate because the population is small and it interacts with larger migrations. Professor Robert May demonstrated that it is impossible to state all conditions which influence a population. This means that it is impossible to predict populations five or ten years into the future. In weather, there is good short-term prediction but not long range because of global complexities in weather patterns. This is the famous 'butterfly effect' described by the late Professor Lorenz of MIT. Hudson's Bay records show that the numbers of Canadian Lynx and snow shoe rabbit pelts follow an eleven-year cycle where populations vary by a factor of ten to one hundred and are modeled with non-linear equations. Gray whale populations have not been modeled with chaos theory.

We have tallied federal court, court of appeals and Supreme Court interpretations of the phrase 'in common with citizens'. We found twenty pages of discussion. Thus, the meaning of 'in common with citizens' is vague so we must apply Chief Justice Marshall's ruling of 1831 that the phrase 'in common with citizens' must be construed in favor of the Native American.

Marsha Waterman: The defense has clearly obfuscated facts. The Native Americans on trial have broken federal laws and ignored the Ninth Court of Appeals rulings. Judge Krieger, your court must find the defendants guilty and set bail. We did not have time to address the briefs of the defense. We will file for a mistrial. Thank you.

Judge Krieger: Objection noted. We adjourn till 2:00 PM tomorrow when I will issue my ruling.

Next Day - Court in session, 2:00 p.m.

Judge Krieger: Having considered Judge Boldt's 1974 opinion pertaining to fishing rights of Makah Indians for their sustenance and cultural ceremonies, and the opinion of the late Judge Franklin D. Burgess, of whose court room I have the honor to preside in, I have reached a decision. I conclude the right to whale is implicit in the 1855 treaty, and the US Government has a duty to preserve that right to whale. The Boldt opinion gave half the catchable salmon to the Indian. Whales were said to be fish in 1858. Therefore, the Makah can catch half the whale allotment permitted by the International Whaling Commission. NOAA and NMFS filed NEPA and EIS impact studies in the 1990s. We don't need more paper work. I find the hunting right is not only guaranteed by treaty for religious ceremonies and tribal sustenance but also for commercial gain. Sustenance implies a manner of living and the Makah historical trade was based on whale products. Considering the Metcalf v. Paley and Anderson v. Evans decisions of the U. S. Court of Appeals for the Ninth Circuit and especially the dissent of Judge Klinefelt, I agree with Judge Boldt, Judge Burgess and Judge Klinefelt in interpreting the 1855 treaty. In my judgment, the opinions rendered by Circuit Judge Trott in Metcalf v. Daley which reversed and remanded the district court ruling of Franklin D. Burgess and the opinion by Judge Berzon do not uphold the obligations that United States Courts assumed when congress ratified the Makah treaty of 1855. Secretary of Interior R. McClelland, in President Franklin Pierce's cabinet, directed Gov. Stevens to uphold the commercial rights of the Makah Indians to trade with the Hudson's Bay Company. It is a sacred duty of United States agencies to carry out the word and spirit of the 1855 treaty as directed by Chief Justice Marshall in 1831:

> "A treaty is to be regarded, in courts of justice, as equivalent to an act of legislation...and... early treaties with Indian Tribes were of the same dignity as treaties with foreign nations."

Ruling on constitutional law, Chief Justice Marshall opinioned that a treaty may be abrogated or superseded only by an act of congress. Article VI cl 2 of the United States Constitution provides all treaties made under authority of United States shall be the Supreme Law of the Land. In 1996, U.S. Representatives Jack Metcalf (R-Wash) and George Miller (D-Calif) introduced a bill in Congress opposing the US proposal to the International Whaling Commission for a gray whale quota. It became apparent that they did not have a three quarters majority to pass a resolution against the Makah Indians. I am embarrassed that the Ninth Court of Appeals failed the Makah Indians, not once but twice, in this sacred responsibility to ensure that the Makah Indians can continue to whale. The United States Supreme Court in an 1899 opinion states:

110

"The treaty must be construed not according to the technical meaning of its words, but in the sense in which they would naturally be understood by the Indians....The language used in treaties with the Indians should never be construed to their prejudice...how the words of the treaty are understood by Indians rather than their critical meaning should form the rule of construction."

The United States Supreme Court from the first to the latest decision has ruled for Indians with the full spirit of the law. The late Franklin D. Burgess ruled for the Makah Indians as did Judge Boldt in 1974. I concur with both. Perhaps Judge Burgess carried his sense of fair play from playing basketball at Gonzaga University to his court in Tacoma. By contrast, The Ninth Court of Appeals has flummoxed the reader with superfluous opinions concerning logging and mining rulings that have no relevancy to the Stevens Treaty of 1855. Considerations of animal activist groups have neither relevancy, merit, nor standing pertaining to the rights of the Makah Indians, as these groups did not exist in 1855. It is the responsibility of the United States Government to uphold the inherent sovereign powers of Indian Tribes and honor treaties.

We will recess for fifteen minutes.

Judge Krieger: Judgment for the Defendants. The Native Americans and First Nation Peoples of Canada have broken no federal law. However, I am not empowered to sit in judgment for Tribal Courts. It is the obligation of the U.S. Government to protect Indian Tribal culture and Tribal sovereign power as outlined by Chief Justice Marshall and reaffirmed by Presidents Ronald Reagan and Richard Nixon in executive orders and that of President Bill Clinton in executive order 13175 issued Nov. 6, 2000. Therefore, the Indians are free.

It's my understanding that the soul, no, I mean spirit, of the whale will not leave its carcass until prayers are said for the whale. Only then can the whale be butchered and the meat distributed. If this traditional ceremony isn't upheld, the spirit of whale will haunt

111

the Makah Village for seven generations. I will instruct the Coast Guard to immediately transfer the dead whale to the Makah Tribal Police.

Bailiff: Please rise. Court is adjourned.

Marsha walks to the defense table, smiles, and says, "We both know that the Ninth Court of Appeals will reverse this ruling. See you in Supreme Court."

Alana nods to Marsha before turning to face the Native Americans. She heaves a big sigh of relief. "Congratulations! We did it. You're free men. See, the Federal Court system does work."

The ten Indians, Alana, and Bernard Edwards file past the gallery. Many in the audience give a thumbs up.

Richard, acting on behalf of the Makah Tribal Police, grabs Quanah. "Not so fast hot shot, tomorrow, early morning, you get to ride home with me."

Not wanting to quarrel, Quanah says with a soft voice he knows will appease his high school football teammate, "Hey Bro, we're on the same team. Grab a bite to eat. Meet you here at seven." Turning to Alana, he asks, "Can you come out to Neah Bay?"

Smiling and nodding to the Indians, Alana moves toward Dr. Edwards. "Bernie?"

CHAPTER 16

Restaurant/Bar in Tacoma

The victors leave the Federal Court Building which is attached to the renovated train station. The building makes a statement for justice and permanence. They hail taxis to McCarver and 31st. The Keel Café/Beer Parlor sports a red neon King Salmon flickering through blue waves.

Climbing out of the car, Alana explains, "This place was recommended by the court stenographer. Good Puget Sound sea food at reasonable prices. The menu lists fish 'n chips, smoked oysters, clams, and wild salmon. Shall we go in?"

Peering into the window Gus utters his first comments since the Indians were apprehended, "I've eaten in tougher looking places. I like salmon. This place is OK for me."

Frowning at Gus, Merle pleads, "I would never go into a place like this in Spokane. I'm certainly not tough like Sherman Alexis' characters. This place will have rednecks."

Alana, high on the win and for the moment not thinking that she loves whales, "Haha, you mean little necks." The menu shows little necks. She looks at Merle and cajoles, "Heck, Merle, I'm kidding, I know what you mean. But, look, the windows are clean and the fried fish smells good. The kitchen is upfront and well organized. You know it's a good place when the air doesn't smell like rancid lard."

Still pressing his concern Merle explains, "Living in Spokane, I'm land locked. I usually don't like fish because our restaurants smell of hamburgers."

Clearly exasperated by the prattle and exercising his role of Chief, Quanah pats Gus on the shoulder, "I'm with Gus, I'm hungry, prices are good, and it's my treat for a great crew. We Indians won. The tides have turned."

With an arm around Gus's and Quanah's shoulders, Alana jokes, "Careful. Maybe you should lose a few court cases, or Congress will change the treaties. Do you know that Congress could pass a law that says there is no such race as Native American? Moreover, I'm not sure I want to defend you guys again. I love whales so much, maybe next time I'll defend them."

The Indians ignore her remarks, as it would be ungracious to whip the dog that just saved them. They enter the bar and file past a piano player who looks ancient. His hair sprouts in all directions, especially out of his ears and nose. He wears an orange sweat shirt that had once been red and a faded pair of jeans. His gnarly hands skip over the keys, as he swivels around for a better look. His weather-beaten face matches his hands, giving him the look of a fisherman rather than a musician. With a smile that exposes naked gums on his lower jaw, he turns back to the keyboard, and starts to sing:

> Ten little Injuns walking' in a line
> One toddled home and then there were nine
>
> Nine little Injuns swingin' on the bar gate
> One fell off and then there were eight.

Alana mutters, "Let's get out of here. They recognize you guys from the newspapers."

Quanah exclaims, "No, we're not leaving. Do you think we haven't heard this shit before? Parents and cheerleaders chanted these songs during warm ups when we played football and basketball in White schools."

Pulling out a chair and sitting in the middle of the long center table, Alana replies, "Of course, I've always known that Native Americans have had to tolerate abusive language. But now I know what it feels like."

The tables are covered with maps of the Inland Passage and are clean, indicating an attentive waitress. The chairs are standard restaurant with green plastic seats to match the green window trim. The inside walls of natural red brick fit well with the trim. The inside is airy with a view looking over Schuster Parkway and past the pier with wheat elevators. The Olympic Mountains rise seven thousand feet above Puget Sound. The interior décor is unusual and timeless. The ceiling is dark green complimenting the oak bar supporting twenty handles for draft beers. The walls—held over from the seventies—are covered with mounted salmon and steelhead jumping into space. The fish skins are tattered, exposing the shavings used as interior stuffing. Moth-eaten trophy elk and deer heads look in every direction. Below the trophy fish are photos of grinning fishermen with huge hands holding fish at arms-length. There are photos of commercial salmon and halibut boats filled to the gunnels. The photos are brown with age, matching the piano player's seasoned face. Framed newspaper clippings attest to the restaurant's reputation of serving the best sea food in Puget Sound.

Looking about the room Quanah says, "Look at all the great White hunters and fisherman. These stuffed fish and heads demonstrate a difference between Whites and Indians."

Alana looks around the room. "Obviously this place is a watering hole for sport and commercial fisherman." Facing Quanah, she asks. "Native Americans and Caucasians both love to fish. What differences are you talking about?"

"Alana, refer to us as Indians. Yes, both Indians and Whites fish. The difference is Indians celebrate fishing with ceremonies like the first salmon feast to honor the return of fish. We eat fish to complete the Circle of Life. The White sportsman kills fish, uses fish's body for a mold, throws meat away, and pulls the fish skin over the fake body. The Whiteman shows no respect for fish."

Merle nods. "Quanah's right. We burn fish parts that we can't use, so that our dogs can't eat them. It would be disrespectful to the spirit of fish to let dogs eat its head, guts, and skin." Looking about, he adds, "This is no place for Indians. We're being ogled."

Overhearing the jibes against White fishermen the piano player squares his shoulders and continues, now louder,

Eight little Injuns pray-in' to heaven
One fell asleep and then there were seven.

115

Sweeping his arm toward his crew members, Merle whispers, "See? This is a Whiteman's club."

Gus smiles and says in a metered tone, "I've heard this from Sitka to Forks. They don't mean nothin'."

The piano man continues.

> *Seven little Injuns cuttin' up their tricks*
> *One broke his neck, and then there were six.*

Alana, jumps up, exclaiming, "This is outrageous, let's go!"

Quanah, grabbing Alana's arm, softly councils, "No, we're not going. This little jerk isn't going to bully us."

The piano player continues,

> *Six little Injuns all alive*
> *One kicked the bucket, and then there were five.*

Quanah, stands, walks over to the piano player, "Man, what's with you?"

The player grins and sings louder.

> *Five little Injuns at the back door*
> *One got drunk, and then there were four.*

Gus positions himself between the piano player and Quanah, "Quanah, let's sit."

The piano player looks at Quanah and sings,

> *Four little Injuns out on a spree*
> *One got lost, and then there were three.*

Merle stands, takes a few steps toward the door and says sharply, "Damn it, I've seen enough rednecks at the Casino in Spokane, It's time to get the hell out of here. I'm Coeur d'Alene. We don't fight; we negotiate. Haha."

All eyes are on Gus as he backs up and quietly speaks, "Merle's right, let's go."

Now sensing he has the upper hand, the piano player, nodding with music, sings louder and slower for emphasis,

Three little Injuns out in a canoe
One tumbled out, and then there were two.

The tavern is quiet except for the piano player who notices that customers are listening. He repeats as loudly as possible,
Three little Injuns out in a canoe
One tumbled out, and then there were two.

Two little Injuns foolin' with a gun
It went off, and then there was one.

With this last stanza, Aaron stands and with a mocking voice:
There is an old fool from Tacoma
Whose words have a hateful aroma
He sings a dumb song
He knows to be wrong,
This brain-dead man from Tacoma.

Alana, pulling on Aaron's shirt whispers, "Jesus, Aaron, sit down! Do you want to start a fight?"

A burly fisherman, with arms the size of a normal man's thighs shoves his table. His bottle of beer crashes to the floor. He stands and walks to Aaron shouting, "You too good for us, for this place?"

Pointing to Aaron and Quanah he says, "I guess you're Tonto and this here blond is the Lone Ranger, huh?"

Immediately the piano player breaks into the "William Tell Overture."

Gus positions himself between Aaron and the big man and, with a smile, says, "Hell no. We don't mean no harm. The music's good."

Startled by Gus's friendliness the big man grunts, "Oh."

With an engaging smile Gus continues, "We're good here. No bad feelings?"

The bar falls silent, all eyes on the big man and Gus.

The big man smiles, "Yeah, no bad feelings. I know you Indians will walk from a fight."

Pointing to the arm-wrestling table Gus offers, "Right, no fighting. Let's arm wrestle for two rounds of beer for everyone."

The big fisherman replies to the challenge, "Sure," and breaks into a wicked smile.

Gus suggested the contest because there are grip bars for the free hand. Outweighed by eighty pounds, Gus wouldn't have a chance without the grip bar that evens out weight differences. The two men take a seat on each side of the table. Noticing that the fisherman is right handed, Gus takes a left hand grip. They settle their elbows into the sockets gouged out of the table top, flex their forearms and wiggle their wrists. The big man doesn't look at his opponent. The bar tender sets their grip. Satisfied he yells, "Go!"

Gus lets the larger man force him off center. Gus's sinewy biceps slightly stretch to where he has the most strength; and conversely, the big man with relatively short arms supporting enormous biceps loses some power as his muscles contract. In this position, they are evenly matched. Gus waits. With sweat dripping from his forehead, the big man yields.

Gus smiles and addresses his opponent, "Sir, I have to admit that I was a choker setter for years, and when not logging, I was a gill netter. I'll pay the first round."

Standing up the big man declares, "Damnation, you're all right for an Injun."

Aaron pats Gus on the shoulder and howls, "Yeah, bro, you good um injun, buy um firewater for pale face. Me pay um with scalps."

Merle interjects, "Hey, Aaron, racial slurs aren't called for. Talk about stereotyping!"

The big man doesn't know whether to laugh or frown but the piano player smiles and starts playing the theme song of *Dances with Wolves.*

Wide-eyed, Alana exclaims, "My goodness Gus, I wouldn't have guessed you are so strong!"

Gaining attention Aaron continues, "We Indians have a long history of athleticism. There was Jim Thorpe, the legendary football player and Olympic track star. There was the Sioux Billy Mills who won the marathon in the Olympics. There was Jay Silverheels, the Mohawk lacrosse player but better known for his role as Tonto with the Lone Ranger." Looking about and noticing no response Aaron continues, "Indians have endurance because we have fast red muscle. Haha."

George interrupts Aaron, "Yes, Aaron, you got that right. Indians have been running from the army for so long that we have been selected to run. That's why we have fast red muscle. We have natural endurance, no training. By the way, if Tonto would have used his given name of Harold Smith, nobody would have taken him seriously."

Aaron elaborates, "I should have been a runner and not a swimmer. Indians weren't escaping the cavalry by swimming. Did you know that Sonny Six Killer, the famous quarter back for the University of Washington was only five eleven and one hundred seventy pounds? Indians are tough. Say, Ben you're really tough. What do you say?"

Ben doesn't respond. His passive-aggressive mood spreads to the other Indians like small pox. Merle, whose job is smoothing ruffled feathers, rises to the occasion. Believing that the conversation is baiting the Whites in the room, Merle changes the conversation, "Did you know that we Coeur d'Alenes have modern humor?"

"Like what?"

"Bro Frank loves golf. He plays at the Coeur d'Alene course near the casino in Worley."

Alana waits, and when Merles says nothing, asks, "That's it? I don't see humor."

Merle smiles as he answers, "My brother loses the ball in the forest, or better, drowns it."

"I still don't get the joke."

"The ball is white!"

"Oh!" Alana shakes her head, not sure whether to laugh or act offended. She does neither, but changes the subject. "In New York before I moved to Seattle, I saw *Bloody, Bloody Andrew Jackson'* in an off-Broadway production. The action in this room is better."

Looking at Alana, Merle says, "This isn't acting, this is real Indian life. The Indian burden. You know, like portrayed in the movie *Smoke Signals*."

Alana wrinkles her brow and says, "Never heard of it"

Merle continues, "Alana, our lawyer, let me tell you something. Every *Reel Injun* knows of *Smoke Signals*. It's a movie played by a cast of Indians, made for Indians, and directed by an Indian. It shows Indian humor. It stars Adam Beech. Adam went on to find fame in Tony Hillerman movies, and starred in *Windtalkers*. By the way, *Reel Injun* is a documentary describing the Whiteman's notion of Indian life."

George breaks into the discussion, "Alana, the title *Reel Injun* Merle is referring to shows how White directors portray us as murderers and rapists. Until recently, the movie Indian was always a white actor sprayed with red paint. One exception is the movie *Hombre* starring Paul Newman where he portrayed a white boy who'd been captured as a child. He played a believable Apache in spite of his blue eyes.

"Even though you Native Americans criticize Whiteman's movies, you know a lot about them. Why do you watch movies if they portray your people so badly?" asks Alana.

George answers, "You can learn about Indians especially Indian humor by watching *Smoke Signals*. Adam Beech shows how to be a stoic Indian. *Smoke Signals* demonstrates the problem of alcoholism on the reservation. It's an honest movie."

"That's funny, George, the two rednecks in *Smoke Signals* almost tossed the two Indian boys from the bus. I love that movie, and it was made on the Coeur d'Alene reservation," Merle says.

Usually quiet, Thomas extends his hand to the middle of the table holding his rolled menu as a talking stick to get attention. "Since this is twenty questions, have you guys heard of Old Shatterhand, the German frontiersman and his Apache side kick, Winnetou?"

"No"

"These western characters were written before the 1900s by the German author Karl May," Thomas explains. "Every German

knows the novel *Winnetou*. Seems to me that we have Karl May's characters here, except the roles have changed in that the Indian has the powerful hand. Isn't that right Quanah?"

Quanah growls, "Let's stop the B.S. and order."

Looking at Thomas, Merle asks, "Hey Bro, who is this Apache and German?"

"A movie was made in 1963 with Lex Barker, an American, for the German frontiersman, Old Shatterhand, and Pierre Brice, a French guy, for the Indian, Winnetou. Even Klaus Kinske was in this international movie. It was recently remade but costumes and props are completely wrong. The story plays in the southwest but they have totem poles and plains tepees, and the Indian clothing is Whiteman's. Seems Europeans don't care." Thomas withdraws his talking stick.

Alana interjects, "I think Will Sampson was very effective in his role of an American Indian in *One Flew Over the Cuckoo's Nest*. In *The Last of the Mohicans,* Wes Studi is terrific. I don't know about *Smoke Signals*, but I do know that Adam Beech is in *Flags of our Fathers* and *Windtalkers*. Beech is believable which shows that movie roles have changed for the Indian."

The waitress, standing patiently asks, "Good evening folks, are you ready to order?"

Quanah orders first. "I'll have the grilled wild sockeye. We also need two bottles of Columbia Gewürztraminer, two Pinot Gris and four bottles of sparkling Loganberry."

The others order. Thomas asks for a Stella Artois, which prompts Aaron to smirk and ask, "How do you know about European beers?"

"Movies have portrayed the Indian as unable to tolerate liquor. We needn't drink to be 'drunk Injuns,'" Thomas replies.

Merle looks at Quanah and asks, "Is Old Shatterhand and the Apache, Winnetou the equivalent of The Lone Ranger and Tonto?"

Quanah ignores the rhetorical question.

After dinner, they taxi back to the court house to join Richard for the drive to Neah Bay. Alana along with two others who don't fit in Richards crew-cab pickup crowd into Quanah's pickup, cluttered with hunting boots, fishing waders, and other gear. The floor is trashed with candy bar wrappers and Burger King bags. Alana thinks, *At least, Quanah doesn't litter the roads.*

They cross the Narrows Bridge, drive past the Bremerton Naval Yards, over Hood Canal, and onto the Olympic Peninsula, a region lying in a rain shadow of the Olympic Mountains.

After two hours of winding roads on Highways 101 and 112 they arrive in Neah Bay. Alana notes the similarities between this Indian village and the Onondaga Indian Reservation near Syracuse. Both have derelict cars, burned out homes, and piles of trash. *All the markings of poor people with little outside income. These villages are the basis for Whites to judge Native Americans negatively."*

CHAPTER 17

Neah Bay - Makah Tribal Headquarters

Makah Tribal Court – Morning
Court hearing against Quanah Tatoosh residing in Ozette
Charges: Hunting and taking a gray whale near Tatoosh Island
without tribal permission

The Makah Tribal Center is a group of twenty, single story structures located three miles west of the village of Neah Bay. The grounds are well maintained, and all buildings are of the same drab brown. As the crow flies, the Tribal court is about twenty miles south east of Tatoosh Island and twenty miles from the waters where the whale was harvested. The court furnishings are modest and modern. The prosecution, defense, and Tribal judge tables are on the same level and are equipped with microphones. The room is not large with chairs for only twenty spectators. The hall joining the court room can accommodate an overflow of fifty tribal members.

Chairperson: Mrs. McCartney will record our meeting. Quanah requested a trial by jury. We drew by lot, nine jurors from tribal enrollment. Seven are here today, that's enough. I remind jurors and audience not to ask questions or talk. Please turn off cell phones. Take no photos. At the end of the proceedings, I will ask for comments from the audience. Quanah, is your residence at Ozette?

Richard: There's only an old shack out there.

Chairperson addressing audience: Quiet, please; no talking or laughing.

Quanah: Yes.

Chairperson: Are you enrolled in the Makah Tribe?

125

Quanah: Yes.

Chairperson: I will read counts where the defendant, Quanah, has broken tribal law:
    1) hunting whale in tribal waters without notifying tribal council
    2) taking a whale without a permit issued by tribal council
    3) taking a calf

Defendant, please stand.

Quanah stands

Chairperson: Did you bring a lawyer?

Quanah: Yes, but I speak for me.

Chairperson: Quanah, do you plead guilty or not guilty?

Quanah: Not guilty.

Chairperson: Did you captain a canoe with nine off-reservation Indians with the intention to take a whale?

Quanah: Yes.

Chairperson: Is it true that during the training program for the canoe regatta we are hosting this coming fall you were training to hunt whales?

Quanah: Yes.

Chairperson: Under Article VI of the Powers of the Tribal Constitution, Section 1, the Tribal Council has the obligation to negotiate with federal agencies like NOAA to obtain permits to follow federal laws and the Constitution of the United States. You ignored this provision, and have endangered our standing with the Department of Commerce, NOAA, and the National Marine Fisheries Service (NMFS). We are attempting to improve our relationship with these federal agencies. We are filing a *petition of certiorari* with the Supreme Court to overturn the opinions of the Ninth Circuit Court of Appeals. You have not helped our cause. Did you know that permits are required to hunt whales?

Quanah: Yes, but Judge Krieger of the District Federal Court in Tacoma found that I have not broken federal laws because earlier permits are valid. They have your signature, Your Honor.

Chairperson: I remind the jury that Makah Court has sovereign jurisdiction over tribal members. Rulings of Judge Krieger aren't relevant on the reservation.

Quanah: The Preamble of the Makah Constitution, ratified by elders in 1936, states that our Tribe established the constitution to promote and develop resources for prosperity. We are to rule in a fashion not inconsistent to federal Law. I have not broken federal law.

Chairperson: Second charge: we find that you broke tribal law part e, Section 1 in Article VI of the powers of the Tribal Council. It is the Council's job to manage all economic affairs of the tribe that require permits from the Federal Departments of Interior and Commerce. You also violated part j, the responsibility of the tribe to regulate trade on the reservation.

Quanah: These charges don't apply to my case. Article VII of our Bill of Rights in our Constitution, Section 2, concerning economic matters states that tribal members have equal opportunities to develop reservation resources. Whales are commodities that our ancestors depended upon. I am descended from Chief Flattery Jack who lived on Tatoosh Island and Chief Ah-de-ak-too-ah of Ozette.

In 1853, the Indians living in Ozette took nine gray whales. An adult gray whale by today's wholesale value is $500,000 dollars.

Since many in the audience ain't too good at math that makes four and a half million dollars or $9,000 for each enrolled Makah. We have one Indian artist with thirteen kids!

Audience: (a ripple of laughter and jeers)

Quanah: Now that I know I have your attention, I'll continue. At the time of the 1855 treaty, Washington Territorial Gov. Stevens knew that our ancestors whaled commercially. Our ancestors sold 30,000 gallons of whale oil, known as trane oil, to the Hudson's Bay Company in Victoria. What is important is that President Pierce and Secretary of Interior McClellan instructed Gov. Stevens to guarantee the Makah commercial whaling rights by treaty. I was exercising this right granted by a President of the United States. Most importantly, Supreme Court Justice Marshall ruled in 1835 that treaties have no time limits.

Chairperson: In regards to the second charge: you have conspired to deceive the Makah People by enlisting help from members of other tribes and bands without permission of the Tribal Counsel.

Quanah: I refer to section 3. of our Bill of Rights that gives all members of the tribe freedom of speech and assembly.

Chairperson: Court adjourned for two hours. We will recommence after lunch. Jury, don't discuss the case with the audience.

Quanah walks over to Alana sitting at the defense table and asks, "Do you approve?"

Alana nods and smiles, "You would make a good lawyer. You were paying attention during the hearing in Tacoma."

"Let's eat lunch," Quanah says. "The women at the Port Café like me. We can discuss my closing argument. It has to be short."

At the restaurant, Alana says, "I sure get a lot of stares. I don't think I'm wanted in court, but it's fascinating, and I'm glad I'm here. I'll be interested to see how many people protest killing the whale when the chairperson asks for comments. I know I would."

"That's because you are White and think White." Quanah smiles and winks. "I may have to work harder to change that."

Two p.m. – Tribal Court Room

Chairperson: Tribal Court in Session for closing arguments. This trial is held by the Sovereign Makah Indian Tribe. We have our constitution that binds our people to certain laws that are important to the welfare of Tribal members. The findings of the United States Federal District Court held in Tacoma are not relevant to our proceedings on the Reservation. The defendant, Quanah has broken Makah Law: first, he failed to inform the Makah Tribal Council of his intention to hunt whales; second, he failed to obtain permits and third he caught a whale. We have been working with Washington State and the Olympic Coast National Marine Sanctuary, and we are filing a *petition of certiorari* with the Supreme Court to overturn the opinions of the Ninth Circuit Court of Appeals. Quanah deceived the elders by not informing them of his intent. The council asks the jury to find the defendant guilty. Quanah, you may sum your plea.

Quanah: Our tribal customs date back thousands of years. We lived in harmony with nature. My ancestry goes back to chiefs who lived on Tatoosh Island and in the village of Ozette. The Ozette archeological dig found that seventy-five percent of our diet was whale. No Indian living in the villages of Neah Bay, Waatch, Ozette, and Tsoo-Yess would have had the audacity, or *bigsteesballs*...

Audience: Laughter. Quanah how do say that in Makah?

Audience: More laughter.

Quanah: In Makah, to have the *Kakloobits* to abrogate…

Audience: Yeah, yeah, abrogate….laughter.

Chairperson: Richard, one more outbreak and you're to throw them out. Is that clear to you in the back?"

Quanah: We still have the rights guaranteed to my ancestors to whale. We were a loosely knit tribe centuries ago; and, at the time of the treaty of 1855 we had the right to live as our forefathers, and the treaty ensures that we have those rights forever. Our name Makah means that we are "The People who live on the end with rocks and seagulls." We live from the ocean. The Makah school teacher, James Swan, recorded in 1850 that whaling is a sacred gift of our creator for spiritual and nutritional sustenance. Charles M. Scammon wrote in1868 about watching a Makah whaling chief— he could have been my great, great, great grandfather—pursue and take the whale in the waters of Juan de Fuca and Tatoosh Island. He should know, because he hunted the same gray whale in Baja California. I conclude that Whites at the time of the treaty knew the importance of the whale to Makah culture. Whaling rights have been promulgated by the United States Supreme Court and canon laws enacted by the United States Congress and signed into law by presidents. In the U.S. v. Winans case the federal court ruled that Indians who were granted U.S. lands retained their rights on both reservations and accustomed hunting and fishing grounds. In 1835 Supreme Court Justice Marshall wrote that treaties are the supreme law of the land and last forever. In taking the whale, I was exercising my tribal rights as a hereditary chief to whale and these rights are upheld by Federal laws. Thank you, Madam Chairperson.

As Quanah sits Alana whispers, "That was impressive. You have information I don't have. Really important. When did you research the federal cases? And when did you learn 'abrogate' and 'promulgate'?"

Quanah whispers back, "You're stereotyping, again."

Chairperson: Now members in the audience may comment. Comments?

Jack, a fisherman: Quanah, did you learn them big words over at that university in Seattle?

Quanah: OK. Jack, I'll give you a lesson, but only for you.

Chairperson: Chair recognizes Mrs. Blackman.

Mrs. Blackman: Quanah, I think you deceived us. We believed you were only interested in the canoe regatta. How can you justify your action?

Quanah: Mrs. Blackman, I deeply regret that I have offended you. I want to return to Tribal traditions. Whaling is central to our customs and religion. I was aware that the Whiteman would object. The Whiteman tells us how to be Indian. White culture doesn't understand Circle of Life and our indigenous way. To keep news people away, we had to make the hunt in secret. I knew that taking a whale would have national impact. However, the taking of a whale can't be simulated with a cartoon and artificial intelligence within our culture. Whales are not threatened today. It is time to whale as our forefathers to maintain our culture.

Chairperson: Jury, please deliberate in the conference room. You must have a majority to decide guilty or not. Please deliver a verdict that considers the welfare of your great-grandchildren and will honor your great-grandparents. I know my great-granddaughter but do not remember my great-grandmother. Yet, I have heard many wonderful stories of her. This is seven generations. Seven generations is our unit of time. We'll reconvene at four.

Conference Room for Jury (not recorded)

Joey says, "Well, I may be a dumb fisherman, and didn't know them fancy words, but Quanah has every right to hunt a whale. It don't matter if the whale is a calf or not. That requirement was put into our laws to make the Whites feel good. They eat veal. I don't care that we're supposed to vote in secret but I know, as well as all of you, that we have already decided. Let's just vote. Fishing season starts next week. We have few salmon, but I need to fish in order to buy new nets. I don't see no difference between fishing for salmon and catching a whale. We haven't been able to catch enough salmon to maintain our boats. Five boats sank at the docks last winter. What will we need the new dock and warehouse for? It could be used to store whales. My vote is not guilty. Excuse me but I need to work on my boat."

May, a grandmother, disagrees. "I think that Quanah was disrespectful and that our Tribe has lost respect. And we worked hard to be involved with the 'Coastal Sanctuary' program. Also, he killed a calf. I say Quanah is guilty."

Mary Ellen, a young stay at home mother, voices her opinion, "I love whales and have read that whales will bring tourists to Neah Bay for whale watching. Quanah broke our law. I vote guilty."

Annie, a restaurant owner, says, "I know Quanah, he's a nice guy. He respects our elders. I think he had the right to harvest a whale. Joey is right, a whale is our culture. In regards to what the Whiteman thinks of us, they have never cared for us. They don't give a damn for us today. They only want Indians for 'dog and pony shows' or during fishing season when they need a guide to catch salmon. Then the Whiteman is very polite to us. As far as the animal rights people, they have enough, they don't live in poverty, they have no idea of Indian culture. Animal rights people should go after White people who eat veal. In regards to the coastal sanctuary, the environmentalists are only giving Indians lip service and pretend they have Indians on their side. The animal protection groups are controlling the press. Quanah has provided us with goals. He is a role model. Our young people will not find respect with iPhones. Quanah is not-guilty."

Jim is an ex-logger with a ruined back. "I'm sick and tired of being told what, when, and where by the feds. We ain't got no casino. Look what the S'Klallam Tribe has done with their Seven Cedar Casino money. They are a smaller tribe. We will never have a casino because we're isolated. Whaling will bring money. Quanah did us a great favor. Not guilty."

Martin, a high school teacher is the jury foreman. "Quanah disregarded Tribal Law. I like Quanah, and in many respects, he is a role model for our young people. Nevertheless, I must vote guilty."

Great Grandmother, known as Granny and oldest member of jury and ex member of Tribal Council, speaks, "I can't make up my mind. On the one hand, Quanah broke tribal law. On the other, the Makah must exert self-determination. I am concerned that we are not holding to traditions that respect the Spirit of Whale. Our young people don't know what the Circle of Life means. Whaling was central to our culture. Whale feeds us spiritually. Yet, we need laws, but we also need to whale. I'm on the fence and withhold my vote."

Martin says, "We are deadlocked. Will anyone change his mind?"

The jurors answer in unison, "No."

Martin says, "Let's call Richard and report to court."

Back in Court Room (recorded)

Richard: Court in session, please rise for Tribal Council.

Chairperson: What's the verdict?

Martin: We're tied. Three for conviction, three for not guilty, and one can't make her mind up.

Chairperson: A guilty verdict would carry a punishment of one hundred hours of community service, so a split verdict means fifty hours. Quanah, arrange your schedule with Richard. We hold you for a court cost of twenty-five dollars and a fine of one hundred twenty-five dollars. The Coast Guard brought Whale to the beach. Let's go to Whale and say prayers. We're adjourned.

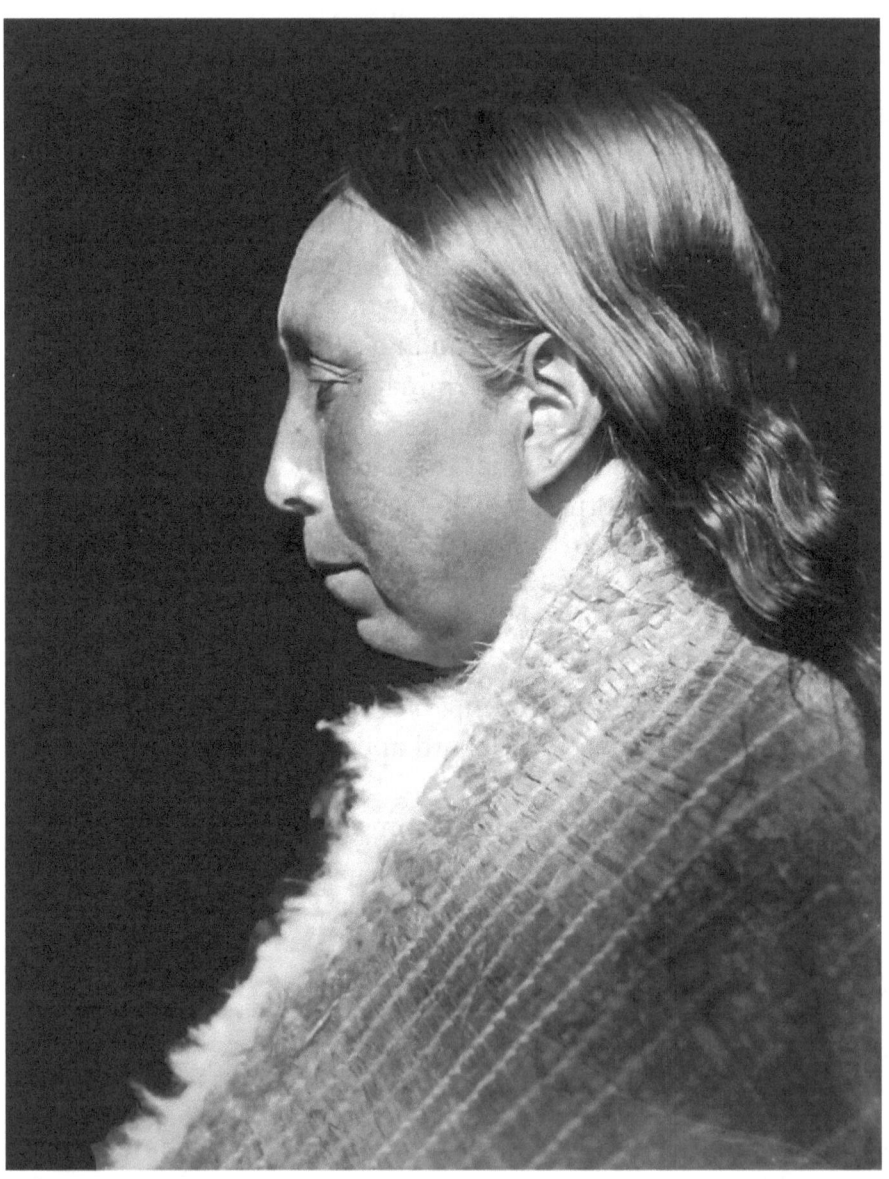

CHAPTER 18

Distribution Ceremony – At Tribal Beach

The Makah Tribal Council members, elders, and jury file out of the tribal center and into waiting cars followed by jurors and spectators. The somber mood changes to one of celebration as Indians from all over the reservation make their way to the tribal beach.

"Hey Quanah, that was a good show."

"Hey Bro, you showed 'em."

Martin, extending his hand to Quanah, says, "Quanah, no hard feelings. You did the right thing."

A stand had been pushed against Whale, and Martin helps Granny mount the steps to address the hundreds of Indians now pressing for a good look. Children hush as Granny grasps the microphone, "In 1918, Grandmother stood here for this ceremony. My mother told me how Grandmother gave blessing for whale. She told me how to do it. She told me many times. Mother died. She never had chance to give prayer for Whale. I am honored to give prayer.

135

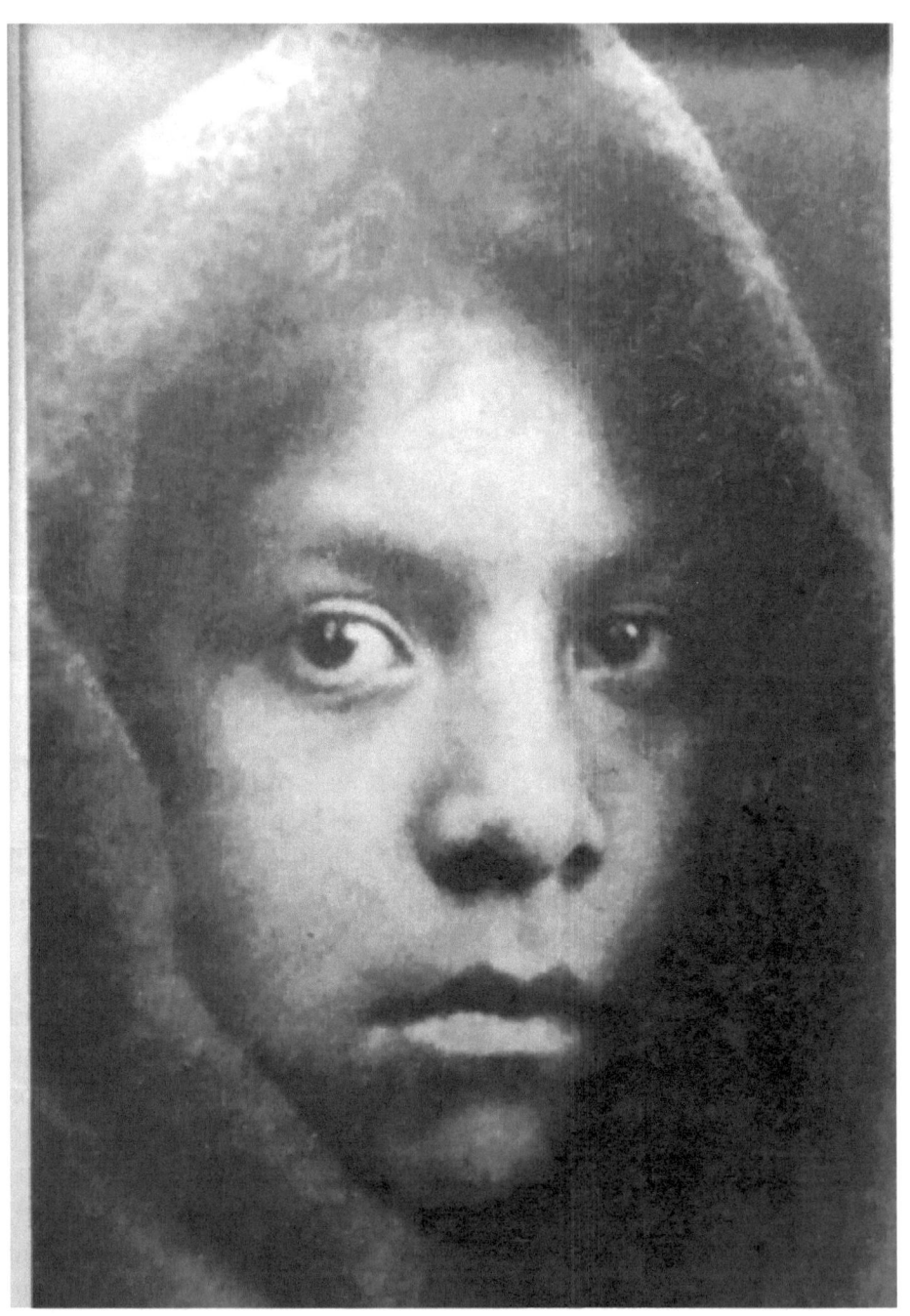

"O' Great Chief from Above,
You brought Whale to waters of Makah Tribe,
You taught Quanah to find Whale,
O' Great Chief from Above, you gave Quanah Whale,
Makah People thank you,
O' Great Chief from Above, you bring People together,
Makah People thank you,
O' Great Chief from Above, Whale will feed us,
Makah People thank you,
O' Great Chief from Above, take Spirit of Whale,
Makah People thank you."

Several old men join Granny and help her remove the back section near the fin. This piece of Whale is sacred because Whale's spirit finds solace when this flesh is removed from his body. Climbing the steps to the platform, Quanah's mother, Monika, receives the first piece of Whale in an ancient woven basket of cedar root lined with newspaper. The basket has mellowed to a golden brown with faded black images of a whale and canoe filled with Indians. Granny and Monika have obviously rehearsed the ritual.

Granny motions Quanah to join her on the platform to bestow a name. "Quanah, it is my honor to give you the name of Flattery Jack for catching Whale. With the body of Whale, we have the ceremony to feed our people and celebrate. We share our wealth with our White brothers. We honor our name Makah, given to us by the Clamath, which means that we share with our neighbors. We, the Makah People, thank Quanah Flattery Jack Tatoosh for providing Whale for this potlatch. We can now share and give as required by custom."

Monika holds the basket toward the crowd and passes it to Quanah. She wears a traditional robe of woven reeds.

Monika says, "Quanah you have the honor of eating the first portion. Then the Whale completes his Circle of Life and makes a uniting force for Makah People."

Quanah strokes Whale Body with an eagle feather. With a barely audible voice gives his rendition of the chief's hereditary prayer,

"O Great Chief from Above, You made me strong as the
Black Rock.
O Great Chief from Above, You brought Whale to us.

Quanah fills mouth with water spouting it upward toward the sky saying,

O Great Chief Above, You made Whale and Me as One.
We honor Whale with Potlatch
Thy Great Name is Daylight- tl'isiiq'ak"

The crowd claps. Some younger members whistle and chant, "Quanah, Quanah, Quanah Flattery-Jack." The mood is like that of a high school football game when Quanah was a star.

Surprised by his reception, Quanah hugs his mom whispering, "Where did you get the dress?"

"I made it when you were born. Your grandmother taught me. It's made of reeds, cedar bark and elk sinew. I have never worn it."

"Nice," Quanah whispers.

He sees Alana approaching and extends his arm. "Mom, this is Alana, our lawyer."

Giving Alana a warm hug, Monika speaks softly into her ear,

"Thank you so much for getting my son out of jail. I'm so pleased that you came to the ceremony. Can you come for dinner tonight?"

Smiling, Alana returns the hug and replies, "Yes, thank you. It's my pleasure." Smiling at Quanah, she adds, "You can tell me stories about young Quanah."

Men appear with large butcher knives and flensing spades and begin cutting long pieces of skin blubber into sixteen-inch-wide by four-inch-thick slabs. After the layer of blubber is stripped from the carcass, men cut long chunks of back muscle which are passed to others. The table crew deftly cuts the skin from the reddish, sinewy blubber and divides the blubber into three-pound blocks. The back muscles, known as tenderloin in the meat market, are cut into five-pound steaks. An old wheel tractor, that forty years ago had been bright orange, turns the body, to expose the large back muscles on the inside of the vertebral column. Indians press closely to receive their piece of meat and blubber. Four hundred portions are distributed.

Meat from fin muscles is sliced into strips to be dried or frozen. Several men assemble three two-burner propane camp stoves. They drop pieces of blubber into six one-gallon pots to melt into oil, called trane oil. Old man Loot and his three sons lug a one-hundred-fifty-pound, cast iron rendering kettle from their pickup and suspend it with a chain from a tripod. It hasn't been used for eighty years. Kids are sent to the beach for dry wood. Fatty flesh from the ribs is removed, diced, and dropped into the kettle. After two hours of stirring, the old man ladles cracklings and pieces of cooked 'bacon' onto paper plates, which are passed to all.

Quanah notices Commander Sorenson and several enlisted men standing off to the side. He picks up plates of cracklings and glistening pieces of red-brown meat and delivers them to the surprised men. He addresses Com. Sorenson. "Sir, we are pleased that you are here. It's important that everyone be included in the festivities, and this means our Coast Guard brothers. Commander Sorenson, I thank you, my crew and Makah Tribe thank you."

"It was our pleasure to help. Any hunter would have done the

same if an elk or deer were involved. Quanah, I thank you for making us feel welcome."

A middle-aged couple makes their way to where Quanah is standing. "Hello Quanah, remember us? We gave you a lift from Ozette to Neah Bay."

"Yes, of course. Please, stay right here, and I'll get you some meat and blubber."

"Oh, no, that's not necessary," Karla exclaims as she takes his arm.

"We are happy that White folks join us. It is important to me that I have this chance to express my gratitude." Quanah thinks that Karla and Bruce probably eat little meat so he returns with small portions, and motions for Alana to join them. "This is our lawyer, Alana. She got us out of jail."

Karla grabs Alana's hand, exclaiming. "We met Quanah a few months ago. You and Quanah make such a handsome pair in the newspapers." Winking at Alana and turning to Quanah, Karla gushes, "Quanah, you are so lucky to be represented by such a striking lawyer."

It's a festive sight. Families who had been bickering for so long that they forgot the basis of their disputes cry and hug. Children are laughing, climbing all over Whale. Stories not told for years are recounted.

Rendered oil is bottled, and meat is packaged to be distributed to Indian Tribes attending the war canoe regatta the coming fall. Elders are pleased to be able to provide these traditional treats while hosting the Makah Tribal Potlatch. The potlatch will now be complete and will be a really "Big Do" with traditional whale meat and trane oil not seen for one hundred years.

Soon only the skeleton remains. Massive sinews are stripped from the vertebral column and distributed to artists for bead work and sewing. Baleen plates, severed from the jaws will become traditional tools, art work, and clothing. Finally, the front loader lifts the skeleton onto a flat-bed truck to be buried near the sea wall.

Quanah, Monika, and Alana are joined by Merle and his pregnant wife, Louise, who gives her high school friend a heart-warming hug exclaiming, "Quanah, we're proud of you. I'm glad that I didn't know what was going on. I mean the hunt. I would've been worried sick. But thank you for including Merle and for watching out for him." Merle grabs both his wife and Quanah loudly proclaiming, "Yeah, thanks Bro. But don't think I'm going on a hunt again."

"Hey man, a good 'Big Do,'" Aaron shouts, as he, Thomas, and George break through the crowd.

Quanah disengages from Louise and Merle and turns to the young men. "I thought you guys had gone home."

Thomas grabs Quanah's hand. "Go home and miss this show? No way! George and I can catch the ferry from Port Angeles. And Aaron lives in Seattle."

Aaron extending his hand to Alana, says, "Hi Alana, we want to thank you again." Turning back to Quanah, he adds, "Quanah, we thought the Tribal Court would murder you."

Quanah shrugs. "Maybe I was lucky. Let's drop over to the Café for a coffee. Alana, you can tell us what you think of Indian Justice."

Giving her son a hug, Monika addresses his friends, "Please go. I expect all of you for a German dinner. See you at seven, German time."

Taking her seat in the restaurant, Alana smiles and motions Quanah to sit beside her. Touching his hand, she asks, "Commander Sorenson arrested you and took the whale. Why did you thank him?"

A blush creeps from Quanah's neck, reddening his cheeks. After a long moment, he gathers his composure and answers. "The Commander had his crew gut the whale. Otherwise, the meat could have gone bad due to body heat which was trapped by the layer of blubber. I guess the Commander is a hunter. He knows that if you leave an elk overnight before field dressing the meat will spoil."

Alana nods and squeezes his hand. "About Indian justice—I like that it's quick. But how can you be half guilty?"

"How can the United States Supreme Court rule five to four so many times? Is it fair that the majority of one becomes law for everyone?"

"Good point." After a few moments, she asks, "Where is your dad, Quanah?"

"Dead."

Taken aback by Quanah's candor, Alana presses his hand, saying, "I'm so sorry. What happened?"

"Shot himself. He is whole again."

Caught off-guard, Alana manages to blurt, "I'm so sorry. I didn't mean to bring up a painful past." After a pause, she asks, "But what do you mean, he's whole again?"

"He lost his legs due to diabetes. I found him where we hunted. He didn't want mom to find him."

Holding his fist high for emphasis, Quanah continues, "I want to explain something. The Makah Tribe is small, and we know every body's business. We have to get along. In court today, people who had something to say, had the opportunity to voice their opinion. I think this is how our ancestors acted."

Alana asks, "Do Indians ever have hung juries and retrials?"

"No, in serious cases the jury quickly comes to agreement. But in many cases, like mine today, both sides have valid points so the decision lies somewhere in between. We don't need to have a winner-take-all verdict like Whiteman's court."

"I thought the prayer was emotional, and I understood. In fact, it sounded very Christian, like the Eucharist. I'm beginning to appreciate why some Indians accepted Whiteman's religion so readily. However, I don't fully understand the phrase, 'Circle of Life.'"

Thomas extends his hand holding his rolled menu for a talking stick, "Indians believe that all animals have a spirit. And, what is essential to the Indian, is that everything composing mother earth has a spirit. Whale has a spirit. The ocean, the ground, rocks, dirt, and water all have Spirit. The Indian believes that the spiritual world is interconnected. Each component, living and earthly, of our world is part of the whole. Each component is born, lives its life, and dies to return to its beginning. This is the Circle of Life. The living can pass into the nonliving and vice versa. The prayer delivered by Grandmother released Whale Spirit so his body could return to earth. Only after the prayer could Indians eat the flesh of Whale. With prayer, Whale Spirit returns to his beginning to complete his

Circle of Life."

Alana protests. "But the whale died so young, he didn't have a full life!"

Thomas tips the menu, his talking stick, signaling he will continue, "Indians don't believe that Whale Spirit died. The fullness of a life span is a Whiteman's construct. Whale was born, he lived, his body returned to its beginning. The Circle of Life for the Indian means that the time of life is a circle. The number of events occurring during the circle is not important. Whiteman sees time as a straight arrow, a progression of events—sequential such that each event must occur to be followed by the next event."

Thomas pauses, but doesn't retract the menu, and continues; "Whale body died. It doesn't matter if Whale died of old age or died when young. How or when Whale died doesn't matter in the concept of Circle of Life because Whale's Spirit continues to live."

Alana, ignoring the talking stick, quietly speaks, "I remained calm while attending the Distribution Ceremony, but now I feel queasy. During the ceremony, everything was natural, peaceful, and joyous. The children were laughing and crawling over the whale carcass. The ceremony was neither disgusting nor distasteful. The butchering appeared as a normal activity. The blood, the skeleton, the smell of cooking oil and bacon seems remote—disconnected."

"Alana you are pasty white, lets change the subject," suggests Thomas.

"No, I'll be OK," Alana says. "I need to work through this. I understand it's necessary to eat the meat of the whale and to render its fat into oil. And to give the artists sinew for thread. How did the men know what to do? I mean, it looked like they butcher a whale every week. I know that a whale was butchered ten years ago, but butchering hasn't been routine for eighty years."

Merle knocks the table to signal it's his turn and speaks, "The butchering skills show the power of Indian oral tradition."

Louise giggles. "Alana, Merle's pulling your leg, we have an extensive collection of photographs in the Tribal Museum showing butchering a century ago. Many photos were by Asahel Curtis.

Some were found in the Library of Congress in Washington D.C. while researching the objects collected from the Ozette dig."

"You mean the artifacts in the museum?"

"Yes."

Alana asks, "But why did the tribe bury the skeleton?"

Quanah answers, "The reason to bury the whale skeleton is to recover clean bones for the museum."

Alana utters, "I still feel sick, but my lawyer instincts force me to ask for clarification. The bones of the skeleton would not appear to be returning to earth if you dig them up and give them to the museum. Please explain."

Looking at Alana, George signals he will explain, "The bones will return to dust in time. You see, Whiteman's mortal time line can't be applied to the Indian way of life. Remember what Thomas said, 'Indians don't perceive time as an arrow, but a circle', never ending. Whiteman's time is controlled by his watch, his calendar, and through his written word. Watch, calendar, and writing are linear. For the Indian, time is when an event happens in the circle of everything."

As George stops, Quanah explains, "In a year, we'll dig up the bones. The bones will be placed in boxes at the tribal museum for children to touch. We already have the mounted skeleton of a whale. With an unassembled skeleton, kids can fit vertebrae together. Find out how joints articulate. Thrust their little fists into the skull to palpate the inside and feel the sutures of the skull. They can contemplate where the brain was located. Discover the foramen of the optic nerve. The kids can experience where Whale's spirit lived."

Alana says, "That's revolting, yet deep."

"You're right, Alana. It's like the work of Georgia O'Keeffe," chuckles Quanah.

"You know Georgia O'Keeffe?"

Aaron immediately jabs; "White woman stereotypes Indian Warrior as blood thirsty. Injuns takum scalps, war dance with tom tom, drinkum much fire water, rape virgins. You, Alana, White woman, makum good squaw."

145

Alana continues, "Don't laugh, I didn't mean to be insulting. I would expect Thomas to know of O'Keeffe, but Quanah, how do you know of her?"

"I hitched to Arizona to acquaint myself with southwest art," explains the whaling chief.

"Quanah, you are so full of shit," Aaron says as he winks at Alana.

George addresses Quanah, "Tell the truth, you speak with forked tongue of your White half."

"During my freshman year we played Arizona State in Tempe. We had Sunday free because our flight home was on Monday. So, I went to the museum."

Smiling Aaron responds, "You speakum half-truth, like-um half Whiteman."

"Coach took the team to the Heard Museum in Phoenix for some culture."

"Yeah, culture for a football team." Thomas laughs

"OK, Coach wanted to purchase a Navajo rug. Most of the team sat in the Caféteria. I spent my time in the Indian Gallery with the frescos. These frescos are powerful and depict the Indian condition. Kit Carson was painted with three arms. One arm representing the army held a spear thrust through the Navajo heart, another arm represented religion, and the third represented government. We could use murals like those in our cultural museum. We could hire Thomas. There was an exhibit of Georgia O'Keeffe. She illustrated the beauty of skulls, vertebrae, and the pelvis of a bat. She painted skulls with the same detail that she used for her flowers. She positioned bleached, white bones in front of desert back drops. The starkness of bones and the soft earth colors of the Painted Desert defy description; they must be seen. I want our Indian children to appreciate the beauty of bones as much as Whites value skin."

Alana gushes, "Wow, that's impressive. But what inspired you for oratory? You're good at it—like during your defense this morning, or for that matter, your Georgia O'Keeffe lecture?"

Extending his hand to the table George indicates that it is now his turn to speak, "Alana, you are stereotyping again. Indians have a tradition of oratory. We can go back seven generations."

"George, I don't mind answering," Quanah cuts in. "The museum also had an exhibit of Scott Momaday's paintings, prose, and poetry. He was a professor—and he was Kiowa. An intellectual Indian! I was impressed. I discovered that an Indian can paint and write."

Thomas, stands, with spiraled menu high overhead for his talking stick and recites:

> *Quit of hope and hurt,*
> *It held a motionless gaze,*
> *Wide of time, alert,*
> *On the dark distant flurry.*

Thomas continues, "You must understand, Alana, Indians love oratory. That was the last stanza of Momaday's *Angle of Geese*. Momaday won a Pulitzer Prize."

The next day, Quanah and Alana drive back to Seattle. Standing on the observation deck of the Bainbridge Island-Seattle Ferry, Alana says, "With the glaciers of Mount Olympus to the west, Mt. Baker to the northeast, and Mt. Rainier rising from Puget Sound, it's no wonder Seattle is a magnet for those loving to sail and hike."

Quanah stiffens and mumbles, "Alana, you must understand that this was all stolen from the Indian."

CHAPTER 19

Whale Museum, Friday Harbor, End of May

Alana was assigned to work on her law firm's defense of the Indians in front of the Supreme Court the coming year. Bernard Edwards was sure that the Ninth Court of Appeals would reverse Judge Krieger's ruling, especially since Krieger chastised the judges of an earlier Ninth-Court ruling. After the recent election with Supreme Court appointments strongly leaning to the right, they would have a tough assignment defending Indians. Moreover, the Sioux at Standing Rock Reservation lost their case to block the oil pipe line just north of their reservation.

Needing a break from preparing briefs, Alana wants to pursue the cold case of her missing grandfather, so she arranges to spend the weekend on San Juan Island at the B&B in Friday Harbor. Maybe she will see Quanah at the Friday Harbor Laboratories.

Alana has a deep, visionary sleep, dreaming of a ferry cutting a skiff in half. Yet, she wakes rested. It's 9:00 a.m. and sunny, when she joins Meg and Charlie for hot cereal. She has never tasted such good oatmeal.

"What's in this?" Alana asks.

Meg cheerfully responds, "Just cooked oatmeal. I'm sure your mom made this, Quaker Oats with Ben Franklin on the box."

"Yes, but it never tasted like this."

Reaching for the milk Charlie explains, "The diced apples are caramelized with butter and natural brown sugar and added to the cooked cereal just before serving. We pick up a half gallon of milk from a local farmer every Thursday. Skim the cream and use skim milk. The blackberries were picked on the Island last fall and frozen."

"No wonder it's so good," she says. "What a treat!"

"What's on your agenda today?" Meg asks.

"I'll walk to the docks and then visit the campus. After lunch, I plan to visit the Whaling Museum."

The Whaling Museum is located in an 1892 historic meeting house, and the generous windows make the inside light and airy. Like her first visit to the museum, Alana is immediately attracted to the mounted yearling gray whale suspended from the ceiling. It is positioned to greet the visitor. Because of her conversation with George, she now sees it from a different perspective. The federal court case and meeting Quanah and his hunting crew have profoundly changed her attitude about many things. She's becoming aware of how her feelings are changing, and in particular, her ideas about life and death. Looking at the skeleton she sees a beautiful creature—the whole animal and not an assemblage of bone. She isn't sad for the whale. She would have been sad last year.

The caption indicates that the skeleton was salvaged from a dead whale found floating in Haro Strait. Alana reads that whales are mammals; she knows that. They have a pelvis which is vestigial and so small that it was not discovered by the scientific world until quite

recently. She did not know that. With essentially no pelvis, the birth process is quick which is a biological necessity, because birthing is underwater and the newborn needs to breathe. In addition, the birth canal is not restricted by a pelvis so the new born is huge, insuring survival of the calf in the hostile ocean environment. Calves grow quickly, because mother's milk is high in fat and protein. For this skeleton, the twelve-inch pelvis is constructed from Plaster of Paris.

Alana walks to wall paintings of skeletons of a whale and man which are scaled to the same length. Before Quanah, she would have by-passed the exhibits of skeletons, because she wouldn't want to think that her skeleton would persist after her flesh had rotted. The wrist and finger bones of the whale flippers are easily compared to the hand of man. Relatively speaking, when looking at the size of human and whale skeletons, it becomes obvious that the whale skeleton can't support the organs when the whale is out of water. Once beached, the huge weight crushes the lungs. Alana started the university as a biology major, but hadn't liked dissecting animals and studying their insides. Another change she notices in herself.

The next exhibit shows a sounding whale with question and explanation:

Question: How does a sounding (diving) whale stay under water for two hours when a man can hold his breath for only a couple minutes?

Answer: *All mammals have hemoglobin in red blood cells that can quickly bind oxygen in the lungs. Even though oxygen makes up only about 20% of the air we breathe, hemoglobin permits each pint of blood to bind three gallons of oxygen gas. The heart first pumps blood to the lungs, then pumps the oxygenated blood to muscles, brain and other organs. In the muscles, brain, and organs where there is a lower concentration of oxygen, hemoglobin gives up its oxygen to the tissues. In muscle, there is a protein called myoglobin which also binds oxygen during a period of rest. Blood flow to muscle during movement can't deliver enough oxygen but muscle* *activity can continue because myoglobin in the muscle fibers gives up its oxygen for muscular contraction.*

There is eighty times more myoglobin in whale muscle than human muscle which is a major reason why a whale can stay under water eighty times longer than a man. Simply put, during a dive, the whale myoglobin gives up oxygen to blood which delivers oxygen to the whale's brain. When the whale surfaces, oxygen is carried to the muscle and recharges the myoglobin with oxygen.

Whales breathe voluntarily. Stated another way, whales must think to breathe. If a whale is anesthetized, it will suffocate because breathing is not automatic, as it is in man. During a dive the physiological response called bradycardia slows the heart, and blood flow is reduced to the musculature but continues to the brain. Therefore, the oxygen bound to myoglobin in the muscle is delivered within a couple of beats to the brain.

A woman can swim underwater for 100 feet or hold her breath for two minutes before oxygen is depleted from her blood. Then she feels her lungs will explode if she doesn't breathe. The waste product of muscle activity is carbon dioxide, the gas of "green" environmental pollution, which builds up in blood triggering the automatic response to breathe; i.e. humans don't think about breathing.

By contrast, the whale chooses when to breathe and can thus ignore the build-up of carbon dioxide. In the case of the human, myoglobin doesn't supply oxygen to the brain during a dive. The relative mass of whale muscle is enormous compared to its brain weight so muscle mass has the capacity to store enough oxygen not only for muscle work during the dive but can keep the brain alive for a two-hour dive. The whale has yet another adaptation for diving in that it has two times more blood volume per weight than a man. The fact that the whale lives in water, which buoys the whale, makes it easy for the whale to not only have the large body mass but to have a relatively large volume of blood. An increase in whale size does not increase the surface area very much. Therefore, an increase in body mass doesn't change the hydrodynamics of a swimming whale.

Alana moves on to the next exhibit.

Question: How do whales find their way during their long migrations?

Answer: *The gray whale migrates from the rich fishing grounds off Alaska to Baja California. A one-way trip of 4,000 miles. After giving birth and mating during the winter, whales migrate back to the Bering Sea. They follow the coast line of continental United States, passing the shores of California, Oregon, and Washington. Most Gray whales migrate around Cape Flattery, Washington, and Tatoosh Island. They cross the Strait of Juan de Fuca to the Western coast of Vancouver Island, proceed along the coast of British Columbia and Alaska and finally to the Bering Sea.*

The question of whale navigation is still a mystery. Whales have good eyesight but this would be of little advantage in the enormous expanse of open sea. For distance, whales probably use the earth's magnetic field, because they have magnetite in special brain neurons which may function as a compass. Near shore, whales may rely on echolocation. Echolocation works like this: whales emit squeaks which travel through water, hit an object, and are reflected back to the whale. The whale ear picks up the reflected sound. This process is similar to an echo reflected from a mountain when a man shouts to the mountain.

Tragically, the specialization in the whale skull for echolocation was one reason for humans to hunt whales because the finest grade of lubricating oil is found in the head of sperm whales. It's strange to think that the weaving industry contributed to the whale's demise because whale oil doesn't foul machinery used in the textile industry. The purpose of the oil to the whale is not lubrication, but for echolocation in that oil in the skull isolates the receptors in the inner ear for spatial perception. Location of objects in front of a whale works like this: the whale emits a click to generate sound waves which are focused by the "melon" of fat in the front of their heads. The waves travel through water. When part of a wave hits a solid object, it is reflected back toward the whale. This reflected wave hits the head of the whale and is transmitted through the jaw bone to the inner ear. The inner ear is suspended in a gelatinous

153

fluid which is vibrated by the wave. The vibrations stimulate the receptors. However, how the brain decodes this information is not well understood. Echolocation is also well developed in bats. When humans hear an echo that is a rudimentary echolocation system.

Alana thinks about the vendetta environmentalists have with the US Navy for experimenting with high energy sonar as she moves to the next exhibit on the whale eye.

Question: How do whales see underwater and in air?

Answer: *The whale eye focuses differently than the mechanism employed by land mammals. The whale can see clearly in and out of water. By contrast, a human doesn't see clearly in water (that is without a face mask). In land mammals, including humans, light is focused onto the retina primarily by the curvature of the cornea. When humans attempt to see underwater, incoming light rays are hardly bent by the cornea so it doesn't function as a lens. Thus, images are not focused on the retina and our vision is fuzzy. The whale eye anatomy is designed to focus images in water as well as in air. The whale lens is round (like a fish lens) so when the whale is submerged the round lens focuses light onto the retina. Another mechanism makes it possible for the whale to focus in air. Out of water, the change in pressure squashes the eyeball to bring the retina closer to the lens to bring the image into focus. This explains why killer whales can catch seals in water and on a beach. Another difference between man and whales regards viewing the world through binocular vision. A human turns his head for a panoramic view. A whale sees a world to the left, and a world to the right. The cervical vertebrae of whales are thin and fused so a whale can't turn his head. However, the whale's eye ball protrudes from its socket and the eye muscles can rotate each eye separately to find objects in or out of water.*

Alana is jolted by the thought that a killer whale could recognize the face of a human in the water as well as on the surface. And a killer whale would not confuse a seal and a human swimming in the ocean. She continues to read:

The whale eye is adapted to seeing deep in the ocean where there is less light. This is accomplished with a reflecting surface called a tapetum which lies just behind the retinal receptor cells. The reflecting surface functions like a mirror and light that passed between receptors is reflected back where some is captured by receptors and the rest comes out the eye. Thus, eyes of nocturnal mammals like dogs, cats, and whales glow when caught in a flash light. Whales have the eyes and the brains to record topological features of their world underwater as well as the shore line and distant objects on the horizon.

Question: In the cold arctic waters, how do whales, who are warm-blooded mammals, stay warm?

Answer: *The body of a whale is wrapped in a layer of fat. This acts like a blanket of insulation. This fat, termed blubber, is one reason why humans hunted whales almost to extinction in the 1800s. A naked human will last only a few minutes in arctic waters before her core temperature of 98.6° Fahrenheit falls to 90°, resulting in the cessation of brain-cell functioning. Breathing stops because the breathing mechanism is driven by nervous activity. Once human temperature falls it continues to fall producing the condition of hypothermia, which leads to death.*

In cold water, a scuba diver needs a rubber wet suit to function like the layer of fat of a whale. The layer of fat surrounding the whale musculature is such an effective insulator that an actively swimming whale experiences the opposite problem confronting a swimming man.

Alana reflects on how lucky Ben was that he didn't die when stitching the whale's lips shut. Lucky that David knew what to do. She would never have thought to hug Ben to warm him up, but would have piled blankets on him. She continues reading:

Question: How do whales get rid of heat?

Answer: *Whales have a system of blood vessels found in their flippers and fluke which function like a car radiator to dissipate heat* *into the surrounding water.*

At the next exhibit about the feeding behavior of killer whales Alana reads,

Answer: *Their powerful jaws and rows of conical, eight-inch-long teeth are ideally suited to grab seals and sea lions. It takes only one crunch to crush a three-hundred-pound seal. Killer whale's teeth are designed for gripping and tearing.*

Alana shudders, wondering if she's solved her grandfather's disappearance. She sighs. *But I have not proven it. I'll have to come back a third time. I need to know more about killer whales, but for now, I'm saturated.*

She decides it's time to call some favors. *I'll email Thomas and get his opinion of killer whale stories.*

CHAPTER 20

Thomas, Kwakwaka'wakw Artist
First Nation Village of Alert Bay, B.C., Canada

Thomas is pleasantly surprised to receive an email from Alana. It has been months since she and Prof. Bernard Edwards kept him out of the federal prison in Seattle. The whaling crew had been detained without bond, no *habeas corpus*. Alana's email initiated a flood of thoughts that he had suppressed. To avoid a full-blown U.S. Canadian incident, the U.S. Feds simply turned the Canadian First Nation People over to respective First Nation Bands. The British Columbia Provincial Government didn't want to get involved. Thomas was surprised that back home at Alert Bay, British Columbia, he's a hero. Yet Thomas wasn't at all proud of taking the whale. He isn't a hunter. He doesn't fish. Animals are an integral part of his being, his art. In fact, he shunned the notoriety of the hunt. Luckily, the Elders are looking forward to hosting the war canoe regatta sponsored by the Makah Tribe. They aren't dissuaded by the negative press of the whale hunt.

The Kwakwaka'wakw council decided it was their duty to honor their commitment to host the war canoe regatta. It's to be a really "Big Do" with potlatches, dances, and ceremonies to honor their great chief James Sewid who led the way for modern bands to gain access into the Whiteman's world. Thomas's middle name is James. His grandfather, James Sewid had invited the Whiteman into the First Nation world as spectators to dances, ceremonies, and a sharing of cultural beliefs using masks and other regalia. Modern day elders decide it's appropriate to honor this tradition and extend invitations to the White community.

Thomas, a taller than normal Kwakwaka'wakw (Kwakiutl) of slight build, enjoyed painting the Sisiutl image (Kwakwaka'wakw name for Wasgo) onto Quanah's canoe at Neah Bay. He developed a close relationship with Sam who had hewn the war canoe from a single Western Red Cedar log. Thomas, a descendent of Kwakiutl chiefs, had inherited the Sisiutl crest. He has an old photograph of two totem poles spanned by Sisiutl in front of Flora Sewid's house at Alert Bay. Today, a Sisiutl gateway greets the visitor at the ferry dock. For the Kwakwaka'wakw, Sisiutl has two heads so Thomas joined the serpent heads at the prow of Quanah's canoe. Thomas's Sisiutl is similar to a Haida Wasgo photo supplied by Sam. Thomas incorporated both Haida and Kwakwaka'wakw motifs because ownership of a totem is not so strong today, and his people have a tradition to create art outside historic conventions. Kwakwaka'wakw totem-pole animals have beaks, wings, arms, and fins painted in color.

The Canadian and U.S. governments passed laws to isolate coastal tribes and bands which had the effect of breaking family and cultural ties. After the ban on potlatches in 1884, Thomas's ancestors went underground to continue potlatch ceremonies. Tragically, the provincial government stole many masks and regalia. The ban was rescinded in 1951 at which time First Nation Peoples had lost much of their culture. Thomas attributes his artistic abilities to ancestors who clandestinely practiced their culture in the face of jail.

Thomas reads Alana's email:

Dear Thomas,

It's been a long time since we have communicated, and I hope that this note finds you in good health. I need to ask some questions. If they are too personal or intrude on Indian culture and tribal traditions not to be shared with Whites, I understand. Some forty years ago, my grandfather disappeared in the San Juan Archipelago. Since the San Juan Islands are part of the Salish Sea inhabited by the Kwakwaka'wakw People and since Port Hardy is a gate into the Inland Passage which brought Whitemen and Indians together, I was thinking that you may know about killer whales and legends of Sisiutl (Wasgo). In addition, I found that the Kwakwaka'wakw shared their traditions many years ago with Edward Curtis during the filming of In the Land of the Head Hunters. I have also been reading the voluminous papers of Franz Boas on the Kwakwaka'wakw (Kwakiutl) language and the legends of Sisiutl and the underworld. I was impressed by the story of *Storm Boy* by Paul Owen Lewis depicted at the Friday Harbor Whale Museum on San Juan Island. I am somewhat troubled by bluntness, but here it is. Do you separate myth from reality? *Storm Boy* refers to the underworld of Killer Whale. But I also know there are similar legends about Sisiutl (also called Haielik or sea-wolf). I want to give you a quote by Paul Owen Lewis because he not only wrote the children's book *Storm Boy* but illustrated it. Therefore, I think that Lewis wishes to share Indian legends. The Lewis quote is: 'Parallel Worlds, Shared Destinies: There is nothing so exciting to me than the idea of interacting with Killer Whales in a supernatural arena. And here—uniquely here—in Northwest Coast Native Art and myth, can you explore this so powerfully.'

The Haida artist Robert Davidson also shared his thoughts about killer whales in the museum. The Davidson quote is: "The word for Killer Whale in Haida is Sgan which

159

means supernatural and also the Chief of the underworld. In mythic times, killer whale was chief of the underworld. They say that when you go underwater to visit the territory of the killer whales, it's no different from being on land, except that, because you're in their world, you see them as humans."

Thomas, could the legendary sea serpent Sisiutl or Wasgo be a killer whale?

Sincerely, your friend,

Alana.

Thomas immediately responds:

Dear Alana: I was pleased to hear from you and am happy to share what I know about our legends. I believe that modern Kwakwaka'wakw want to inform Whites of our culture and customs to follow the example of our great chief James Sewid. Let me give you some of my background. I majored in European Art at the University of Victoria. I could readily interact and was completely at ease with Whites. But then these students were art types which by selection have an international *Zeitgeist*. After graduation I spent a year in an exchange program at the University Constance, Germany. Initially, I was very apprehensive because American movies often portray Germans as ruthless killers bent on murdering all Jews and minorities. We First Nation Peoples are a minority. However, the citizens of the medieval town of Constance accepted me, and I soon learned the *Alemannic* dialect of German spoken in Baden-Württemberg. Moreover, Germans are interested in First Nation Peoples. This was a wonderful surprise. I was intrigued to discover that Constance is on the Swiss side of the Rhine River and was thus spared from bombing raids in World War II. Nevertheless, The University which was constructed in the 1960s has an architecture which breaks traditions, like my band can break from artistic traditions. In Constance, Germans reject the

Teutonic Herr Professor mentality. I found that Germans love Indian stories and movies such as those based on the Tony Hillerman novels. I remember that we discussed these at the Tacoma bar. I have found German ideas about Native Americans are largely from the author Karl May so they have a very romantic notion about us. They use Red Man as a word of endearment. I was amused that German people thought I should wear an eagle feather. The University of Tübingen offered me a stipend to lecture about First Nation Peoples. I return every year for a four-month appointment. It was in Tübingen that I discovered the art of Tilman Riemenschneider who had carved religious altar themes bigger than life out of linden wood in the mid-1500s. What a wonderful wood, it takes on the patina of flesh over the years. Now you know why some of my Kwakwaka'wakw mythological art looks gothic. I also know that my band accepts new versions of stories. Did you know I have a German wife? We named our son Tilman. When I was on the whale hunt, I didn't know of Quanah's German heritage, not until I met his mother, Monika, in Neah Bay. Small world, *nicht wahr?*

Of course, I'll share Kwakwaka'wakw legends with you. But first let me tell you about carving as an integral part of legends. I love carving alder. There's no grain and therefore this wood cuts smooth. If I need to sand, I use dogfish skin. I feel the work emerge with my fingers, and that feeling is more important than what I see. My spirit passes into the carving through my fingers. And the spirit of wood passes into me. This notion is expressed by the Iroquois who carve masks from a living tree so that the spirit of tree is kept within the mask. I don't use oil finishes as they darkened the wood discoloring the grain while obscuring Spirit. I am currently working on two house posts commissioned by an industrialist in Stuttgart. And can you believe this? The two posts are bridged by the Kwakwaka'wakw version of Sisiutl. One post is of human beings. The second post tells the abduction of a woman by Thunderbird. The mother-in-law is at the top of one post dressed in shaman robes. She holds two salmon and stands on a seal and a sea lion. My Sisiutl have wolf heads, wolf teeth, ears, eyes and a wolf tail connecting the two heads. My Sisiutl has a body of a killer whale.

I seem to have rambled but this reflects my band of People who share in our stories. And, I have turned into a Whiteman academic. To get to your question about killer whales. The killer whale is an important crest for our village of Alert Bay. In regards to killer whales catching humans, we have a traditional story of killer whales who carry a beautiful young woman to their lair under the sea into the Underworld. The Curtis film has Wasgo on one canoe and a killer whale on a second canoe. The killer whale is attacking a human being who wears a mask. Thus, there is a legend in our band that killer whales take humans. We think that the two creatures are different. We have transformational masks that change from killer whale to man and also Sisiutl masks which open to reveal a masked man. Killer whales and Sisiutl are different creatures.

Alana, I didn't like the whale hunt or the taking of the gray whale, but I did enjoy the comradeship of men. After the hunt I thought of myself as a warrior for the first time. But remember I don't hunt. On a very personal note, Whale has visited me. Not regularly and not to reproach. Whale asked me a simple question: why had humans picked him? Whale didn't hold it against me. Whale asked, "Why me?" I said, "I don't know, just by chance I guess."

I studied the Edward Curtis photos and watched his movie, which was made around 1913 depicting a Kwakiutl love story. I understand why my People have divided feelings about Curtis. Some People claim we shouldn't honor Curtis, whereas others state that he provides a window back into time. You probably know that he staged the photography. Thus, many of our People feel that the photos are fake. As to the movie, the Kwakwaka'wakw think it's funny and a great joke in that White folks believe it's an accurate portrayal of our customs and legends. My opinion is that my forefathers had fun making the movie and dreaming up the love story. It is loosely based on customs before Whiteman, so it would have some historical value. From my perspective, I believe that Curtis provided an important link to our heritage. By the way, did you notice how thin the Kwakwaka'wakw were in the Curtis movie?

The famous ethnologist, Franz Boas comes to mind as how Whites view us. I have read Boas's book and know that he didn't interview many of my ancestors. Many elders think that Boas portrays our ancestors correctly, but others believe that Boas has perpetuated stereotypes because he didn't understand our language. Kwakwaka' is very difficult. If you have any additional questions, let me know.

Be well.

 Your friend,

Thomas"

Alana is pleasantly surprised that Thomas answered so quickly. Apparently, he was not on Indian Time, for lengthy emails are not an Indian trait. *But I know that Indian oral presentations never seem to reach an end. I guess that Thomas's email is like a speech.*

Feeling successful with Thomas's reply, Alana decides to write to Ben. He lives on the west coast of Vancouver Island, which is very remote. *He should know about killer whales and Wasgo.*

Chapter 21

Ben, Member of Nuu-chah-nulth First Nation,
Kyuquot Bay, West Coast of Vancouver Island

Ben's grandmother left the letter on his bed. Ben, the Nuu-chah-nulth who almost died after sewing Whale's lips together, seldom receives mail. Having just returned from work to his grandmother's home in Kyuquot Bay, Nootka Sound, British Columbia, Ben is tired.

His life hasn't changed with the whale hunt. His grandmother saved him from alcoholism after his wife left him and took his son with her two years ago. Ben is still raging against almost everyone. He blames the Whiteman for his drinking problem.

His grandmother and uncle had written Quanah about his abilities, and Ben agreed to participate only because of his love for Grandmother. Ben hadn't liked Sam, the Haida steersman, and he didn't think much of the others, often quarreling with them. He admired Quanah, accepted him as the whaler chief, but then the Nuu-chah-nulth and Makah are related. He still hasn't reconciled with how David saved him during the hunt.

He decides he'll read Alana's letter after he showers and eats at the only restaurant in the village. It's been a grueling week on the tramp steamer, Ucluelet, and he'd looked forward to a good night's rest. Tomorrow, they will steam back to Muchalat Islet on the west coast of Vancouver Island for their next load of supplies and curious tourists. Ben doesn't like the idea of having tourists on board, as they're always asking questions and getting in the way. The reason for tourists is that the west coast of Vancouver Island has few roads. Supplies are first trucked from Campbell River to ports serving the west coast. The supplies are delivered by ship to villages along the western coast of Vancouver Island. The only way to reach Ben's village of Kyuquot is by boat. Thus, tourists can experience the travel of years past.

Not that much has changed in the village since Capt. Cook dropped anchor in Nootka Bay two hundred years ago. Cook was met by Indians in war canoes who shouted "Nootka, Nootka" which means "go left to miss the rocks." The Indians were friendly and eager to trade. Hence, the bay was christened Friendly Bay.

Ben is pragmatic and the Whiteman's name, Nootka, for his tribe doesn't bother him. The proper name is Nuu-chah-nulth which means "people with hat with knob."

To supplement his income made from salmon fishing, Ben works on the small steamer delivering all kinds of stuff along the western coast of Vancouver Island. The steamer makes deliveries at Muchalat Inlet, Nootka Sound, isolated wharfs on Nootka Island, Ceepeecha, Esperanza, and Homebase. The steamer crew needs four days to load at Muchalat Inlet which is thirteen kilometers from the town of Gold on Vancouver Island. Their load included a four-month supply of fish food for the salmon farm where Ben works part-time as a scuba diver, mending salmon pens ripped by seals and sea lions. A young killer whale had taken up residency in Nootka Sound, and the operators of the fish farm fed him. He was a good omen. Passengers loved to watch him surf the bow wave of the Ucluelet. The orca kept the seals from the salmon pens.

The Ucluelet exchanged drums of machinery oil for used oil, garbage bins, and other junk to be trucked to landfills on Vancouver Island. They also dropped pallets of groceries onto logging and fishing camp docks. On this trip they carried all the components for a cabin—windows, doors, toilets, and roofing nails —to be off-loaded on Nootka Island. As goods are hoisted from the hold, tourists watch crew members load cargo nets with all sorts of supplies. For Ceepeeca sport fishing camp, supplies were offloaded into a boat. At the next stop, two tons of food and three tons of supplies were passed by hand to a fish processing plant by a human chain. Ben's job was operating the cargo boom. A demanding job because a slight miscue would knock a man into the hold or crush him against a bulk head. Ben stood on the foredeck, looking aft into the hold. The captain rode the cargo net with load from the hold onto a waiting truck or wharf. The crew trusted Ben with life and limb.

At a logging wharf on Nootka Island, it was Ben's quick response that saved a pickup from plunging through an old rotten dock. When Ben sat the two tons of equipment onto the Chevy pickup the truck broke through the decking and snapped stringers. The crack of wood cued Ben to immediately lift the load from the truck. Ben was well known for his quick reactions, a reason why elders had selected him to participate in the War Canoe regatta at Neah Bay. His grandmother was very pleased that her grandson had been selected.

The passengers debarked into a Boston Whaler at the final destination of Kyoquot. The crew needed three hours to offload and load for the return sail.

After showering and eating, Ben opens Alana's letter:

Dear Ben,

I'm on a quest to learn about killer whales and other marine mammals. I know that you are very busy, so I'll not beat around the bush. There are Indian legends about killer whales and a sea monster called Wasgo. Do you think that a killer whale would eat a swimming man? I would very much like to hear the Nootka perspective. Do you know of a sea serpent called Wasgo?

Your friend,

Alana

167

During the trial in Tacoma, Ben had learned to trust this lawyer— a White lady at that. Otherwise, he would not have written back:

Hello, Alana.

Here at Kyuquot, I'm not involved in tribal activities and don't know much about legends. I have worked on the Ucluelet steamer for a few years and have seen killer whales. I know of Wasgo but haven't seen him. I saw killer whales grab a swimming deer, tear him apart, and eat him.

I talked to grandmother and she says deer, dogs, otter, a cow, and even bears are eaten. Uncle says that killer whale would eat a man who fell overboard. He says that whale would grab a man like a seal, shake him out of his clothes, snap his head off, and crush his chest like a seal. Grandmother says killer whale take women from the beach, and people ride killer whale. Uncle says killer whales are important to Human Beings because the spirit of a dead chief is reborn in killer whale.

The young killer whale that strayed into Nootka Sound a couple years ago was our chief Macquenna, my grandfather. He'd just died. That was the reason we didn't help White people return the young whale to his family in the San Juan Islands. The young whale was called Luna by White Folks. He was tame. He rode bow waves of our steamer. Luna stole salmon from fisherman. The Whiteman thought Luna was a nuisance.

Luna was murdered when the tug captain reversed his boat. Sucked Luna into the three-foot propeller driven by 750 HP diesel marine engine. The spirit of Macquenna will not rest until Luna's death is avenged. Many Whites will have to die by killer whales.

Be well,

Ben

Chapter 22

Merle, Coeur d'Alene Indian from Plummer, Idaho
Lives in Spokane - works at the Kalispell Indian Casino
Louise, Makah, Merle's wife

As Alana tugs her overnight bag from the carousel, she hears, "Alana, great to see you! Did you see the Columbia River and the Great Columbia Plateau from the plane?"

Alana turns to greet Merle with a smile. "Good to see you, Merle. And yes, magnificent sight from the air, but I didn't expect to see a desert in Washington State. I also noted several fires. Are these normal?"

"Lately, springs have been dry, so fire seasons are longer, now." Taking Alana's bag, Merle says, "Louise is waiting in the car. We are pleased that you decided to spend the week end. To answer your questions with emails is impersonal. This way we can show you our casino and reservation—and," Merle adds with a twinkle in his eyes, "I have found your family farm." As they walk to the car he says, "We'll take you to lunch at Anthony's at Spokane Falls."

"Thank you for finding the time for me."

"It's our pleasure. After lunch, we'll drive to Coeur d'Alene. Then, if you're not exhausted, we can take a tour through the mountains to the Coeur d'Alene Casino hotel?"

"I would like a tour," Alana assures him.

As they approach the car, Louise jumps out and embraces Alana. "Hi Alana, we are so glad to see you!"

When Alana looks in the back seat for a baby," she says, "I was hoping to see your little one."

"He's with grandmother." Louise explains. "We have a full two days planned, but you'll meet our baby tomorrow."

During the drive from Spokane, Merle keeps up a narrative

171

about the Plateau Indian Battles of 1858. "Do you recall the Judge Krieger comment about Col. Wright hanging Indians?"

"Yes, sure."

"Look to the left towards the Spokane River, just past the weigh station, that's where Col. Wright had his troops shoot 840 Indian horses. This occurred after the Battle of Four Lakes and the Battle of Spokane Plains. Both battles took place near the airport. They weren't decisive wins for the army, which had new rifles with a range of 400 yards, because the Indians realized they were outgunned and stayed out of range. The Indians attempted to set the prairie on fire but a thunderstorm had greened the grass and it wouldn't burn."

Alana exclaims, "I guess that's an example of the so called 'winds of war?'"

"Yes, providence was on the side of the army. If the grass had burned, the airport and all of Spokane would be Indian land. Anyway, the soldiers captured the Indian horses, and Wright figured to kill them would break our spirit, which it did."

"Why?"

"The horse is part of our family. The army also burned seven barns of wheat and camas cakes for our winter food supply. Oral tradition tells it was impossible to fight the paleface who had such disregard for horses and food."

The drive from Spokane to the city of Coeur d'Alene is only 30 minutes, barely enough time for Merle to retell the US Army march that took place 160 years ago. Approaching Coeur d'Alene Lake Merle exclaims, "Wright and his 700 soldiers camped where the Spokane River comes out of the lake at an Indian village. Father Joset sent Wright a message that the Coeur d'Alene Indians were ready to sign a peace treaty. We will follow their route to the Mission on the Coeur d'Alene River."

Leaving the city of Coeur d'Alene on Interstate 90, Merle continues, "Our main village was at the site of what is now the city park. My ancestors used canoes on the lake and rivers to reach into the Bitterroot Mountains. Nevertheless, there was a trail over the mountains to the Catholic Mission where my ancestors were waiting to sign the treaty."

As they leave the lake Alana marvels, "This pass is really narrow and steep. I can't imagine how the army got through it without our modern roads."

Merle nods, smiles, and says, "The trail was so narrow that the soldiers marched single file and the cavalry walked their horses. The column stretched for eight miles. We could have beat the soldiers in the mountains but the priest convinced my ancestors it would be pointless because ultimately, the whites would overrun us."

Merle stops at the top of Lookout Pass. "My ancestors controlled this pass for trade. Dried salmon was transported east, and dried buffalo meat and hides were sent west. Plains Indians loved dentalium and abalone shells for jewelry. Elk teeth went west and shells went east. We were wealthy. Dentalium shells, called tooth shells, were used to buy a slave or a wife."

With this last comment Louise interjects, "Ha, ha. You didn't have six tooth shells, and Dad didn't think you were much of a hunter, either."

Taking her chance to elaborate on her heritage, Louise continues, "Abalone are found in intertidal rocky beaches and are easy to pry from the rocks. Plains Indians prized the black abalone for medallions. The tooth shell was used for currency. Tooth shells are found burrowed into the sand below low tide in protected bays. It was a mystery as to how ancient Makah gathered them until the dig at Ozette where they found long pipes of cedar wood."

Alana asks, "How did the pipe work?"

"Standing in a canoe, an Indian covered one end of the pipe with his hand, and pushed the pipe into the sand. When he removed his hand, the vacuum forced sand and shells into the wooden pipe. The collector again covered the open end, quickly lifted the pipe from the sea, and dumped its load of sand and tooth shells into the canoe. My ancestors held this gathering technique as a tribal secret. A string of twenty, two-inch-long tooth shells, termed a fathom, was the standard unit of trade between Indian tribes before the Hudson's Bay trade blanket was introduced."

173

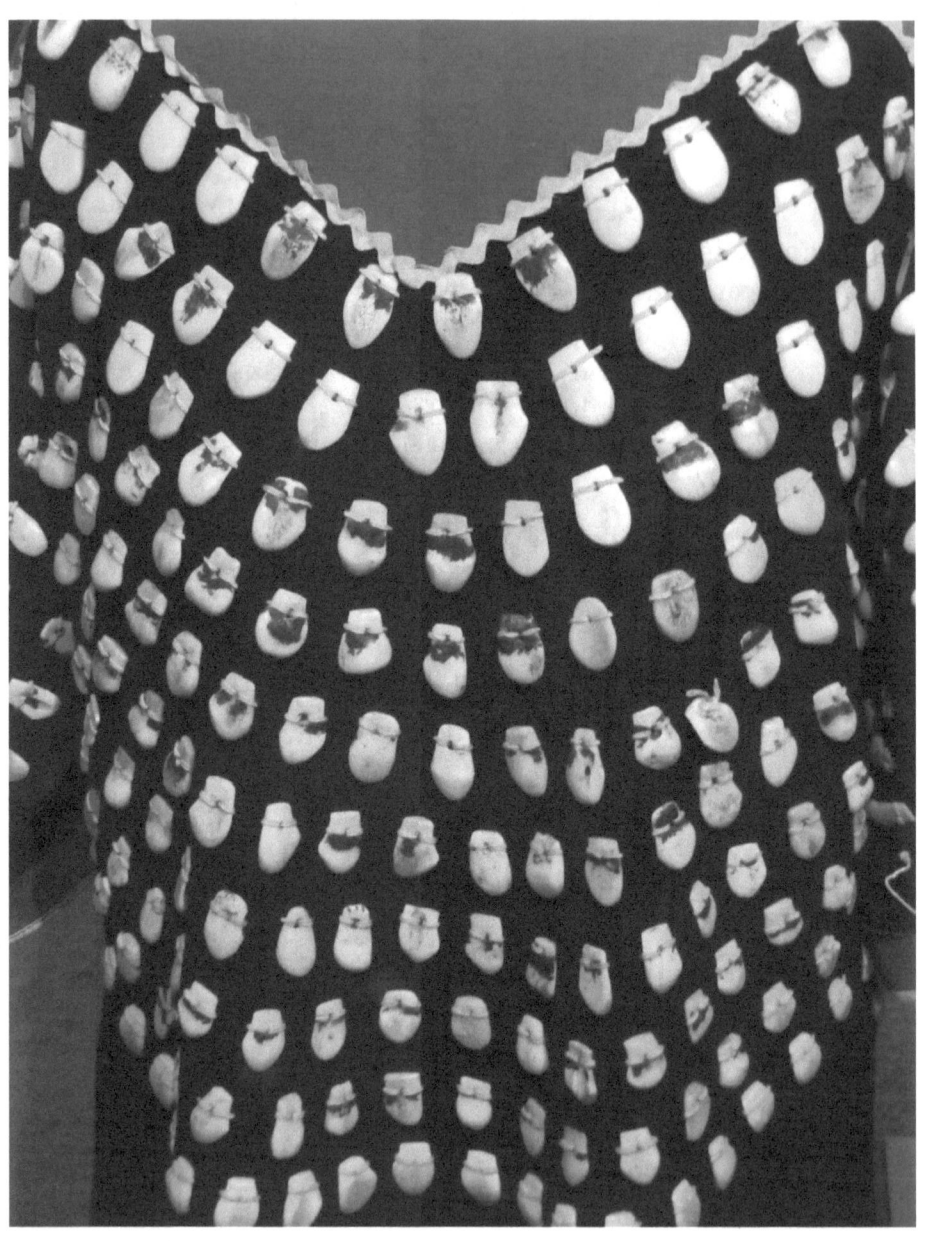

"I would have had to pay Louise's dad at least five fathoms as a dowry," Merle laughed. "A slave was worth a fathom. During the whale hunt I was thinking that I would have had a value of only a few shells."

Laughing, Louise pushes on Merle's shoulder. "You don't have a chief in your history. My dad worried about you. You were to redeem yourself during the hunt. I guess you did."

"Wow," Alana says, "the Makah were both Fort Knox and the Federal Reserve."

"Yes, you could say that, Louise agrees. "Coastal Indians traded for buffalo meat and hides, bitterroots, and camas cakes. The introduction of trade beads displaced shells upsetting the balance of Makah commerce and wealth. Plains and coastal Indians simulated the two-inch-long tooth shell with a string of eight or more small, pearl beads. White ethnologists call this beading technique 'lazy stitching'. There is nothing lazy concerning Indian bead work. The beads also replaced porcupine quills."

Merle cuts in, "Now you can appreciate why we, the Coeur d'Alene Indians, did not allow the Hudson's Bay Company to establish a fort on our lands."

"Yes, but my Makah ancestors were adaptable," Louise quips, "With the Hudson's Bay Company, we had a market for our whale oil. At $1.50 a gallon we were rich. When the whale industry collapsed, we purchased a fleet of seal and otter vessels. The Chinese paid hundreds of dollars for an otter pelt. Many present-day whites think Indians are slovenly, dirty, and drunk," Louise says bitterly. "Our history demonstrates that perception is not true. We adapted to markets. Historically whites were jealous of our industry and passed laws to keep us down." Louise continues, "So, you can understand why I so admire Quanah for his attempt to reinstate whaling. Whale products could bring wealth to our nation."

Turning off Interstate 90, Merle pulls into a parking lot explaining, "This is the Mission on the Coeur d'Alene River, now called Cataldo, where Col. Wright forced my relatives to sign the treaty. This mission was built by Indians. It's the oldest building in the state of Idaho!"

As they walk about the grounds and into the mission Alana remarks, "Truly a wonderful statement left by the Jesuits and your ancestors."

The drive from the mission to the Coeur d'Alene casino is along the river before crossing a small divide into the St. Joseph River Valley. Merle tells how his ancestors ferried the troops across the river in canoes and swam their cavalry horses across. He points out where ancient Indian villages and the troop camp sites were located. "At the St. Joseph River, Col. Wright took a warrior for a hostage."

Merle, Louise, and Alana check into the casino at six. Merle had arranged to have dinner with the cultural affairs director, Mr. Mathews and Laura, a tribal spokeswoman. Mathews was eager to explain his ancestral history, "The French traders gave our ancestors our name in deference to our bargaining prowess. Coeur d'Alene roughly translates into 'hearts as sharp as a leather awl.' In years past, Columbia Plateau Indians asked permission to pass through CDA territory to the Great Plains for hunting and trade. Even the Nez Perce Tribe, who numbered 8000, would send a runner in advance of a buffalo hunting party to obtain permission. We don't control Interstate 90 today, haha, but our business acumen is used to manage the casino. My People practice environmentally sound logging and cattle industries and rent tribal properties on Coeur d'Alene Lake."

Laura interjects, "We not only take care of our enrolled members, but we also provide substantial funding for health care and education for the entire population. Moreover, the casino employs over 1000 people, and many are white."

Alana says, "That's admirable considering what the federal government did to your people." After a pause she continues, "Merle tells me that a Jesuit brought Christianity to your tribe."

Laura agrees, "Yes, but many enrolled Indians still practice old customs. Birth and death customs remain tribal. The Jesuits taught us wheat farming. In fact, we were so successful that the Federal Government passed the Dawes Act so they could take half of our lands for White homesteading in the early 1900s. I apologize and must warn you that we are still bitter about this land theft. Our savings from wheat farming helped keep many small banks afloat during the great depression of 1929."

The next day as Merle, Louise, and Alana drive through Lovell Valley Alana exclaims, "Your reservation is really big!"

"Not so," Merle replies with a distinct edge to his voice. "Remember the feds reduced our reservation to half in 1907 by selling homesteads to white people."

At the western edge of the reservation they crossed the state line into Washington State. A mile east of Tekoa, Merle turns onto a dirt road which they followed for three miles where he stopped by an abandoned farm. Getting out, Merle tells Alana she is standing on her family farm. "Alana, you are the seventh generation to stand here, you should honor your ancestors and return."

Alana looks at the windmill derrick, inspects the foundation, where the house once stood, and a pile of partially burned timbers.

Rusted, twisted sheets of metal are the remains of the barn roof. Stooping by a pile of rubble, she pockets a couple shards of pottery.

Alana's heart swells, and tears sting her eyes as she stands and surveys the homestead of her great-great-great-grandparents.

Back in the car, Merle says they have time to take a circuitous route back to Spokane so he can show Alana a very sacred place of the Spokane Indians.

En route, Louise looks at Alana and says softly, "The morning of the whale hunt, as I stood at the beach, I connected with my ancestors. I never felt such an emotional pull—Maybe you felt something similar here."

Alana nods, grateful for Louise's empathy.

Louise continues, "I walked to the Coast Guard Station because I had a woman's intuition that the canoe was in trouble. I grew up with Quanah and have faith in his vision, but I was still worried sick. I could not lie quietly in bed as required by tradition. I knew there was something wrong. I have always feared the ocean stemming from childhood stories that grandma told me when I behaved badly. Alana, you asked about stories we tell. My grandma said that I would be carried into the ocean by a sea serpent. This story is so terrifying that I never learned to swim."

"No wonder you were afraid. Did your grandmother believe it was true? And do the Makah still believe the sea serpent will come after people? This is the story I'm trying to confirm."

Louise takes a deep breath, starts to say something, and takes another deep breath before slowing answering Alana's question, as if finding her way as her narrative unfolds. "Alana, an answer to your question is very deep. Native Peoples have been able to accept western religions because they have the ability to accept two points of view. Some aspects of indigenous religions have a counterpart in a western religion, for example *Creator* and *God*. And, an afterlife for *Soul* and *Spirit*. However, we believe that *Creator* endowed everything with *Spirit* and everything is part of *Mother Earth*. Christians believe that only man has a soul. White people seem to need to know all, whereas we accept that man can't know all. Therefore, it does not bother us to acknowledge the existence of both beliefs. Sea serpents are real."

Appreciative of Louise's explanation, Alana turns to Merle and asks, "Why did you agree to take part in the whale hunt?"

"To stay married. Haha. You now understand that Louise is a deep thinker. My job at the casino is to arrange entertainment, and the tribal council thought it appropriate for a CDA Indian to join the canoe regatta because our People were the gate keepers of trade between coastal and plains Indians. Actually, they wanted to honor Louise's request. Louise and I love to talk about our tribal histories and conclude it was destiny that we married."

At this comment Louise interjects, "Yes, two hundred years ago Merle and I would have forged a dynasty in trade. I was quite surprised when the judge in Tacoma referred to our plateau wars. It may seem strange how the past comes back to the future as to where the past helped us in court. This is the Circle of Life that all Indians talk about."

Alana nods. "I'm beginning to appreciate this notion of Circle of Life"

"I think Quanah picked me as a puller because of Louise. Part of my casino job is working with dilettantes with big heads; i.e., the entertainment crowd. Therefore, I was not surprised that ten Indians from different tribes were a source of friction. Ben, the Nuu-chah-nulth, who almost died during the hunt, hardly said a word. He did not like Sam, the Haida. During the hunt I kept thinking if I were in this canoe two hundred years ago, Sam, the Haida Indian behind me at the tiller would have trussed me up as a goat. Ben didn't like Gus either. They were on the verge of quarreling all the time. I don't think that Ben liked anyone. I was pleased to have the role of conciliator. Tribal animosities are slow to heal. By the way, we Coeur d'Alenes are still angry with the Nez Perce who were the scouts for Col. Wright."

Merle's narrative spun out as they drove through the rolling Palouse Prairie until Alana challenged, "Merle, you must be lost, these hills all look the same. And there are few road signs."

"No, I know where we are," Merle assures her as he drives over a small creek. Merle stops and they scramble out to admire a granite monument. A cold testament to the history that unraveled seven generations ago. This is where Col. Wright immediately hung seven Indians after they confessed to being in one of the battles. Actually, they weren't hung but garroted. Idaho legislated to name this creek Hangmans [sic] Creek but Washington State changed the name back to the Spokane Indian name of Latah Creek."

Alana softly says, "The name change would signify a rejection to acknowledge history. However, since this is the hanging site on which Judge Krieger based his decision to hold a very quick trial, his ruling was redemption."

Louise, shaking her head, says, "Well, maybe. In 1858 Indians did not appreciate that white people could hold such grudges. A potlatch with gift giving should have appeased Col. Wright, but he didn't know the Indian way. That's why the Indians so readily admitted to being in the battle. To Indians battle is noble."

Alana sighs, stretches her legs against the bulk head and is thankful no one sits in the middle seat. She hadn't realized how tired she was. The lights of Spokane disappear, and soon the few scattered clusters signaling small villages recede, leaving the void of the Great Columbia Plateau below her. She dozes, thinking of all the information she has received in just two days. She snaps awake, pushes the overhead light switch and opens the brown paper bag that Louise had slipped into her carry-on. The note reads:

Dear Alana, we so enjoyed your visit. You had asked about Wasgo and so we thought you should have this drum painted by one of our Makah artists. Note that the canoe is actually Wasgo. Wasgo appears in many art forms and plays a central role in many narratives. You should use it. Love, Louise and Merle.

CHAPTER 23

Quiet Weekend in Seattle

The weather forecast for Seattle is drizzle. Not conducive to catch the ferry to Friday Harbor and go fishing with Dr. Bob Black along the eastern shore of San Juan Island. They planned to go in the same type of skiff that her Granddad had used forty years ago. Dr. Black calls to postpone.

Alana decides to make it an Internet weekend. *I'll find out about orca behavior and sea monsters who may have killed grandfather.* She doesn't think it could have involved a collision with another boat, as someone would have known about it, and it wouldn't have remained a mystery. *I wonder if killer whales are lovable as portrayed in the movie Free Willy or "gentle giants" as espoused by staffs at marine parks?*

In articles in Wikipedia, Alana finds it difficult to separate scholarly works from nonsensical material. Quite by chance, she discovers an article by Paul Bartsch in the *Smithsonian Treasury of Science,* published in 1960, near the time of her grandfather's disappearance. The article with the same title as Bartsch's earlier book, *Pirates of the Deep - Stories of the Squid and Octopus,* includes old lithographs showing huge octopus and squid in mortal combat with boats. Coming from the Smithsonian suggests to Alana that the Native American stories are credible. Sea monsters could be more than just tribal folklore, as they are still carved into totem poles, house posts, and artistically executed in art and jewelry.

With further reading Alana finds that in 1913, the Kwakwaka'wakw painted a Wasgo sea serpent on the bow of a war canoe for the Edward Curtis movie, *In the Land of the Head Hunters.* Alana found many stories relating animals to the spiritual, told by all coastal tribes. For example, the Bella Coola band in Canada tell of a giant man-eating octopus which compliments the octopus mask in Curtis's winter dance.

The story of Wasgo that she read about in the Whale Museum in Friday Harbor is prominent in all tribes. There are variations but the theme is similar. A mother-in-law gossips that her son-in-law is lazy. To prove he isn't, the son-in-law kills Wasgo. He skins Wasgo and wears his hide to acquire its hunting prowess. Early, each morning, he deposits seals, sea lions, Chinook salmon, and halibut on the beach in front of the village. His mother-in-law finds the animals and claims she caught them with mystical power. She feeds the village and achieves shaman status. Finally, the son-in-law manages to kill three killer whales. However, in pulling them onto the beach he so expends himself that he falls into the surf and dies as Wasgo. His mother-in-law, looking into the eye of the dead sea serpent sees her son-in-law. She is so ashamed that she dies right there on the beach.

Alana concludes, *These are powerful stories. Indians mix mythical creatures with real animals for family crests and totem poles, which may indicate that Indian legends have a basis in reality.*

With further searching, Alana finds images of totem poles with Wasgo occupying a central position. Paradoxically, some totem poles show both Wasgo and killer whale. Alana wonders if there is a connection between the two creatures? *To solve my grandfather's disappearance, I need to evaluate all aspects. This is what good trial lawyers do. They make connections and weave the smallest pieces of information into the fabric of a defense or prosecution.*

Alana finds a 1991 Michael D. Swords article with the title, "The Wasgo or Sisiutl: A cryptozoological sea-animal" in the *Journal of Scientific Exploration*. Swords compares stories of Northwest Coast Indians to European legends such as the Loch Ness Monster. Swords suggests there is a basis for a sea monster because the Indian legends describe Wasgo in great detail. Alana proposes, as if writing a brief, considering the enormous shore line of Alaska, British Columbia, Washington, and Oregon, a large animal could escape scientific detection. After all, transient orcas were not recognized as a distinct race until the 1970s, and the offshore orcas escaped detection until the 1990's. Resident, transient, and offshore orcas do not intermingle and each has its unique language and specialized hunting behavior. Perhaps there is another orca subspecies that could be Wasgo.

Alana finds the legend of She-he-took-a-muck, which is about a ferocious whale that swallows Indians along with their canoes. She thinks, *This legend could be based on a fourth race of killer whales? Considering that most coastal Native Americans hold the orca in high esteem, and carve orcas on totem poles and house fronts, a human-eating orca would present a quandary for the Native American.*

By noon the skies clear. Alana looks over Puget Sound to Mount Olympus. The lawyer side of Alana muses, *I may have solved my cold case with the existence of Wasgo. It seems logical that Native American legend would have a separate creature to preserve orca as a benevolent totem and family crest. My closing argument before the Olympic Mountains is that Indian legend fuses killer whale with wolf which solves the dilemma of good and bad whales. The offspring, Wasgo eats man; killer whales remain to protect man.*

As Alana gazes at the mountains, her mind swims with contradictions. *The blue sky is a beacon. It's time for a run, I need to clear my head.*

Alana had great luck finding an apartment with a westward view of the Olympic Mountains across Puget Sound and Bainbridge Island, and, sixty miles to the south, Mount Rainier rising 14,000 feet from the Sound. The Magnolia section of Seattle is isolated from Seattle proper which reduces traffic, making the area a runner's paradise. When Fort Lawton closed in 1970 it became an urban Indian reservation with access to the adjacent park.

As a student, Alana worked hard to develop thigh muscles and was particularly proud of strong calf and butt muscles. Trails from the beach to the hilltop gain 350 feet, and maintaining a running schedule has kept her in shape. The beach circling West Point is great for sand running.

Today, Alana decides to time herself on the track near the tribal center and is surprised to find the parking lots full of cars, teepees, and hundreds of Indians. Approaching a man wearing a Pendelton vest directing cars into parking spaces she asks, "What's going on?"

"We're having our yearly powwow."

"I thought that powwows were only held on traditional reservations. Is this a real powwow?"

"Yes, the Daybreak Star Powwow is open to everybody."

"May I take photos with a digital camera?"

"You bet, we encourage photography. But you should ask the dancers first. And a token gift is appreciated."

Alana runs home and returns with her camera. What an amazing exhibition with at least 500 Indians dressed in costume for dance competitions. An angular Indian with an aquiline nose immediately catches her eye as he is a head taller than most. The tall Indian sports number 417 pinned to his shirt. Alana guesses he is a Plains Indian. Many Whites and Indians are photographing and mixing with the dancers. She can't keep her eye from the tall Indian with burnished red-brown skin. A swatch of red ochre covers his forehead. White-lead finger bars extend from eye folds and ears on each side of his face. The man is about sixty and in terrific shape. On his head, he wears a roach made from the tail of a whitetail deer. His bustle is of eagle feathers with tufts of rabbit hair. His silk satin shirt is adorned with shoulder straps in the Seminole patchwork style. The design pattern is Plains Indian. A breast shield, made of hundreds of deer bones signals a great hunter. His attire is complete with a red silk neck scarf, a beaded neck choker, a red, fulled-wool loin cloth, beaded knee chokers, and moccasins. His regalia fits together so well that the complexity is not obvious. In fact, it looks simple compared to the elaborate, colorful regalia of many dancers.

Alana waits till the drumming stops and follows her stately Indian to a tent where he slumps into a camp chair. He opens a can of Coke. Mustering courage she asks "Sir, would you mind if I take a couple images? I love your regalia."

The Indian growls "No photos." But, as he notices the shy girl with hair falling over wide, brown shoulders, his voice softens. "You may take pictures when I dance."

Alana smiles, her almond eyes sparkle as she breathes, "Thank you so much. I'll use a telephoto lens, and you probably won't know that I am taking your photo."

The Indian, the age of her Austrian grandfather responds with a nod, signaling the interview is over. The next hour is a swirl of dancers performing in different dance categories. The master of ceremonies announces the snipe dance, the grass dance, and the grouse dance. The feather dance is described as the dance for peace. The ladies paddle dance follows. An ancient, stooped lady wears a red dress, shoulder shawl, and a traditional coned hat indicating she is a member of a Puget Sound Tribe. She dances in the fancy shawl dance. Number 418 is a fifty-year-old man, offsetting his portly countenance with an enormous bustle and war bonnet. Women are covered in yellow, green, and red deerskin dresses with long feather thongs. A forty-year-old lady wears an elegant white deerskin dress, a medallion is attached on the back of her head between two luxurious braids that fall below her waist. She, as well as the other women, dance ramrod straight as they glide over the earth. The announcer calls the dancers to the War Bonnet Dance, then announces the Rabbit Dance for couples. A young boy of about eight dances continuously, in all dances, to the delight of the onlookers.

The host drummers beat out the pulse for the Grass Dance, which is mainly men and boys. The finale is a dance-off between two dervishes making swirls of red and orange. She set her camera on 'Sports Action'.

The drumming transports her into a different culture, time, and place, so she doesn't immediately notice a horse quirt laid over her shoulder from behind. When a voice loudly proclaims, "Me tak'um squaw." Alana jumps. Spinning, with her hand over her heart, she gasps, "Don't do that!" She squints into a face painted half black and half white split down the middle from forehead to chin in the shape of a lightning bolt. It would be a scary sight if the Indian were not laughing uncontrollably.

"Aaron?" she asks tentatively.

He nods, still grinning. "Who else?"

"Who else, indeed," Alana says, unable to keep from giggling. "You're the only Indian I know who would pull such a prank."

"Yeah, probably so. I'm an urban Indian. I learn from the Whites."

Aaron, a half blood, grew up on Seattle's Mercer Island where the inhabitants are isolated and protected from the throb of Seattle. Aaron grew up white and privileged. His dad, a Nisqually Indian and an engineer, made sure that Aaron knew his Indian heritage. Aaron was also his high school class's comedian. Scaring Alana is not an Indian prank.

"I'm trying to learn the meaning of the costumes I see today. Yours is yellow and your head piece is red yarn and feathers with tufts of cotton. Your shoulder straps sport rows of silver medallions. What tribe do you represent—or does it stand for 'Urban Indian'?"

"No specific tribe, my regalia is a composite, like my beliefs."

Alana, with a nod of her head, says, "See that tall Indian with the pink shirt, a head taller than everyone else; do you know him?"

"I don't personally know him, but he's Greg Red Elk, a Sioux Indian from Montana. I saw you talking with him earlier. He seldom talks to anybody."

"Well I'm honored that he spoke to me. Does he think I'm a professional photographer?"

"No, I'm sure he doesn't, but if we could have lunch tomorrow, I'll explain why Greg Red Elk talked to you—and anything else you want to know about us Injuns, Urban or otherwise."

"Sure. Let's meet at the restaurant opposite the main entrance at Pikes Market."

Chapter 24

Aaron a Half-Blood
Nisqually and Tulalip Tribe of Puget Sound & White

Aaron attended high school with children of the Microsoft and Boeing crowd. He is an only child. His mother is a high school teacher, and his father works for an engineering firm in Redmond. Thus, it's not surprising that Aaron was raised with a work ethic and couldn't help but be diligent. From age seven, he swam 20-30 hours a week. In high school, he realized that he had a high tolerance for pain which gives him incredible stamina. In his freshman year, he took first in state in 500- and 1650-meter races. His work ethic paid-off, as he won an athletic scholarship to attend the University of Southern California. It probably helped that he was part Salish Native American. Aaron made the USC swim team, swam third in the relay, and competed in the backstroke and long-distance races. Distance races are events that only parents watch, and they take place early in the morning. They are lonely events. Aaron is outgoing, but his desire to compete compensated for swimming in boring races.

He was competitive at the university level but during his sophomore year he knew he wasn't big enough to beat the Michael Phelpses who stand over six feet, have a barrel chest, long arms, big hands and feet, and are strong as bulls. Nevertheless, Aaron competed and won a few matches because he was fast in turns and had good technique. Aaron tackled his engineering courses with the same ferocity and discipline. By the end of his second year, he knew he had picked the right career in electrical engineering and planned to attend graduate school in bioengineering.

The solitary nature of swimming makes for lonely practice. By his junior year, Aaron decided to try-out for the lightweight rowing team. He had an ideal weight of 145 pounds to offset heavier rowers so that an eight-man team averaged 155 pounds. Aaron was a "weight maker." He enjoyed the comradery, and they won the PAC TEN in light shells his senior year. Races are 2,000 meters, which requires about 300 strokes, meaning that endurance is important. Races are not exactly a sprint, and competing shells are visually separated by 3 to 5 seconds. Therefore, there is no room for error in technique. The slightest oar "crab" loses the race. Crews are a model of discipline and hard work. A basketball player can make a mistake early in a game with the chance to make it up later. Not so in racing. Aaron's crew didn't compete in the Nationals because, unlike basketball and football, his crew would have had to pay their way. Hence rowing is called a "club sport." His quick wit was greatly appreciated by his teammates.

After six years in public schools and two years at USC, Aaron had spent 12,000 hours in the water making 100,000 turns. For arithmetic he traveled 60,000 yards underwater which is about 30 miles. In addition to all that, he spent summers as a life guard at Seattle beaches, making ten bucks an hour.

However, it wasn't Aaron's fast tongue and swimming ability that had caught Quanah's attention. It was rowing that attracted Quanah to Aaron's list of accomplishments. Pulling is different from rowing but Aaron knows how to get men to perform together. Aaron also knows swimmers in danger, so during the whale hunt, when Ben had raised his hand, Aaron knew Ben was drowning. In an instant, by reflex, Aaron had pulled his tennis shoes off, dropped his pants and tore his shirt off. As Ben disappeared, Aaron dove from the gunwale and hit the water under the whale. He swam straight down and held his nose at twelve feet, blew to clear sinuses, and continued down until his head throbbed. The canoe was ten feet from the whale, and Ben was down ten feet on the opposite side. Aaron knew that Ben would be above him. Even with salt water burning his eyes, when he looked up, he saw the blurred shadows of Whale and Ben. Because of years of early morning practices in cold water, Aaron is immune to cold and shock. He has an extremely high pain threshold. He grabbed Ben's hair and kicked hard to break surface. Now, several months after Alana sprang the Indians from jail, he was meeting their lawyer.

Alana figures that Aaron wouldn't know much about whales, but she is interested in his knowledge of dance costumes and face painting. Aaron emailed to confirm lunch at the little café opposite the main entrance of Pikes Market.

"Good to see you, Alana."

Grabbing Aaron's hand, Alana replies, "Thanks for bucking traffic."

"Oh, I didn't. I know how to get here by going west from the University to 15th Avenue, then to Elliot. I like coming down here for lunch."

"Me too. I live just off 15th in the Magnolia area." Dropping Aaron's hand, she asks, "How's grad school coming?"

Smiling, Aaron says, "I finally see the reasons for course work in undergraduate school. I was prepared. And, I have a great dissertation topic."

"Tell me."

"It concerns ultrasound effects on fetal rats. There are published studies that the energy levels used for the human fetus alter nerve transmission and transmitter release. This is really exciting because there isn't that much difference between rats and humans."

"You must be kidding. Of course, I know about ultrasound. My first law firm in Syracuse is preparing legal cases against businesses specializing in making photo albums of developing babies for their mothers. I decided to leave the firm because parents of disabled babies are so sad."

"So, Alana, now you understand the Indian perspective concerning the United States Government and health."

Perplexed, Alana responds, "I don't understand your argument?"

With a devilish smile Aaron elaborates, "For us Indians, it was blankets laced with small pox. And we do share in the problem of lead poisoning."

"I don't see the connection."

"Let me explain. The feds tried to poison poor Whites by permitting landlords to rent them houses with deteriorating lead paint. For Indians, they used lead balls."

Alana smirks. "Ha, ha. That's Indian humor!"

"OK, Alana, let's be serious. I did a search for your name and found you rowed. I thought you were still in Syracuse. Funny, we didn't meet, as I rowed for USC, but in light shells."

Alana acknowledges his comment with a nod and a smile. "Now wouldn't that have been fun." But she has something else on her mind. "My firm is preparing to argue your case, the illegal hunt, before the Supreme Court. Personally, I'm on a quest to learn about whales, especially killer whales and Indian culture. From your comments at the Tacoma bar I thought you had broken with your heritage. That's why I was surprised to see you at the powwow."

"I am zealous about my heritage. I just don't wear 'hey, Whiteman, I'm an Indian' on my sleeve."

"Doesn't it bother you to see Indian culture such as masks and totem poles for sale in The Old Curiosity Shop which has been a Seattle tourist trap for decades?"

"Yes and no. Masks and carvings are art. Modern pieces are made for sale. Their sales support Indian artists."

Frowning, Alana says, "Well, it would bother me if I were Indian to see my heritage for sale along with shrunken heads from Peru and dried human mummies."

Aaron responds, "The antiquities of civilizations are in museums. The only difference between White culture and ours is that Indian stuff ended up in museums of natural history and university museums of ethnology like the Peabody in Boston."

"Yes, I know," Alana agrees. "I've been at the Harvard Peabody and the Museum of Natural History in New York City. Nevertheless, the Iroquois don't sell false-face and corn-husk masks."

Nodding in agreement Aaron continues, "The philosophy of sharing ceremonial objects varies between tribes, and we respect differences. In regards to cultural artifacts, most museums agree that these items should be repatriated. So, yes it does hurt to see historic masks, rattles, and ceremonial objects that have been stolen from our ancestors for sale."

"Aaron, I have a personal question."

"Ask."

"In regards to your face makeup for the powwow, what is the symbolism of having your face painted half black and half white?"

Aaron turning his face from side to side says "You are probably thinking that this reflects my half Indian, half White DNA. It doesn't. The human face isn't symmetrical. Do the right and left sides signify two personalities? Many Indians think so. Asymmetry is accentuated by Iroquois carvers of false-face masks."

"Yes, but coastal Indians carve mainly symmetrical masks."

"True. Symmetrical masks and totem poles represent animals and spiritual creatures. The idea of multiple forms or personalities is expressed differently in different tribes. For coastal tribes, duality is expressed with transformational masks used in ceremonies where a dancer demonstrates that one being or one spirit can take on two forms. What mask did you wear when talking with Greg Red Elk at the powwow?"

Alana thinks, *There is a trick here, and I need to be careful how I answer.*

She changes the subject. "I love this mixed plate of wild salmon, halibut, and cod."

Looking up, she asks, "What do you know about whales?"

As quick as Alana and with a smile Aaron presses, "You didn't answer my question."

"I'm not sure I understand."

Aaron, with a laugh, teases, "You don't know what I mean, do you?"

Alana thinks she knows what he's getting at, but stalls. "I guess not."

Arron chuckles and says "Alana, you needn't be a lawyer with me. You wore a mask when asking permission to take Greg Red Elk's photo. You assumed another face in court, and you definitely wear another mask with Quanah. You wear a mask now, talking with me. We present an appropriate face for a given social activity. Indian masks play on this theme." Putting down his fork, he adds, "The only thing I know about whales was learned from Quanah." Smiling, he adds, "It's still good to see you and visit."

"We should do this more often."

Aaron asks "By the way, did you visit the Glass Museum in Tacoma during our trial?"

"No, why?"

"Next time you're in Tacoma, stop and visit. The museum has art by Preston Singletree, who renders Indian legends in glass. He demonstrates that Indians don't have to be traditional. To answer your earlier question, his art is powerful and conveys Indian culture. Preston has captured the importance of sharing our culture."

Alana replies, "Sounds good, and the glass museum will be interesting, so I'll make sure to visit it. Let's do this again."

CHAPTER 25

Whale Scientist and Sheriff at Friday Harbor

The work preparing briefs for the defense of the Makah whale hunters brought by Green Earth and other animal protection groups to be argued in the Supreme Court is progressing in a timely fashion. As expected, the ninth circuit court of appeals reversed Judge Krieger's ruling.

Alana is ready for a break and a meeting with Larry Driscoll, an expert on whales, at Friday Harbor, is the diversion she needs. Alana uses the ferry ride to review questions to ask him. Time passes quickly as she rehearses the various aspects of her knowledge of whales.

Stepping from the ferry and tasting salt, she muses, I *should become a marine biologist. I love Friday Harbor, and there isn't much legal work here on the island.*

She looks over the bay to the University Laboratories, and says,

195

"Maybe my attempt to solve granddad's disappearance is just an excuse to visit the labs and relax. Darn it, I spend all my free time addressing a jury, real or make believe!"

Charlie and Meg are out when Alana arrives at the Lottia B&B. She lets herself in and reviews what she knows about Larry Driscoll. He began studying whales as a hobby, and since the success of his first book, he devotes full time to his passion. He receives enormous support as everyone wants to learn about killer whales.

Walking into the café the next morning, Alana recognizes Larry Driscoll from the dust cover of his book, even though he is now bald and has gained a few pounds. His clothes are rumpled but clean. As Alana approaches, he rises and extends his hand. "Hello, you must be Alana."

"Good morning, Mr. Driscoll."

"Please, call me Larry. Have a seat, a cup of coffee, and a roll. Jane makes them every morning."

"Coffee would be nice."

Smiling, Larry asks, "Orca brings you to Friday Harbor?"

"Yes. To get right to the point, I started studying killer whales for a personal reason. My grandfather disappeared forty years ago when fishing in San Juan Channel. He was a student at the labs. The authorities never found his body, and they ruled out homicide. Do you think it's possible that he was killed by a killer whale?"

Larry clears his throat and responds, "I haven't heard of a wild orca attacking a boat or a swimming man, but I can't rule out the possibility. Listen, you're here at a good time. The J-pod family has been staying in Haro Strait feeding on spring salmon. There is a good chance to observe them from Lime Kiln Lighthouse. Want to join me this afternoon?"

"I don't have much planned, so if it's no trouble, I'd love to go with you. We could continue our talk while whale watching."

"Wonderful. Let's meet after lunch. Say 2:00, here at the Wharf Café?"

"Thank you so much. The timing is great. I will visit the court house this morning."

The courthouse, a few minutes from the café, is a lovely, two-story brick building with basement windows. It was built in 1906. The large addition, also of brick, houses the police station and county departments. Alana thinks, *The Island's history is here, so there is a good chance that grandfather's Case Report is collecting dust in a basement corner.*

Alana enters the police station and looks about. The waiting room is small. A locked door leads into dispatcher offices. An unlocked door leads to the toilet.

An officer opens the reception window and asks, "Good morning, Miss. Can I help you?"

"Yes, I have a peculiar request. Could I talk with an officer about a disappearance that occurred forty years ago?"

The dispatcher disappears. When he returns, he announces, "Yes, Sergeant Leonard will be able to spend a few minutes with you. Please have a seat."

The green walls with trim of a darker hue have a soothing effect. Alana sits on one of the battered chairs. One wall is covered with photos of the San Juan County Police force—the sheriff, two under sheriffs, fifteen deputies, two sergeants, two officers, and twelve dispatchers. *Seems like a lot of policemen for a sleepy village and a few islands. With this police force there should be a lot of lawyers.*

Five minutes pass. Alana stretches. Photos of Island sheriffs from 1892 to the present line the wall over the chairs. She pauses to read Eric Erickson was Sheriff from 1951 to 1970, the period of her granddad's disappearance.

An elderly couple comes in, and the woman, breathless, addresses the dispatcher, "Young man, we want to report an erratic driver, he almost ran into us!"

The dispatcher asks, "Did you get the car's license plate?"

The lady replies "Yes, it's on this piece of paper."

The dispatcher takes the paper and says, "We know the party. We'll send an officer out. Thank you."

Alana overhears the dispatcher yell, "Hey, Mike, we have another complaint about old man Harder. Yeah, stop by and visit with his son. They have to keep him out of the car."

Alana thinks, *These people care about neighbors. I should get some help here.* She walks to an old photo of Friday Harbor. A carousel is loaded with pamphlets: "Missing Person," "Theft," "Accident Report," "Boating Accidents," "Dog Regulations," "Lost Property," and "Found Property." She stuffs the "Firearms Safety, the Law and you, basic safety, general laws, and regulations" booklet into her pocket.

Alana returns to her chair with a "Voluntary Statement" pamphlet. She sighs "I'm not making a statement, I'm seeking information."

A sergeant opens the door saying "Good morning, may I help you?"

"Yes, I know this request is unusual, I would like to look at a Case Report filed in 1964. Could you help me?"

"Come in, I'm Sergeant Leonard. So, you're interested in a case in the 1960s?"

Alana, thinking how nice it is to deal with these people, inquires "I wonder if there's a Case Report concerning a missing person in 1964?"

"We hold records only for twenty years. Even on these small Islands we have mounds of paper work."

"My grandfather disappeared from a fishing skiff and he was a strong swimmer, I was thinking ..."

Smiling, the Sergeant interrupts, "I would really like to help but we only keep cases open when there is a strong suspicion of foul play or insurance fraud. We only have four open cases, and there's none about a missing person."

"I understand, thank you for your time."

"Don't mention it, my pleasure. You could visit the Historical Society because they keep old copies of the San Juan Journal. Their building is only a couple blocks from here. Walk west on Spring Street. Oh, this is too complicated. Here's a map and I'll sketch the route. If you find something pertaining to the disappearance come back and we'll talk."

At the San Juan Historical Society, Alana asks the receptionist, "Do you have the local newspapers from the 1960s?"

"You're in luck, our archivist, Ed, is in today. He loves helping folks."

Ed, pleased to be interrupted "Good morning, young lady, what can I help you with?"

"I'm interested in the San Juan papers in the fall of 1964. This is about my grandfather who disappeared while boating and was never found. His boat washed up on a small island to the north of San Juan Island. Does the archive have digital or microfilm records of the paper?"

Ed smiles and responds "Well, that's before my time but I'll check the filling cabinet. I think that a story would have been filed because it would've been big news on the Island."

After a few minutes Ed returns "Miss, you're in luck. The archives have all of 1963 and 1964, probably because of the Kennedy assassination. Come with me and I'll help go through the papers. Our archives are in the little building next door. What month?"

"September, 1964. I appreciate your help. I haven't had much experience hunting through old newspapers."

Ed, obviously pleased to assist, says, "Look, here's an article about the fisherman who spotted the row boat on the North Bay of Waldron Island. No tracks were found on the beach. Some thirty officers, county and state, combed the island for your grandfather. They also deployed bloodhounds. No indication that he made it to shore. Here's a photo of the skiff."

"Could I take this article to show Sergeant Leonard?"

"We normally don't allow materials out on loan, but since I know Leonard, you may."

Sergeant Leonard takes the newspaper from Alana and explains as he examines the photo, "It was a very light skiff, about thirteen feet long, and probably weighed two hundred pounds. A two-bencher with two sets of oar locks. There is one oar, still in the oar lock. The floor boards are in place. Look, there's a fishing net, a bucket, and what looks to be a fishing box wedged under the rear bench. It also looks like there is a life vest under the front bench. Obviously, the boat hadn't capsized because there's a fishing pole. Let's scan the photo and clean the image electronically."

Leonard scans the newspaper image, enlarges it, and fuses the dots of the newsprint. With color adjustments, he eliminates the brown background.

Alana gasps "This image is fantastic, a plus for the digital age!"

"I used a five-point moving average program to smooth out the dots. You can now see a lead weight which hangs in space from the pole because we can't see the line. The position of the weight, reel and pole indicates that your granddad wasn't fishing when he separated from the boat. This is strange, the knife scabbard is empty, where's the knife? The caption reads that blood was found on the port gunnels and floor boards. The newspaper states that the blood smudges on the starboard gunnels match your grandfather's blood type."

Looking perplexed Alana asks "Everything looks normal but the missing knife, right?"

Leonard points to the port side of the skiff and states "There seems to be a dent at the water line. And, the port wooden gunnels at the bench show a split, possibly due to a blow which smashed the side inward pushing the starboard side outward. These indentations could result from the skiff hitting a channel marker when running with the tide."

Alana enthusiastically replies "Possibly but another scenario is that the skiff was rammed by a boat or a killer whale."

"I think the dent is real but there isn't a comment about boat damage," exclaims Leonard.

After a pause Leonard continues "Lets say your grandfather fell overboard, and tried to pull himself into the boat. Thus, he could have pulled the pin out of the oar lock and lost the one oar trying to

200

get back into the boat."

Alana, with a slight smile "Remember, he wasn't my grandfather at that time. He was only twenty-six, a powerful swimmer because he swam in the Snake River as a kid. Most importantly, my mother told me he snorkeled at Woods Hole, in Massachusetts. I don't think he would've had trouble climbing back into the boat unless he was injured."

Leonard chuckling "I envisioned a 50- to 60-year-old man who had a heart attack."

"That's understandable. I keep thinking he is like my other granddad. It's spooky to read about my young grandfather and not to know anything about his life after his 26th birthday! My God, he was my age!"

"The article says that Sheriff Eric Erickson made all tests possible. Erickson had the reputation of a very thorough officer. The paper states he checked the boat and gear for finger prints. Found only one set. In the 1960s the AFIS data base wasn't developed. I guess that Erickson would have checked the State Identification Designator Number and found no matches. If he had been arrested, even for a misdemeanor, your grandfather would have had an FBI number which was kept at the national Crime Information Center. I surmise that Erickson found nothing there."

"Thanks so much, you are a real help."

CHAPTER 26

Lime Kiln Lighthouse - 2:30 p.m.

The village of Friday Harbor is small. The distance from the Historical Society to the Wharf Café where Alana is scheduled to meet with Larry Driscoll is only a half mile. As she walks to the café she considers her good fortune. What luck, to watch killer whales with a whale expert.

Alana and Larry are at the lighthouse parking lot within thirty minutes. They walk to a bench strategically placed overlooking the bluff with a clear view of Haro Strait with Vancouver Island to the west. After the Pig War of 1859, Kaiser Wilhelm of Germany determined that the border between the British Colony of Canada and the United States should be Haro Strait which placed the island of San Juan in Washington Territory. This boundary is the reason that her granddad was a student in the Friday Harbor Laboratories on the island and the reason he disappeared forty years ago and why Alana took her job in Seattle. Alana concludes that history and human activities are a series of large and small interconnected events. *And, these events are the reason that I'm here today!*

As Larry sits, he motions Alana to a seat saying, "Let's get comfortable and wait. So you want to learn about orcas?"

Alana, immediately presses her new idea. "It seems to me that killer whales could flip a fisherman out of a small boat and eat him. Something like killers washing seals from an ice floe. What do you think?"

"I haven't heard of such a case, and I think it unlikely. Killer whales would have plenty of chances to kill fisherman. There's so much boat traffic in the San Juan Archipelago and Inland Passage an attack would be noticed, and there haven't been any reports. No, wait a minute. A couple years ago a killer whale aborted its attack on a swimmer."

"Yes, but I've read that there are several people who disappear each summer without a trace."

Larry answers without taking his eyes off the water. "I've spent time on the Internet looking for attacks and even though kayaking with killers is popular, no attacks have been reported. Killer whales steal salmon from fisherman by grabbing fish from their lines. I believe that killer whales aren't afraid of man and have innumerable opportunities to attack, but don't. Moreover, it's documented that wild spinner dolphins frolic with humans and solitary killers seek human company. Orcas are the largest of the dolphin family of toothed whales, and I wouldn't expect a different behavior of orcas from that of spinner dolphins."

Not to be deterred, Alana presses, "What do you make of the male killer whale who drowned his trainer in Florida?"

"I think that whale was just exuberant. Something akin to a big dog that plays too rough. In the case of orca weighing 12,000 pounds, his play can be deadly. Trainers become too casual, which explains why there are so many examples of orca bouncing trainers about."

Alana, still pressing as if Larry were an expert witness, "I noticed that trainers in Florida wear black and white wet suits with the killer whale pattern. Could the killer whale have thought the trainer was a baby whale?"

"No."

Alana presses on. "Monkeys interact with humans, and in most cases, the two species tolerate each other. However, in Florida a pet male chimp tore a women's face and hands off, showing that chimps can't be trusted. The victim knew the animal and was a good friend of the monkey's owner. Indian elephants are known to kill Mahouts. Then, there is the tiger who almost killed Siegfried. Wild animals can't be domesticated; they remain wild by nature. Is it possible that the captive orca planned to kill his trainer?"

Larry suddenly breaks off the conversation. "Hey, look toward Bellevue Point, here they come."

Alana trains her binoculars to the north. "Wow!"

Several whales turn into the small cove one quarter mile north of the lighthouse. Picnickers on the beach see them and begin to yell and point.

"The whales are spy hopping and putting on a show for those folks," offers Larry.

He continues, "Notice the people on the beach are clapping and yelling, and the whales seem to respond by breaching and splashing."

Alana asks "One whale is standing on its tail. Is she responding to the crowd?"

Larry, "Yes, the matriarch is looking at the beach."

"I read in the museum they see in air as well as underwater."

Larry asks, "Did you like the exhibits in the museum?"

"Yes, the eye is interesting, and other exhibits explain whale behavior."

"Glad you like them. Several are mine; thanks."

"Would these killer whales swim onto a beach for a seal?"

"Not these, because they're residents to this region and eat only fish. If they were transients or off-shore orcas, yes, certainly."

Alana looks intently at Larry. "So why wouldn't a transient swim onto the beach and take a human?"

"You are persistent. Are you a lawyer?" Larry asks, chuckling.

"Yes, sorry, I'm not able to control myself."

"It's OK. I like being on the defensive. I believe that orcas have a sense that humans can be vengeful. Thus, orcas know they must not kill humans."

Alana asks "You mean that killer whales have consciousness?"

"Maybe not like we have. They communicate with each other. They show complex hunting tactics. They know about boats and that humans run the boats."

Alana asks "How do whales relate boats to humans?"

"Boats and humans would be perceived by orcas as dangerous, therefore they don't ram boats."

Alana continues to press, "Trainers at marine shows interact with killers, and they appear to like human interaction. It would seem to me that the interaction could be either deadly or mutually beneficial."

"See? You are persistent," Larry says, smiling. "Orcas learn that humans will not harm them. Something akin to a wolf accepting food from a zoo attendant. However, wolves in the wild avoid human contact."

After about thirty minutes, the lead cow decides enough play and starts across the cove toward lighthouse point. All but one whale follow her.

As the whales round the point, Alana whispers, "This is fantastic!"

A yearling whale has remained behind and continues to interact with the beach crowd. The pod stops by the lighthouse bluff. The large female turns and swims the length of a football field back to slap the surface several times with her fluke.

"Tail slapping is a signal for her laggard calf to join the family," Larry explains. "This behavior reminds me of watching spinner dolphins and snorkelers interact in Capt. Cook's Bay on Big Island a few years ago. Swimmers stroked and rode dolphins for several hours. Both man and dolphin enjoyed the contact. After playing, the spinners suddenly disappeared as if responding to a lead command."

"Would you swim with killer whales?"

"No." Larry laughs. "You are a lawyer!"

The female orca splashes a couple more times until the young whale starts toward his mother. Swimming rapidly, the pod passes Deadman Bay a couple hundred yards south of the lighthouse.

Jumping up, Larry says, "Come on, let's get in the car and follow them along Westside Road. We'll have a fantastic view for two miles."

Larry drove the Bailer Hill Road and circled back to shore on McGinette Road.

"There, just past Charlotte Rock...Now they're swimming to the cove. I've never witnessed this before; the whales are napping."

Larry and Alana are looking straight down on the napping

whales. They look like logs. Every few minutes, a whale rises to the surface and blows, and sinks back into the water.

"They aren't completely asleep because they need to think to blow." Larry explains.

CHAPTER 27

George - Coastal Chilkoot & Tlingit

Alana had much to think about after watching killer whales with Larry in Friday Harbor. To relate that experience to the distribution of the gray whale meat at Neah Bay, she talks to herself, *It's clear that Indians and the Whiteman see their place very differently in nature. Do all Native Americans have similar view points? I must ask Quanah how he selected his crew. They're so diverse. Many are university educated and several have university positions. Ben, the Nootka, is a typical quiet Indian. Aaron wasn't raised on a reservation and he seems too White to understand the Indian condition as it relates to nature. George was quiet, but seemed talkative at the restaurant at Neah Bay. I need to contact him.*

On the phone, Alana asks, "Hello George, is everything going well?"

George answers, "Yes, who is this?"

"George, it's me, Alana."

"Oh, Alana."

"George, could I come up and visit this coming week end?"

"Yeah, sure."

After making reservations, Alana calls back. "George, could you pick me up at the Victoria Airport. I'll arrive on Alaskan flight 821 from SeaTac at 9:30 in the morning?"

"I will be there. It will be good to see you."

George had been quiet during Quanah's practice sessions at Neah Bay and even during the whale hunt. He maintained silence during the arrest, the imprisonment, and the trial. George was named after Chief George, who played with Clint Eastwood in the movie, *The Outlaw Josey Wales*. Chief George is known for succinct words, and George the Third continues the tradition.

During the Tacoma trial, the Indians were known as the "Makah Whale Hunters," a name given by the press. The press never learned that George is an Associate Professor in First Nation Studies at the University of Victoria, British Columbia. George's academic area is legends and oral traditions. An attentive and patient man, George spends long sessions listening to elders relate stories. Patience is not a strong trait of White ethnologists, which may explain academic inaccuracies. After his release from the federal prison in Seattle, George told Alana to call if he could help her. He was pleased when she called for a visit.

George finds Alana at the Victoria International Airport. He is reserved as usual. Alana doesn't force conversation as they silently drive on highway 17A. When George turns at the Butchart Gardens exit, she wonders why he didn't take the throughway to Victoria.

George breaks the silence. "I know a nice restaurant for lunch. Afterwards I think you will enjoy a tour of Butchart Gardens."

They order, and Alana remarks, "This grilled Coho over greens and fennel sounds delicious."

George opens the conversation. "I guess you are interested in Indian traditions?"

"Yes, I would like to know what your thoughts were during the whale hunt?"

"I found the summer training program and hunt very interesting, because Quanah placed so many different Indians into the canoe. I couldn't help but think of atrocities perpetrated by northern tribes, even though those events happened 125 years ago. Indian oral traditions are effective. We don't forget," answers George.

Alana nods. "That would be seven generations."

George continues, "Yes, stories are told with such fervor that children think they occurred recently. Indians think of time in blocks of seven generations."

Alana asks, "What generation were you thinking of during the hunt?"

"The oral accounts of my people, the Tinglet Chilkoot, and related Salish Bands of the Inland Passage tell us we never engaged in all-out warfare. We had squabbles and altercations with neighboring bands, but these never resulted in taking slaves or genocide.

The perpetrator of an act against a member of another village could reinstate his family with a potlatch. The original purpose of a potlatch was to show good will toward neighboring tribes."

After a pause George goes on, "The earliest known example in written records of unprovoked warfare was when a northern Tlingit band killed the Russian Vitus Bering landing party in 1741. In 1852, the Chilkoot Tlingit sent a war party to destroy the Hudson's Bay Company's trading post at Fort Selkirk located now in Alaska. However, the Tlingit spared the traders and sent them away with a warning to stay out of their territory."

Alana is patient, and after another pause, George remarks, "This is surely boring you. I think the Indians in the canoe had mixed feelings. Are you in contact with Quanah?"

Alana feels a hot blush creeping from her chest to her neck with this personal question, but she answers with an evasive "Well yes, we see each other, occasionally, in Friday Harbor."

George continues, "I'm comparing Whiteman's written narratives of First Nation warfare to Indian oral tradition. It is written that northern bands practiced warfare with the intent of killing entire bands in land grabs for trading and trapping. The northern Tlingit were said to have severed the heads of victims and placed heads on pikes in front of their homes alongside totem poles. The northern Tlingit drove the Eskimo from Kayak Island but were subsequently expelled from Prince of Wales Island by Haida clans. The Xaihais Bands were brought to the brink of extinction by Tsimshian and Bella Bella Tribes. Both Nootka and Haida were known for raiding into Puget Sound for slaves. Death of a chief was cause to mount a raiding party. Wealth was shown by sacrificing a slave during a potlatch. They even had special slave killing clubs! My work is to question the veracity of Whiteman's written accounts."

Alana replies, "Those are awful stories."

"Yes, they are gruesome. During the whale hunt, while paddling in sync with the crew, I was thinking that a hundred and fifty years ago, ancestors of some of these men would have been rowing south to raid our villages. Yet today, canoe regattas bring tribes together for a show of First Nation unity. During the whale hunt, I was stuck in the past, thinking of how my band was routinely raided. We had wonderful robes made of sea otter and marmot pelts. Unfortunately for my ancestors, the northern bands knew we weren't fierce warriors. Even today, robes and blankets woven by Chilkoot women are highly prized by all coastal Indians. Our women make yarn spun from mountain goat wool and dog fur. Warp twine for garments and blankets is from the core of yellow cedar bark. My wife has learned this art from family pattern boards. She is very beautiful. When I was paddling during the hunt I couldn't help but think that warriors would have captured my wife for a slave."

These stories were not what Alana wanted to know, but she had learned enough about Indians to be patient. George would get to whales and Wasgo, so Alana just says, "Really interesting. Please go on."

After a sip of water George adds, "Oral traditions confirm the White narrative. Tsimshian, Tlingit, Haida, and Nootka bands had traditions of war, slaving, and territory expansion back to the beginning of time. These activities were based on sea worthy war canoes so they could raid Peoples who couldn't retaliate. Our villages were prime targets because our women are not only attractive but are skilled weavers. Only Chilkoot women know how to weave the famous goat hair blankets."

Alana interjects, "Yes; I know Chilkoot blankets—absolutely stunning craftsmanship as well as artistic."

After lunch, George drives Alana to the hotel, there is no conversation "Here we are. I'll pick you up at 10:00, and we'll visit the museum and talk about whales."

213

214

CHAPTER 28

Following morning - Thunderbird Park & Museum

George points to the array of small buildings, exclaiming, "I admire these recreated Indian lodges. In this setting, they portray the grandeur of early Indigenous Life and show the relevancy of totem poles."

Alana, walking up to a carved and painted house facade of a giant creature whose mouth serves as the entrance door, exclaims, "I'm impressed, is this animal Wasgo?"

George answers, "Yes. I did some research concerning Wasgo and orcas. The idea behind this modern museum is to make the visitor feel at home by creating a meaningful experience. I want to show you a reconstructed chief's house from the Prince Rupert region."

As they walk into the museum, George continues, "Tony and Richard Hunt carved the house poles to represent Fort Rupert in the 1800s. The family has retained ceremonial rights to this house. They feel it important to show visitors how their ancestors lived before Whiteman. Museums have an important role to educate the public and especially school kids. We stress that the so called 'primitive Indian' could not have created this wonderful art."

Alana says, "David, from the hunt, has invited me to Prince Rupert for Winter Ceremonies. I'm beginning to understand the basis of Indian cultures. A totem pole or a blanket chest standing alone in a museum doesn't capture a way of life. To see the massive carved house posts, the large storage chests, the benches, and items of everyday use displayed in a natural setting illuminates the complexity of ancient Indian life."

George motions Alana to look inside. "Dancers wearing costumes depicting animals and the spirit world would perform in this house. The masks carved by the late Mungo Martin of Raven and

Crooked-beak were made with love and reverence to detail. These birds were attendants of the Cannibal of the North. Notice the symmetry and precision of these sculptures."

After a moment of quiet George says, "Much of the symbolism has been lost, but thanks to early ethnologists, there are written accounts. We can match stories with historical carvings. Even though recent carvings were made for trade and later for tourists, modern carvers follow specimens preserved in museums."

Alana asks, "What about Wasgo?"

"The sea serpent is a recurring theme in all coastal Indian religions."

"You mean Wasgo is true?"

"Not necessarily. Creatures depicted in religious ceremonies tend to blend into known creatures and known animals can transform into mystical spirits. Indians feel that creatures central to religious beliefs are real. White culture distinguishes mythology from religion. Raven, eagle, owl, orca, and coyote are animals that both Indians and Whites recognize. They and other animals are used as family totems and crests. In winter ceremonies, Wasgo, Thunderbird, and Cannibal of the North are prominent in many stories. Spirits move from human into an animal and back with transformational masks. In our creation stories, animal spirits transform into man." George pauses and smiles at Alana. "You will have a wonderful experience with David during the winter ceremonies."

Alana presses, "Do your People believe that an animal can morph into another creature?"

"Certainly. This characteristic is basic to our religious beliefs. Blending animal attributes represents our concept that all aspects of nature are linked together in the harmonious whole, the Circle of Life. This wholeness of nature is the basis of our spiritualism. Religious themes can be expressed artistically in totem poles, rattles, storage chests, utilitarian objects, and ceremonial regalia. This explains why our religion is part of all daily activities and is our way of life. Our place of worship is everywhere and all the time."

Alana adds, "White people separate church from daily life."

George nods so Alana continues, "Do you think Wasgo is a form of killer whale?"

George's eyebrows knit as he answers, "This is a complex and serious question. Wasgo is a blend of killer whale and wolf. There are depictions where killer whale spirit morphs into man with a transformational mask. Haida argillite carvings exhibit complex relationships between women and killer whale."

After a pause George adds "Ceremonial rituals are elaborate and follow scripts passed to the next generation with great fidelity. A given family owns a particular performance as well as the masks and regalia to support the narrative. Plots steeped in tradition usually tell history and present a moral. While Whites have the written word, Indians use oral tradition. Your culture minimizes the importance of the oral tradition because of books. The book preserves White perspectives. During our ceremonies, oral stories must be accurately told or the audience will complain. To answer your question if killer whale can morph into Wasgo, I don't know of a story that addresses this issue. Perhaps Gus and David can help you. Gus grew up in a remote community with little off-reservation influence. David's family is traditional."

"George, will Gus and David be as open as you?"

"With you, Alana, yes. But I caution that most Indians will politely deflect direct questions. Your relationship to Quanah's crew is unique and special in that we trust you. By all means, contact Gus and the other crew members. I suspect that Ben will be reserved. He is traditional. Sam operates a sport fisherman's outfit in the Queen Charlotte Islands. David is a physician for both his tribe and Whites."

CHAPTER 29

Gus, Mixed Blood. Tongoss and Tatitlek, Skagway, AK

Quanah chose Gus to be his front right puller because he is extremely strong and agile. Gus has a powerful grip resulting from summer work in logging camps on the Islands around Sitka where he earned enough to attend Ketchikan Community College. He is one of the few Tatitlek/Tlingit Indians to go to college to escape the numbing gilded-cage environment which has sapped Tatitlek Indian initiative. To compensate, Native Americans whose hunting grounds were thought to be adversely affected by environmental damage, oil revenues from the Alaska pipeline are used to buy the Indian. Environmentalists predicted that the pipeline would disrupt wildlife migrations that inland Indians needed to survive. With Washington's autocratic logic, the money was also distributed to coastal Indians, even though they don't hunt inland game. Tatitlek has a population of only 400 souls. Two adults out of 100 have a valid driving license. Fast food, alcohol, marijuana, and TV, have deprived most tribal members of heritage and pride. Gus's dad, Big John, and a school teacher from Oregon intervened to save Gus from a life of destitution and maybe suicide. Gus had called his teacher a bitch. And he decided his dad and teacher could go to hell. He had friends who were smart, had money, and were tough guys. He didn't need an education. When his dad learned that Gus, along with several other boys, had been shooting at ravens perched on the blue steeple of the Russian Orthodox Church with .30-06 rifles, his dad confronted him.

Red-faced, with a quiet, internal rage, Big John grabbed Gus. "Don't you know that Raven is sacred to our tribe, your Tlingit ancestors? Raven is our friend and protector."

Big John's action and unusual reprimand, surprised Gus. Indian

219

parents seldom grab and never hit their children. Shocked and feeling the shame, Gus squeaked, "Yes, no."

Big John, making an exception to Indian tradition where parents stay out of school affairs, marched Gus to the teacher's trailer. "We must set this straight."

He knocked, and the teacher appeared at the door. "I'm Gus's dad. Mr. Marvin, was my boy shooting in town?"

Mr. Marvin responded, "Yes, I saw the boys shooting toward the church, and the ravens scattered. I asked the kids to stop."

Big John grasping Gus by the shoulders and giving him a quick shake, asked, "Did Mr. Marvin say this?"

Gus stammered, "Y…yes."

It seemed as if all the town was watching. Gus had expected his dad to side with the other dads, but Big John, uncharacteristically squeezed his son's arm until Gus cried for mercy. From that day on, Big John and Mr. Marvin were friends—and Gus diligently did his homework.

Big John was proud to be from the small Tlingit village of Yakutat near Skagway. Honor and respect were traits his people valued, and his son needed to know that. Big John moved to the Alutiiq village of Tatitlek after marrying Gus's mom. After his wife died, Big John moved to Metlakatla where Gus attended his last year of high school. Gus excelled. The Indian village of Metlakatla on Annette Island is on the only Indian reservation in Alaska and is close to Ketchikan so Indians can get an education.

After graduation, Gus was accepted into management school at the University of Alaska in Anchorage, a huge move into White society. The move was a challenge for Gus. To supplement his Indian stipend, and to help his dad who was suffering from a logging accident, Gus worked in logging camps during summers. During his first year, he bumped knots with an ax and chain saw. The work of a knot bumper starts after a tree is felled. Knot bumpers cut limbs from the tree so that logs can be cut to length and skidded to loading ramps. Gus's foreman noticed that Gus was agile and strong, so he offered him the job of choker setter. Choker setters have one of the most dangerous jobs in the woods. The choker setter places a looped cable around a log and signals the cat skinner to tighten the cable. As the inch-thick braided steel cable snaps taut, the choker setter jumps free as the log is skidded down the mountain slope by a D6 Caterpillar tractor to a dump ramp where logs are bound together and pushed into the water. In logging operations on steep mountain slopes, loggers leave a standing tree. A "topper" drops the fifty-foot crown with a chain saw. He attaches a giant pulley to the snag which makes the spar pole. The topper threads the winch cable through the pulley at top. One end of the cable is attached to the choker cable and the other to a diesel-powered winch called a donkey or in Indian language, a Thunderbird high liner. The donkey swings the log from the high line tree down the mountain side. Chokers also wrap logs into bundles to make log rafts. Logs are loaded onto logging trucks with donkeys. In this dangerous task, the choker setter places a giant tong at the end of a log. As the cable snugs against the log, with points digging into sap wood, the choker setter must jump clear or be bashed by the log.

After two seasons as a choker setter, Gus was promoted to timber scaler. A scaler measures log diameters and lengths to calculate the board feet which can be sawed from the log. Gus is fast and accurate, and his intimate knowledge of logging landed him a management job after graduation.

When Big John heard about the Makah

canoe regatta, he asked his son to apply. The lumber company thought it good press and gave Gus time off with pay. Big John was so pleased with Gus's participation, he overcame his fear of flying and watched some of the training sessions in Neah Bay. Even as a 'timber cruiser' (a forester who determines the amount of lumber in a forest) Gus kept himself in shape. College and demanding jobs changed his outlook of life. He didn't want to lead a lifestyle as an overweight diabetic Indian living with parents and depending on welfare. Gus was surprised by Quanah's whale hunt proposal because Gus had not imagined that his logging experiences would be applicable for whaling. Gus's logging experiences suited him well to operate under pressure where men's lives would depend on his skill to keep the front of the canoe off the whale, toss the harpoon rope into the prow notch, play-out rope as the whale sounded and to have the hand strength to gather rope and coil it into a basket as the whale tired. After Gus returned to his village from practice sessions at Neah Bay, he shot four seals and made floats from their skins. He peeled cedar bark to weave the traditional rope to be attached to Quanah's harpoon point. With a new, burning interest in ancestry, Gus learned that Yakutat, his father's village, means "place where canoes rest." His return to the canoe was a good omen.

Perhaps in years past, the skills of whaling and manning ocean-going canoes were the reason that coastal Indians worked in logging camps and on whaling boats. Gus thought he might bring whaling back to both his father's Tlingit Yakutat Tribe and mother's Alutiiq.

During the canoe practice sessions in Neah Bay, Gus learned to play rope over the bow notch of the canoe. He could hold the war canoe against a ten-horsepower outboard. Therefore, during the hunt, after Quanah harpooned the whale and yanked the shaft free from the point, Gus pulled the rope snubbing the point against the inside of the whale's chest cavity and threw the rope into the bow notch, a task for a choker setter with powerful wrists. Of course, Gus had been the perfect Indian for arm wrestling in the Tacoma bar. Big John was proud because Tatitlek is now on the map.

After the whale hunt and federal trial in Tacoma, Gus had not been in contact with Alana. He was surprised by her phone call.

"Hello Gus, how are things up in Alaska? How are you?"

"Fine; staying out of prison."

"Gus, it was my pleasure to represent you in Tacoma. Now, I need to ask a favor of you?"

"Sure, of course."

"Have you watched killer whales?"

"Yep."

"Did you ever see some kill a seal?"

"One day in Valdez Channel we saw a killer whale leap out of the water along the edge of a rocky beach. It turned onto his side and splashed so hard that a wave washed a seal from the beach. The pod of six or seven killers played with the seal until only the hide and head were left. They threw the seal to one another like kids playing catch. They seemed to be having fun. They didn't eat the seal, I guess they were not hungry."

"Have you heard of killer whales attacking humans?"

"My dad has told stories that Indians have been eaten."

Alana, breathless, asks, "Do you believe them?"

"Alana, you are quick. You could be a logger. I now understand how you kept us out of prison. I have heard many stories, like Sasquatch carrying Indian women into the mountains. Or like killer whales grabbing girls digging clams and carrying them to their lairs."

"Thanks Gus. If you get to Seattle, call and we'll have dinner together."

Chapter 30

Google & YouTube

Alana wakes at seven, looks at the clock and groans, "I wanted to sleep in." To the west, the Olympics glow in the early morning sun as she plans her day. She wanted to catch the ferry to Friday Harbor to visit the Applegates. *No*, she chides herself. *That's an excuse. I wonder how Quanah is doing in his studies. No, that's another excuse. The truth is I simply want to see him, and the ferry ride would be fantastic. But, no, I should continue looking into grandfather's disappearance. I'll search Google and You Tube for documentaries and videos about Wasgo and killer whales.*

Watching *The Wild Discovery* program "Dolphins: the Ultimate Guide," Alana learns that orcas are dolphins. They can reach speeds of thirty-five miles an hour and can swim at twenty-five miles an hour all day. Terry Williams, a physiologist, determined their oxygen consumption per pound during swimming is larger than that of a swimming man. With cameras attached to the back of dolphins, researchers report dolphins make a couple fluke motions to start a dive, and plummet like a rock, as their lungs compress with the increasing water pressure. Therefore, they use little metabolic energy for the dive. They spend a short time swimming at the end of the dive which is terminated by a couple kicks upward. As water pressure decreases, lungs expand, sending dolphins rocketing to the surface. When they blow, hot blood rushes into fins where it is cooled in a network of small blood vessels, functioning like a radiator.

Alana thinks, I can see why people study whales. Their biology is interesting, but I'm off track with physiology. I need to learn about behavior, and more specifically, how killer whales interact with humans. She finds there is more written about small dolphins than their larger cousin, the orcas. There are many more dolphins than orcas. Both wild and captive bottle nose dolphins are tractable

225

and have been extensively studied. Their friendly grin results from anatomy, and they grin while killing harbor seals. The most disturbing characteristic of these beguiling creatures is that male bottlenose dolphins kill juveniles of their own species. In other mammals like bears, boars kill cubs to bring the sow into heat (estrus). "My God, that's not a nice characteristic. Yet people think they're so cute," Alana sighs.

She learns that orcas hunt as a family and that each family develops specific skills for a given prey. For example, some pods force herring into a dense ball and then swim into the ball to stun the fish with powerful fluke strokes. A killer eats 400 herrings in a day. Pods off New Zealand hunt in pairs where one orca grabs a sting ray by the tail, flipping it so its partner can safely bite off the snout and brain. A similar hunting behavior was observed off the California coast where a killer whale turned a great white shark onto its back where it became immobilized. The killers easily killed the shark without risk. These hunting behaviors demonstrate that orcas understand that prey can do them harm. Alana found that this conclusion is backed by Dr. Ingrid Vieser who concludes that large male killers grab baby seals from the beach—a dangerous maneuver since the whale could strand itself. Juvenile seals don't fight back. An adult seal or sea lion could inflict serious wounds.

Alana has an epiphany. *Killer whales don't usually kill humans because humans would retaliate. Learned self-preservation behavior would be passed to future generations. The learned social behavior is to stay away from close human contact!*

She grabs a pencil and paper and begins making a list.

1) Pods of each population scattered over the oceans, have unique languages which evolved for particular prey. Some populations are skilled at hunting smaller dolphins by wearing them down, others feed on seals, rays, salmon, herring, or sardines.

2) Orca populations are 'opportunists' which makes a dilemma. Why hasn't a pod developed a taste for humans? Maybe they did in the past. Over 60 young orcas were captured along the Pacific Northwest Coast in the 1960s and 1970s. These populations learned

to avoid humans. And before this period, "devil fish," as fisherman called orcas, were shot and killed. Therefore, learned avoidance behavior would be passed to future generations living in the San Juan Archipelago.

3) It seems reasonable that along with avoidance behavior, there could be retaliation by whales whose young have been kidnapped. This notion was the basis for the movie *Killer Whale*. I haven't found documented examples of killer whale attacks in the wild although the captive male Tilikome has killed three humans. His last victim was Dawn Branshaw during a performance in sea world. After grabbing Branshaw, Tilikome swam vigorously around the pool to drown her. On YouTube, I found home movies where orcas attacked trainers at many marine exhibits, and a trainer was killed in Tenerife in the Canary Islands.

Alana begins again, more succinctly.

1) Orcas know they can kill humans.

2) A mother orca "cried" for days after her calf was taken from her.

3) They are playful when tossing seals into the air and catching them like a ball.

4) Females bite males in captivity.

5) Orcas hunt together.

6) In captivity, orcas are bribed by humans with handouts.

7) Spinner dolphins in Hawaii play with humans.

8) Orcas learn vocalization and language dialects.

9) They have homicidal tendencies.

10) Orcas kill other mammals for sport.

11) They recognize self in mirrors.

12) Pairs exhibit sexual foreplay by caressing flipper, penis, and mouth with tongue.

13) They show empathy (as in a mass suicidal stranding).

Alana sends an email to Quanah asking, "What do you think?"

Email from Quanah: "Alana, Indians have known about killer whale behavior from the beginning of time. That's why totem poles integrate humans with whale."

Alana emails back, insisting, "Yes, but I have made a list!"

Quanah replies, "Alana, of course you made a list. You are White!"

CHAPTER 31

Sam – Haida
Masset, Queen Charlotte Islands, B.C.

Unsatisfied with Quanah's response, Alana thinks Sam might help her. She reasons, *It seems to me that Sam has a good relationship with tribal elders because they immediately sent money for his defense. Moreover, the Queen Charlotte Islands are surrounded by transient killer whales and if anyone should know about elusive transients, it would be the Indians of the Haida Gwaii who live a remote existence one hundred miles from the mainland of British Columbia..*

She finds his card:

HaidaGwaiiguidesam.com
Fish the Queen Charlotte Islands for record salmon
Sam (Two Fish) Hanson.
Masset, Skidegate, BC. Phone: 800 251 4444

Alana recalls that Sam told her he is a scion of canoe builders. He had proudly shown her a photograph of his dad, granddad, and his great-grandfather holding him on his lap while sitting in a canoe. He was two when his great-grandfather died.

Alana was surprised that Sam had been so open with her in Tacoma. Maybe because he was far from home, lonely, or simply wanted to talk to a white person who wasn't a threat. Or, perhaps, his openness is the result of his guiding business. Alana learned he deeply loves his uncle, his mother's brother, and it was this man who taught him seamanship. He said his earliest recollection is in a small canoe, and he was completely soaked. His mother hadn't been pleased but understood her brother.

Sam was a teenager when his uncle took him to Hetta Inlet, across Dixon Entrance, 80 miles north of Graham Island in the Queen Charlotte Archipelago. Dixon Entrance is essentially Pacific Ocean, so his uncle used a traditional square sail. Once they reached Cordova Bay, the trip to Hydaburg between Dall Island and Prince of Wales Island was easy. Hydaburg is historically the northern most boundary of Haida territory. The coastal region north was Tlingit. This trip had been Sam's initiation into open ocean sailing. It was on this trip that his uncle showed him the petroglyph of Sgan (the Haida sea monster, called Wasgo in Makah, or Gonakadet in Tlingit) on a rock in Hetta Inlet. This ancient rendition is the basis of many modern Wasgo paintings.

Sam is proud that Franz Boas selected this image of Wasgo for the cover of his *Primitive Art* book. Sam's family crest is Wasgo, and his family painted or carved Wasgo into many traditional utilitarian objects. The Haida sea monster has a snake-like head with broad flat teeth, a wolf nose and face. The body supports either wolf claws or whale flippers. Sometimes dorsal fins and an orca-like fluke are incorporated. When Quanah decided to have Thomas paint Wasgo on the war canoe, Sam readily consented to man the steering paddle.

For the Neah Bay war canoe, Sam had located a red cedar in Naden Harbor on Graham Island. Its straight, four-foot-diameter trunk was perfect for the ten-man hunting canoe. When finished, they towed it to Prince Rupert and sent it by steamer to Vancouver where the Makah picked it up. Thomas painted Wasgo onto the canoe in Neah Bay.

During the hunt, Aaron sat in front of Sam, behind Ben. It was during the first canoe trip into the Strait of Juan de Fuca when a personality conflict arose. Sam shouted for Aaron and Ben to pull harder. Of course, Aaron made a smart-ass comment. Taking the joke the wrong way, Ben pushed his paddle into Aaron's midriff. It was Merle, the overweight CDA Indian, who defused the incident with "When life gives you apples, make applesauce." At this non-sensical play on words, Ben relented.

After the whale hunt, Sam returned to his fishing guide business working out of Skidegate. Fisherman from all over the world fly into Sandspit across the bay from Skidegate for the finest King salmon fishing in the world.

Sam was surprised to find an email from Alana buried in customers' email:

Hello Sam.

I hope this email finds you in good health. I would appreciate information about killer whales and Wasgo. I realize some information is restricted for family, so I understand if you are selective. Have you witnessed killer whales eating seals and land mammals? Are there stories about killer whales attacking Indians? What oral traditions concerning Wasgo can you relate?

Thank you,
Alana

Sam emailed right back:

Hi Alana. Yes, I have seen killer whales kill seals and sea lions. Because of my guiding service, I see many pods that live around Graham Islands and the Gwaii Haanas. One day near a seal rookery on the west shore of Graham Island, I had a boat full of fishermen from Los Angeles, and we saw a killer whale chase a seal onto the beach where he grabbed it and squirmed back into the water. I told the guys they would need to pay me extra. My uncle watched a killer whale kill a swimming deer.

We Haida believe that killer whales will kill anything they find in the water. If they are not hungry, they will play with it, as they do with seals. Once I saw a group of sperm whales form a rosette around their babies, and they warded off the killers with powerful fluke splashes.

Come up fishing, and I will show you some orcas. Sgan in our language is Wasgo and means supernatural and chief of the underworld. Sgan is part of our religion.

Your friend

Sam."

The next day there was a second email from Alana to Sam, asking if any Haida have been eaten by an orca.

Sam emailed:

"Hi Alana. I have heard stories from elders about killer whales carrying people into the ocean. But those elders are now dead. Haida teach that when a killer whale enters the deep ocean, he becomes human, and that's why they steal Indian women. I will ask around the village for more information. I will start a log on killer whales that I observe when guiding, because I know that you and Quanah are very interested in our transients.

Be well,

Sam.

In the third email, Alana asks, "Sam, do you believe that Wasgo is real?"

Sam replies, "Yes. There's a lot of ocean for Wasgo to disappear in."

234

CHAPTER 32

Flight to Prince Rupert
Alana and Quanah attend a Tsimshian Winter Ceremony

When making arrangements to attend the Tsimshian Winter Ceremony with Quanah, Alana contacted David to meet them. In his return email, David said, "I will pick you up at the Prince Rupert airport. If you have time, be sure to see the Bill Reid sculpture, *The Spirit of Haida Gwaii,* in the Vancouver airport lobby."

During the flight Alana asks, "Quanah, did you know much about David before the whale hunt?"

"I knew he was a tribal doctor."

"Me too, but did you know The Provincial Government removed his parents from Port Simpson to Prince Rupert? David told me he felt like an outcast at Simon Fraser University."

Quanah answers, "Indian schools are a shared burden. Federal policies kept Indian children from society. Indians feel a collective shame."

"I don't understand. The White man should feel the shame. You interact with Whites at the labs, don't you?"

"Sometimes. Usually conversation is forced."

"What about Daniel?"

"He's different."

"Have you thought about quitting?"

"Sometimes."

Alana continues, "David said each time he fled back home, his mother convinced him to continue his studies. By the end of his sophomore year, he realized that his tribe needed doctors, so he changed his major to pre-med. David told me he was lucky, because calculus was easy, which made physics and chemistry easy." Alana pauses and looks at Quanah. "Quanah, are you listening?"

"Yeah."

"David was the first of his tribe to get a medical degree."

"Oh." Quanah's tone is noncommittal.

Alana continues, "Even in medical school, David took part in winter ceremonies and tribal affairs. David's uncle sponsored him to attend the Makah war canoe festivities because of his position as a tribal doctor. David is a member of Hamatsu, an ancient society that encourages tribal traditions. Tsimshian People were proud of his participation in the canoe ceremonies representing Tsimshian loyalty to First Nation Peoples." Alana remembers more of her conversation with David. "After taking Whale, David was surprised to feel connected to Whale through its death. When he touched Whale, he said he felt Whale Spirit pass through his being. The feeling was monumental. Did you have a similar feeling?" she asks Quanah.

"Yes."

"David told me the bonding of men to nature and the unity of all sentient beings is difficult to put into words. You had just killed a beautiful creature whose mother followed your canoe for miles."

Quanah asks, "How do you know so much about David?"

"David wrote about the hunt for the tribal paper but hasn't sent the article to the paper. He let me read it. He said his feelings didn't transfer well to paper. In print, he says, the hunt seems trite, super-ficial, and an attempt to justify killing.'"

Quanah doesn't respond as they prepare for landing.

They meet David in the baggage room. "Hi Alana. Hi Quanah."

There is no question that the hunt bonded the men of two tribes, separated by traditions and 600 kilometers. There is no need to dis-cuss the hunt, so they don't. Quanah talks about the progress of his studies. David proudly talks about his boy and girl. "My girl, now twelve, looks like Naida in the Curtis film, *In the Land of the Head Hunters.* This is not unexpected, as one of my ancestors married a Kwakwaka'wakw."

They drive into Prince Rupert to the Harbor Inn. After checking in, they eat local fare at the Waterfront Restaurant. Leaving Alana and Quanah at the Museum of Northern British Columbia, David suggests, "I'll pick you up at 5:00 and we'll walk to the Metlakatia Ferry Dock for the thirty-minute sail to the village of Metlakatia."

Looking toward the shoreline from the small tribal ferry, David explains, "I have offices in Prince Rupert, Port Simpson, Ona River, and Metlakatia. This appears to be a complicated practice, but I enjoy flying and boating. Most importantly, I help my people although most of my patients are White. They don't mind that I'm a First Nation person."

Disembarking the small ferry Alana remarks "This is a lovely place. Metlakatia is only eight miles from Prince Rupert, but it is a different world. If I stay too long on San Juan Island, I get cabin fever. Do tribal members ever feel hemmed in?"

David explains, "This has been our homeland for thousands of years. We don't suffer from cabin fever, and I don't think isolation is a cause for alcoholism and poor eating habits that lead to diabetes as some suggest. I think First Nation health problems relate to the rapid loss of our culture. I lecture in the pharmacology and psychiatric departments at BC Medical School in Vancouver and offer a course with the general theme, "Drugs or Placebo." The placebo affect may explain the shamans' healing powers. We must bring back old traditions to save our people. My Uncle Cliff is a practicing shaman, now eighty-seven, and is influential in the village. You will meet him later."

After dinner they walk to Uncle Cliff's small but neat house. Uncle Cliff is attired in western clothes, wears his hair short, and doesn't look like a shaman. But this notion is a Whiteman's perception of what a shaman should look like. Alana is no exception. Uncle speaks with a lilt with many pauses, indicating that English is his second language and acquired with difficulty.

With a pleased look, Uncle Cliff takes Alana's hand saying, "You must be Plains Indian. Our winter ceremonies are open to all First Nation Peoples."

Alana softly protests, "No. I'm not Native American."

Uncle Cliff persists, "I understand many American Indians wish to keep their heritage secret, but here in Canada, today, our government supports our heritage. For example, there is an enormous First Nation sculpture in front of the Canadian embassy in Washington D.C. It was made by Bill Reid."

"We just saw the second sculpture in the Vancouver airport. Very powerful," Alana answers.

The old man seems to look back in time and forward simultaneously. Alana thinks, *This man reminds me of the chief guiding the canoe in Bill Reid's sculpture. I wonder if Uncle sees himself as guiding his People.* She asks, "Did you know Bill Reid?"

"Yes," replies the old man. His face has softened with a blanket of folds and creases. He smiles at the young lady and says, "There has been a change. Indian life is not like the old days where I was forced to attend Indian School in Prince Rupert. We don't harbor hatred for Canadian authorities who thought they were doing the right thing. I will be an Indian for a thousand years." Smiling, he asks, "Where did you grow up?"

Alana answers, "My first ten years were spent in Austria because my mother married an Austrian. My father's family is from Eastern Austria. I still carry an Austrian passport along with the burden of the Holocaust."

Quanah says, "You look like the Blackfoot that I met at Fort Hall, Idaho, a couple years ago."

David comments, "I guess the Holocaust explains your interest in Indian Law and the Indian Holocaust."

Alana nods.

The old shaman strokes Alana's black hair and gently runs his finger along her cheek stopping at the edge of her eye. He pats her chin and whispers, "Tomorrow's ceremony starts in the afternoon with tribal feasts."

Arriving back in Prince Rupert David remarks, "Alana, I'm surprised that Uncle Cliff invited you for the Hamatsu ceremony, which is usually restricted for men. He took to you!"

"In 1911 Edward Curtis was initiated into the Hamatsu society by the Kwakiutl," Alana muses. "Your Uncle is modern."

Stopping at the motel David announces, "I got it. The Hun's leader, Attila, led a wave of Asiatic people to conquer Eastern Europe. They got to Salzburg."

Quanah, with a chuckle, adds, "Alana, you're the fourth migration to the new world, a wave of one."

Blushing, Alana retorts, "Ha. David, did you hear that? Quanah has a sense of humor after all."

Alana and Quanah are subdued on the return flight. Quanah looks out the window at a jagged shoreline of inlets, fjords, and passages running against a backbone of rugged mountains. He touches Alana's arm. "I like this region. There is little footprint of the Whiteman. I accept your invitation to kayak in Principe Channel this coming fall."

Alana dozes and thinks, *My mind is full of memories. The four days and nights went so fast with potlatches, gift giving, food, dances, masks, and story tellers. The events are jumbled together. I'm reminded of the Edward*

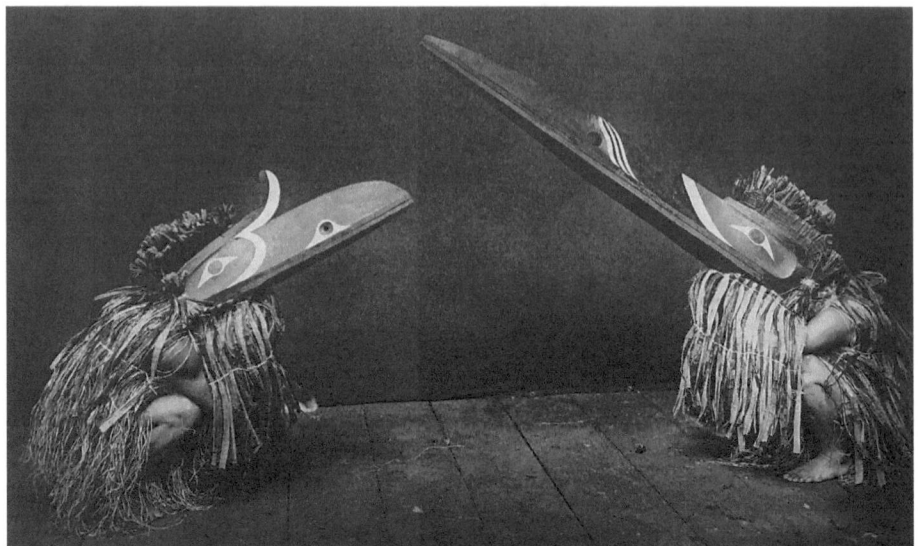

Curtis film, In the Land of the Headhunter. *There is one major difference in that the Curtis film shows all the dancers at the same time, whereas during the Tsimshian ceremonies, each dancer had the arena for his story. The men with the huge bird masks of Crooked Beak, the long-billed Kotsuis, and short-billed Hohhug were always dancing.*

Alana nudges Quanah and asks "Do you know which character David played?"

Quanah grumbles, "Maybe one of the birds."

"Well, the dancers and drumming were mesmerizing. I was transported to a different time and place—a different era. I was part of the ceremony. I lost objectivity. I, the lawyer, lost control."

Quanah grumbles again, "It seems you learned something. Dancing and drums give life to masks. Quite a contrast to the hundreds of masks collecting dust on shelves in the Anthropology Museum in Vancouver. When masks are in rows, they are inanimate."

"Yes, indeed. The winter ceremony presents the world of bear, wolf, raven, otter, mountain goat, and orca. I saw Thunderbird and Wasgo. The dancers, no the creatures, were ethereal, surrounded by mystery. The story of warrior and Wasgo was my favorite. I loved how the audience chanted approval."

As the flight wore on, the throb of jet engines has the same effect as drums, and Alana whispers to Quanah, "Transformational masks are the key to relating real life to spirituality. The white man views Indian stories as mythology, which differentiates the two cultures. Orca, along with bear, eagle, raven, coyote, and other animals have totem status used for family crests. All tribes hold these animals in high esteem. I'm beginning to understand that with the crest and linage, the Indian assumes the identity and prowess of the animal."

Quanah responds with a sleepy, "Yeah."

Alana pokes Quanah and says, "Ceremonies, masks, and regalia are central to Indian heritage and the passage of culture. A written word is not necessary because living theatre is more powerful than words."

Alana organizes her thoughts. "Indian cultures are complex. The Whiteman's interpretations distort it. The dances are the product of generations of renditions, and their themes define Indian life. In one dance an orca carried a young girl to his land in the deep ocean. Bear, Wolf, and Eagle also carried people away. These rituals demonstrate how Indians acquire totems. The transformational masks permit spirits to move from animal to man and back. Wasgo and Thunderbird totems occupy a unique position in space and time."

Alana whispers to Quanah, "Do you believe that killer whales and Wasgo are related? I think so because the spiritual characteristics of Wasgo are universal to all coastal tribes, and Indian stories show a dark side of the killer whale. To preserve orca as a crest, maybe the Indian story of Wasgo evolved from the dark side of orca."

Alana nudges Quanah in the ribs exclaiming, "Quanah, listen to me. I know the meaning of Winter Ceremonies. They are like opera, maybe more like Chinese opera, which is also based on masks. The themes must be performed precisely according to tradition."

CHAPTER 33

Boeblingen, Germany - February

Quanah fishes his smart phone from his back pocket. "Hi, Mom, what's up?"

"Your German relatives are giving your grandfather his 90th birthday next week. I bought direct tickets from Seattle to Frankfurt on Lufthansa/Delta. We'll take the ICE to Stuttgart."

"But Mom, I haven't seen him for fifteen years. I don't speak German. I don't know him."

"Please don't argue."

"Mom, I have course work. You go. I shouldn't take the time."

"Would you attend a birthday for an Indian relative?"

"Of course." Quanah sighs and concedes, "OK, I'll go with you."

Driving to Sea-Tac International Terminal, Quanah remarks, "This is enjoyable—compared to my arrest."

His mother elbows him and says, "Be nice."

At the check-in desk Quanah is surprised to notice his mother still retains her German passport. The flight is comfortable. The stewards are friendly and the meals tasty. His mom speaks German with a flight attendant who responds, "*Sie sprechen gut Deutsch für eine Americanerin.*" (You speak good German for an American.)

Monika blushing, answers, "I've lived in the States for thirty years and haven't kept up my German."

"I'm sure German will come back. Enjoy your visit," replies the attendant.

The flight is uneventful. The Frankfurt terminal is large and everyone is in a hurry. Quanah follows his mom as she bee-lines, darts past walkers, and wiggles through clots of friends to arrive at the Inter-City Express train, the ICE, to Stuttgart.

243

In the Stuttgart train station, he falls behind as his mom rushes up escalators, past parents wheeling baby carriages, and pushes between clusters of school children. As they near the Boeblingen local train platform, he yells, "Monika, not so fast!"

His mom slides past the closing train doors, and then shoves on one door so it reopens for her son. Settling into a seat Quanah remarks, "Mom, I've never seen you move so fast."

Monika reminisces, "I took this train every day to the *gymnasium* in Stuttgart. In those days, trains were crowded and not so nice. People were in a hurry, and if you didn't push, you didn't get a seat."

Monika keeps a running discourse, like a tour guide, on places and childhood experiences. As they disembark from the car, an elderly woman races toward them crying, *"Liebchen Moni, Ich bin so froh das du hier bist."* (My dear Monika, I'm so pleased that you are here.)

After embracing her daughter, Marie pulls Quanah hard against her ample bosom, *"Und du mein Enkelkind; du bist, ah, tut mir leid.* My grandson, you are all grown up."

Pulling from the bear hug, Quanah manages, "Grandma."

Sonia, embracing her sister-in-law, says, "Monika, let me help with a bag, Uwe is waiting with the auto."

Stepping onto the sidewalk, Monika's brother, Uwe, takes a bag. *"Hallo, Moni,"* Grasping Quanah's hand, he says, *"Hallo, Neffe, mein Gott, du bist ein man!"* (Hello, Nephew, My God, you are a man!)

Smiling sheepishly Quanah asks, "What?"

Uwe, grabbing Quanah by the shoulders, exclaims, "You look like Dad, *nicht wahr Moni?"*

Quanah, not expecting to be hugged so hard by a grown man, stammers, "What?"

Uwe relinquishes his hold. "We'll need to give you a crash course in German, because Dad doesn't remember English. Otherwise, his memory is good."

Uwe stacks the luggage into the trunk of the Mercedes sedan. Noting Quanah's surprise, he explains, "We get a discount from management on slightly used vehicles."

Quanah asks, "What do you do at Mercedes?"

"I test drive new models. I'll give you a tour of the plant in Sindelfingen and take you for a drive on the test ring at Rottweil, if you want to."

Quanah replies, "Yeah, sure."

Pulling onto a bricked driveway, in front of Uwe's three story, plastered house, Uwe explains, "You'll be staying with us."

Monika hugging her dad and sobbing, says, *"Pappa, wie gehts dir?"* (Papa, how are you?)

Pappa, slightly stooped, yet tall, tears on cheek, utters, *"Meine liebe Moni."* (My dear Moni.)

"Pappa, hier ist dein Enkel, Quanah Siegfried, es ist schon Fünfzehn Zahre hier." (Papa, here is your grandchild, Quanah Siegfried. It's been fifteen years since we were here.)

Pappa, teary-eyed, says, *"Hallo,"* as he extends his left-hand toward his grandson.

Quanah, pulling his right hand back, and extending his left manages, "Hello."

Pappa Siegfried embraces his grandson. *"Es tut mir leid.* I do not speak English anymore; I understand little bit."

Quanah replies, "I don't speak German." He can't help thinking, *This man, my grandfather, was probably a Nazi in World War Two. But he looks normal enough. Not as fat as most Americans.*

The two men assess each other, separated by two generations but related through a daughter-mother, men of two eras and two different cultures. The older, with remnants of white hair clipped short, not a wrinkle on his coat, shoes black and polished, teeth strait, aquiline nose, cheeks sunken, with blue penetrating eyes surveys the young man who looks surprisingly like he did sixty years ago.

The younger man, muscular, broad shouldered, with blond hair tied into a pony tail, locks eyes with his grandfather. All eyes are on the two in this awkward situation.

Uwe breaking the silence, says, *"Pappa, in einer Woche, wird Quanah Deutsch sprechen."* (Pappa, in a week Quanah will be speaking

German.) "Isn't that so Quanah? Here, come, let me introduce you to your relatives."

It was a swirl of names and relationships: *Tante Petra, Tante Ursula, Tante Klaudia, Onkel Kurt, Onkel Wolf, Onkel Dieter*...Hans, Claus, Maria, Sylvia, Thomas...

Uwe continues, "Now, Quanah, the next level of relations. My sons, Frank and Claus, your cousins Kurt, Annie, Maria, Peter, Willi..."

There is no way Quanah can remember. He is jet lagged and feels lost.

"Hi Quanah, I'm Frank. I have heard a lot about you from papa. All of us and Germans in general will be asking you hundreds of questions. We love Indians. The author, Karl May wrote extensively about the American old west. So you see, you're our Indian."

Overwhelmed by Frank's openness, Quanah manages to answer, "I'm sorry but I haven't read him. Mom talked about May on the train so I know a bit of the story. May wrote about southwest Indians, and I'm a coastal Indian. We live by the ocean and fish salmon."

Frank, grabbing Quanah's shoulder, exclaims, "That's even better, because we know little about your people and culture."

Uwe comes to Quanah's rescue. "Come, let me show you and Moni your rooms. Freshen up, and we'll walk to the *Stille Winkel* for dinner."

Eighty people attend dinner. Lots of wine and beer. There are many dishes to choose from including a rack of *Hirsch, (Hirsch* is stag in German.) pork chops, and chicken. Quanah is surprised that the gathering is like an Indian potlatch held in the tribal long house. The difference is that there are no alcoholic beverages on the Rez.

The next morning, Uwe knocks on doors saying, "*Aufstehen,* good morning Moni and Quanah. *Frühstück!*"

At the table Monika says, "In the states I miss the fresh breakfast rolls, the sheep and goat cheeses, and of course smoked hams. But, we do have wonderful smoked salmon."

After lots of coffee, bread, cheeses, cold cuts, and fruits Uwe announces "Quanah, let's take a small outing, *wir machen ein rundfahrt,* (we will take a short car trip.)"

As his uncle navigates the small streets, Quanah remarks, "This car is nimble."

The S Mercedes is soon on the autobahn. It is Sunday, modest traffic, and no trucks. It is obvious that his uncle loves to drive as he lightly holds the top of the steering wheel with his right hand. As they pass the sign 130 with lines through it, his uncle accelerates to 180 explaining "The V8 is a 324 Kilowatt, 4.17L engine. I had the electronic limit of 250 Km/hr removed."

"What does 324 Kilowatt mean?"

"435 horsepower."

"How fast will this car go?"

"When limited, about 250, when unlimited 300, or about 180 miles per hour!"

Quanah, looks out the window as they shoot past several cars. "Yes!"

They pass Stuttgart, Heilbronn, Crailsheim, and take the exit to Rothenburg.

Driving between two towers, Uwe explains, "This city has remained untouched by war for centuries. The towers were the city gate in the Middle Ages. Even Napoleon didn't find Rothenburg, or he would have burned it to the ground. There was no industry during World War II, so Americans didn't bomb the city."

They walk on top of the wall circling the old, inner city and then stop at a coffee shop as Uwe explains, "I want to show you the Tilman Riemenschneider alter in the gothic church. Where you have totem poles, house fronts, and masks, we have a tradition of carving alters."

After a pause, Uwe continues, "Quanah, I have a sensitive question to ask; may I?"

Nodding approval and muttering a weak, "Yes," Quanah gazes over the old town.

Uwe continues, "My son Frank, who is studying biology at the

247

university noted you have blue eyes. Yes, your mom is blue eyed but your dad had brown eyes. Did he have a blue recessive gene?"

"My great grandfather on my dad's side was Scandinavian. He jumped ship in Seattle, drifted to Port Angeles, and became a logger in the Olympic Mountains. My great-grandmother was working in the cook shack. I guess his blue-eyed gene is expressed in me."

"As you saw last night, Germans love Native Americans."

"We prefer to be called Indian. Native American is an academic reference, so Whites think it's politically correct. Thanks for showing me the church. I liked the carved altar figures."

Uwe says, "Of course Indian and German carving styles are completely different. However, both totem poles and altars are rigorously executed with rules defined by culture. Interesting that Nati… er, Indians and Germans have this same passion for careful detail in art. I think that totem poles and masks are one reason for German infatuation with Indians. Today, we still practice the ancient traditions of carving masks to celebrate the solstice. Our Celtic winter ceremonies are expressed in *Fastnacht* or *Fashing*."

The two men walk in a narrow alley lined with six-hundred-year-old homes, Uwe pauses to appreciate the scene and explains "Various Christian churches celebrate the same forty days of fast or lent. Mardi Gras, best observed in New Orleans is like our *Fastnacht*."

Quanah perks up. "Coastal Indians have winter ceremonies too. With masks. Why do Germans have masks?"

"Yes, masks. You will learn more and see many kinds the day after tomorrow. We will drive to Rottweil and drop Dad at the town hall."

After a few moments of silence, Uwe notices Quanah's preoccupation. "What's on your mind? Surely not this old city."

"Was grandpa a Nazi?"

After a pause, Uwe answers, "Yes, during the last war, almost all German men belonged to the party, especially young men and school children. From their perspective they thought the Americans were invading our fatherland. Your grandfather had just turned fifteen toward the end of the war. He along with his entire class in the Esslingen *Hochschule* were given world war one uniforms and old 1870 Manlicher rifles and told to hold the bridge over the Neckar River. I looked into this and found that most of his classmates were killed at the bridge. That's why he will not talk about the war. He was shot in the right shoulder and couldn't pursue his love of playing the piano."

"I can relate to Grandpa. My People were defending our homeland against White invaders. We still are."

The next morning, Quanah makes a call on his phone. "Hello Thomas, it's me, Quanah."

Thomas manages, "Quanah, what? Where are you calling from?"

"I'm here in Germany, Thomas. What are you doing this afternoon?"

"Are you OK? Where are you? Is this a joke?"

"No. I can drive over and see you this afternoon. Can you believe it? I'm here in Boeblingen with Mom. We're visiting her dad to celebrate his 90th. It's been a long time since the trial in Tacoma; we have some catching up to do."

They arrange to meet at noon in Tübingen at Thomas's office.

"Hi Quanah. I guess this isn't such a coincidence—me with my German wife and you with a German mother." Smiling, Thomas gives Quanah a shoulder hug.

"That's true. Boeblingen is only 25 kilometers from Tübingen. I guess that's why Uncle Uwe let me use his Mercedes."

Thomas asks, "What do you think of Germans?"

"They have a mentality not unlike western White people. When I was younger, I was ashamed of my mom. I thought that Germans were Nazis like you see in the movies. They killed Jews, Gypsies, communists, and other minorities. As an Indian, I grew up thinking I would have been killed during Hitler's time. I dyed my hair brown. It wasn't until basketball that I appreciated being tall. In grade school my classmates were always beating on me, especially

Richard. You remember him, the Makah Harbor Policeman?"

"Yeah, sure, I remember Richard." Thomas looks out the window. "As to your Uncle letting you have his Mercedes today, I'm not surprised. Germans are generous and love minority peoples. Of course, Germans are ashamed of the Hitler years. And I must defend the German people because they have openly denounced Nazi Germany. Most cities have memorials dedicated to the Holocaust. Much different from the American government that has not formally apologized to us for the Indian Holocaust."

"White Americans don't even accept that they attempted to exterminate us," Quanah growls. To change the subject, he asks, "So why did Hitler turn his back on Jesse Owens in the 1936 Olympics?"

"Because the Olympic committee told Hitler he had to stop shaking hands of winners. This does not exonerate Hitler. He was a monster. When I watched film clips of the Olympics, the German people roared with approval every time Owens won an event. In preliminary broad jumps, Owens fouled twice. His German competitor advised him to start his jump at least ten inches before the line and placed his T-shirt alongside the take-off board to mark

where Owens should step from. Owens took his advice and as a result, not only didn't scratch, but eventually won the gold.

Even though Germans didn't understand American football they adored Jim Thorpe. By the way, today, most German basketball teams have black players, and they are well respected. Germans, by and large, accept minorities. After all, your mother married an Indian."

"Be honest, Thomas. How are you treated?"

Thomas thinks for a moment. "Your question surprises me. I have more invitations to present talks about Indians than I can possibly accept and still write. The university allows me a lot of time to be away, but I need to publish articles and work on my book."

With a sly smile Quanah asks, "Are you writing about 'drunken Injuns'?"

"Haha. You have been around Aaron too much. Germans have an interest in the Old Shatterhand character and his side-kick Apache called Winnetou, published by Karl May in 1893. The May story plays out after the American Civil War. I am writing about German and American western heroes like the Lone Ranger and Tonto."

"What do you say about them? I don't like the subservient role played by Tonto."

"Interesting. You should read Winnetou because Karl May develops a partnership between the Apache, Winnetou, and the German, Shatterhand. I think writers for the original radio scripts of the Long Ranger got the idea from Karl May. Maybe the *Katzenjammer Kids* came from *Max und Moriz,* written by Wilhelm Busch."

"Sounds to me that you are getting an education in Germany, *nicht wahr?*"

"*Jawohl.*"

After leaving their dad at the Rottweil town hall the next day, Monika, Uwe, and Quanah make their way through the dense crowd of spectators lining the streets in the Rottweil town of several thousand.

Monika puts her arm around her son's shoulder. "We think you will enjoy *Fastnacht* because it's very traditional and personal."

The crowd is yelling, screaming, and dancing. Masked marchers are tossing candy and fruit. Kids are running helter-skelter, unsupervised, releasing a year's worth of stored energy. Groups of people in costumes with masks, representing fruit, hideous monsters, and animals, march along the street. Suddenly, witches and monsters pull Quanah and Uwe away and push Monika into a cage mounted onto a wagon. It disappears into the maelstrom.

"What the hell?" Quanah shouts to his uncle.

Smiling, Uwe pats Quanah's shoulder explaining, "That's Dad's group. They carry young girls and women off in their carts."

"I guess it compares to stories we have where sea monsters carry young women to their undersea world and a mountain wild man carries women to his cave," Quanah says. He asks, "Who is that guy with the big nose? The one pestering those guys in suits standing on the bleachers?"

"Oh, the guy with the big red nose is the town fool. And, he is making fun of the town mayor and other city dignitaries. Too bad that you don't know German, the fool is really giving his mind to the mayor."

"In our winter ceremonies, we also have a fool who makes fun of the chief. He throws snot at the chief."

On the flight home, Monika remarks, "I can't believe Dad gave you his Fashing costume. Did I tell you what your Indian Grandma told your dad when he went into the army?"

"*Nein.*"

"Don't be surprised, but your Indian Grandma told your dad not to bring home a black wife, a Mexican, or an Anglo. Your dad got on well with Germans and learned German quickly. He was so handsome. Grandma eventually accepted me when you came into the world. Yet, she had trouble acknowledging a blond, fair-skinned grandchild. Strange prejudice, since I learned later that her dad was Scandinavian."

Quanah responds, "Wow. I guess we had to be trapped in this plane to learn about family."

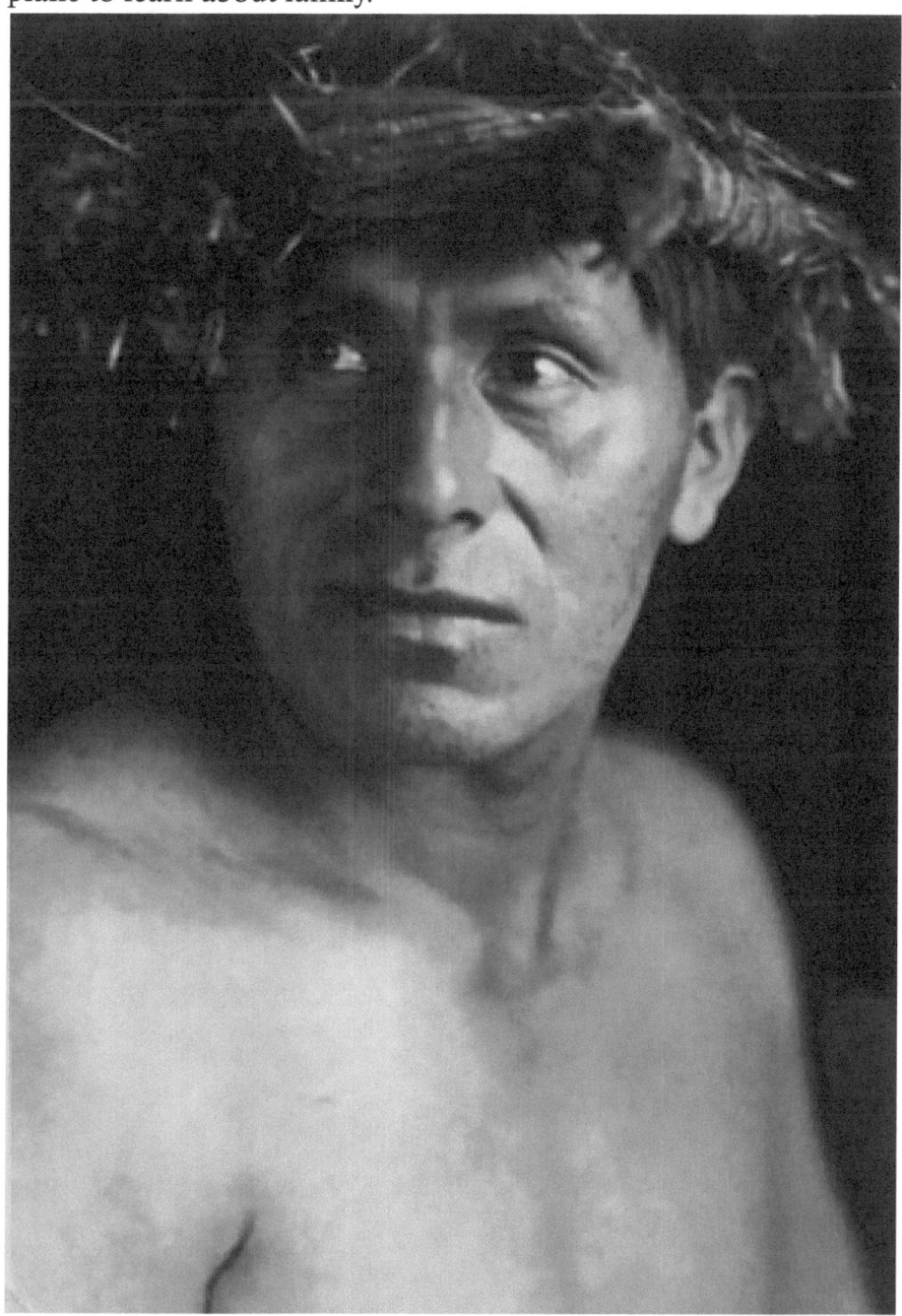

CHAPTER 34

Spring Quarter- Friday Harbor

The University of Washington research ship, Century, smacks against the standing wave of the upwelling flood tide. The boat swerves as the auto pilot applies rudder to keep the southerly bearing while maintaining eight knots against the four-knot current. Captain Rathmeier disengages the auto pilot and nudges the boat back on the transect run before re-engaging the auto pilot. The jog in the course appears on the computer screen as the boat repositions into the transect run. Every week the Century makes the run for marine bird and mammal counts. The six graduate students standing in front of the wheel house, training binoculars to their sectors, feel the ship shudder against the power of the surging tide into San Juan Channel between Cattle Point on San Juan Island and the western shore line of Lopez Island.

This part of the strait squeezing the flood tide is known as Cattle Pass. The immense volume of sea water flowing from the Pacific Ocean through the deep, wide Strait of Juan De Fuca sweeps south into Puget Sound and North into the Strait of Georgia separating Vancouver Island from the Canadian mainland of British Columbia twice every day. The northern flush is diffused into smaller, shallow channels between a clot of peaks rising from the sea floor. These peaks are the San Juan Islands which were shaped by the grinding power of the Puget Sound Glacier 10,000 years ago. The United States and the English Empire almost went to war over which channel should be the boundary. England claimed that Rosario Strait, to the east of the cluster of San Juan Islands was the natural shipping boundary. The Americans claimed that Haro Strait, to the west was the boundary. In 1872 Kaiser Wilhelm I of Germany ruled in favor of the Americans. The Kaiser could have cut the San Juan Archipelago in half with San Juan Island going to Canada and Orcas

Island to Washington Territory. Wisely, Kaiser Wilhelm chose not to make the small San Juan Channel, in which the Century is presently bucking the current, the boundary.

It is the strength of the tides through San Juan Channel that brought the Century, the course director, Captain Rudiger Rathmeier, Quanah, and five other students to this spot. Historically, the archipelago was an important fishing and clamming station for Indigenous Peoples. The cold currents rising from the Pacific Ocean floor pick up nutrients deposited during the ice ages when glaciers pulverized mountain meadows, valleys, and plateaus surrounding the northern reaches of the North American continent. The pull of gravity deposited mineral-laden river silt onto sea floors. Today, sea water flowing into the Strait of Juan de Fuca wells up from the depths into the sunlight and diffuses through the myriad of channels of the San Juan Archipelago. Phytoplankton bloom, and the food chain is jump-started each spring. Shrimp forage on microscopic organisms. Shoals of herring devour clouds of shrimp. Salmon, ling cod, and rockfish feed on herring. The top predators, the resident killer whales, harbor seals, Dall's porpoises and Stellar and California sea lions prey on predatory fish, the salmon and ling cod. The plankton bloom nourishes beds of clams which historically attracted Lummi Indians to dig clams for smoking. And, today, Quanah, a Makah student, finds himself counting birds and mammals.

At the urging of instructors, Quanah migrated out of his comfort zone of anonymity in the thousands of students at the University of Washington to be a student in small classes at the marine laboratories, studying with professors he doesn't know. More troubling is that he has to stay in a dorm and eat in a mess hall. Socializing is not a priority. Rez Indians do not interact with White students, and professors think that they are inattentive or stupid. The university doesn't have a retention officer. Quanah had been a loner when playing football. Nevertheless, the attraction to biology is strong, and he finds himself at the Friday Harbor Laboratories, sharing a room with Daniel,a man a little older than Quanah but worldly. Neither of the men belong to a particular generation. Both are headed for new careers. They are culturally far apart. One has fished for salmon; the other has fished for stories. One attended an eastern Ivy League college and succeeded with relative ease whereas the other struggled with English and humanity courses.

Daniel knows Quanah is Native American, so most mornings start with a fishing question, "Quanah, I don't mean to be nosy, but why do you care if a football team is called the Washington Redskins?"

"I shouldn't need to explain," is Quanah's patent response.

"That's no answer," is the little man's standard response.

Today, Daniel challenges, "My favorite football team is the Washington Redskins."

To which Quanah snaps, "The expression 'redskins' refers to scalps. Have you heard of the Soaring Kikes basketball or Wop baseball teams?"

Daniel whines, "That's an unfair comparison. I don't think team names were intended to be derogatory."

Quanah steps back, glaring. "Team names are used as mascots and mascots are not real. The United States Military took scalps. President Grant offered rewards for Indian skin. Skin has bad meanings."

"Hey, you're right. I hadn't thought of that comparison. But the use of Indians or Redman is not meant to be derogatory. For example, the Florida Seminoles," replies the little man with thick glasses.

Quanah takes a step toward Daniel, asking, "Do you want to be paraded around as a money lender, looking like Dickens' Fagin before games? That is mascot mentality."

"I got it, like Shylock in Shakespeare's *The Merchant of Venice*. Please accept my apology for being so insensitive. We're on the same page. Let's go for breakfast," pleads the man who is a head shorter than Quanah.

That evening, as Daniel pulls a chair to the table located far from those used by the female students, he smiles and quips, "Guess we have our own ghetto."

"What?"

"Historically, Jews were pushed into ghettos in Europe. Native Americans were first sequestered in Oklahoma Indian Territory and later onto reservations."

"No, we are not the same. Reservations belong to Indians. On the reservation we are sovereign nations," replies Quanah.

Danial quickly replies, "O.K., but Indian tribes were initially dispersed by the federal government. That's a diaspora, like the twelve tribes of Israel. And in 1948, Jews returned to the biblical lands for a new Israel. We Jews have lots in common with the American Indian because many Indian tribes have returned to their original homelands."

Picking at his salad Quanah decides to engage with Daniel. "Never thought of that comparison. However, very few tribes were able to keep their sacred grounds. They were given lands that the Whiteman didn't want. We will not have our lands back until the white buffalo is born."

"There's more similarities. Jews survived slavery by building the pyramids. During the Spanish inquisition we were forced into Catholicism and finally the Holocaust. Children of Native Americans were forced into federal schools in order to extinguish native languages and to teach the Indian to farm. The federal government first tried to exterminate the Indian, then to assimilate them by destroying their language, culture, and religion, and finally, in the 1970s, to dissolve Indian reservations by buying out the Indian. So, you see, we have lots in common."

Quanah answers softly, "I know our history."

Smiling, Daniel continues, "Jews and Native Americans are survivors. We both are the chosen people."

With a flat monotone, Quanah says. "My grandfather was in the German army during World War II. He was a NAZI. How does that make us similar?"

David leans close to Quanah and whispers, "My family name is Uhlenbeck. My Dutch ancestors were shipping merchants. I think of Shylock in *The Merchant of Venice*. My family was in the 'rum, cotton, slave triangle' of the 1800s. We have similar family histories, but you and I can't remake history. We can only move forward with understanding."

Quanah looks hard at Daniel. "I'm surprised to be talking about history. All Americans, including Indians, are taught about the Holocaust and anti-Semitism. The average American knows little about Indians."

"I know that."

"No, you don't understand. We learned about the Holocaust in school at Neah Bay. Yeah, you learned about the Custer massacre, but do you know of the Indian massacres in Oregon and Washington Territories? The deplorable conditions on the first reservations and the high death rates of babies?"

"Not details."

"That's my point, we were shown movies of German death camps. Nazi's made lamp shades from Holocaust victims. The Jews have successfully educated the world about the Holocaust."

"You have a point. I know of the '70s American Indian Movement. Dennis Banks and Russell Means were successful. You could be the new leader. I know of your whale hunt; it was awesome!"

"I'm not an activist."

Grinning broadly Daniel replies "You, my friend, are a born leader. Yes, like Moses."

"No, this is where Indian spirituality is different from that of Jews. Each tribe believes that it has been placed on earth by the Great Spirit, and each tribe has its own unique origin. At least today, no Indian believes his tribe is 'The Chosen One' over the other tribes. Makah believe that Thunderbird brought us to earth, other coastal tribes teach that raven opened a giant clam to let their people out. And…"

Daniel interrupts to proclaim, "There are more similarities. You have a chief, and we have a rabbi. You recount endless stories based on traditions, and so do we. We both have relics, rituals, and sacred religious artifacts. Both Jews and Indians love ceremonies."

Pausing, Daniel leans toward Quanah asking, "Will you take me on a whaling hunt?"

259

Within a week the students knew Quanah is Indian. The girls flood him with questions like, "Do Indian men help in the kitchen?" "Can Indian men have two wives?"

Joking aside, Quanah enjoys the outings on the research vessel, because students focus on mammal and bird counts and analyze dredge hauls. He is a quick learner, recognizing silhouettes of birds and mammals. Consequently, his eye for nature induces stereotypic comments, not in a derogatory manner, but with humor and admiration like "scout" and "eagle eye."

Diving birds remain on the surface for such a short time that quickness counts. Unintentionally, Quanah's classmates emulate his posture, focus, and dedication, calling out names of mammals and birds observed within 200 yards in each sector. After the third trip Quanah emerges as the class leader.

Quanah Tatoosh and Daniel Uhlenbeck are the two males in the Marine Biology 419 class of eleven students. This advanced undergraduate and graduate program of 15 hours consists of three courses to be selected from six classes. Each course is composed of lectures and field work designed to engage the student in marine and oceanic studies. Quanah signed up for Ecology and Conservation of Marine Mammals and Birds and was pleasantly surprised to find Pelagic Ecosystems interesting. He also took Creative Writing in Marine Biology because Dennis recognized his weakness in writing.

When the Century passed over the shoal from San Juan Channel into the Strait of Juan de Fuca, Quanah counted bull and cow Stellar Sea Lions perched on rocks. The bulls held heads high as if on guard duty. The female sea lions were hunting salmon in the rip tide, and salmon were foraging on herring which were buffeted about by currents. The research boat passed the sea lion rookery to end its 30-kilometer course for mammal and bird counts.

Captain Rathmeier held the boat at a "station" where Quanah lowered the 12-bottle Niskin Carousel from the main boom. This morning, the deckhand had reported sick. Quanah had helped on previous outings, so Captain Rathmeier had no reservation suggesting to the course director that Quanah could be the deckhand. Otherwise, they would have cancelled this scheduled outing. Considering these bird and mammal counts and water samples have been conducted faithfully for seventeen years, the course director had agreed.

After the 300-pound carousel splashes into the water, Quanah lowers it by ten-meter intervals. An array of tubes is designed to collect water samples, determine temperature, oxygen levels, and salinity at each depth. After finishing these experiments, the carousel is secured on deck. A smaller winch drags a five-meter-long net with a meter-wide opening, for ten minutes to collect plankton. The final experiment consists of pulling a bottom dredge with a ten-meter-wide mouth, held open with otter boards, to sample bottom fish such as flounder, rock fish, and crabs for a pull of 200 meters. The Dugus trawler winch is not that different than the one on Quanah's uncle's gill netter which he manned in the Strait of Juan de Fuca and off Tattoosh Island for salmon. On the research vessel, Quanah controls the winch and dumps the dredge contents onto the sorting table. There are few fish, explaining the moratorium on trawling in these waters. The unregulated fishing from 1950 to 1970 destroyed the stocks of bottom fish. *Another example of Whiteman's greed,* Quanah thinks. *Do they appreciate that a seven-pound rockfish is fifty years old?* Not wanting to engage in conversation, he doesn't vocalize his thoughts.

Finishing the work at the southern collecting site, they motor back through the strait to the starting position for the return bird and mammal count. They hoped to see killer whales but don't. Two Doll's dolphins ride their bow wake for about ten minutes; then, just as they had appeared from nowhere, they disappear. Reaching the northern collecting site, they repeat the carousel experiments, sample plankton, and make the fish-trawl.

As the Century approaches the Lab dock, Capt. Rathmeier uses the 16-inch hydraulic bow-thruster to nudge the vessel into berth. He yells, "Quanah, tie the stern line first." Rathmeier eases the boat against the line yelling again, "Now tie the bow line to the cleat."

It isn't that Rathmeier is chauvinistic, but the girl students aren't familiar with equipment. Winches, cables, trawls, and hooks, mixed with a pitching boat are a recipe for accidents.

CHAPTER 35

Spring - Underworld - Ebb Tide at Friday Harbor
Alana staying with Meg and Charlie - Early Morning

Alana can't hold her breath any longer. The automatic drive to breathe is pounding her head, her eyeballs are pushing from her skull. Suddenly, as the dive deepens, she is released from pain. She has plenty of oxygen. She gasps as she and Wasgo, who plucked her from the rowboat on the horizon, pass through the world of ocean into the underworld. She is surprised to suck air and not water. She can breathe!

She is riding on Wasgo's back!

Wasgo swims to the castle, through the open doors, and into the King and Queen chamber. On thrones are Wolf and Wife, Orca. Their eyes glow a threatening yellow-green. Wasgo swims to King and Queen. Dropping Alana, he declares, "Mother and Father, I present my bride!"

Octopus, King's first court jester slithers to King complaining, "She's skinny."

King Crab, second court jester, clatters before the Queen clicking, "She has only four legs!"

King Wolf barking, "Summon my advisors."

Queen Orca echoing, "Summon maids-in-waiting."

Ponderous Walrus, the Court Bailiff, balancing staff on nose, bellows, "Yes, Your Majesties."

The chambers soon overflow with creatures of all makes and sizes. Each pushing and shoving to get close to King Wolf and Queen Orca. There is no sun, no moon, no horizon, and no firmament. Alana has entered the World of Undersea with a dimension of chaos.

Bailiff Walrus of ponderous mass with bulbous nose and brushy mustache, proclaims, "Jury of seals take stools. Here comes Judge Coyote; court in session."

Judge Coyote slinks to his desk and barks, "This is my court. I tolerate no tricks."

263

Bailiff Walrus, slobbering from jowls, bellows, "Court in session."

Judge Coyote, sitting bolt upright, with cold, steel eyes and slicked hair, yaps, "Trial of Human has begun."

Beaver, the buck-toothed, beady-eyed prosecutor, charges, "Human is guilty. She has defended those who kill gray whales."

Transient killer whale for the defense, "She's innocent. What's the charge?"

Squid jet here, there, and everywhere recording court proceedings with trails of black ink.

Giant worms, the size of fire hoses, wiggle and glow.

Beaver says, "Your Honor, the accused is Human and White, therefore guilty."

Giant clams, with no legs at all and necks high, flap to no avail as they are chased by sun stars.

Sea Otter sucks at a Sea Urchin.

Transient killer whale says, "The accused, Alana, has committed no crime."

Beaver, lips curled exposing yellow teeth, chatters, "She's not part of the Circle of Life. Therefore, Alana, the White girl, is guilty of Whiteman's deeds."

Torpedo marmorata, creature with proper name, discharged, discharged, and discharged to charge the chambers to fifty volts.

Jester Octopus dances with Jester King Crab. Octopod declares, "You, my fine crab, have two too many legs."

Decapod insists, "No, you my friend have two too few legs."

Salmon declares, "I prefer herring."

Dolphin, chasing herring, says, "I have them rounded up."

Humpback whale, gulping herring ball, murmurs, "Mmmmm, good."

Kelp scream, "Help, help, sea slug is eating me."

Judge Coyote, hackle hair raised, howls, "Order. Bailiff, throw the ruffians out!"

Pounding floor with tusks, Ponderous Walrus trumpets through bulbous nose, "Jury of seals, how find you?"

"Your Honor, the verdict is sealed. Guilty, guilty, guilty of all crimes against nature," sing the jury of seals as they seal the defendant's fate!

Sitting upright Alana cries, "Wow, that was influenced by *Alice in Wonderland!* I haven't had a dream like this since middle school". She looks around sighing with relief. "Oh, I'm at Meg and Charlie's B&B in Friday Harbor."

Meg, knocks lightly, asking "Dear, are you OK? Did you have a nightmare?"

"Yes, I'm fine. I'll shower and be right down."

"Take your time, I'm just starting the waffle batter."

Alana thinks, *That dream is a premonition. Should I row a skiff from the Friday Harbor Laboratories along the eastern shore of San Juan Island to re-enact my grandfather's disappearance? I don't believe he simply fell overboard and drowned. He was killed by some creature.*

It was something Alana wanted to do, but fear of what she might find had caused her to procrastinate. The chief of police claimed that most recovered bodies of drowned fishermen had their flies open indicating that they fell overboard while taking a leak. Alana doesn't buy that. Had her grandfather fallen, he could have climbed back into the skiff. She'd procrastinate no longer.

Dr. Bob Black, her granddad's friend forty years ago, agrees to let Alana use his skiff. He asks her to meet him at the town boat ramp and suggests they have a cup of coffee at the Wharf Café. He explains, "When the labs auctioned the old skiffs, I bid thirty-four dollars and eleven cents on the best one and got it by one penny. It's a twin of the skiff used by your grandfather forty years ago. Quanah and I launched it yesterday."

Alana asks, "Why can't I start from the labs?"

"Since your grandfather disappeared, the university requires that skiffs can only be rowed to Brown Island or into town. As they walk to the skiff, he says, "Alana, you must keep in touch with your cell phone. I'll read in the library until you call to be picked up at Roche Harbor." He drapes a life jacket over her arm.

Alana jumps aboard exclaiming, "Don't worry. I'll call, and I'll wear the jacket."

Doctor Black motors over to the labs in his twenty-foot Boston Whaler and ties up at the dock. He watches Alana row around the bluff where sea water is pumped for the laboratory. The pumping dock that jutted from the bluff forty years ago has been replaced by intake pipes, which follow the contour of the bluff into the bay.

Alana rows out of the harbor and into the channel, aware of the humming from the sea water pumps. She can see the Applegate's house. They insisted she bring Eugene Kozloff's guide book, *Seashore life of Puget Sound, the Strait of Georgia, and the San Juan Archipelago.* Meg had also packed her a sandwich and three quarts of water. Relieved at how effortlessly the skiff rows, she tells herself, *I will easily reach Roche Harbor on the northwest shore of San Juan Island.*

Peering into Quanah's lab, Black asks, "May I come in?"

"Sure. What's up?"

"I just watched Alana row out of the harbor, heading for Roche Harbor. She's strong and a good rower, but I fear she won't be able to buck the tide at Davison Head."

"She has a high opinion of her ability," Quanah says.

Black ignores Quanah's comment, saying, "Would you take my Boston out in about three hours and follow her around Limestone Point? Spieden Channel will be dangerous."

"She needs a lesson." But Quanah continues, "OK, of course I'll go."

Alana experiences little tidal current in Friday Harbor, which is protected from tides in San Juan Channel by Brown's Island. Rowing into the Channel, the tide catches the bow of the skiff, spins it, and sweeps her along like flotsam. The inlet pipes for lab sea water were placed at this location because the strong tide ensures fresh, uncontaminated sea water for the laboratories. As Alana rounds Point Caution, the little skiff is caught in a large eddy. Even though Alana is a powerful rower in a shell, rowing a skiff is different. The skiff requires back and arm muscle whereas legs provide most of the power in a shell. The skiff oarlocks are too high for optimal transfer of body energy to the oars so she "crabs" the blades when they catch water too early and are forced deep into the water becoming a brake. The eddy swirls the little skiff and she feels helpless. A flash of fear sweeps over her as she realizes she can't row back to the harbor. Her immediate challenge is to escape the whirlpool. She can't row in a straight line and quickly learns to go with the swirling current in ever widening circles. She is making progress until tangling into a mat of kelp spaghetti near the shore line. After a frustrating few minutes she is ejected from the grip of kelp floats and swept along with the tide in San Juan Channel.

Alana grunts, "I can't get back so I'm committed to go with the current." She examines her map, finds her phone, and calls, "Hi, Dr. Black, I'm past Point Caution. An appropriate name."

Black responds, "Keep 100 yards from shore. Watch out for ferries. In about five miles you'll see an Island in the middle of a bay where, if you want to pull into the bay, I can fetch you. Or, you can continue past O'Neal Island and Limestone Point where the channel turns due west. Continue around a second prominent land mass projecting into the channel. This is called, 'Davison Head.' From there, row south, and you'll come to Roche Harbor."

Alana cheerfully replies, "It's a wonderful day, I'll make for Roche Harbor and meet you at the customs house. Thanks."

It's easy rowing with the two-mile-per-hour tide pushing from behind. Most of the rugged shore line is exposed, and she decides to pull into the little bay. Dr. Black suggested that she bring a viewing bucket with a Plexiglas bottom so she can peer into the inter-tidal world. The iridescent kelp and reddish sponge covering the rocks are wonderful. She sees bright orange brittle stars, purple and green sea urchins, and brightly colored turban shells with black and orange rings. Green and White sea anemones form solid mats of waving tentacles. Rocks are covered with chitins and limpets. Attempting to detach a limpet from its rock Alana muses *I bet this limpet is the Lottia.* The limpet pulls its conical shell tightly against its rock so she can't dislodge it. Brightly colored nudibranchs slide over sea grass. The lemon nudibranch looks exactly like a lemon. She beaches the skiff and scrambles along the shore line. Black mussels hang from rocks to the high tide level. She tugs at a cluster of them,

MAHLON KRIEBEL

but tough threads glued to rocks anchor the bivalves. Alana notices what looks like grapes hanging in rock crevices. She pinches one and it squirts a jet of water. "Ha," she exclaims, "You must be sea squirts, the little animals whose hearts my grandfather studied. He wrote your hearts have electrical signals similar to ours."

Kneeling by a tide pool, she shoves kelp fronds and algae aside, exposing a menagerie of crabs, sculpin fish, and worms. The animals in Kozloff's field book are readily found. *No wonder students love marine biology*, Alana thinks.

Grandfather may have explored this very shore because it's remote. Mom told me he ran wild rivers such as the Salmon River of No Return in Idaho and the Rogue River in Oregon. He was an explorer. I don't know what I'm looking for, but unexpected details surrounding cold cases usually provide clues.

As she stands by the tide pool, she sees rivulets of blood running from cuts where her knees had brushed acorn barnacles. She exclaims, "Ouch! Shorts aren't appropriate for beach combing."

Alana hauls out on the sandy beach of O'Neal Island. It's low tide, so each step is answered with jets of water. "Clams," she says to sea gulls screaming overhead. When a plop splashes against her hat, she retreats to the skiff.

Approaching Limestone Point, she spots a family of otters swimming through kelp beds and breaking sea urchins against their bellies with a stone. She thinks, *Such cute and curious animals. I wonder if they were always fearless. If so, this behavior would explain why they were nearly killed off by coastal Indians in the 1800s for pelts to be sent to China. I should talk to Quanah about this as an example of 'Indian greed.'*

Daydreaming, Alana doesn't notice the ferry from Sidney to Orcas Island and the city of Anacortes pass the ferry from Anacortes to Sidney until their colliding wakes nearly swamp the skiff. *Wow that was close! And the wind is forcing me north. I'm losing ground—or water,* she tells herself. *Was granddad swept north by the same tide and wind?*

Alana spies a boat approaching from Davison Head and wonders why it's coming right at her.

268

With a devilish grin Quanah yells, "Hi, how you doin'?"

"OK."

"Where're you headin'?"

"To Roche Harbor."

"Oh, I thought you were going north into the Inland Passage."

Davison Head continues to recede as Alana puts renewed strength into the oars. Tide and wind conspire to push the skiff north past Speiden Island into Boundary Pass between Canada and the States. The vastness of the Salish Sea and power of tidal currents soon loom in her mind as insurmountable. Pulling hard with oars she can't help thinking, *Grandfather may have experienced the same sense of helplessness forty years ago as he was swept into the Inland Passage.*

CHAPTER 36

Caught as Illegals at US – Canadian Water Border

At 78 km/hr., the 45-foot Coast Guard response boat bores down as Quanah pulls Alana into the Boston Whaler. Tide and wind are simply too much for Alana. The twin diesel engines generating 1650 HP are surprisingly quiet. The Coast Guard boatswain cuts power some two hundred yards from the wayward boaters and the sleek, aluminum hulled boat silently glides to the Boston Whaler. A seaman mans the fore twin .50 caliber M240B guns.

The boatswain yells into the bull horn, "Cut engine! We are going to board you."

Alana yells back, "What? Why?"

The boatswain answers with a clipped military voice, "Freeze forward, I'm boarding."

Alana, with an exhausted voice, manages, "You can't. You don't have a warrant."

A seaman pulls the Boston Whaler to port side of the Coast Guard 45 with a boat hook.

The boatswain, unsnapping the holster strap over his Beretta M-9 instructs the boaters, "Ma'am, sir, don't move. I'm climbing aboard."

Alana shouts, "I'm a lawyer and know this is an unlawful search. We haven't done anything to give you cause to stop and search us."

As the boatswain jumps into the Boston Whaler, he addresses Alana, "Ma'am, I'm following Coast Guard legal practices and procedures."

Alana quickly replies, "That's bullshit."

Quanah bends to Alana's ear and softly utters, "Dammit, Alana, don't mess with these guys. Do what they say."

The boatswain, with precise diction, directly addresses Alana, "Ma'am, I'm losing patience. Under maritime law enforcement, I

271

have jurisdictional authority to enforce Federal law."

Alana, with a softer but forceful voice, "What do you expect to find?"

Quanah says, "Alana, please cooperate!"

The boatswain addressing them both. "Ma'am, sir, please hand me two pieces of identification."

Quanah opens his wallet and retrieves a couple pieces of paper. "Here are my driver's license and Makah Indian Tribal ID."

"You can plainly see that we don't have anything in the boat but life jackets. I don't have my driver's license with me, and I don't need one for a skiff. We're still in the United States," Alana asserts.

The boatswain again addresses the young lady with a calm voice, "Under U.S. Code: Title 14, paragraph 99, section 70, I have Homeland Security authority to arrest you without a warrant. Ma'am, you are only five miles from the U.S. Canada Border, and I believe you are an alien immigrant. And this Native American is illegally bringing you into the United States of America. It is my duty to apprehend illegal aliens. Ma'am, what is your relationship to this Native American?"

"I'm Quanah's attorney."

"Sir, what is your relationship with this woman?"

"We're friends."

The boatswain asks, "Why do you have two boats?"

"I was rowing to Roche Harbor and couldn't make headway against the tide and wind," Alana quietly explains.

"Sir, were you picking her up?"

"I was rescuing her."

"Where do you live?"

"Seattle," Alana says.

Quanah answers, "Neah Bay and Friday Harbor."

With a weary voice Alana insists, "You're conducting an illegal search and arrest."

The boatswain tells them, "Please step aboard the Coast Guard boat. Seaman, pull the skiff into the Boston Whaler and tie it to our boat."

Climbing into the cutter, the boatswain addresses both, "Please turn around and place hands behind your back. Seaman Jamison, cuff and escort our prisoners to the galley."

Alana argues, "You're seizing our boats and breaking our fourth amendment rights."

The boatswain follows them into the galley explaining, "Ma'am, as an agent of Homeland Security, I have statutory authority to arrest you and transport you to the Coast Guard Station at Port Angles. If you will cooperate, I can remove the handcuffs."

Alana, with a condescending voice replies, "Thank you. I won't jump ship. I need a bathroom."

Seaman Jamison interjects, "At 40 knots, you would probably die if you jumped."

The boatswain, with an amused grin, points. "The head is forward."

As Alana returns, she asks, "May I make a phone call?"

She calls Charlie in Seattle. "What? You've been arrested by the coast guard?" he asks. "Yes, of course, I'll see what I can do."

As the 45 Response Boat is tied to the Coast Guard wharf at Port Angeles, the boatswain is surprised to see his commanding officer approaching. "Commander Sorenson, Sir."

CDR Sorenson says, "Bruce, I see you have apprehended some suspicious persons of interest. What do you think of these two?"

Boatswain Bruce answers, "I think the lady, who is clearly not an American, was attempting an illegal entry, and her companion, a Native American, was going to take her to the University of Washington Laboratories on San Juan Island. They were going to scuttle the skiff when we caught them."

Sorenson says, "Bruce, please handcuff and escort them to my office."

On entering Sorenson's office, Alana, quietly asks, "Sir, may I use the restroom?"

With a hint of a smile, CDR Sorenson issues a command, "Bruce, ask my secretary to escort the young lady to the ladies' room."

As Alana is escorted from the room, CDR Sorenson takes a seat behind his polished desk, and looking sternly at Quanah, asks, "Well, son, what do you have to say?"

"I guess there's not much to add, I was going to take Alana back to the labs. She wasn't able to row to Roche Harbor where I was planning to meet her."

Sorenson smiles. "This is certainly a suspicious story. And if I didn't know better, I would be required to lock you up. Quanah, please have a seat. Of course, I know who you are. I towed your whale. And, you gave me and my crew pieces of it in Neah Bay. By the way, what happened to the canoe crew?"

After a second or two, Quanah says, "The First Nation Indians returned to Canada. I don't think any lost their jobs. David, the Tsimshian is a doctor in Prince Rupert. Thomas and George are university professors. Can you believe that? Ben works as a boom operator on the Ucluelet Steamer on the west coast of Vancouver. You probably know the ship?"

"Two professors and a doctor, and yes, I've heard of the Ucluelet."

Quanah continues; "Merle is still working for the casino in Spokane, and his wife, Louise, had their baby. Aaron is working in Seattle as an engineer and is finishing his doctoral dissertation. You have probably read about Darrell Leshi Ross, because he's very active in salmon and water-right issues. Gus returned to his logging operation in Skagway. Sam still operates his salmon guiding service in the Queen Charlotte islands."

Sorenson, looking attentive, says, "You don't say. Can you give me Sam's address? I'm due for some first-rate salmon fishing, and I'm looking into guide services in the Inland Passage."

Returning with the secretary, Alana hears the last bit of conversation and says, "Sir, I'm sure that Sam would like to see you under different circumstances where Sam would be the Captain, and you would be his guest. Give me your business card, and I'll forward his address to you."

Sorenson nods. "Here's my card."

Quanah whispers in Alana's ear, "Alana, do you always have to have the last word."

CDR Sorenson, smiling, but with a stern voice says, "It's late. I'll have Boatswain Bruce take you back to Friday Harbor in the 44."

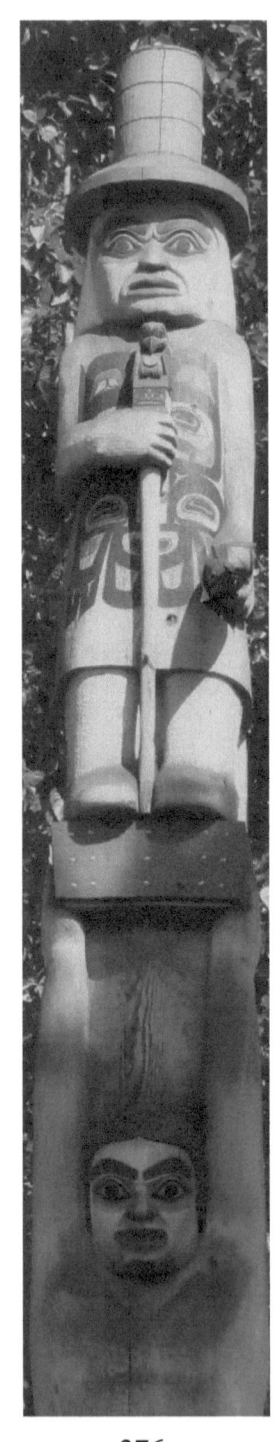

276

CHAPTER 37

Darrell Leschi Ross
Nisqually Half Blood Mother & Chinook-Salish Father

Darrell, an enrolled Nisqually, was a natural pick by the Makah Elders to be part of the canoe regatta. The Nisqually Tribe has organized Intertribal canoe races since 1900 in Puget Sound, so the elders didn't object to Quanah's request that Darrell be part of his multitribal canoe. The Nisqually Tribe has good relations with the Seattle press, and newspaper coverage of Nisqually canoe races has been favorable to Indians. With a tradition of cooperation with Whites, Nisqually Tribe members participate in the Puyallup Daffodil Parade and Washington State Fair.

Lately, however, ill will has developed over the 1974 Boldt Decision, which gives the Nisqually Tribe the right to fish historical waters located outside their reservation. White fishermen claim that Indians should fish only on the reservation. A generation after the Boldt Decision finds emotions between the Indian and Whites contentious.

The Makah Elders specifically maintain that the regatta is to be educational and must not repeat the American Indian Movement (AIM) that took place at Rosebud, South Dakota, in the 1970s when the feds invaded the reservation with tanks. AIM achieved international news and was successful in defining the Indian cause, but it increased the division between Whites and Indians. The goals of the regatta are reconciliation and education.

Darrell's middle name, Leschi, is after his great-great grandfather Leschi who fought in the Seattle Treaty Wars of 1855. The reason for this war was the Medicine Creek Treaty which did not provide for tribal fishing rights. The treaty was drafted by Washington Territorial Governor Stevens who was also the Indian Commissioner and an Army Surveyor. Isaac Stevens also drafted the Makah

277

Indian treaty. After the Willamette Valley in Oregon had filled with pioneers, they turned north into the Puget Sound in Washington Territory and settled before treaties had been made. Gov. Stevens drafted treaties to permit settlers to occupy tillable land and designated forest lands for Indian reservations.

Because the original Nisqually reservation did not include historical fishing grounds, Chief Leschi fought the Whites and lost. Leschi was taken into custody, imprisoned, and tried in civil court for the murder of a white man. The U. S. Army contended that Leschi fought as a soldier, defending his homeland and argued that Leschi was a military prisoner of war and couldn't be tried as a civilian. Justice did not prevail for Leschi, and he was prosecuted as a civilian, found guilty, and hanged. Gov. Stevens could have intervened, but didn't because he was occupied with subjugating the plateau tribes of the Columbia River. The Nisqually Tribe has kept the story alive. The spirit of Leschi burns deeply in Darrell Leschi Ross. Darrell was the first to shout his approval of the whale hunt.

Darrell knows treaty law and history and readily shared his knowledge with Alana during the preparation for the upcoming defense of the whalers to be argued in the Supreme Court. It was expected that the Federal Ninth Court of Appeals would reverse Judge Krieger's Tacoma decision which freed Quanah's whaling crew. Alana appreciates Darrell's assistance, because he also understands the position of the White fishermen. Darrell is only one quarter Indian. He played high school and college football. He is married to a White woman. Alana once asked Darrel, "How can a person with only 1/4 or even 1/8th Indian blood be classified as Indian?"

Darrell is bicultural, speaks Nisqually and some Chinook Jargon. Most Nisqually have White blood which is traced to the trapping period when the Hudson's Bay Company looked favorably on traders marrying Indian women. This created an environment for early pioneers to also marry Indian women. This heritage explains why Nisqually Indians know White culture. In contrast, the Makah Tribe has remained isolated on the tip of the Olympic Peninsula. Darrell's mother is one half Nisqually and his father has a trace of Chinook-Salish. The tribe registered Darrell as one quarter Nisqually. Darrell carries only one sixteenth of the genetic material of his gg-grandfather's genome. Nevertheless, Darrell's passion for Indian rights burns with the same intensity as in the original Leschi. This passion has been maintained through five generations to be expressed in Darrell Leschi Ross.

Listening to Darrell's intriguing heritage, Alana had asked, "You are of mixed races, so why are you Indian and not White?"

Darrell explained, "Indianness isn't like mixing paint because gene complexes can be passed from generation to generation. There are recessive and dominant genes in regards to everything from behavioral traits to skin and eye color. Consequently, a human of mixed parentage may have characteristics traced to each side. This is observed in large Native American families where siblings may show different racial characteristics. Several years ago, Indians with mixed blood were ashamed of their White heritage. Today, it's 'cool' to look Indian. In fact, many liberals, especially young women, have dug into their past to find their Indian connection. I know that I don't look Indian, so I sometimes dress Indian and have braids. Logic doesn't apply to a perception of who I am because my genome is three quarters White meaning that I should be described as White. James Luna, an Indian comedian, has addressed this paradox in the 1970s describing what characteristics make an Indian. He introduces himself, dressed as a Whiteman, to a White audience as an Indian. He asks if anyone would like to have their picture taken with a 'real Indian'. Nobody responds. Luna excuses himself for a minute and changes into a loin cloth with a feather tucked into his pony tail. Luna reappears and repeats his question. Now everyone wants their picture taken with 'a real Indian.'"

CHAPTER 38

Seattle - Incident at Ballard Locks

Alana wakes to a sunny morning. It is Saturday, with sun and no drizzle. It's a morning that requires a run to Discovery Park, along the Hiram M. Chittendan Locks, through the Daybreak Star Indian Cultural Center, to the beach around Western Point, and back home.

Alana makes the choice of which trail to use at each branch point depending on her wind. *Changes in routes expand my mind. Just like in court where I make an immediate change in tactics when presented with evidence not disclosed.*

Running is one of the advantages to living in the Magnolia Section of Seattle. Today, as she runs north along 34th NW, several news panel trucks pass her. Sirens are converging onto the locks at the shipping canal. There is a huge commotion. The usually orderly walkways, filled with joggers and retired couples enjoying the Lake Washington Ship Canal, are seething with human drama. There are hundreds of Indians and Whites shouting and shoving.

An Indian without shirt and sporting a head band anchoring a couple of feathers is shouting at the crowd with a megaphone, "It is our right to net salmon in the canal. Federal law has upheld our treaty rights. You Whites should go home."

Indians and Whites are pulling at a fishing net with entangled salmon thrashing about. Indians are throwing salmon into ice chests. Whites are throwing salmon back into the canal. Mayhem!

Alana shouts, "Good grief, that's Quanah and Daniel tugging on the net." Suddenly, pushing and pulling turn ugly as several Whites with baseball bats start swinging wildly at the Indians.

With war whoops, Darrell Leschi Ross leaps into the fray wielding a salmon killing club as if it were a tomahawk. As his namesake, Chief Leschi, Darrell is clubbed into submission. Out of nowhere,

Gus appears, and, just like at the bar in Tacoma he extends his hand in friendship to Whites. A burly man with a wrist the size of a stove pipe comes behind Gus and smashes him in the back of the head. Quanah rushes to Gus, but it is too late. Gus collapses. Just as quickly as the brutality had started, the fracas abates.

George, with headdress, Aaron, and Daniel join Quanah holding Gus. Gus doesn't respond. Adrenalin controls Alana as she shoves people aside to kneel beside Gus. Shouting stops as police separate Whites into isolated clots. Danial holds Gus, and Quanah lays the unconscious Darrell Leschi Ross on a park bench.

Ambulances arrive. With blood gushing from his nose, Quanah climbs into the ambulance to join Gus. With police escort, they head to Swedish Medical Center. Gus has no pulse and the technicians administer CPR. Adhesive defibrillator pads are applied to his chest and shocks are delivered. Gus's body shakes but his heart remains still. Adrenalin is injected hurriedly through an IV and another jolt of electricity is sent into Gus's chest. A tiny electrical bump appears on the EKG monitor. Gus's heart begins to weakly beat.

Paramedics lift Darrell into a second ambulance, which heads to University Hospital. Darrell is unconscious and will need to be admitted into surgery immediately. However, his breathing is steady and his heart beat remains that of a warrior. Dr. Cordell Grossman, the neurosurgeon, saves Darrell Leschi Ross to fight another day.

Alana climbs into a third ambulance with Daniel, Aaron, and Chief George. Daniel and Aaron realize they are covered with contusions as they arrive at the Fred Hutchinson Medical Center Hospital.

Alana, in a state of shock over the brutality she witnessed from fellow whites, wonders how to comfort her friends. She can only mutter, "I'm so sorry. So sorry."

The nurses and doctors manipulate limbs and probe soft tissues. Two Indians, one white male, and one white woman have sustained many punches but miraculously have received no serious injuries.

Aaron quips, "George, you're not scratched. Your chief's bonnet saved you."

George doesn't smile.

Daniel Uhlenbeck shrieks, "I'm on an adrenaline high. Jesus Christ, this is what human rights is about. No, this is 'The American Indian Movement' and I'm part of it!"

At the hospital, they are seated in the ER waiting room. The news on TV catches their attention.

"This is James Brouton, reporting from Seattle Locks. Several minutes ago, the police were called to break up a fight between Native Americans and white fisherman over Native fishing rights. In the midst of the melee, an unidentified woman with a long black pony tail, wearing a red head band, and dressed in running clothes, thwarted fists to save her fallen comrades. Several victims, mostly Native Americans were carried away in ambulances. If you know the name of this warrior princess, please call me at this number. James Brouton for special news reports."

Alana shakes her head. "And that's the part they think is newsworthy?"

Meanwhile at Swedish Hospital, Doctor Jim Holzbirn tells Quanah, "There's no time for a scan. It's obvious the problem is at the base of Gus's skull and there's little sign his brain is functioning."

Quanah asks, "Can you save Gus?"

"The best I can do is decompress the brain by removing some skull and any swollen brain that can be spared. The odds of success are very low, but we can try."

Hours later, the doctor returns to the waiting room. "I'm sorry. We did what we could but there's been too much damage and several major vessels were destroyed."

The next morning, Big John, Gus's father, meets Quanah, Alana, and Daniel at the Tatitlek airstrip. It is a short hop from Anchorage. The longer plane trip from Seattle to Anchorage was uneventful.

Alana embraces Big John. The others grab Big John's shoulder. There are no words. Big John has arranged for an Anchorage mortuary to transport his son to Tatitlek. The rosary is in the afternoon at the Russian Orthodox Church, which sadly needs a coat of paint.

Most of the 400 residents attend. Mr. Marvin, who had been Gus's teacher comes from his retirement home in Anchorage to give the eulogy.

At the reception, Big John presents Daniel Uhlenbeck with Gus's .30-06 rifle. It is a Winchester Model 70, made before 1970. Gus had oiled it religiously to maintain bluing. The rifle is still in mint condition with a bolt action as smooth as a hot knife through butter. Rising from his chair with a chalky face, Daniel protests, "Sir, please, I can't accept this precious gift."

Gently pulling on Daniel's shirt Quanah explains, "To accept an object of the deceased is to forever hold his name in memory."

With tears in his eyes, Daniel accepts the rifle.

Big John places a beaded jacket in Alana's hands saying, "Alana, this jacket is made of split moose hide. Gus spoke very highly of you and would be proud to see you wear it."

Alana sobbing, manages to say, "Thank you."

As Big John moves to Quanah he partially pulls a hunting knife with a carved deer antler handle from a moose raw-hide sheath. "Quanah, Gus would want you to have his hunting knife."

Big John presents Quanah with a box explaining, "These things have a name attached for the rest of the whaling crew."

Prayers are said. The pastor closes the ceremony with a poem.

Within seconds men move benches and chairs around tables. Ladies set tables, and the pastor announces all should stay for food. Village girls bring plates of smoked salmon and roasted moose. There is no alcohol, and most drink cans of Pepsi. During dinner, many Indians rise to recount Gus's adventures. Mr. Marvin retells the story of Gus shooting at ravens perched on the church steeple with his .30-06 that Big John had presented to him for his 16th birthday.

The funeral takes place in the church the next day. A marine military guard opens a folded American flag, holds it over the coffin, and crisply refolds it. The material snaps as the two marines, highly decorated, stretch the flag before folding it lengthwise into fourths. They tightly fold the flag into a triangle and tuck the edges so that the flag won't open. Their white-gloved hands are quick and exact. They have performed this ceremony too many times for Indian veterans who died of diabetes and alcoholism. The marines stand at attention, salute Big John, and present the flag to him. At that precise moment, outside, four Indians dressed in uniform fire the three-shot solute.

The church is filled with sobbing and wailing. Six of Gus's former classmates somberly bear the coffin out the double doors, down the steps, and proceed up the path to the cemetery. Most of the grave markers are simple iron crosses. The few grave stones have either toppled or are leaning. There is no grass. It is a bleak place. But, perhaps a cemetery should look this way. The congregation follows behind. The reverend gives a prayer, the coffin is lowered by ropes into the hole onto a bed of hemlock branches. Gus now rests near his mother. There is no rug shrouding the hole to sanitize this solemn event. The reverend kneels, grabs a handful of earth, and tosses it onto the coffin. Mourners follow suit. Quanah, shoulders drooping, stands for an eternity before tossing the gravelly dirt onto his friend.

As Daniel approaches Quanah, he manages a tearful question, "I didn't know Gus had been in the marines. I'm surprised to see so many Indians from this small village that were in the service: marines, navy, and army. I don't get it. The US government screwed the Indian so many times. Why do they fight for the United States Government?"

"They fight as warriors for their homeland—for the Indian homeland. They see themselves as warriors and are damn proud of it!"

Daniel nods and whispers, "I wouldn't have thought of it like that!"

CHAPTER 39

An Offshore Encounter

It's five in the morning when Alana's phone rings. Dennis, Quanah's advisor and museum director, shouts into the phone, "I received a report from a tanker captain that a pod of killer whales is traveling south along the Vancouver coast. They are probably offshores. Alana, you can catch the seven-a.m. ferry if you hurry. We have a chance to intercept the pod near Cape Flattery."

Alana dresses, skips breakfast, and drives to Anacortes. There is little traffic and the lights are with her. As she purchases her ferry ticket, the attendant leans out the window, "I'll call down so you can make the ferry." The crew members smile as they toss the hawsers.

Quanah and Daniel meet Dennis for breakfast at the Wharf Café and wait for Alana. Dennis informs them, "We'll have a good chance to find this pod, because it's keeping a southern bearing. Several whale-watching boat captains first saw offshores out of Tofino, on the West coast of Vancouver Island. The pod was next spotted off the villages of Long Beach and Ucluelet Island and then between Rim and Bamfield in Barkley Sound. Last night a tanker captain, delivering oil to the Everett refinery, reported he saw killer whales as he turned into the Strait of Juan de Fuca."

Quanah explains, "Daniel, the whales are making twenty miles-per-day which will put them in the vicinity of Cape Flattery."

Dennis adds, "The weather is clear. We'll fly to Neah Bay and refuel. I'm going down to the plane and check it out."

Dennis bled fuel from the Cessna 180 into a bottle to look for water from condensation and found the fuel clear. He looked inside the pontoons for bilge water which would add unwanted weight. He loves his little "Betsy" but it will be crowded with four.

Running into the café, Alana breathlessly addresses her friends, "Good morning. What are our chances to spot offshores?"

Dennis answers, "If they keep their heading, we will intercept them."

As they fly over the southern extent of Haro Strait, Quanah reports, "There's the matriarch Hilda of the resident J pod and her new calf. Her older children swim dutifully behind."

Alana remarks, "I watched this pod off the Light House. They like to perform for people."

"Quanah, this is great," Daniel says. "I appreciate the chance to come along."

"Daniel, we're now over the Strait of Juan de Fuca," Dennis says, "To the north is Vancouver Island, and the Olympic Peninsula is south. Mount Olympus is the highest peak."

Dennis refuels in Neah Bay. No new reports have come in, so he heads to Tatoosh Island.

Quanah worries, "I have yet to see offshores. Maybe they aren't a good theme for a dissertation."

Offshore killer whales are man-eaters. They killed my grandfather! Alana thinks.

Dennis is excited, thinking, *This may be our best chance to study offshores.*

"There!" All four whisper, as if they are watching a skittish herd of Olympic Elk.

Quanah says, "See? They aren't deterred from their death hunt by the engine. There are seven killer whales chasing a pod of gray whales. They used the tidal surge between Cape Flattery and Tatoosh Island to cover their ambush."

Dennis says, "We'll follow the gray whales through the channel. I see they're turning south along the shoreline toward Fuca Pillar. They will probably head west into deeper water."

Quanah, snapping photos, remarks, "This is where we got the gray whale. Did you see the grays sound to take evasive changes in direction? This is a cat and mouse hunt although the killers are smaller than their prey."

Dennis announces, "I'll level to 2000 feet and stay to the side of the killers because killers stay over the grays with echolocation. The killers don't sound. They wait on the surface."

Quanah switches his camera to video and asks, "Can we get closer?"

Dennis reaches to the center of the panel and pulls the small knob marked 'Carburetor Heat' to divert heat from the engine to keep water from condensing in the carburetor. He pulls the throttle back, reducing the engine to 1800 rpm. After adjusting trim, the plane obediently begins losing altitude at about 500 feet per minute. Dennis adds a little more power and reduces the flaps an additional 10 degrees. The Cessna's speed drops to 75 knots as it levels off at 1000 feet. At 55 knots and 1000 feet Dennis adds power to keep the airframe from stalling. As an experienced bush pilot, Dennis is aware of the dangers of 'low and slow' flying but the chance to film a pack of offshore killers zero in for a kill simply overpowers caution.

Dennis drops the Cessna speed as much as possible with flaps down and adds more power to prevent stalling. Nevertheless, he still needs to circle to keep the whales in sight. After about 10 miles, the grays slow and spend more time on the surface.

Dennis reports, "We are just off Makah Bay."

Quanah exclaims, "Look! See the two bull killer whales pursue a calf and mother while others dart among the pod to disorient the grays. Wow! I recorded the two bulls separating the calf from his mother."

Alana says, "That's just like a quarter horse cutting a calf from a herd of cattle. This is a water version of a pack of wolves pulling a calf elk away from its mother. Now I see why Indians fuse a wolf and a killer whale into the creature, Wasgo."

The mother gray whale tries to force the killers from her calf by smashing them with her fluke. The top predators are not to be deterred and are quicker than the gray. The calf appears to be too tired to sound. The mother gray tries every maneuver to protect her calf but can't prevent a bull orca from ramming it. After three dead-on butts, the calf rolls onto its side. The killers swim on top of the calf to drown it.

Alana murmurs, "Orcas know death by drowning. This is similar to a lioness suffocating an antelope by biting its mouth and nose shut or collapsing its wind pipe. Killer whales understand life and death. I would guess that this killing technique is passed to the next generation of killer whales just like cubs learn from lionesses."

Breathless, Daniel interjects, "I can't believe I'm watching this. Somehow the reality of witnessing the brutality of nature is different than seeing it on TV. I wouldn't watch this on TV. Yet, I'm not turning away."

The orcas ram the calf's head, and when the calf's jaw opens, they tear his tongue out. It's horrific, and Alana looks away. Quanah is getting fantastic footage as well as stills. The pod of gray whales has abandoned the mother and calf. The mother still attempts to force the killers from her calf, but it is too late. The water is crimson as the killers eat the tongue. The four watch as the calf sinks out of sight. The orcas continue south.

Quanah exclaims, "This was a sport kill! They didn't eat the gray."

Betsy coughs. Dennis mutters, "Damn, our air speed is too slow."

Alarmed, Alana asks, "Why are you switching the fuel selection switch to 'off'?"

"Carburetor icing," Dennis explains, "It's caused by high humidity and the shape of a carburetor's horn."

"What does that mean?" Alana asks.

"The carburetor heat should have prevented icing. Time to ditch," replies Dennis as he tightens the primer lock and snaps the master to 'off.' "Alana, open your door about three inches and push the handle lock to the closed position."

"Why?" cries Alana, even as she rushes to comply.

"The protruding lock pin will keep the door from locking closed which could prevent an escape," Dennis explains.

Then he tells his passengers, "We can't make Ozette Lake or even the beach."

Alana holds her breath as they glide, eye level, with Spike Rock at Point of Arches. The Sea Needles are a frothing row of teeth. Dennis struggles to keep the nose up because there is no propeller wash to hold the tail down, and there is no rudder control. A dead-stick emergency landing in rough water is something that pilots don't practice. Predictably, Dennis has thought it through, because an experienced pilot continues to fly regardless of events. There is no time to radio May Day. They hit hard and bounce off the first three or four waves like a flat pebble skipping over a lake. The tail lifts and as the plane drops into a trough the floats knife into the swell. The right float struts snap collapsing the right float, dipping the wing into the swell. Betsy flips. The four are dangling upside down like puppets. Water rushes into the cabin through the two open doors. Dennis is the first to undo his seatbelt. Alana is struggling to open her belt latch while Quanah hangs unconscious upside down in his harness.

The plane is now bobbing like a $5.00 carnival ride. Within seconds the inverted cabin is half full of sea water, the plane is sinking nose first at a 10-degree angle. Wing tanks are providing some buoyancy with captured air bubbles, but the contribution is quickly overpowered by the forces of gravity and the upside-down configuration. Alana, with Dennis's help, frees her seat belt and they are helping to untangle Quanah, who has regained consciousness. Quanah drops head first into the water filled cabin.

As Daniel falls from his seat, his thigh catches a broken strut which penetrated the cabin's thin skin. He yells, "I'm bleeding!"

Moments later the cabin is flooded. Quanah and Alana hang onto the starboard pontoon. Dennis is on the port side. Dennis hopes that the pontoons will keep the inverted 180 afloat and that some fishing boats have seen his little plane ditch. Dennis, Quanah, and Alana pull themselves on top of a float.

Daniel weakly pleads, "I can't get onto the pontoon, you'll have to pull me up."

When Dennis sees blood pulsing from Daniel's pant leg onto the wing he yells, "Daniel's cut his femoral artery, pull his leg strait so I can get my belt as far up his leg as possible."

Alana shouts, "Do you realize that offshore killer whales probably eat humans. If the whales don't eat us the wind will blow us into the rocks where the plane will break apart, dumping us into the surf."

"Alana, don't be so analytical," says Quanah.

Alana, holding Daniel, "I think that the bleeding has stopped. We're safe for the time being."

Dennis, "Yep, four humans sitting on the float like seals on a log."

"Perhaps," quips Alana, "Do you guys know that killer whales see in air better that we do?"

Dennis replies, "Yes," and Quanah replies, "No."

"Well, if the killers come within two miles and spy hop, they'll see us sitting on the floats," Dennis says.

The "sitting pigeons" don't know that several commercial and sport fishing boats watched the plane go down and immediately called the Coast Guard Station. The Coast Guard Cutter, Wahoo, is returning from Kalaloch and is patrolling just south of Umatilla Reef with Commander Sorenson. The cutter arrives within minutes, and a rescue team is lowered in a Zodiac.

The Zodiac pulls to twenty yards and a seaman shouts with a bull horn, "It's too rough to attempt to approach the plane to take you into the Zodiac. A helicopter has been dispatched from Westport. They'll be here in 45 minutes. We'll stay with you. If you drift toward the rocks, you will have to swim from the plane toward us. Are you injured?"

Dennis yells, "Yes, we need to get Daniel to a hospital immediately. He's lost a lot of blood."

"Do you have life vests?"

"No, they're in the plane."

Quanah asks, "The cameras?"

Dennis says, "I got 'em in the sea bag."

The seaman yells, "We're sending a swimmer with a line. Tie it to a strut."

"Daniel has lost consciousness!" cries Alana as she struggles to keep him on the float.

After thirty minutes that seem like an eternity, the sound of the chopper is music. It hovers above and lowers the harness. They slip Daniel into the harness and watch as he is winched up.

"Go! Leave us," yells Quanah.

As Dennis, Quanah, and Alana are pulled into the Zodiac a seaman asks, "You look familiar. Didn't you kill that whale? How'd that turn out for you?"

Quanah weakly replies, "No trouble. We had a judge who ruled that we didn't break the law. We're sure happy to see you this time around."

The seaman says, "All in a day's work."

Quanah, Alana, and Dennis are transferred to the cutter and are met by Commander Sorenson, "I'm pleased to see you on board. But I'm saddened to inform you that your friend didn't make it to the hospital in Port Angeles."

"Oh my God. I feel terrible," Alana moans. Guiding Alana to the ship's phone, Commander Sorenson says, "You can use our phone to call his relatives."

Obviously in shock, Quanah responds, "I don't know his parents first name but maybe there aren't too many Uhlenbeck lawyers in Poughkeepsie, New York.

CDR Sorenson calls information, "Here, Quanah, take the

phone, it's ringing."

"Hello, Mrs. Hendrik Jacob Uhlenbeck?"

"Yes."

"This is Quanah Tatoosh from Friday Harbor. I'm a friend of Daniel's. Is Mr. Uhlenbeck also home?"

"Yes, I'm on the other line."

"I have some very bad news. Daniel is...dead."

"Oh! My God!"

"What? How?"

"He died this morning while we were watching whales and our plane went down."

Quanah, shaking gives the phone to Alana, "Hello, Mr. and Mrs. Uhlenbeck. My name is Alana Svoboda. Daniel was a dear friend. I'm so sorry."

Alana hears sobbing and asks, "Will you want us to fly Daniel back home? I can accompany the casket."

Mrs. Uhlenbeck sobs loudly and can't answer. Mustering composure, Mr. Uhlenbeck answers the question, "No, Daniel found a home on the Island. He discovered a love for marine biology and was writing us regularly about his new Native American friends. He wrote about a young woman lawyer; I guess that's you. Until his stay at Friday Harbor, we hardly heard from him. During these last months, Daniel wrote weekly. He didn't like his previous job as a reporter. We will honor his new home and bury him in the local cemetery. It's important that his new friends can attend the funeral."

Alana stifles her sobs to say, "Mr. and Mrs. Uhlenbeck, if it's OK with you, I'll arrange a room at the same B&B that I stay at in Friday Harbor. You can fly to Seattle, rent a car and drive to Friday Harbor, in which case you will take the ferry from Anacortes, or you can fly with a small charter."

"We have friends in Seattle. I'm sure they'll drive us. How did he die?"

"We had to ditch our plane, and Daniel fell onto a broken wing strut. It severed his femoral artery. We applied a tourniquet, but the wound was too high. The coast guard rescued us in thirty minutes, but Daniel didn't make it for the 45-minute flight to the Port Angeles hospital."

"Where is Daniel now?"

"At Port Angeles Hospital. We are on our way there now. Would you like us to send him to the funeral home in Friday Harbor? I'm sure that they can arrange a Jewish funeral."

"Yes."

"We'll send you the telephone number of the funeral home. My cell phone number is 509 358 8867." There is a long pause as Alana composes herself, "Please feel free to call about anything. We all loved Daniel. Quanah was Daniel's roommate at the labs. They had joint projects on the University research vessel and became very close. Daniel has been teaching Quanah how to write."

"Yes, we know. Daniel wrote high praise about Quanah and his Native American friends. We feel as if we know all of you. We'll plan to be in Friday Harbor tomorrow. Alana, could you request that the funeral home provide a very simple pine casket?"

"Yes. Certainly. Is there anything else?"

"Yes, please let me speak to Quanah."

"Hello, Quanah, could you accompany Daniel to Friday Harbor?"

"Yes."

"Thank you, we wish that we could meet under happier circumstances. Our Seattle friends will arrange for a Rabbi."

Perhaps the weather is fitting for such a sad event. It is unusually cold with a heavy mist shrouding the island, suffocating the mourners at Mill Street Cemetery, Friday Harbor, as if they were under water. On a bright day, to the east, Mt. Baker rises above Pear Point Bay and Lopez Island, and, to the southeast Mt. Rainier majestically hovers over Cattle Point and Puget Sound. But today, there is only sorrow, with moisture condensing on grass. The cemetery looks over Griffin Bay into San Juan Channel where Daniel, Quanah and other classmates carried out marine studies on the lab research vessel. Friday Harbor students and faculty are gathered to pay final respects.

Gradually, one after another, they look to the woods a hundred yards to the north where a small cluster of people are standing under an enormous oak. They are not an apparition in the mist. One wears a headdress and several have pulled buckskin jackets tightly against their necks to ward off the chill. Others have a feather tucked under a head band. Quanah bends down and whispers to Mr. and Mrs. Uhlenbeck, "Those are Daniel's friends."

The Rabbi didn't know Daniel. Many friends spoke of their love and admiration of Daniel. Quanah couldn't speak. The simple ceremony concluded with tossing a fist full of dirt onto the coffin. Daniel's Indian friends made their way to the grave and tossed a handful of dirt onto the coffin along with a sprig of cedar as is the custom for an Indian burial.

After the grave is filled, Mr. Uhlenbeck says Kaddish. He doesn't mention his deep sorrow of Daniel's death but refers to the glory and holiness of God. After the prayer, Mr. Uhlenbeck steps back from the grave. Mrs. Uhlenbeck weeps.

The laboratory personnel and Quanah wear yarmulkes and shawls. They file past the parents, followed by the American Indians, each culture paying their respects to a young man so capable of understanding others.

Mr. Uhlenbeck, facing Quanah, asks, "Would you please accept the rifle given to Daniel by the Native American because our home is gun-free, and Daniel would want you to be guardian of it."

CHAPTER 40

Interview with Robert Zachary Gould - Neuroscientist
Retired from Uni. Oregon - Lives in Portland, Oregon

After several months, Alana has recovered from the accident and is making progress on the Supreme Court Briefs to defend the whaling crew. She'd expected that the ninth court of appeals would reverse Judge Krieger's ruling in Tacoma. She has also started to think again about the cold case of her disappeared grandfather.

While waiting for her teeth cleaning appointment, she opens an issue of Smithsonian and finds an article by Ingfei Chen on "The Social Brain." Chen describes unique neurons found only in mammalian brains that show complex social behavior. Humans, great apes, elephants, whales, dolphins, and orcas share the distinction of possessing these simple, spindle-shaped nerve cells dispersed among the more numerous and complex neurons composing a distinctive layer of brain tissue. These sparsely distributed neurons are found only in two defined areas of the human brain termed the anterior cingulate cortex and the frontal insula. Since these collections of cells are buried deep within the convoluted recesses of the brain and compose only one ten thousandth of the brain mass, it is hard to imagine they would play an important role. Prof. John Allman proposes that they are responsible for emotion and self-awareness and

thus important for social behavior.

Alana thinks, *It's serendipitous that I found this article. The von Economo neurons provide a link between human and killer whale behavior. Awareness of self implies the existence of a soul. Thus, the killer whale must also have a soul.*

Alana breathes deeply and sighs. *I'm not an animal behaviorist, but if killer whales have a sense of self and thus a soul, it's appropriate to anthropomorphize their behavior.*

Alana recalls some unnatural killer whale traits. In marine aquaria, they permit trainers to ride them and kiss their lips. People don't want to know that killer whales rip out the tongue of a gray whale or play ball with a live seal as a cat plays with a mouse before killing it and leaving a pile of mouse guts on an oriental carpet. Killer whales don't like the taste of harbor seals so they leave the carcass to drift on the horizon. *Maybe humans don't taste good.*

Why should man, a mammal, be defined differently than a killer whale? Alana answers herself, thinking, *Since transient and offshore killer whales kill for sport, it's not a stretch to envision orca attacking man. Moreover, deviant behavior could be the basis for Indian legends of bull killer whales carrying women to their lairs under the ocean surface.*

Alana decides, *I need to talk to a neuroscientist to find out if the brain of a killer whale has the complexity and analogous morphological structure of the human brain to support a range of human-like behaviors.*

In an internet search for neuroscientists, transmitters, brain, anatomy, and animal behavior, she found, "Robert Zachary Gould—retired."

Robert Z. Gould rose through the ranks to Professor of Neuroscience at the University of Iowa before accepting a position at Rockefeller University, New York. His career is impressive. His doctoral training was under a neuroscientist who studied basic electrical properties of squid axons at the Marine Biological Laboratories in Woods Hole, Massachusetts. Gould traveled to Australia for postdoctoral training with Sir John Eccles, where he identified the inhibitory neurotransmitter, the amino acid glycine, and characterized the postsynaptic receptors of neurons in the cat brain. Gould has written popular articles on memory, brain function, and amino acid transmitters. "Good grief, Dr. Gould may have known my grandfather!" Alana mutters to herself, "He lives in Portland, just a few hours from Seattle." She calls him to pose her question and to see if he'd meet with her."

As Alana pulls into Gould's driveway, she notes that the yard is a chaotic mix of rocks, fescue grasses, prairie flowers, and Canadian thistles. The adjoining yards are expanses of green without a single dandelion. *Thistles probably reflect Gould's personality,* she thinks as the door opens.

"Come in," Gould commands, "Yes I knew Ernst Kepler, and no, I didn't know your grandfather. Would you like some tea?"

"Yes," Alana replies, taken aback by Dr. Gould's terse greeting. She follows him into the kitchen. The house is clean and cluttered with books and magazines. Many issues of the *New Yorker* (all open to some article), *Audubon, Nature Conservancy,* and *National Geographic* are tucked here and there, unopened. *The National Enquirer* and years of *Foreign Affairs* are stacked in the corner. There are piles of scientific journals such as *Neuroscience* and *Nature.* Alana thinks, *Dr. Gould stays current. He's read the Chen article on von Economo Neurons.*

Alana asks, "I don't see *Scientific American* magazines."

Gould exclaims, "Bullshit articles! And I might add the *National Geographic* has also lost its direction. The recent articles about sugar and diet have no physiological basis." He peers at her. "I like talking with young folks with free thinking minds. Are you of this class?"

Alana doesn't answer. *Is this to be an adversarial meeting?*

Gould is a heavy-set man, with a prominent nose supporting glasses that were popular in the '70s. Twenty pounds lighter and twenty years younger, he would have commanded a presence in the lecture hall. Alana looks away as his dark eyes penetrate her soul.

Gould continues, "I like your ideas in general. However, the Chen notion that a small group of cells confers social behavior is folly, analogous to the Grandmother Neuron Hypothesis, where a given neuron located in the cortex stores the information for a unique human face. Face recognition requires fidelity and long-term retention. People simply don't forget their grandmother's face. A competing theory, one I support, is that brain functions, and I mean all aspects of brain activity, are accomplished with arrays of neurons acting in unison. I believe that emotions are carried out by all cells in the limbic part of the brain."

Gould pauses, catches his breath, and continues with an all-knowing smile, "There are not enough von Economo neurons to support emotion. Moreover, a distributed small number of cells could not form arrays to perform given responses."

Alana recognizes that the professor is not expecting a discussion. He's lecturing.

Gould settles deeper into his chair and continues, "In other words, to put it simply, the distributed von Economo neurons do not make enough mass in a given part of brain tissue to generate a meaningful signal capable of emotion and thought."

Alana interjects, "But Professor Allman claims they would have a role in transmitting information throughout the brain because they would have fast-conducting nerve fibers."

Gould answers, "Von Economo neurons are small and would therefore have small axons which would conduct relatively slowly." Gould takes a deep breath and continues, "In summary, what is important to your investigation is that killer whales and man share many behavioral characteristics and both have complex brains."

Alana persists, "Please tell me more about the complexity of the mammalian brain."

Gould pulls a model of the human brain from a book case. "This model is twice as large as a human brain." Gould wipes the dust off. "I can explain all you need to know about brains with this model. We don't need scientific jargon. Yes, it looks complicated but think of it as a three-dimensional puzzle. Each color represents a distinctive part of the brain with identifiable anatomical and cellular characteristics. We don't have to worry about the names that each color represents. The areas marked with different colors were identified in the late 1800s, because the neurons making up a particular part of the brain stain differently when subjected to dyes. All of these differently colored regions are connected by axons which form tracts and pass through the brain to given target areas. When tracts of axons reach their target, they branch and make contacts with neurons in the target area.

"To demonstrate this idea, let's examine the visual system. Light enters the eyeball, photons are captured by rods or cones in the retina. The energy of a photon stimulates a rod (for animals with both color and with shades of gray vision –night vision) or cone (for color vision) which are specialized retinal cells called receptors. When stimulated, minute electrical currents decrease which in turn decreases the release of chemicals, neurotransmitters, onto bipolar cells. Then minute electrical currents are generated in the bipolar cells which in turn release a transmitter which stimulates a ganglion cell. The ganglion cell generates an electrical signal that is carried into the brain by its axon. So, in the retina, there are three layers of cells, the rods and cones which are the receptors, the bipolar layer of cells which connect the receptors to the ganglion layer of cells. The ganglion cell axons carry information from the eye into the brain. Hence, it is said that the retina is a window into the function of the brain."

Reminded of college days when tedious lectures droned on and on, Alana fights to stay alert. She doesn't want to miss anything that links whales and humans. Nor does she want to embarrass herself by looking inattentive.

Dr. Gould is saying, "The axons of the retinal ganglion cells terminate in a brain region called the lateral geniculate, which is a way station in the flow of information. In the lateral geniculate, the light stimulated spots of adjoining receptors are grouped together by geniculate neurons to represent a line of light entering the eye. The neurons of the lateral geniculate pass the lines of information to the rear of the brain called the visual cortex. In the first layer of cells, the lines are grouped into angles of lines that we see. In the next layer of visual cortex cells, the angles of lines are put together to form surfaces. So you see, at successive levels of nerve cells in the visual cortex, lines and angles of the lines are put together to make ever increasing complex patterns to represent the field of vision. Finally, the information in the visual center is passed onto association centers where we think and recognize patterns."

Gould, with a satisfied look, concludes, "This is how the brain works. The basic physiology of the retina and first stages of signal integration within the brain explains why cubism is powerful. Lines and angles are carried to the first levels of our visual cortex."

Alana presses her expert witness, "But, where do emotions and recognition of self reside?"

Gould looks surprised. "Your question dates back to Descartes who concluded that our soul or self resides behind our eyeballs. Today, we know that the seat of emotion resides deep within our brain in an area called the hippocampus."

Gould opens a door in the model to explain, "This red part is termed the hippocampus. It controls emotion. 'I', my soul, reflects activity of this area. Elephants, whales, orcas, great apes, and man have this area in common."

Alana wonders if this man is an insufferable know-it-all, or if he's real. She did follow his arguments. Seeking to distract him with humor, she asks, "If hippopotamuses have the hippocampus, where is the campus?"

Without missing a beat, Gould answers, "The potamuses indeed have clubs and play croquet."

Alana laughs. She points to the model. "Exactly where am 'I' in there?"

Gould smiles, saying, "Yes, yes, that is the question! Where are we, our soul, and our self? We know how the brain processes visual information. We know that chemicals called neurotransmitters carry information across synapses between neurons. We know the electrical basis of nerve conduction. We know the chemistry of the brain. We know the basis of the smallest electrical signals that are generated across nerve membranes. Each neuron, each cell in our body is like a small battery. In the brain, neurons are connected by axons. Information travels as electrolytic current, and chemicals are released at nerve terminals. These chemicals, or transmitters, produce electrical currents in the postsynaptic neuron."

Gould raises his eyebrows and shrugs, "This recitation is reductionism. Reductionism has not answered the question of soul, mind, or memory."

He points to the middle, top surface of the brain. "Here, within these convolutions of billions of cells, is a representation of our body parts, our left side is represented on the right surface, and our right side is represented on the left surface of the brain. All body parts are represented linearly, but some body parts have more space such as the fingers and face. The sensory space represented on the cortex surface for fingers is adjacent to the wrist, arm, shoulder, and neck such that the brain surface represents the body surface. Just behind the sensory area on the brain is the motor cortex, which controls motion. Again, the facial muscles get more than their share of cortex. The cortex areas have been mapped making a 'homunculus' which is a two-dimensional characterization of our body. One homunculus is for sensation and one for motor control. Because the fingers and face compose so much of the surface, the homunculus is a very oddly-shaped being. In regards to orca brains, the part of the brain dealing with hearing and echolocation occupies an extremely large percentage of the brain. It is known as Brockas' area in man."

Alana interrupts. "Thus, thinking of whale echolocation, it makes biological sense that the hearing area of the orca brain is large. I understand this idea. But I still don't know where the "I" or "self" is located in this model."

"I don't know either. Perhaps the concept of self or soul is intractable. Maybe it will be informative to reflect on Freud."

Alana wonders how he will bring Freud into this lecture.

Gould asks, "Why Freud? Freud was a gifted neuroanatomist at the beginning of his career. He studied with the renowned physiologist, von Bruecke, who in turn had studied with von Helmholtz. And von Helmholtz was the personage who demonstrated that nerves generate electrical signals. Up to Helmholtz's time, scientists thought that nerves were a conduit for vital spirits, which were transported with the speed of light! Von Helmholtz determined the speed at which neurons conduct an electrical impulse. Freud was present, as a young scientist at the birth of neuroscience. He studied giant neurons in hagfish ganglia to show that neurons are distinct entities and not connected together. Thus, neurons are the basic anatomical unit of the brain. His drawings are not only accurate, but are first rate art. Freud thought primitive brains would lead to understanding the brain of man. This notion didn't help, and Freud left the so called 'primitive' nervous systems to describe the origin of the acoustic nerve in fetal mammals. He published his ground-breaking work in an article called 'Ueber den Ursprung des Nervus acusticus' ('The origin of the auditory nerve')."

Gould pauses, as if to be sure Alana is listening. "Strange isn't it? Freud found the brain center that is important to the whale for echolocation. Brains of whales and other mammals are not all that different. Therefore, what we know about man's brain would apply to the whale."

Alana begins, "Yes, that is simple enough…"

Gould interrupts, "Freud's study on the auditory center in the brain was based on painstaking anatomical work where mammalian brain tissue was stained to show hearing neurons and axons. The stained tissue was cut into thin sections. The thin sections of brain were stacked to make a three-dimensional reconstruction of nerve tracts from their origin to their destination. Freud imagined that this type of brain analysis would lead to understanding brain function or dysfunction, and he proposed that these studies would explain aphasia. In 1891, Freud published a schematic of how a word would be processed by the brain. He had the concept that axon arrays transfer information throughout the brain. Freud thought in diagrams and imagined that the "I" or "*Ich*" in German, was the product of brain activity generating our psychic characteristic. However, Freud eventually reached the conclusion that basic neuroscience could not solve the question of where and how 'we' reside in our brain."

Alana is now overwhelmed. *Each part of his lecture is simple enough, there are simply too many levels. I should have brought a recorder.*

Gould smiles and continues, "Freud drew diagrams of the brain with *Ich,* (I) *Ueberich,* (super-ego) *Es,* (it) *unbewuesst* (unconscious) *und vorbewuest* (subconscious) printed over circles representing the brain."

Alana says, "Yes, I understand, but haven't nuclear magnetic resonance studies shown that our emotional centers of the brain would be the 'I'?"

Gould quickly responds, "Nuclear magnetic resonance studies are the modern phrenology."

Alana asks, "What?"

"Neuroscientists bad mouth phrenology because they know nothing about it. Gall formulated phrenology in 1800 as an empirical system to be employed in the study of psychology. It is based on three principles that can be used today with slight modifications."

"But Professor Gould, everybody knows nuclear magnetic resonance studies are..."

Gould cuts in, "Nuclear magnetic data reflects blood flow in the brain, not nervous activity, therefore, those beautiful pictures of the brain purporting to show nervous activity misrepresent brain activity just like bumps on the head used in phrenology!"

Gould looks wild. His eyes are dilated, Alana thinks. *Here comes the next lecture.*

Gould explains, "There are a few principles of phrenology: The mind resides in the brain, there are independent areas of the brain for our various faculties, each faculty controls the size of the particular part of the brain, and the size of each part of the brain in turn influences the size of the skull. Hence, bumps on the skull reflect the size of a given faculty of the brain. In the context of 1800, this formulation demonstrates critical thinking."

"Well, how does this relate to modern nuclear magnetic resonance imagining?" Alana asks, thinking, *My God, his temple blood vessels are throbbing, I hope he doesn't have a heart attack.*

Gould sits back into his chair. "Modern imagining is measuring 'something' on the surface of the head. The more activity somewhere within the skull, the brighter the image. Ergo, modern phrenology! Brightness is scaled to the rainbow. Color is much more dramatic than shades of gray. Not bumps but color. Freud thought of brain areas interacting to produce 'self.' This is a global concept such that 'I' does not reside in a given part of the brain that will light up in color. We will not find a spot for 'I'. The modern phrenologists think that they will find the 'I' in color. Not so!"

Wow! Alana thinks, *He tied Descartes, Freud, Picasso, phrenology, and modern psychiatry in one long breath! I just received a keynote address at a scientific symposium.*

Alana asks, "Does the whale brain work like man's?

Gould answers, "Of course, the basic principles of nerves, synapses, and chemistry are the same in all mammals." Gould's demeanor changes. "Now there is something to be said about the usefulness of modern imaging techniques. They indeed demonstrate which areas of the brain are active during specific tasks, and this data supports previous conclusions about brain function. The MRI does have wonderful clinical relevancy in identifying the region of a stroke. After examining the literature on orca brains, I conclude that killer whales have the capacity to recognize 'self' and perform complex social behavior. However, it would be impossible to perform these studies on a living orca as performed on man."

Gould rises from his chair. "I have arranged for us to have lunch with Carmen Lorenzo, tomorrow. She is a behaviorist. You'll enjoy talking with her, because her area of expertise is the limbic system of mammalian brains."

CHAPTER 41

Interview with Professor Carmen Lorenzo
Mt. Hood Community College in Gresham, Oregon

Professor Gould has the ultimate in take-charge behavior. He could have arranged for Alana to meet alone with Professor Lorenzo, but he didn't. Alana would have preferred a one-on-one. During the ride to Gresham, she is trapped and has to listen to Gould launch into a tirade about would-be scientists with little if any formal training in the field of animal behavior.

After the introduction, Gould becomes surprisingly quiet. Professor Lorenzo is a head taller than Gould, who is short and stocky with rumpled clothes. Lorenzo is slim with black hair, tied into a tight bun. She wears black slacks with a navy-blue, hip-long sweater. Her face is delicate with high cheek bones, and her demeanor presents a misleading fragile countenance. She motions for Alana and Gould to sit at the round conference table in a tastefully decorated office. The chairs are modern and comfortable. Light streams into the room, illuminating rows of books neatly arranged on glass shelves, grouped for topic. The floor is oak, covered with oriental carpets. Lorenzo's desk is cherry with a writing pad

307

and a beaker of pencils and pens. The desk supports a neat stack of scientific papers and several books held between alabaster bookends. Pages of books and scientific papers are marked with stick tabs of several colors. The walls are decorated with wood block and copper plate lithographs of birds, plants, and mammals. Alana thinks of the contrast between Gould's disorganized office, albeit at his home, and Lorenzo's office.

Dr. Lorenzo, sitting straight-backed at the table, starts the conversation, "Dr. Gould tells me you're interested in killer whales and their evolutionary position in the hierarchy of mammals."

"Yes, I'm particularly interested in anecdotal stories of fishermen and Indian legends. Does the scientific community take these stories seriously?"

Lorenzo displays the opposite personality of Gould's as she calmly addresses the question, "I believe that scientists have not paid enough attention to folklore and anecdotal stories—those referred to as common knowledge. For example, there is a wealth of information about dog intelligence that can be learned from shepherds. In the past, behaviorists dismissed working dogs and fell back on the old notion that working dogs follow instinct. I don't know the anatomical basis of instinct and ponder where 'instinct' could reside in the DNA genome. Dog owners passionately contend that the family dog thinks and is part of the family. Ranchers know that dogs love to ride in the back of pickups and recently to ride on ATVs. The dog obviously thinks about the vehicle as a source of transportation. Hunters have unique bonds with hunting dogs and tell that their dog 'knows' a shotgun kills birds. The ability to know the function of a vehicle or gun shows that the dog adapts to new situations not present during evolution."

Pleasantly surprised by Dr. Lorenzo's calm and to-the-point demeanor, Alana pushes toward her objective, "What about mammals with social organizations?"

"We can continue with dogs. Dogs have evolved from wolves and a pack of wolves shows complex social behavior. There is the top female wolf. Subordinate females do not mate so the pack devotes its attention to the alpha female and her pups."

"I'm especially interested in killer whale behavior and their interactions with man. I know that killers haven't been studied to the degree of elephants and apes. Do you think there are generalizations applicable to all mammals with complex social behavior?"

Holding up a finger, Dr. Lorenzo pushes from her chair, explaining, "Coffee's ready. Would you like cream or sugar?"

Both visitors declare black. Dr. Lorenzo answers as she pours, "We can make generalizations. In regards to elephants, Indians have had close associations with these beasts of burden for hundreds of years. There is no doubt that elephants interact with man on a thinking level. As to African elephants, they are certainly different from Indian elephants. It has been reported that the members of a herd will attack a hunter with planned organization."

"Do you believe that elephants learn to become killers?"

"Certainly. Bulls turn rogue and are excluded from herds. Rogue behavior occurs in both Indian and African elephants. Females refuse to mate with old males. Rogue bulls attack humans and this behavior has been well documented during the British colonization period."

"Why do bull elephants turn rogue?"

"Interesting question. Maybe the same reason that some old men turn mean."

"I don't see a connection."

"The connection tying elephants, whales, and man together is loss of sexuality in males."

Alana notices that Professor Gould is squirming a bit, and a faint blush appears on his forehead. It's obvious that Professor Lorenzo is comfortable discussing sensitive issues. Alana smiles at Gould and asks, "Do male whales and elephants lose their ability to breed?"

"Of course," Dr. Lorenzo answers. "Sexual behavior is a major component of studying the life of any animal, and especially mammals and birds. Male elephants, whales, and humans lack an anatomical feature of great importance for procreation. They don't have an os penis, or penial bone, which is found in almost all other mammals."

"I can guess what that means."

"The human, whale, and elephant penial erection is a function of blood pressure, and age changes this dynamic needed for erections." With a twinkle in her eyes Carmen Lorenzo continues, "And, the females of these mammals select males with which to mate."

Alana changes the subject. "Do elephants recognize 'self'?"

"Elephants recognize themselves in a mirror. Yes, they have a perception of self," explains Lorenzo.

"Do they have a concept of death?"

"Certainly. When a herd approaches bones of a dead member they vocalize and fondle the skull with their trunks. When a calf dies, the mother stays with the corpse for days. Two elephants will attempt to hold a dying family member upright."

"Where would you place orcas in the thinking ability of mammals?" Alana asks.

"Very high. Training facilities that make a living with orcas are closed to the public. Therefore, it's difficult to judge whether orcas and dolphins can perform more tricks than dogs or learn faster. They certainly enjoy performing in front of an audience, just like dogs do. In the wild, I have observed orcas off the shore of Lime Kiln Beach, San Juan Island. I've seen them spy hop and breech much to the delight of onlookers. The whales certainly seemed to respond to clapping of the beach crowd."

Alana exclaims, "I also had the good fortune to witness an impromptu performance at Lime Kiln with Larry Driscoll, a whale expert working at Friday Harbor. Dr. Lorenzo, this brings me to the question of comparing orca behavior with human traits. Many writers anthropomorphize orca behavior. Is this proper science?"

With this pointed question, Dr. Gould looks agitated but remains silent. By contrast Dr. Lorenzo looks very pleased as she answers, "Yes, it's easy to anthropomorphize orcas, elephants, and most mammals. Just a generation ago, scientists were quick to say that mammals don't think; therefore, they can't have human traits.

Parrot owners know their birds have a command of several hundred words. Crows use sticks as tools and interact with humans."

Alana continues her questioning as if Dr. Lorenzo is on the witness stand. "Wouldn't it be accurate to describe animal behavior in human terms? To dismiss a behavioral trait as instinct could be misleading, and to use the expression 'don't anthropomorphize' could misrepresent animal behavior and create inaccuracies when defining animal behavior. Would you agree?"

Without hesitation, Lorenzo replies, "Yes, certainly."

Alana continues to press her witness. "Larry Driscoll told me whales have a sixth sense with which they communicate complex social behaviors. I know that whales organize into hunting packs, and hunting is specialized for specific prey. Resident killers hunt salmon and vocalize, whereas transients approach seals and sea lions in silence. Larry wasn't able to define the mode of killer whale communication, but he believes they 'tell' each other to leave humans alone with their sixth sense."

Dr. Lorenzo says, "I know Larry. He has performed a service to educate people that whales need our protection. It does seem that orcas know to leave humans alone. Up to fifty years ago, fisherman shot killers with rifles. Avoidance behavior could have been reinforced because of the capturing techniques used in the 1970s."

After a pause, Alana asks, "But, Dr. Lorenzo, if killer whales know that they can readily kill humans and eat them, why don't they utilize the human as a food source?"

"This is a good question, and I have given it a lot of thought after the killing of Dawn Branshaw at Sea World. We know that different world populations of killers have preferred foods. A young whale will learn from his mother how to kill and eat specific prey. They become accustomed to a given taste and therefore continue to hunt this prey. Resident killer whales are not opportunistic whereas offshore and transients are nonspecific."

Alana smiles and says, "The French, Swiss, and Italians eat horse meat, whereas, Germans, Brits, and Americans find eating horse meat repugnant."

"Precisely."

Alana presses on, "Thinking of Dawn Branshaw, I watched the documentary, *Blackfish,* which examines why Tilikum killed her. The producers interviewed Lori Marino, a neuroscientist, who made studies on orca brains. Do you know her work?"

Professor Lorenzo shakes her head. "I don't watch documentaries. I find them sensational."

"Dr. Marino found that orcas have a brain region not found in the human brain that extends into the limbic region. The limbic region expresses social behavior in mammals," Alana says, "Marino concludes whales have a sense of self and emotion forming the framework for social behaviors."

Dr. Gould interrupts, "Alana, Alana! Remember, conclusions in a documentary are an example of unsubstantiated correlations based on anthropomorphic notions."

Not to be drawn into a debate with Dr. Gould, Alana changes the subject. "Dr. Lorenzo, what about stories of porpoises and whales rescuing drowning sailors by pushing them to a beach or showing fisherman the direction to shore?"

Lorenzo takes a deep breath and smiles at this question, "It could be luck. We wouldn't hear from the sailors that followed dolphins out to sea, would we? By the way Robert, I'm not sure that anthropomorphic statements are so incorrect." Before Dr. Gould can respond she continues, "Robert, let's have lunch next week and discuss this further."

"Dr. Lorenzo," Alana asks, "how do you interpret Native American stories of killer whales and the sea serpent Wasgo?"

"Behaviors of a pack of wolves and a pod of orca are similar. Somewhat removed from our discussion is a report on recently discovered fossils showing that wolves and orcas have a common land-based ancestor. This could explain why wolf packs hunt similarly to a pod of orcas. The Indian legend of the sea serpent is interesting because Indians blend wolves with orcas to make the mythical sea monster."

"Is the sea monster mythical, or could it be based on reality?"

Frowning Lorenzo explains, "Indian renditions of Wasgo are blends of wolf and killer whale bodies. Coastal Indians appreciate behavioral similarities in the wolf and killer whale. We whites believe Wasgo to be mythical, but the Indian believes Wasgo is real. Nevertheless, it is possible that there is a dolphin species not known to science."

Alana takes a deep breath and says, "Great. My Indian friends claim Wasgo is real."

Dr. Lorenzo nods in agreement. Alana changes the direction of questioning. "Many researchers make statements to the effect that because whales have a larger brain than humans they must be as intelligent as man, if not more so. Is there a relationship to brain size and intelligence?"

"I'm aware of this argument for correlation of intelligence to brain size. First, let's think of dogs. Tiny dogs are just as smart as large ones, yet brain volumes vary by a factor of three. A large animal has more muscle cells, receptors for pressure, heat and other senses. Therefore, there must be more motor nerve cells to drive the muscle fibers. The axons that communicate between nerve cells of large animals have longer distances of communication which require larger cell bodies. A larger cell body needs more energy. Ergo, large mammals such as whales have a requirement for more neurons, and a larger number of neurons requires a larger brain."

Dr. Gould offers, "There's another factor when thinking of brain size. This is array theory. In mammals, neurons are bundled together to perform a given task. The larger the mammal, the larger the bundle of nerve fibers. Whales have a larger brain than man, but this doesn't substantiate the notion that the whale is more intelligent than say a dog or cat."

Dr. Lorenzo nods toward Gould that he should continue, and of course he does. "Just think what dogs and other mammals can do. They can catch a ball or jump onto prey. This means that their brain, as our brain, can perform complicated mathematics. That is, project where the ball will be in the future and intercept the ball in space. The dog catches the ball with his jaws, man catches it with his hand. The brains of dog, man, and orca use sophisticated calculations to catch prey."

Alana interjects, "Yes, but man knows he uses calculus."

Smiling, Gould parries, "Some men, yes, but the baseball player doesn't think at bat, if he does, he's in a slump."

Dr. Lorenzo looks to her wall clock, "Oh, my! It's 12:45 and I have a faculty meeting at 1:30. I need to give myself time to prepare. Dr. Gould warned me you're a lawyer, Alana, and I have enjoyed our conversation." Smiling, she hands Alana her card. "Email any time, and let's keep in touch."

CHAPTER 42

Solved Cold Case: How Robin Morton was killed
Robson Bight, Vancouver, B.C.

At three in the morning, Alana is tossing and turning with sublim-
inal thoughts: *Spectators watch in horror as a tiger drags his trainer by*
his head...a bullfighter scoops his guts back after being gored...an arrow
of geese brings down a jet liner with 250 passengers...a pet male chimp
severs the hands of his keeper and bites the keeper's nose off...a giant skate
impales a skin diver with its tail barb....a killer whale pulls an entertainer
wearing a wet suit looking like a seal from the pool deck...a woman trainer
collects ejaculate from Tilikum...a bull elephant goes berserk and tramples
hundreds in a circus...three pit bulls rip apart a jogger...vampire bats drain
the blood of a sleeping man...a Burmese python escapes into air shafts with
swallowed child...the Lions of Tsavo suffocate workers by crushing their
windpipe...New Guinea head hunters eat Michael Rockefeller's brains...
piranhas bite off toes, fingers, ears and nose from a biologist swimming
naked in the Amazon River, and he lives...Tilikum, a trained orca kills a
human in Victoria and in Florida...

After a couple of hours or tossing about, she drifts into a period of deep and restful sleep. Morning light filters into the bedroom window facing west. She hadn't drawn the shades. Nor had she set her alarm. She drifts back into that dreamy state between consciousness and sleep. Not a deep REM state which we don't remember, but a stage that we think we control. The truth is Brain controls Us. A state of Brain which mixes dreams with our world of wakefulness. A state where Brain reviews recent events. A time when Brain determines whether it should move short-term memories into long term memory banks, and, how to integrate memories into repositories. A time when Brain creates false memories, and deletes painful ones. Brain must throw out the myriad of short term events which it deems not worth keeping. Brain integrates newly stored memories with old memories in order to retrieve both new and old memories with fidelity—usually. Memories have associations. Should seal pup be filed with children, with drowning, with mothers, or murder? Or, should seal pups be filed with food, fish, or cannibals? Brain decides how to cross-reference. Brain sometimes prolongs this dreamy state. This dreamy state is a time of invention and a time of problem solving. A delicious state of clarity:

Killers shred a seal
Killers ram Stellar Sea Lions
Two Killers team to pray on sting rays
Killers play catch with a seal pup used as a ball
Killer picks toys from aquarium floor to delight children
Killer can see with acuity and clarity under water
Killers drown baby gray whale by lying over it
Killer whale gently holds trainer's arm
Killer tosses trainer from his nose
Killer and trainer French kiss
Tilikum, the killer whale in SeaWorld is a man killer!

Alana rises and goes to the window. The morning is crystal clear. The Olympic Range appears so close she could touch it. Mt. Olympus glows as a sapphire surrounded by crystals. "My God, perhaps I've solved the cold case death of my grandfather and of Robin

Morton," says Alana.

Alexandra Morton has described many details of how her husband drowned in Robson Bight while preparing to film killer whales at the rubbing site in her book, *Listening to Whales.* Alexandra writes that she and her husband, Robin, chased after a pod in Johnstone Strait in their Zodiac outboard, passed them, and predicting the pod was heading to the rubbing station, raced ahead. Robin donned his wet suit and slipped from the Zodiac to take a position where whales rub against the pebbly ocean floor. Alexandra motored some distance from the rubbing site so as not to disturb the whales. Soon, the known pod swam toward the site. She signaled Robin that they were coming. He gave a thumbs-up and dove to take a camera position. Alexandra wrote she heard whale vocalizations she didn't recognize through the hydrophone. A couple minutes later, the matriarch surfaced near the Zodiac and rapidly sounded. Alexandra didn't see the other pod members. Time lapsed. No more vocalizations. Alexandra grew anxious for Robin's safety. However, she didn't want to check on him for fear of ruining his chance to film whales scratching their bellies against the ocean floor. After an excruciating wait, she started the outboard and found Robin in eight feet of water on his back. Robin's mouth piece had fallen out. Mustering enormous courage, Alexandra dove to her husband, released his weights and brought him to the surface. She managed this heroic feat with her five-year-old son in the Zodiac.

The Royal Canadian Mounted Police initially concluded that killer whales had killed Robin. However, there were no abrasions on Robin's body, and his wetsuit was intact. An inspector found the rebreathing valve was slightly clogged but still functional. The rebreathing device permits the scuba diver to rebreathe air because the carbon dioxide from the exhaled breath is removed so that the air can be rebreathed for the remaining oxygen. Thus, this device permits longer times under water, and there are no distracting bubbles. Alexandra Morton concluded that the rebreathing valve malfunctioned, so her husband continued to rebreathe and inhaled more carbon dioxide than oxygen. Thinking that our brain has no warning mechanism to detect increasing levels of carbon dioxide, Mrs. Morton proposed her husband went to sleep. She wrote that the same process happens when people commit suicide by running their car in a closed garage. Mrs. Morton concluded that her husband stopped breathing, fainted, and drowned.

Alana had learned in the Whaling Museum that whales voluntarily breathe. If whales had an autonomic brain mechanism for breathing, their brain would force them to breathe underwater and drown. By contrast, land mammals, including man, breathe automatically. The rate of breathing is determined by the concentration of carbon dioxide in the blood stream. Carbon dioxide in blood makes carbonic acid. As acidity increases, brain sensors are stimulated to increase the breathing rate. When we hold our breath, carbon dioxide increases, the acidity of blood increases, and we feel the need to breath. Finally, we gasp for air.

Alana, summing up for the prosecution, looks to Mount Olympus as the jury, "Ladies and Gentlemen, Killer Whales are guilty of the murder of Mr. Robin Morton while he was underwater at the rubbing site. Their motive was sport, comparable to a White hunter killing a trophy bull elk for a rack or shooting an old lion for his black mane. One of the matriarch's sons stayed out of Robin's camera range as a distraction, while the second son stealthily approached Robin from behind. Like two wolves stalking a rabbit. Mr. Morton did not start his camera. The stalking young male suddenly appeared over Robin, rolled him onto his back, and pressed against Robin's chest holding him against the gravel. In his struggle to escape, Robin lost his mouth piece, inhaled sea water and drowned. The matriarch mother whale witnessed this deed, made vocalizations of alarm and disapproval, or maybe of approval, which Mrs. Morton heard. The matriarch surfaced near the Zodiac and rapidly left the scene. The two young males, having silently bagged their trophy retreated not to be detected by the lady in the Zodiac. The two killer whales drowned Robin Morton as if he were a hapless seal. Their motive was sport. They killed like the family cat suffocates a field mouse by pressing her paw over the rib cage. The defendants, the young male killer whales, killed Robin!"

As a good trial lawyer, Alana now summed for the defense, "Members of the jury, it is true that a pod of killer whales was near the rubbing beach. The rebreathing device malfunctioned. Carbon dioxide gas was scrubbed (removed) from the air that Robin was rebreathing so that carbon dioxide was also depleted in Robin's blood system. Since the drive to breathe is due to carbon dioxide in blood, Robin did not feel an urge to breathe. Since oxygen was depleted in his blood he simply passed out. When unconscious, Robin's mouthpiece fell out and he drowned. Whales understand death and realized that Robin Morton was dead. The matriarch vocalized in horror and left the scene after surfacing near Alexandra. Realizing that Robin was dead, the young males left without surfacing. Robin had died before the whales had reached the rubbing site and that explains why there are no whale scenes in his camera. The killer whales were innocent bystanders."

Alana moves to her window. "The jury is out. Did a killer whale kill her grandfather or did Wasgo? Does the whale-like creature, Wasgo, inhabit the ocean, the inlets, and channels of the Pacific Northwest coast line? Is Wasgo a rogue, psychopathic killer whale? Now it's time to scout the area of the Inland Passage. I'll call Quanah and see if he'll go with me. First, I need to send an email."

Dear Dr. Lorenzo and Prof. Gould,

Hi, I appreciated our conversations last week. You both gave me much to think about. And, I have a couple thoughts to run past you. Humans have a complex social behavior, we have language, and we write. Animals have complex behaviors but don't write. Animals also interact with man. Man and animals rely on body language. My thought is that interaction between animals requires the greatest part of the thinking brain. And, the actions of talking and writing require little more of the brain. Would you agree?

Sincerely,

Alana

CHAPTER 43

Tragic News from Prince Rupert

Looking at the caller's number Alana is not surprised that David called, as she and Quanah are planning to see him in a couple days. "Hi David. What's up?"

"Sam's disappeared."

"What! How?"

"His dad called. A couple months ago, while guiding fishermen, Sam discovered a pod of killer whales to the north of the Haida Gwaii Islands. You would know these Islands as the Queen Charlotte Islands. It seems all Sam could talk about was your quest to understand killer whales and Quanah's study of offshores. He started staying out all night and motoring farther out in the ocean. His dad said elders weren't surprised by his disappearance, because they warned him not to paint Wasgo on the war canoe. Haida elders think Sam has entered the World of Undersea."

"Oh my God, this is the third casualty. Two Indians and one white man. My quest is jinxed! I had a dream last night about the death of Robin Morton. This seems to have been a premonition for Sam. Did they find Sam's boat?"

"No."

"I should give this up, who'll be next?"

"Now, Alana, who's superstitious?"

Alana stifles a sob and says, "I'll call Sam's dad immediately. And David, could you join us to visit Sam's dad when we fly up to Prince Rupert? Your presence will ease tension."

"Yes, certainly. Sam's dad wouldn't hold you responsible. We can take my float plane."

"No, I'd rather not."

"Oh, I forgot, sorry. A boat is really out of the question because Skidegate is 200 miles from Prince Rupert and ferries are infrequent. I'll make arrangements on the commercial flight."

"Thanks, David. I appreciate the chance to visit with Sam's dad. I do feel responsible. Three friends are dead because of me.

Before David can argue, she clicks off and makes another call.

"Hello, Mr. Charles. Am I speaking with Sam's father?"

"Yes."

"This is Alana, Sam's friend."

"Yes."

"Mr. Charles, I'm so sorry about Sam. I feel responsible. Is there anything I can do?"

"No."

"Mr. Charles, Quanah and I would like very much to visit with you. Would it be OK?"

"Yes." After a very long pause, Sam's dad continues, "Sam's spirit is strong."

There is a long, awkward pause and not knowing what else to say, Alana finally says, "Goodbye."

After a couple minutes Alana calls Quanah. After a greeting, she asks, "Did David call you?"

"Yes."

"I called his dad. I think he holds me responsible for his son's disappearance."

"No, he doesn't blame you. On family matters, such as death, Indians do not talk about spiritual issues. Families respect the deceased by not gossiping."

There is a long pause as Alana mulls Quanah's assessment, "Quanah, we're still going to Prince Rupert, aren't we?"

"Sure. I promised Sam's dad that we would visit. He wants me to have Sam's computer. It seems that Sam kept extensive notes on offshore killer whales. Sam was pleased to be able to help with my studies. I guess I'm the one to blame, not you, Alana."

"Quanah, I think I'll call Commander Sorenson."

"Sure," Quanah says.

Sorenson answers on the first ring.

"Hello, Commander Sorenson. This is Alana Svoboda. Did you hear about Sam?"

"Yes, we were notified by the Canadians, and we sent helicopters and cutters from our Alaskan bases. His boat hasn't been found. No 'mayday' transmissions were noted."

"Commander, this is the third death of people that I really cared for. Sam would not have been motoring out to sea if it hadn't been for me."

"Now, Alana, don't blame yourself. I took my kids to Masset and spent a week with Sam. He has a thirty-foot Duckworth with double Yamaha outboards. All the latest electronics." Sorenson sighs and in a wistful voice says, "Sam was wonderful with my kids. We caught lots of fish. Sam talked highly of you and Quanah, and we spent hours discussing killer whales and this ocean creature called Wasgo. He was excited and honored that he could help Quanah with information about offshore killer whales and pleased to help such a great lawyer and nice person as you in your mission to find out what could have happened to your grandfather. Sam knew he would never go to college and found solace in the chance to help Quanah." Sorensen continues, "Sam was a very competent guide and sailor. I'll miss him. His disappearance may always remain a mystery, but you didn't cause it."

324

CHAPTER 44

Port Alberni, British Columbia

Quanah and Alana decide that Principe Channel, a branch off the Inland Passage, is a probable site to find an elusive beast that preys on humans. In addition, they can visit Skidegate in the Queen Charlotte Islands to pay their condolences to Sam's father. Hopefully, Sam's father will provide insight to his son's disappearance. They look at Internet maps and information of the islands and channels along the British Columbia Coast and find that Principe Channel is compatible with First Nation legends of Wasgo and the Warrior. Principe Channel is located between Banks Island and Pitt Island, it is deep and large enough to encompass the territory required of a large carnivore. It is readily reached from Prince Rupert and yet is remote because ocean traffic uses Hecate Strait.

Principe Channel is confined by steep mountains, which plunge into the water, making a perfect place to set a giant trap as described by Indian mythology. When Alana and Quanah attended the Tsimshian winter festivities, David's uncle told them that Ona River People avoid the channel because, forty years ago, a tribal member, while fishing for ling cod, disappeared, leaving no trace. Principe Channel is centrally located in respect to Haida, Tsimshian, Tlingit, Kwakwaka'wakw, and Bella Coola villages which have similar Wasgo totems and legends. Both resident and transient killer whales feed in Hecate Channel, which is connected to Principe Channel.

When Alana and Quanah had marveled at a Haida totem pole with a sea monster holding a person in his jaws in the Anthropology Museum, Alana remarked, "See? Indians relate killer whales to Wasgo."

Alana tells Quanah, "Considering that Sam was such a competent guide and knew the Queen Charlotte waters, he must have had an encounter with killer whales or Wasgo. I bet Sam's computer notes will shed light on his disappearance.

Alana and Quanah learned from Tsimshian shamans that the best time to lure Wasgo into a trap is at a full moon during spring high and slack tide. With these conditions the trap can be anchored to the shore and not seen by Wasgo because the horizon fuses to the world of sea. This notion is important as Indians recognize four worlds: Sky, Horizon, Sea or Earth, and the Underworld. Each realm has unique spiritual qualities. Alana muses, "Maybe the realm of Sky is Whiteman's heaven, Earth is the world we live in, and the underworld is Whiteman's hell. The fourth Indian realm of Horizon may be purgatory."

Quanah mutters, "Maybe."

Alana and Quanah drive from Seattle to Vancouver. The Nanaimo Ferry to Vancouver Island doesn't take reservations so they stay in the village of Delta and are up at five to make the six-a.m. ferry. George meets them at the Nanaimo ferry dock.

Quanah, extending his hand to George, says, "Hi Bro, here's a little something from the Olympics."

George smells the package and says, "Jerked elk. Thanks."

Alana extends her hand. "Hi George, it's great that you can spend a little time with us."

George takes Alana's hand. "Hello, Alana. Twice in a couple of months. I'm honored and pleased to see you both." His smile fades as he adds, "I still can't believe that Gus was killed. He always knew how to make peace between the Whiteman and Indian. But when it came to shove, Gus could hold his own in a barroom fight. And now Sam. There was never a better skipper than Sam." George shakes his head and adds, "Did you know that Daniel drove up a couple of times to visit me? I really came to like that little guy. I hope Quanah's whaling crew isn't jinxed. I may be next."

Alana sighs. "I know. It's all so sad. But I'm not surprised Daniel visited with you. He was writing a book on Indians and Jews. He was a reporter in his previous life."

Quanah adds, "Daniel could be irritating when getting the truth. He was always writing everything down. He pestered for written reports to verify everything I told him. He had trouble believing oral tradition." Quanah looks away and says, "I miss him. I learned a lot from Daniel."

After a few moments of silence, George changes the subject. "I'm always happy to talk about whales and Indian legends. I think it's important that you see the whaling sculpture at Port Alberni. Follow me on Highway 19 to Coombs. At Hilliers, you can ride with me to Port Alberni. Years ago, this sculpture was located in the main lobby of the Anthropology Museum in Vancouver. When it became politically incorrect to support whaling, the museum authorities moved the sculpture to Port Alberni."

In Port Alberni, walking to the sculpture of a whaling scene—now covered by a roof—Alana exclaims, "I see why you wanted to show us this sculpture. It's terrifying and beautiful at the same time. But it appears to have been left outside for years. Such a lovely piece of art should be inside."

George grimaces. "For Whites, yes, always protect everything."

"I don't understand."

"Everything in nature returns to its origin. Time is irrelevant. We believe this sculpture will return to nature, it is destined to rot as part of the Circle of Life. It doesn't bother us to watch totem poles rot."

"Ah," Alana says, "another thing my culture doesn't grasp. Like whaling. I love whales, and I must admit it hurts me that you guys want to whale again. This whole thing of hunting and killing gives me nightmares. I wake up thinking of whales, killer whales, and men drowning. In Syracuse, I knew what I stood for. Now I'm not sure, because you Indians have introduced me to a new realm of perception."

"Do you thank our creator every morning and night?" asks George.

"No, why?"

"Prayers keep bad spirits from entering your body."

"I don't believe everything you tell me."

Touching Alana's arm, Quanah looks deep into her eyes as he explains, "Most Indians accept living in two cultures. We have no other choice."

George points to the sculpture. "Alana, Indians say we 'catch' or 'take' a whale. We don't kill the spirit of Whale. Whale spirit joins the Great Spirit to complete the Circle of Life. Whiteman kills. Trophy hunters slaughter rhinos and lions for horns and capes. We honor the spirit when we take its body to feed our village. All animals and things have a spirit, which is why we respect all animals and nature."

Seeing Alana's perplexed face, George remarks, "You have discovered the difference between Whiteman and Indian. We think that White hunters aren't spiritual, and they don't see the interconnection of life. We have a circle of being such that Indian life is part of the circle. Everything has a spirit, and that's why spirits can pass between the living and all things in the world. The spirit of animal is as important as that of a man in the Circle of Life."

Alana retorts, "That belief is animism."

"No. We believe in a creator—and that all things and animals have a spirit. This is not animism because we don't worship animal spirits, we honor their spirit as part of what the creator made."

Alana slowly nods.

Quanah, admiring the sculpture, exclaims, "This is fantastic. The signboard says that a Vancouver artist, Lionel Thomas, designed the sculpture, and First Nation artists Godfrey Hunt and Douglas Cramer carved it. The harpoon is longer than the one I used. But the floats and lanyard draped over the paddles depicts the precision of the hunt and conveys the danger of getting tangled in the line. Look! The artist even placed two lances along the gunnels of the canoe. I see Sam at the tiller. By the way, the tiller paddle in the sculpture has been replaced with a normal sized one. The man representing Gus is playing out line. We could have posed for this sculpture, except the sculpture has a crew of eight and we had ten."

Alana, points to the sculpture. "It makes sense that the sculpture is realistic because the carvers are Nuu-chah-nulth." Turning to Quanah, she asks, "Why did you need a crew of ten Indians?"

Quanah answers, "I figured we needed ten to have the strength of eight traditional whalers."

Alana, still struggling with the concept of death and spirit, asks Quanah, "You have just thrust the harpoon into this beautiful, intelligent creature. It's going to die. How can you relate to this killing?"

George, resting his hand on Alana's shoulder, explains, "Alana, I just explained we didn't kill Whale's spirit."

Excitedly, Quanah points to the whaler, "Look, the canoe approaches Whale from the left, and the harpooner is left handed. I'm a lefty, and we also approached on the left side of Whale."

Alana says, "So, whalers always approach on the side of their dominate hand?"

Quanah answers, "To thrust the harpoon into Whale, you must have the correct stance to position your shoulders for maximal strength. Note that the whaler's feet are pressed against the gunnels for stability. His thrust is along the axis of his body for maximal power. Exactly like a quarterback throwing a football."

"I'm not a football fan, but I see your analogy." Looking at George she continues, "I think I understand your concept of spirit. Nevertheless, I can see why the officials moved this sculpture. To white people it's gruesome."

Standing back George muses, "As I recall, there were no smiles in our canoe. We knew that Whale body was dying. We felt his spirit leave his body." George sighs and continues, "I guess you have to be there to know death."

Quanah explains, "Yes, you have to be part of a hunt. I felt a spiritual connection to Whale through the harpoon. A very powerful feeling, because at that moment, Whale and I were a single being. Whaling started when Thunderbird caught Whale to feed our People. Thunderbird used lightning, which he hurled into Whale to catch it. That's the reason I carved a lightning bolt into the shaft of my harpoon. We gave pieces of whale to our People to connect all

People to Whale."

"That's true, and I felt part of the ceremony. Nevertheless, I have difficulty understanding the killing part on a gut level as you do, but I want to understand," sighed Alana.

Quanah, taking a folded, tattered piece of paper from his wallet, says, "Mattax, an Aleut, sent me this song from his village of St. Laurence Island, Alaska. I wanted to read it at the 'Distribution Ceremony' but I couldn't find it. Listen to this Whaling Song from Prince William Sound, written by an Aleut:

> '*After I have killed you,*
> *Do you want to see me dance?*
> *I would not feel bad, if the whale*
> *Dined with me!*
> *After I have killed the whale,*
> *He will feel fine with all*
> *The people around here.*'"

George adds, "Alana, this poem is a good example of the problem of translating an indigenous language into English. The English version sounds simple, because the complexities of indigenous syntax do not translate."

Pausing to let his comment sink in, George continues, "You will need to join Quanah on a hunt or when he fishes. After the Whiteman kills an elk, what does he do? His Buddy takes his picture. In Canada, the great White hunter has an Indian guide. The hunter gives the Indian the meat, has the head stuffed, and mounts it onto the wall. He doesn't care about the meat. That shows no respect for Animal's Spirit."

Alana is surprised as she hadn't seen George so animated, and she only manages, "Oh."

George asks, "Alana, have you heard the expression 'plinking' squirrels?"

"No."

"Whiteman shoots ground squirrels with his .22 rifle for sport. We don't understand this sport. This is killing to kill, and the squirrel is left to rot. Killing coyotes and wolves for fun is only Whiteman's sport. If we killed for sport, we couldn't honor an animal as a totem or portray the animal in ceremonies."

Smiling, as understanding dawns, Alana murmurs, "I've got it! In our ethnocentric, Eurocentric understanding of life, God created man with a soul and placed the animals on earth for man's use. Consequently, animals have no soul or spirit."

Quanah and George look at her and nod.

Alana continues, "Explain, why you didn't use a high-power rifle to dispatch the whale in what Whites believe to be a more humane manner?"

Pointing to the harpooner, Quanah explains, "Look at the sculpture, note how large Whale is. Exactly where is the brain? And think that the canoe would be pitching about in waves and that the shooter would need to have a steady stance. A well-placed lance will dispatch Whale better than rifle slugs."

"But the veterinarian for the legal 1999 hunt said that the rifle is humane."

Quanah explains in a condescending tone, "With all due respect for Dr. Allan Ingling, I don't think he understands hunting from a canoe. He doesn't understand Indian spiritualism. The use of the rifle was to appease the White community."

Pointing to the whale George explains, "Yes, we take Whale, we release his Spirit, and thus we can eat his body. We do not have the notion of 'humane killing' because we don't kill for sport but out of necessity. It is sacrilegious to kill for sport."

Quanah adds, "What you see in the sculpture is the end of the hunt. Standing here, we are not part of the preparation, the discussions of equipment, the rituals, and customs, the picking of crew members, and where they should sit. The practice. Getting ten men to function as one warrior and be part of the canoe. I'll take you fishing. It will help you understand." Quanah continues, "The Alaskan Aleut who wrote the poem told me that a few years ago, his People used a rifle to dispatch bowhead whales. The rifle didn't prove to be effective and they returned to the traditional lance. The rifle is an example of Whiteman telling us what to do."

George asks, "Alana, have you been in a sweat lodge?"

"Of course not. Why?"

"The sweat lodge makes the connection to the spiritual world, it is the link to tradition. It is where the past—our heritage—becomes present."

Quanah asks Alana, "Do you eat meat?"

"Yes?"

"Would you kill a cow?"

Alana doesn't attempt to hide her irritation, "Of course not."

Quanah pushes, "What happens to Cow's Spirit?"

Startled, Alana retorts, "You surprise me. I've never thought of this question."

Quanah thinks, *She has grit. Even outside the court room, she's holding her own. And, she's so attractive when she's mad. Her body language betrays emotion she hid in the court room. Standing by this magnificent sculpture she looks defenseless.*

"Quanah, what are you thinking?" Alana asks.

Instead of answering, Quanah reads from the information plaque and explains, "What really upsets me is that this sculpture was in a museum, and the directors decided it was politically incorrect. But the purpose of the museum is to preserve Indian culture. The carvers used Indians for models, reality is caught in solid yellow cedar. Whaling doesn't fit into the Whiteman's perception of our culture, so it was discarded."

George joins the tirade. "Yes, you're right, bro. A prime example of Whiteman's attempt to make us fit into their idea of who we are." Looking at Alana's solemn face, he adds. "Hey, let's give Alana a break, quit arguing, and have lunch."

After a pleasant lunch, the three friends say goodbye, with Quanah and George sharing a bear hug. Alana and Quanah continue north along the eastern coast of Vancouver Island to Port Hardy where they will catch the BC Ferry to Prince Rupert the following day.

They find the motel in Port Hardy. Alana insists they drive the eight miles to the ferry dock for practice. Reservations were required by the Circle Tour. Quanah pleads that a reservation means that they could arrive at 4:55 and still make the 5:00 A. M. sailing.

Alana argues, "We can't be on Indian time."

So, Quanah and Alana are in line at four a.m. It seems like there are hundreds of vehicles in front of them. To increase anxiety, the ticket taker motions them into a boarding lane for trucks. Cars keep loading and they sit. Finally, an official walks to the car with a long hockey-like stick. She stands it by the car and declares they are over-height and will have to pay another 198 Canadian dollars to board. The kayak on the roof makes their vehicle two inches too high.

Quanah says in a low voice, "I'm not superstitious but this is a bad start. Let's wait till tomorrow, and I can tie the kayak directly to the roof. Whites are always ripping off the Indian."

"Well, I can pay the extra."

Perplexed, Quanah asks, "Alana, you spent a lot to fly Gus to Alaska, and now this trip. How can you afford these?"

"I received a nice bonus after the lead poisoning case in Syracuse. After this trip, it will be gone. I should complain about the extra surcharge, but it wouldn't do any good."

To add insult, the deckhands had them park in a car lane where the roof deck was three feet above the kayak!

With the ferrying nightmare behind them, the fifteen-hour sail through the Inland Passage to Prince Rupert is lovely and relaxing. They are treated to the sight of several pods of feeding humpback whales. Arriving at 8:00 p.m. they find the Betty & Bruce B&B.

The next day they drive to Port Edward, the skeleton of a once thriving fish-canning town owned by The North Pacific Cannery. The town has been saved as a National Historic Site. It's one of the few remaining 19th century salmon canneries of nearly a thousand that were scattered from Alaska to California. Canneries at Port Edward along the Skeena River were the reason for the Grand Truck Railway of the Canadian Pacific to Prince Rupert.

Quanah and Alana pay a modest entrance fee and take the tour.

History is everywhere. The cannery buildings cover five acres. It once employed hundreds of First Nation Indians, Chinese, and seasonal white workers from Seattle, Vancouver, and Victoria.

Quanah can't resist, "An excellent example of Whiteman's exploitation of our People!"

Alana quickly replies, "Not just Indians. Yet, even with a history of intolerance, it saddens me to see the wharf pilings sinking and rotting into the muck. I see all this rusting equipment, canning ovens, carts with racks ready to be filled with cans of salmon. A whole industry is dead."

Their guide directs their attention to the only remaining automatic fish gutter in the world and tells them, "The conveyor belt dumped salmon into the hopper where whirling knives gutted and beheaded fish and spewed fillets out the other end. The machine processed a fish every 10 seconds and replaced twenty men."

Quanah reads the brass plate affixed to the cast iron frame, "The Iron Chink," and remarks, "This machine shows how the industry thought of their workers. It was OK when the Whiteman used Indians to work in the salmon and whaling industries, but now when we want to whale, the Whiteman forces his morality onto our tribe to keep us from our legal rights."

Squeezing Quanah's arm, Alana answers, "I see your point. Salmon distributors are now Japanese and Chinese companies, and Whites work for them."

Alana and Quanah watch salmon and halibut boats dock. Halibut are unloaded one at a time, weighed, tagged, and iced. A First Nation person keeps a tally for the Provincial Fisheries Department. Salmon caught with hooks by longlining are individually graded whereas those purse-seined are efficiently offloaded with a suction pump. They watch an older Indian with a young girl, probably his daughter, shove a hose into the hold. A pump sucks the slurry of salmon, ice, and sea water into a ten-inch tube which dumps the slurry into a dock hopper. Two rows of sorters grab fish as they whisk down a sluice and toss them into boxes labeled Chinook, Pink, Sockeye, and Coho. Battered fish are chucked into a separate bin. Once a box is full, it is weighed. All boxes are tallied for Provincial Government records and attributed to the boat that unloaded them. A forklift places boxes into a refrigeration trailer. The fish tallies are used to determine when Indian and White quotas are reached. The best fish are trucked to a fast freezing facility to be shipped to U.S. and Japanese markets.

Quanah, obviously upset, says, "Working here, the Indian loses his heritage. It is not possible to respect the salmon. Today, few Indians are employed. The Whiteman moves the Indian to the company town, but, when the canneries close, Indians are forced to move to cities. A diaspora."

Surprised Alana asks, "Where did you learn diaspora?"

"You're stereotyping, again! If you must know, Daniel and I have discussed the similarities of Jewish history to Indian's."

Having been counseled to patiently wait until fishermen received their catch receipts before approaching a boat captain, Alana and Quanah watch the Indian father and daughter finish unloading. They work as a good team. When the fisherman takes out a cigarette, they approach the boat.

Quanah says, "Hi, your catch is impressive."

The boat captain replies, "Thanks."

"Good year?"

"Yeah. Where're you from?"

"Neah Bay."

Boat captain looks to Alana. "My girl, she loves to fish. Do you fish?"

Pleased to be noticed, Alana responds, "No, but I love to eat fish. My man here, he fishes."

Blushing, Quanah quickly changes the subject. "Do you know Dr. David? The doctor who was part of the Makah whale hunt?"

The boat captain climbs up the ladder to the dock and extends his hand to Quanah. "Of course I know David. We are proud down at Ona village. David is our doc. I'm Frankie."

Taking the captain's hand, Quanah continues, "Do you know someone who could take us to a camp site in Principe Channel where we could kayak for a week? After hearing stories from Dr. David, we thought it would be exciting to explore the region."

Alana offers, "We can pay."

"No, you don't pay, I'll take you. You're the chief whaler on the hunt, aren't you?"

Quanah manages a soft, "Yep."

Alana and Quanah don't tell Frankie their real objective, fearing he would not approve of their quest and not ferry them to Principe Channel. He could be superstitious and believe that Stick People would make mischief.

The next day they meet Captain Frankie, load their kayak, supplies, and equipment onto the fishing boat, and motor to Principe Channel. Frankie knows the perfect spot with a long beach at the end of an inlet. He offloads supplies and cautions them to watch for sudden squalls and rip tides.

Taking Quanah's hand, the boat captain advises, "If you see trenches in the beach as if someone had been digging clams, be sure to move, because the digger would be a grizzly. I will return in a week."

Quanah and Alana find a protected, level spot fifty yards from the beach for their campsite. The place is a midden (shell heap) of clam shells and fire pits. Pushing a pile of clam shells with his foot Quanah remarks, "Yes, this is a good spot to connect with my spiritual past."

CHAPTER 45

Camping at Principe Channel

The first evening, they walk the beach. The tide is low and Quanah is able to rip exposed mussels from rocks. They also find a bed of rock scallops in a talus slide that disappears into the channel. Though protected by law, they gathered a few anyway. Quanah found three red rock crabs tucked into rocky crevices.

Pointing to a black abalone tightly adhering to a rock Quanah explains, "These are prized by Indian artists for inlays and medallions. They are protected in the US and Canada, but it wasn't the Indian that depleted them. Whiteman destroys the environment, exterminates animals, and blames the Indian."

Looking over the beach Alana asks, "It's low tide, and no holes dug by bears; why not dig clams?"

Smiling, Quanah answers, "It's not the bears that are a problem. Even though there's no evidence of a red tide in this channel, the protozoa that make toxin are found everywhere in British Columbia waters."

"What does that mean?"

"Clams are filter feeders and filter poisonous protozoans. The toxins are absorbed into the clam tissue. During a plankton bloom, people shouldn't eat clams."

"What about grizzly bears eating poison clams?"

"In the fall, bears should be catching salmon that are spawning in creeks and rivers. I hope we see one. I'd like to have his claws."

"You're kidding?"

Quanah just smiles.

Returning to camp with the spoils of nature, Quanah builds a fire and starts boiling water. He adds potatoes, carrots, celery, and onion. He steams a rock fish, which he caught with a hand line using a clam as bait, in aluminum foil. After the veggies cook, he adds mussels, crabs, and scallops to the pot. When the mussels open, he adds fish chunks and spices. Quanah exclaims, "Voila, bouillabaisse." He cracks a giant purple sea urchin and scoops out the eggs in a spoon and holds it to Alana, "Here try this for an appetizer."

"Too salty. I don't know why the Japanese and sea otters relish these."

The second day Quanah and Alana troll along the shore with a piece of rock fish skin. A ling cod takes the bait and pulls the kayak into a kelp bed. Finally, Quanah brings the fish to the kayak and they tow it to the beach. Ling are lovely with mottled reds, rusts, and brown patterns to blend into forests of kelp.

As she watches Quanah grab his knife, Alana blurts, "Don't kill it. Let it go."

"O' Chief from Above. You gave us Great Fish." As Quanah thrusts his knife into fish's brain he softly continues, "Thy Great Name is Daylight. *Sahalce Tyee*"

"What did you say?"

"Nothing."

"I distinctly heard 'great fish.' Did you offer a prayer?"

"Maybe."

Exasperated Alana asks, "Why are you so evasive? It's like you're hiding something. You talked about Circle of Life in the Tacoma bar and with George at the whaling sculpture in Port Alberni. Are you practicing your religion?"

Quanah doesn't answer. He leaves the skin attached to the fillets, ties them to a bleached piece of driftwood with a kelp rope. He shoves the driftwood into the sand with flesh toward the fire. Within minutes, fat is glazing the surface and the fillets are grilled.

Resigned, Alana opens her mouth for the offered tidbit. She thought to refuse the peace offering but decided not to. "It tastes like halibut but milder."

After the meal, Quanah stuffs the back bone and head into a shrimp pot, adds a rock, ties a rope and tosses the trap into the channel. He lashes the rope to a large rock.

Alana asks, "What did you feel when you killed the ling cod?"

"Alana, you're not in court, and I'm not on the witness stand. We caught the fish."

"I know. I don't want to be rude. I want to understand."

After a long pause Quanta whispers, "I don't know that I can explain my feelings."

The camp fire is burning brightly. Quanah pokes at the burning logs, producing showers of sparks, shooting upwards, leaving red oscillating ribbons, tangling through smoke. Flames dance as the night shadows close about Quanah and Alana. They sit close to avoid smoke. The smell of her soap mingles with his aroma of red cedar boughs.

Sensing that she has an edge and with an attempt to break the tension pushing them apart like aligned magnets, Alana quips with a girlish laugh, "Sir, the question before the court is?"

Quanah's feelings are electric. Personal gratification must be pushed aside for a whaler. They don't fit into a hunt. And, they are on a hunt. Quanah returns to the present. "What?"

Alana presses her argument, "You were talking to the fish. Were you spiritually connecting to the fish before killing it?"

Quanah looking at her face thinks, *She does look Indian. In fact, she looks more Indian than I do. She knows who she is. She is lovely and smart, but not Indian. White, through and through.* He turns away, thinking, *I need to focus on the upcoming hunt.*

Both stare into the fire when Alana begs, "Quanah, talk to me."

"Oh, yeah," he says with a sigh. "Where are we? Remember what George said, 'We don't kill animals, we catch them and their spirit continues to live outside their body. I don't think of the spirit as a soul. The spirit isn't unique, in that every animal and every thing in nature has a spirit. Everything is part of Mother Earth."

Alana pokes at the fire to release another shower of sparks and asks, "You were telling me how you feel when you kill a fish. Remember, you're not on trial. Take your time. We have all night. I think I'm starting to understand Indian spirituality."

Quanah shakes his head slowly, his resistance broken. "I have never attempted to explain my feelings in words. I grew up with an understanding that life is sacred." Pausing a moment to think, he continues, "My dad took me elk hunting when I was young. We had been hunting for several days with no luck. It was almost dark, and we were walking back to the pickup when we saw this bull elk standing on a ridge. Dad shot and Elk just stood there. Elk didn't even jump. Then the bull was gone. As we walked up the slope, I thought Dad had missed. He hadn't. Elk lay crumpled against an alder tree, his neck bent backwards. He was looking at me. I touched his nose. I felt Elk's spirit pass through me. I touched Elk's eyeball. It had turned to glass."

After a pause, Quanah continues, softly, "Elk didn't blink. His body was dead. Dad told me we had to thank Elk's spirit, because his spirit was still about us."

Alana whispers, "Wow, that's poetic."

"Dad closed Elk's eyes. He thanked Elk for giving us winter meat. That big bull dressed 350 pounds, and Dad distributed all but 50 pounds to the elders. When an Indian gets his first deer or elk, our culture asks that we offer the meat to our elders."

"That's spiritual. Is that why you knew where to find your dad? Oh, I'm sorry, I didn't mean to pry."

They both poke about in the fire when Alana finally asks, "You thanked Cod?"

"I had a feeling, not words. Now you understand why it's important that we catch Whale."

"I'm beginning to understand. I admire you. The Indian gives thanks directly to the animal. In the Whiteman's religion, at the table, we thank God for providing food."

As the fire dies, the Milky Way brightens. A great horned owl announces his presence.

On the third day, they find a giant red cedar, with a three-foot diameter base that toppled into the channel leaving its roots anchored into the rocky shore. The crown, sticking 150 feet into the channel, floats up and down with the tide. Quanah bumps the limbs and tops the crown. The pieces float away. Alana is surprised how easily they split the trunk in half with wedges made from driftwood. Quanah pries the initial split apart with levers and keeps the two halves spread with spacers. The split trunk makes the jaws of a giant trap. The trunk resembles the Haida petroglyph that Sam claims depicts a trap used by his ancestors to catch Wasgo. Quanah constructs the trigger mechanism from two six-foot logs of eight-inch diameter and a six-foot 2 x 6 board they gleaned from the beach. He hacks notches near the ends of the logs. He uses the board for the horizontal part of a figure-4 deadfall trap, binding the ends together with kelp. The vertical log functions as a spacer to keep the jaws apart. The second log forms the angle of the figure 4 to keep the spacer upright which in turn holds the jaws open.

While Quanah was making the trap, he noticed a trail of crab legs and carapaces leading to an octopus lair under a flat rock. Using the ax handle as a lever, he pries the rock up and down. When the octopus squirts out, Quanah is ready and grabs the slippery, eight-armed mollusk. The octopus immediately wraps Quanah's arm with some of his and seeks anchorage with other arms thrust into the rock pile. Quanah is careful to keep the octopus's bell, which houses a sharp, parrot like beak, off his arm. The suction cups make welts on Quanah's arm. One octopus arm comes free, holding a rock, and Quanah severs two which stubbornly hold into a rocky crevice. The severed arms continue to wiggle about like eels. They seem to have a mind of their own. The remaining five arms encircle Quanah's chest. Out of water the boneless creature has no

shape. The battle is over when Quanah thrusts Gus's hunting knife between the eyes of the slippery mass of writhing flesh. Within a second, the red skin fades to ghost white, signaling death. This is only a ten-pound animal.

Quanah notices Alana is as pale as the dead mollusk. He thinks, *Wow, she looks more like a little girl than a tough lawyer.* Taking her in his arms, he murmurs, "Alana, you're trembling. Are you OK?"

She doesn't answer, but she doesn't pull away.

At camp, Alana whispers, "Thank you for helping me regain my footing. I did feel faint." She watches Quanah deftly skin the arms and cut the white flesh into sections. He stirs the pieces into sizzling oil and adds them to spaghetti garnished with sea weed, pepper and caramelized onions.

"Octopus is tender and tastier than calamari," Alana exclaims, "What a treat! How do you know how to cook so well?"

"Remember, my mother is German."

After supper, Quanah washes his upper body at the beach.

Alana shouts, "You don't need to dry off with cedar boughs, we do have towels." As he comes closer, she asks, "What's with the tattoos?"

"I had an identity crisis."

"What's the symbolism?"

"My heritage."

"I didn't see those diagrams in the Makah Museum, and they aren't Germanic. Are they occult?"

"No."

"So...?"

"So! What do you want to know?"

Alana thinks, *Why couldn't he just answer a simple question,* but says, "I don't have you on the witness stand."

"They link to my heritage."

"You already said that!"

"There are many Indian types. Anthropologists think that coastal Indians migrated across the Bering Strait during the last ice age from China. The Plains Indians are taller and may have roots back to Mongolia. But Indians believe we have been here from the beginning of time."

Alana nods. "The Bering Strait route is an old idea. Recently anthropologists found that DNA of American Indians is a unique blend of Mongolian and Eastern Chinese, DNA not found anywhere else in the world. So, you're correct that Indian DNA is unique and has been here from the beginning of Indian occupation."

Impatient, Quanah replies, "Again, you are interpreting our heritage to fit White perceptions."

"And you?" asks Alana.

"Some Haida and Nootka are tall. It is quite probable that we also have Maori and Pacific Islander/Hawaiian blood from Captain Cook's crew. Japanese and Russian people were ship wrecked along Cape Alava, too. Spanish, English, Filipinos, Americans, and Scotts have also left DNA in the Makah Tribe."

Sensing a chance to make a point against whaling, Alana jumps to catch Quanah off guard. "Did you know that the Maori of New Zealand don't whale anymore?"

"I didn't know that. The Icelanders and Japanese whale and whale watch. What people do in other countries is their business, and they follow their belief. Other cultures don't alter my wish to reinstate whaling for the Makah Tribe. The eleven Aleut villages in Alaska take fifty bowheads a year. The Aleut who sent the song told me they have kept their customs. They are too far north for the animal activists to interfere."

"Too cold, too," answers Alana. "I can understand the Eskimo needing to kill whales for sustenance, their villages are so remote. Icelanders and the Maori's of New Zealand have whale watching guides. By the way, the Maori towns are remote. Whale watching would provide work and income for the Makah," Alana suggests.

Quanah walks off to gather more firewood saying, "Whale watching would be a good project, and you could help organize it."

When Quanah returns with wood, Alana continues, "Thinking of the origin of Native Americans, I read in *Smithsonian Magazine* that Kennewick man, whose skeleton was found in Washington

State, was probably Asian. You said that Indians don't believe in the land bridge. What do you think?"

As Quanah pokes about in the fire, Alana persists, "Are you ignoring your German heritage?"

Quanah stands and steps closer to Alana. "Aaron said you won a big legal case in Syracuse. Why did you move to Seattle?"

"For a change."

"As you would say, that's no answer. Why did you defend us in Tacoma?"

Alana pushes sand about with her feet and answers, "I didn't mind defending you because a lawyer must distance herself from her client. I still love whales. As to leaving Syracuse, my firm was about to litigate a class action suit representing children with deformities and conjoined twins."

"Since you won the first case, why not continue?"

"These deformities are sad, and parents suffer. I didn't think I had the stomach to continue."

Quanah drops to the sand beside Alana. "Describe conjoined twins."

Alana nods. "The common name is Siamese Twins. It just means that the two babies' bodies are connected. Our case was two heads attached to one body. Each head is a person, and they share the same trunk, organs, and limbs. Lead in drinking water may cause the fetal cells to remain together instead of completely separating into twins so that the developing fetuses remain joined."

Quanah presses closer, "A strange world we live in. Some versions of sea serpent are called Sisiutl. This serpent has one body with two heads."

After breakfast, Quanah, looking serious, says, "Alana, I want to show you an interesting place I found yesterday. The walk will take an hour. OK?"

"Sure, what's the intrigue?"

"You'll see. Let's go."

They hike about two miles to reach a bench four hundred yards from the shoreline. Torches of sunlight filter through the canopy of giant Douglas firs, illuminating the forest floor like spots on a leopard. Moss hangs from limbs and covers every surface with a thick green carpet.

Pushing against a stump, Quanah remarks, "See this broken trunk?"

"Yes." Looking around, she says, "This is an eerie place; let's go back."

"We're in a cemetery, probably not used for 80 years. The Indians that made the middens at camp buried their dead here. Mortuary boxes have toppled from tree trunks and rotted."

Quanah picks a seven-inch yellow slug from its gossamer track on the green carpet. Smiling, he holds it out for Alana, "Look at this lemon slug."

"No," she replies, retreating a couple steps.

Scraping moss and slug slime from the rotting log, Quanah says, "You can make out the eyes of a carved bear. This fallen log was a mortuary pole, and the bear totem protects the dead person."

Looking about wildly Alana whispers, "This is a sacred place. There are probably real bears stalking us. I'm ready to go."

Quanah, rummaging around the base of the tree stump and stacking bones into a pile, says, "No, we aren't ready to leave. I haven't smelled any bear poop."

"Quanah, those are human remains. Let them be, please."

"Hey, White woman, I thought you were not spiritual." Quanah continues to sift through decades of the detritus of decay to triumphantly exclaim, "Come here. Look!"

Alana watches as Quanah wipes the skull clean. The upper jaw is smooth. The teeth had fallen out long before death as the sockets are filled with bone. The smooth mandible indicates an ancient person.

Quanah kisses the skull, stained green with chlorophyll, between the eye sockets. He calls, "Alana, come here, please."

"No, I'm not kissing that skull."

"For our hunt tonight, it is important, because Spirit will protect you."

Alana, now pale as a ghost, answers, "I don't believe that!"

"White folks visit cemeteries all the time and pray to loved ones and ancestors. The only difference is that Whites bury their dead in expensive coffins, so they won't imagine worms at work. In the past, Indians placed their dead in a grave or left the bodies exposed until the bones were picked clean by ravens and coyotes. To the Indian, the body must return to earth. Bones are bones, covered or not. White people display bones of saints in cathedrals and pray to them."

"How do you know that?"

"My German Uncle showed me a crystal reliquary containing *Gutta sanguinis Christi* and an ivory box containing St. Jacob's bones. We were in the Rothenburg cathedral in Germany."

"Wow, you remember details. What's your point with the blood of Christ and the bones of Jacob?"

"Both Indians and White folks worship bones and relics. Honoring bones of dead ancestors protected my crew during the whale hunt, and this explains why Whale gave himself to us. It is a tradition of the Hamatsu to pray to bones. A skull of ancestors connects to the Spirit. Alana, if you don't believe in spirits, you shouldn't care."

Alana stiffens. "David's Uncle's ceremony was personal, and it seemed natural. Kissing a skull is quite different. Maybe if David's Uncle were here, I would feel differently."

"You were initiated by David's Uncle. Here, kiss the skull."

"My God, you remind me of Mel Gibson in his movie rendition of *Hamlet*."

"*Hamlet*; never saw the movie."

"*Hamlet*, by Shakespeare. When gravediggers dug into an old grave for a new one, they dug up the bones and skull of Yorick, Hamlet's teacher. Hamlet, played by Mel Gibson, talked to the skull as if Yorick still resided in it."

Quanah approaches Alana holding the skull to her lips saying, "Yes, Hamlet was addressing the Spirit of his teacher."

As if under the spell of Uncle, Alana places dry lips on the slick, damp forehead. Quanah returns the bones and skull and covers them with moss as he had found them.

Walking into camp, Alana exclaims, "Quanah, the clam shells under our sleeping pads were tossed by the person belonging to that skull!"

They have shrimp for supper. Quanah produces a bottle of Riesling.

"You're full of surprises," Alana exclaims, "A Cabernet Sauvignon for yesterday's bouillabaisse. You ordered wines in the Tacoma bar. How do you know about wines?"

"My mother is from a wine producing region in Germany."

After supper they paddle to the trap to watch the sun—a deep red disk—fall into the horizon. Quanah stuffs a burlap sack with bodies of dead shrimp, of which they'd eaten the tail meat, and ties the sack to the floating tip of the trap for a chum slick.

Alana, taking the seat on the horizontal board of the figure-4 trap manages a meek, "I don't appreciate being bait. Yet, according to oral tradition, I will attract the beast that prays on women and men." Alana sighs and continues, "I have to face the jury foremen to hear the verdict. So, let's do it."

Quanah fumbles with the rope as he passes it around Alana's chest. With a wavering voice, he says, "Don't worry."

She gulps and asks, trembling, "Will the Whaler or Wasgo get the girl in the deadfall?"

He ties the rope, answering, "When Wasgo comes for you, and if you don't jump, I'll pull you from the figure-4 to spring the trap."

Alana, leaning against the upright post of the figure-4 deadfall trap which keeps the jaws apart, resolutely asks, "Indian legends, coyote and raven stories, these are grandmother tales for grandchildren. Who is the Wasgo legend intended for?"

Quanah ignores her question while adjusting the horizontal trigger into the notches of the vertical post of the figure-4 trap. Alana sits on the part of the horizontal board, which sticks past the vertical post. Thus, her weight keeps the vertical spacer between the trap jaws.

Trembling, Alana whispers, "I'm now not so sure I want to attract Wasgo! But I have invested so much research. I need to know." Alana pauses, then whispers, "Will I die?"

Holding Alana's shoulders Quanah asserts, "You will not die. When I pull you from the horizontal trigger board, all three parts will fly apart, and the tree trunk jaws will snap together and catch the beast. You'll see."

"Three parts?"

"The three parts of the trap form the number 4. Thus, the name, 'figure-4 trap.' A primitive but effective deadfall trap."

"This is pure witchcraft. Where will I fall?"

"Just stay on the trigger board. If you fall asleep and don't jump into the water, I'll pull you from the seat, and you will fall into the water. You don't have to do anything." He pauses. "Are you sure you want to do this?"

"I'm sure," she says.

Quanah plays the rope and sits against a beached log, sixty feet away. Alana squirms. Little sand crabs scratch along the tree-trunk. The red horizon turns orange with a flash of green, then blue, then gray, and finally black. The Milky Way appears with the North Star. The moon breaks the horizon and hovers to illuminate the shore. Quanah looks to be asleep. By 3:00 a.m. nothing has happened. High tide slacks. The trap is horizontal to merge with the horizon. Alana drifts, thinking, *I should have drunk more coffee.*

Visions of a decaying humpback whale that had floated onto a beach north of Seattle are intermingled with an oil tanker which killed it. Now, this beautiful, intelligent creature is a lump of one-hundred tons of putrefying muscle, fat, and guts. No form, just a stench emanating from an undefined hill. She has never, in all her life, smelled anything so revolting. It is worse than rotting clams. Some beach combers puked.

Alana opens her eyes. "What smells?" she wonders. The full moon is soft, filtered, and enlarged by a blanket of thick air. Not a ripple on the water. A school of squid dart about catching red-eyed shrimp. Squid eyes reflect a yellowish light from the lantern that

351

hangs from a limb behind her. Squid dart erratically, here and there, leaving tangled ribbons of phosphorescence when colliding with unicellular *Noctilluca phosphorescence* protozoans. Exploding rings of yellow-green light indicate squid are bumping into jellyfish. A ling cod drifts from the kelp bed to snatch a squid. Alana is suspended between worlds. She is in the horizon, the world between sky and water. Groups of foot-long sandworms swim upwards, converge and wiggle frantically to release clouds of eggs and sperm. Patches of silvery spawn indicate the horizon, keeping plankton, shrimp, squid, worms, and ling cod in their world of sea, and Alana in her world of Horizon.

Time is suspended. Alana composes a poem for squid:

Melody for Loligo
In the soup of life
dressing to survive
Speckled for catching
the red-eyed shrimp
Banded for escaping
the toothed Ling
Pulsing, fawning, jetting
with a prospective mate.

This is strange as Alana has never composed a poem. Perhaps the reason for this poetic revelation is that she has entered the dimension of the Fourth World, that of Horizon. A world of vision, thoughtfulness. The Horizon, a world of meaning and creativity. She is bait for a creature living between worlds of sea and undersea. She is in the Horizon, the interface of life and death.

Alana is jolted back to reality by the putrid smell to ask, "Why the smell?"

With jet propulsion, squid dart into the depths, others rocket over the log. Light from the lantern is reflected from an enormous eye drifting toward the trap. It glows like a dog's eye caught in headlights. She thinks of Edward Munch's painting, *The Scream*. The eye, now with head, drifts closer. There is not a ripple. The creature floats on the Horizon. Its mouth opens exposing long rows of white, conical teeth. The creature's pink tongue slides along the tree-trunk. Now Alana understands the reason for the barb which Quanah had fashioned from a yew. He had fire-hardened the point and swaged the base into the upper trap jaw. The two-foot barb is positioned to hit the hole in the lower trap jaw when the trap is sprung. She looks into the maw. She can think, but can't yell or jump!

"Am I dreaming?"

As the creature's tongue presses her leg, she answers, "No."

354

CHAPTER 46

September - Friday Harbor
"Alas! Poor Yorick. I knew him…
Here hung those lips that I have kissed…
to mock your own grinning?"

Alana sits upright in bed exclaiming, "That's what Hamlet said to the skull of Yorick as he dusted the cranium of dirt. Yorick, the court jester who carried young Hamlet about on his back."

It's been five years since Alana took the course in Shakespeare. The night had not been restful but full of monsters and skulls. She thinks, *There is something to the Indian legend of spirits protecting hunters after all. Am I becoming Indian?*

The past few months had been quite stressful, but interesting and successful. Her law firm is preparing to argue before the Supreme Court because the Ninth Court of Appeals overturned Judge Krieger's ruling. The animal activists have lots of money to fight the Makah whalers in court.

Alana routinely escapes Seattle to stay with the Applegates for weekends. Having no children, Meg and Charlie have unofficially adopted her. It is mutually beneficial, as Alana's mother, living in Syracuse, is too far away to offer a sympathetic shoulder.

It's about eight, and Alana hasn't had the luxury of sleeping this late for weeks. The smell of ham and eggs permeates her upstairs room.

"Ouch," she gasps. Absentmindedly, she rubs her left armpit and gasps again. Her three broken ribs are painful. They broke when Quanah jerked her from the trap. She can't remember what the monster looked like except for its yellow eye. *I was like a deer frozen by headlights. I don't remember what happened next until I was in the kayak.*

Meg knocks at the door asking, "Alana, are you OK? You were yelling."

"I'm fine. Please come in."

"My goodness Alana, you are covered with scabs! What happened?"

"I was bait for Wasgo, and when Quanah jerked me from his jaws into the water, the thrashing creature pushed me into the shore. The gashes were made by barnacles covering the rocks."

"You shouldn't pick at the scabs," Meg warns. They'll get infected. How in the world did you get out of the water? You're lucky to be alive!"

"Quanah got me into the kayak and back to camp. I was unconscious. I guess Quanah learned how to revive someone from hypothermia from David when the crew saved Ben. When I came to, I was in a sleeping bag. Quanah lifted me back into the kayak and paddled toward the Tsimshian village of Kilkatla, ten miles to the north. The tide was strong, and we were swept past the inlet, so we missed Kilkatla village."

"Oh, my goodness, you must have feared for your life," Meg exclaimed.

"No, because I wasn't aware of our predicament. The next village is Ona River, an additional fifteen-mile paddle. Quanah didn't talk but paddled like a wild man, and we made the Tsimshian Village of Ona River. We knew the spiritual power of Uncle's Hamatsu watched over us when we saw David at Ona River. I had a perforated lung, so he flew us to Prince Rupert."

Meg gasped. "You poor dear! And what made the burn under your armpit?"

"It's from the rope Quanah used to pull me to shore."

Looking into the mirror, Alana sighs, "That trip was a mix of survivor and extreme sports. I was a lure for Wasgo, and now I can't remember what he looked like. Hopefully, we'll try to find the creature again next year."

Meg replies, "I hope you reconsider, you could have died!"

"No. I was protected by Uncle's Hamatsu ritual. As to what

happened to my grandfather? I believe that some sea creature killed him. But is the sea creature Wasgo or a rogue killer whale?"

Smiling, Meg hugs Alana and says, "You're spending too much time with Quanah. You can't believe in all that Indian baloney he's telling you. *Circle of Life*, what nonsense."

When Alana only smiles, Meg adds, "We have breakfast ready. Come down when you're dressed."

Looking over the harbor to the Lab, Alana ponders, *I'm pretty sure Quanah remembers what the creature looks like. He won't tell because of his Indian thing. I'll have to pander to his German heritage.*

As Alana comes down, Meg says, "Alana, good. We have eggs and ham and your favorite blackberry jam. Charlie made fresh muffins."

Looking puzzled, Charlie asks, "Did you see the harpoon in the hallway?"

"Yes, it's a Makah whaling harpoon."

Charlie's demeanor doesn't change. "The locals are really divided about the whaling court case. As you would expect, the academics and fisherman are against the Indians, but for different reasons."

"Yes, I know."

"Now Charlie, let the poor girl eat."

"No, it's OK to talk about the case."

Charlie says, "I found the harpoon sticking in the lawn in front of the B&B sign. Is it some kind of threat?"

Alana, blushing, replies, "No."

Meg, always sympathetic and calm, says, "Well dear, you obviously know what it means, but you don't have to explain."

"It's clear to everybody in town and at the labs that I spend a lot of time with you folks and that you have sort of adopted me." Alana takes a bite, chews, and says, "These muffins are delicious."

Charlie asks, "So, what about the harpoon?"

"Yes, my goodness dear, you are certainly a Pauline!"

With a confused smile, Alana asks, "Pauline?"

Meg continues, "In just the short time we've known you, you've been in a plane crash, adrift in the ocean, lost in the Inland Passage rowing a skiff at the mercy of wind and tide. You had a punctured lung, were in a barroom brawl, saved Indians during an Indian battle in Seattle. You were the bait for some sort of sea monster, arrested as an illegal alien, and now harpoons. And, we don't know what else."

Meg stops for a breath, then continues, "To answer your question, Pauline refers to the *Perils of Pauline* serials which played in the 1950s in movie houses. Long before your time, but the era of your Granddad's childhood. The Pauline episodes followed news clips and Mickey Mouse cartoons before the main feature. The heroine, Pauline, escapes from being tied to train tracks in front of an oncoming train, she swims in a raging river after being spilled from a canoe, survives an airplane crash, and wanders in a desert to escape marauding Indians waving blond scalps. You, my dear, are our Pauline." With a soft giggle, Meg continues, "But you, my dear, have only one cat-life left."

Alana, blushing and with a halting voice, "There wasn't a barroom brawl, simply a confrontation. I didn't stop the fight at the shipping canal in Seattle, the police separated the Whites from Indians. The harpoon is symbolic of a contract, not danger."

Meg and Charlie exclaim in unison, "This isn't a Whiteman's threat? It's Indian?"

"Yes, Indian. But not a threat. You are my parents to the lab folks."

Exasperated Charlie complains, "You know how to beat around the bush."

Alana takes another bite as she decides how to answer.

Suddenly, solitude is shattered by war whoops and hollering. They rush to the front window. On the lawn are ten Indians, dressed in costume, wearing masks, waving paddles and spears and beating drums. Alana recognizes Louise and her baby. The tallest warrior is dressed in a bearskin robe, he wears a fierce mask covered with matted, long hair, supporting a big red nose, with red lips wide open exposing a toothless grin, except for one errant tooth. A wild, hideous grin. A wild man.

Now smiling Alana says, "That mask on the tall Indian doesn't look quite right to be Indian. Maybe German." She giggles and continues, "I think the last stanza of the Little Indians played at Keel Café in Tacoma is happening."

"What are you talking about?"

Alana explains, "You know the old children's song about the ten little Indians,

"Two little Injuns foolin' with a gun
it went off, and then there was one."

Meg and Charlie exclaim, "Oh my," as the man sporting the German *Fashing* mask throws a lance into the lawn in front of the Lottia B&B sign.

Charlie gasps, "That's where I found the harpoon this morning!"

Meg stammers, "Yes, yes, you are Pauline reincarnate."

The masked man picks up a stack of Pendleton blankets and dances up the steps.

Now, Meg has lost her usual composure and exclaims, "What's he doing with the blankets?"

Alana, giving Meg a hug, "The blankets are for you and Charlie. They signify an engagement dowry."

Alana sings the last stanza:

"One little Injun, buck free,
found me and there'll be three."

Modern Six-Man Race
After one mile the Makah and Nuu-chah-nulth teams
are neck and neck. Neah Bay (MEK photo).
A testament to today's vitality in Indian villages

Circle of Life - End and Beginning
A toppled totem pole of a man holding a talking stick.
The end, symbolized by decay and return to earth.
Grass growing in the decaying wood symbolizes the beginning.

Figure descriptions

Cover: Makah waiting. Thunderbird carrying Whale. Painting by Amrita Stützle.

Chapter 1a: Whaler chief. A. Curtis, 1903. (Library congress, MEK photo) -*page 1*

Chapter 1b: Western tip of continental United States. (MEK photo) - *page 7*

Chapter 2: Cape Alava. (MEK photo) -*page 8*

Chapter 3a: Cape Flattery. Entrance into Strait of Juan de Fuca. Mount Olympus in background, Tatoosh Island in foreground. (Library of Congress, MEK photo) -*page 13*

Chapter 3b: Thunderbird with Whale. Alert Bay. (MEK photo) -*page 17*

Chapter 4: Syracuse Federal Building. (Amrita Stützle photo) -*page 18*

Chapter 5a: War canoe. Edward Curtis, 1911. Alert Bay, B.C., Canada. Canoe used in the 1913 Curtis movie, *In the Land of the Headhunter* (Library of Congress, MEK photo) -*page 28*

Chapter 5b: The Reluctant Conscript paddler – Figure in bronze sculpture by Bill Reed. Human paddling in figure is "The Reluctant Conscript" inspired by a Robert Frost poem. -*page 37*

Chapter 5c: Ship of Fools. Bronze sculpture by Bill Reed in front of Canadian Embassy, Washington DC. (Oliver Brown photo) -*page 39*

Chapter 6a: West coast map of North America. Gray whales mi-

361

Chapter 45d: Trap for Wasgo. Haida. Note warrior on top of trap. Wasgo has caught woman who was used as bait. From F. Boas *(Primitive Art) -page 353*

Chapter 46a: Ritual of 'Hamatsu'. E. Curtis 1911. Library of Congress. (MEK photo) *-page 354*

Chapter 46b: Pendleton blankets *-page 359*

Back cover: Dancer mask with red and green sea serpents. "T'sil – Pit Took". Makah Nation. Wyaatch Village. C. Wade Greene, artist. (MEK photo)

Makah drum. Wasgo is used as a canoe. Spencer McCarty, artist.

Publisher Photo Credits:

Chapter 33a. Tilman Riemenschneider photo by Helga Schmidt-Glassner. Courtesy of Langewiesche Nachfolger KG, Koenigstein/ Taunus, Germany.
Chapter 43. Relief carving by author after Franz Boas cover, *Primitive Art.* Dover Publications, Inc.
Chapter 45d. Heida trap for Wasgo. Franz Boas, *Primitive Art.* Dover Publications, Inc.

References

General Native American:
Adams, G. *The Coeur d'Alene Indian Reservation.* Ye Galleon Press
Boas, F. *Primitive Art.* Dover
Coté, C. *Spirits of our Whaling Ancestors.* University of Washington Press
Drew, L. *Haida: Their Art and Culture.* Hancock House
Drucker, P. *Indians of the Northwest Coast.* The Natural History Press

Erikson, P. P. with H. Ward & K. Wachendorf. *Voices of a Thousand People*. University of Nebraska Press

Haeberlin, H. and Gunther, E. *The Indians of Puget Sound*. University of Washington Press

Hillaire, P. A *Century of Coast Salish History*. Works

Krause, A. *The Tlingit Indians*. University of Washington Press

Pascualy, M. and Carpenter, C. *Remembering Medicine Creek*. Fireweed Press

Rohner, R. P. & Rohner, E. C. *The Kwakiutl Indians of British Columbia*. Holt, Rinehart and Winston

Spradley, J.P. *Guests Never Leave Hungry: The Autobiography of James Sewid, a Kwakiutl Indian*. McGill Queens

Stein, J. K. *Exploring Coast Salish Prehistory*. University of Washington Press

Sullivan, R. *A Whale Hunt*. A touchstone Book, Simon & Schuster

Wallas, Chief James & Whitaker, P. *Kwakiutl Legends*. Hancock House

Native American Art:

Ashwell, R. *Coast Salish: Their Art, Culture and Legends*. Hancock House

Gunther, E. *Art in the Life of the Northwest Coast Indian*. Portland Art Museum.

Halpin, M. M. *Totem Poles. An Illustrated Guide*. University of British Columbia Press

Keithahn, E. L. *Monuments in Cedar*. Superior Publishing Company

Shearar, C. *Understanding Northwest Coast Art*. Douglas & McIntyre.

Steltzer, U. *The Spirit of Haida Gwaii: Bill Reid's Masterpiece*. Douglas & McIntyre

Worley, J. & Woodcock, D. *Totem Poles of the Jamestown S'Klallam Tribe*.

Native American Novels:

Erdrich, L. *The Round House*. Harper Perennial

Alexie, S. *The Toughest Indian in the World*. Grove Press

Alexie, S. *The Absolutely True Diary of a Part Time Indian*. Little, Brown

James, C. *Catch the Whisper of the Wind*. Health Communications, Inc.

Jans, N. *The Last Light Breaking*. Alaska Northwest Books

Dove, M. Hum-Ishu-Ma. *Cogewea, The Half-Blood*. University of Nebraska Press

Northrup, J. *Walking the Rez Road*. Voyageur Press

Owens, L. *Mixedblood Messages*. University Oklahoma Press

Petterson, P. *Out Stealing Horses*. Picador

Power, S. The Grass Dancer. Berkley Signature Edition

Trafzer, C. E. *Earth Song, Sky Spirit*. Anchor Books

Welch, J. *Winter in the Blood*. Penguin Books

Native American Legal & Political:

Brown, D. *Bury My Heart at Wounded Knee*. Owl Books

Calloway, C. G. et al. *Germans & Indians*. University of Nebraska Press

Colwell, C. *Plundered Skulls and Stolen Spirits*. The University of Chicago Press

Deloria, V. Jr.& Lytle, C. M. *American Indians, American Justice*. University of Texas Press

Farb, P. *Man's Rise to Civilization*. Dutton

Laduke, W. *All Our Relations*. Haymarket Books

Lyons, O, et al. *Exiled In the Land of the Free*. Clear Light Publishers Santa Fe

Moore M. *Genocide of the Mind*. Thunder's Mouth Press/Nation Books

Murray, K. *The Pig War*. Washington State Historical Society

Philp, K. R. *Indian Self-Rule*. Howe Brothers

Stannard, D. E. *American Holocaust*. Oxford

Steiner, S. *The Vanishing White Man*. University of Oklahoma

Treuer, D. *The Heartbeat of Wounded Knee*. Riverhead Books

Wilkinson, C. *Messages from Frank's Landing.* University of Washington Press

Ziontz, A. J. *A Lawyer in Indian Country.* University of Washington Press

Native American Historical References:
Indians, North American. The Encyclopaedia Britannica. 11th edition Vol. 14.p. 452.

Krieger, H. W. Indian Villages of Southeast Alaska. The Smithsonian Institution 1927.

Palmer, R. A. North American Indians. The Smithsonian Institution 1927. Series 4.

U.S. Military:
Schlicke, C. P. *General George Wright: Guardian of the Pacific Coast.* University of Oklahoma Press

Stevens, I.I. *A True Copy of the Record of the Official Proceedings at the Council in the Walla Walla Valley 1855.* Ye Galleon Press. This account gives insight into Gov. Stevens attitude towards Indians.

Non-Indian Novels:
Kingsolver, B. *Animal Dreams.* Harper Perennial

Ivy, E. *To the Bright Side of the World.* Little, Brown and Co. Hatchette Book Group

May, K. *Winnetou.* Preposterous Press

Yalom, I. E. *The Spinoza Problem.* Basic Books

Special Movies & Videos
Curtis, E. *In the Land of the Head Hunters* (1913). 1972 release – *In the Land of the War Canoes*

For the Next 7 Generations. 13 Indigenous Grandmothers. The Laughing Willow Company

Hillavie, P. A *Century of Coast Salish History.* Works Group

Norman, D. & Kramer, R. *The Return of the Buffalo Horses.* Soar Corporation.

Released Movies:

Smoke Signals, Pow Wow Highway, Reel Injun, Hombre, Gray Owl, Wind River

TV Series:

Longmire

Museums:

Alaska Native Heritage Center. Anchorage, AK.

Burke Museum. Seattle, WA.

Daybreak Star Indian Cultural Center. Seattle, WA.

'Ksan Historical Village, Hazelton, B.C., Canada.

Makah Museum. Neah Bay, WA.

Museum of Anthropology. Vancouver, B.C., Canada.

Museum of Northern British Columbia. Prince Rupert, B.C., Canada.

Squaxin Island Tribe Museum Library and Research Center. Squaxin Island, WA.

Suguamish Museum. Suquamish, WA.

The Whale Museum. Friday Harbor, WA.

Thunderbird Park. Victoria, B.C., Canada.

Totem Poles of the Jamestown S'Klallam Tribe

U'mista Cultural Centre. Alert Bay, B.C., Canada.

Gray Whales:

Busch, R. H. *Gray Whales: Wandering Giants*. Orca Book Publishers

Carwardine, M. et al. *Whales, Dolphins & Porpoises*. Time Life Books

Cousteau, J-Y & Diole, P. *The Whale: Mighty Monarch of the Sea*. Doubleday

Eder, T. & Sheldon, I. *Whales and other Marine Mammals of British Columbia and Alaska*. Lone Pine Publishing

Ellis, R. *Men and Whales*. Knoff

Hand, E. *Gone Whaling*. Sasquatch Books

Kelsey, E. *Watching Giants: The Secret Lives of Whales*. University of California Press

Peterson, B. & Hogan, L. *Sightings: The Gray Whales' Mysterious Journey*. National Geographic.

Russell, D. *Eye of the Whale*. Simon & Schuster

Killer Whales & Dolphins:

Baird, R. W. *Killer Whales of the World*. Voyageur Press

Cousteau, J-M. *Sea Ghosts and Call of the Killer Whale*. PBS Home Video

Ford, J. K. B. & Ellis, G. M. *Transients: Mammal-Hunting Killer Whales*. UBC Press/Vancouver

Ford, J. K. B. et al. *Killer Whales*. UBC Press/Seattle

Hoyt, E. *Orca: The Whale Called Killer*. Camden House

Knudtson, P. *Orca: Visions of the Killer Whale*. Graystone

Mason, A. *Whales, Dolphins & Porpoises*. Altitude Publishing

Physiology:

Florey, E. *General and Comparative Animal Physiology*. Saunders

Kandel, E. R. et al. *Principles of Neural Science*. 3rd ed. Appleton & Lange

McCann, F.V. *Comparative Physiology of the Heart: Current Trends*. Birkhäuser Verlag.

Prosser, C. L. & Brown, F. A. *Comparative Animal Physiology*. W. B. Saunders Company.

Ruch, T. C. & Fulton, J. G. *Medical Physiology and Biophysics*. 18th ed. W. B. Saunders Company.

Shanes, A. M. ed. *Biophysics of Physiological and Pharmacological Actions*. AAA Science.

Chaos Theory:

Berry, M. V. et al. Eds. *Dynamical Chaos*. Princeton

Baker , G.L. & Gollub, J.P. *Chaotic Dynamics. An Introduction*. Cambridge

Pickover, C. A. *Computers Pattern Chaos and Beauty*. St. Martins Press

Chapter Notes:

Chapter 1. Neah Bay – Western tip of continental United States.

Whaling is one of the most contentious issues facing Indian-White relationships in Washington State. This is not surprising because there have been over 4000 treaties and statutes written to provide relationships between US citizens and Indians. As social norms have changed, the relationships between Indian and White have changed and therefore law. The complexity is mind boggling. Cohen's Handbook, Federal Indian Law, helps to untangle legal issues resulting from changing cultural attitudes. The first edition, 1941 summarizing law, recognized tribal culture and advocated that all Americans are morally responsible to support Indian rights and self-governance. The second revision of Cohen's handbook written in 1958 shows that the federal government sought to strip Indians of their rights by de-emphasizing tribal sovereignty; stated bluntly, Indians were seen as thorns in the sides of American Government. This attitude festered to spawn the Indian Civil Rights act of 1968. New federal laws tend to protect Indian's self-governance and autonomy, promote legal traditions and protect land and water usage as well as fishing and hunting rights. However, the Supreme Court has not been consistent with its ruling. Most troubling is that Presidents have exercised a complete range of policies which are mandated because the Sec. of Interior makes policy for his president. In 1839, Pres. Martin Van Buren said "no state can achieve proper culture, civilization and progress as long as Indians are permitted to remain". President Andrew Jackson and the State of Georgia scoffed at Supreme Court Marshall's rulings and demanded the removal of the Cherokee Indians from Georgia to Oklahoma Indian Territory – known as the "Trail of Tears." On the other hand, R. Mc Clelland, Sec. of Int. in Pres. F. Pierce's cabinet directed Gov. Stevens of Washington Territory to uphold rights of Makah Indians. Pres. Nixon told congress that Federal Indian Policy was a black mark on our nation's character, "evil" for 150 years. Nixon felt that Federal Indian policy should promote Indian sovereignty in order

to uphold Indian society. The Clinton-Gore administration supported Indians but didn't sign any law. This extremely short summary is
intended to show the lack of a historical policy which would have
set guide lines for Indian-White interactions. Consequently, the lack
of federal consistency fuels emotions that govern present day Indian-White cultural conflicts.

The whaling controversy shows the incompatibility of Native beliefs with the animal rights movements. Conflict has been expressed
at all social economic levels. U. S. Representative Jack Metcalf was
against whale hunting. U.S. Senator Slade Gorton suggested that
whaling is "an aggressive effort orchestrated by the Tribe to show
they can avoid laws that govern the rest of us". NOAA – NMFS
federal agencies completed a 900 page draft outlining seven options
how to kill a whale. The Indians interpret federal agencies as how
White culture attempts to dominate the Indian. Robert Friedheim
argues "Native Americans do not want to give up distinctive features of their cultures in order to be consistent with postmodernist
values of metropolitan societies." Charlotte Cote' termed the 900
page draft dictating how to kill a whale as federal interference based
on "Cultural Imperialism" which ignores the Indian "sacredness
and gratitude for being given the spiritual gift of whale as food."
The Sea Shepherd Society attacked the 1999 Makah plan with "not
a trace of aboriginal whaling". Progressive Animal Welfare Society
(PAWS) attempted to discredit the identity of the Makah claiming
that the Makah's do not practice real Indians. Whaling opponents
used terms "savage Indian" and "barbaric." To their credit, Green
Peace and World Wildlife Fund remained neutral. In 1993, Pierce
Bronsan and Martin Sheen noted their position on whaling. Marlon
Brando did not attend the 1973 Academy Awards ceremony and
Sacheen Little Feather, representing Brando, declined the award of
best actor. She read Brando's acknowledgement of how poorly the
film industry treated American Indians. The audience jeered. For
the Indian view of Hollywood watch "Reel Injun." Brando sided
with the Nisqually Indians for salmon rights and urban Indians for
the establishment of the Daybreak Star Reservation in Seattle on

deserted military ground. Sen. Warren Magnuson and Sen. Jackson worked with Bernie Whitebear for the Indians to obtain the surplus government land. A new "Marlon Brando" has not surfaced. The United Nations upheld Indigenous Rights with only New Zealand, Australia, Canada and USA voting against the declaration. And, thus the USA took a formal position against Native Americans. To refer to Charlotte Cote' again: "the New Age dogma is pious and inflexible and a product of the corporate "Save the Whale" culture is a brand of super-racism and a style of ethnic cleansing."

This novel unfolds under this history.

Chapter 3. Cape Flattery, Washington State.

Kirk, R. & Daugherty, D. *Archaeology in Washington*. University of Washington Press.

Chapter 6. Whales off Tatoosh Island.

Purrington, P. F. Curator. *The Whale*. Crescent Books.

Scammon, C. M. *The Marine Mammals of the Northwestern Coast of North America*. Dover Publications

Additional information about Gray Whales: In 1853, there were 30 – 40,000 Gray whales. They eat 4% of their body weight in krill, herring and sand shrimp a day (1,600 pounds). A lactating cow in Baja produces 50 pounds of milk, of which 25 is fat, a day for her calf. Most of this milk is from the mothers fat stores (this is over 112 Kcal).Some grays feed in Baja as bottom feeders and are thus known as 'mussel-digger' and 'clam-digger'. Touch is important between whales, they use tongue and penis, and this behavior may explain why whales seem "to enjoy" human touching.

Chapter 7. The 'Taking' of Whale.

Theron Parker. Harpooner of Whale on May 17, 1999. Quote: "To take such a creature you must be clean in your heart, mind, body and soul."

Ingling, Allen Dr. Veterinarian with the National Marine Mammal Laboratory of the National Marine Fisheries Service.

Sproat, G. M. 1868. *Scenes and Studies of Savage Life.* Smith, Elder, and Co., London

Chapter 8. Morning, Friday Harbor, May 12

Richardson, D. *Magic Islands. Treasure-Trove of San Juan Island Lore.* Orcas Publishers

The San Juan Story. C. T. Morgan San Juan Industries. Friday Harbor

Chapter 9: Morning, Friday Harbor, May 12.

Paul Owen Lewis quote from *Storm Boy* and Robert Davidson (Haida Artist) art is at the Friday Harbor Whaling Museum.

Scammon, C. M. *The Marine Mammals of the Northwestern Coast of North America.* Dover Publications

Chapter 10. West entrance of Strait of Juan de Fuca; Late morning, 12 May.

Richard calls Quanah *"Go-Ge-We-A* which means "The Half-Blood" or "Half-Breed."

Chapter 11. Wahoo Sails to Neah Bay, Noon, May 12.

Hudson, G. J. *They Had to Go Out.* Xlibris Corporation.

Chapter 15. Court in Session – 14 May, 8:00 A.M.

Lorenz, E. *The Essence of Chaos.* University Washington Press. [Butterfly effect]

May, R. M. 1976. Simple mathematical models with very complicated dynamics. Nature 261 (5560): 459-467.

May, R. M. How many species are there on earth? Science 214: 1441-1449.

Scammon, Charles M. 1868. "Makah pursue and take Gray Whales about Cape Flattery."

Executive Documents 2nd secs 33d Cong. Vol I, pt 1 1854 – 1855. Isaac I. Stevens. Gov. & Sup. Ind. Affairs.

18th Ann. Report of the Bureau of American Ethnology 1896 -97 part 2.

Second Indian Intercourse Act of 1793; States that Indians born in U.S. are citizens.

NCAA – 1998 sanctions that Makah could harvest 25 whales in 5 years. In 1998, Judge Franklin Burgess upheld the Federal and Makah proposal. In Metcalf v Daley, 2000- ninth court of appeals overturned Burgess.

Chief Justice John Marshall opinions: Cherokee Nation v Georgia 1831 and Worcester v Georgia in 1832 that tribes are nations, tribes are a political society and tribes are domestic dependent Nations.

Gov. Terr. Washington. I. Stevens. in Terr. Gov. reports, 1853-1858. No. 83. Dept. of the Interior of Indian Affairs. May 9. Includes Indian Agent M. T. Simmons report.

Chapter 17. Neah Bay – Makah Tribal Court – Morning.

Micah McCarty – 1995 noted that 76% tribal members voted to whale.

Historical information: 1840s – In N.Y. City whale oil was $1.20/gal. 1877 Geo. Gibbs wrote that Makah sold 30,000 gals oil (40 whales). 1885 – Makah harvested 20,000 seals. 1896, sealing peaked. 1883- Chief Peter Brown owned three sealing schooners. 1900, Makah fisherman earned $3 to 30/day. 1907 Makah harvested last whale whereas White whalers continued.

Chapter 18. Whale Distribution Ceremony.

Makah believe that *Maa'* the Gray Whale gives its life for food, not its spirit. The sharing of Whale is extremely important to adhere to the Clallam name for Makah "Generous with food". The feather used by whaler to stroke Whale is symbolic of the spear. In Makah culture, whaling is central to the relationships within families and reinforces intertribal alliances and fosters sacred gift giving between tribes.

N. Scott Momaday received the Pulitzer Prize for House Made of Dawn. He received the National Medal of Arts from Pres. G. W. Bush in 2007.

Chapter 20. Thomas – Kwakwaka'wakw Artist;
First Nation village of Alert Bay, B.C., Canada

1918 – Was-go photo on totem pole in front of James Sewid's home.

1950. Big Indian Dance. White people invited to potlatch which had been reinstated by Canadian Gov.

Chapter 21. Ben – Member of Nuu-chah-nulth First Nation;
Kyuquot Bay, Vancouver Island.

Jewett, J. R. *White Slaves of Maquinna.* Barnes & Noble.

Friendly Cove (Yuquot) was the most important port north of Mexico at the time of Capt. Cook. Sea otter pelts fetched $300 in London. Indians were paid $3.

Chapter 22. Merle – Coeur d'Alene Indian
from Plummer, Idaho, Lives in Spokane.

Bassler, R. S. et al. The Smithsonian Series 10. Chapter III. P. Bartch, The Toothshells.

The Coeur d'Alene Indians were forced to give up half their reservation with the passage of the Dawes Act of 1880-1900s (The Allotment Act). This is an example of constitutional law which implies that a treaty may be abrogated or superseded by a subsequent act of congress. Yet, in 1871 Indians were not aliens. As late as 1924, non-citizen Indian groups were made Indian. The Indian Re-organization Act protected reservation lands. However, no Indian Nation or tribe is recognized as a nation. What does this mean?

Chapter 23. Quiet Weekend in Seattle.

Bartsch, P. Pirates of the Deep – Stories of the Squid and Octopus. Smithsonian Treasury of Science II. Ed. by True, W. P.

Chapter 24. Aaron – Half-Blood. Nisqually and Tulalip Tribes
of Puget Sound and White.

General federalist position regarding Indian rights has changed over the years because treaties are subject to interpretation, modification and repeal. Generally, rez Indians are not subject to local and state law. Rez Indians are governed by Tribal constitution. Feds sometime rule that 1/16th Indian blood gives Indian status. A white man can be adopted by a Tribe. Tribal enrollment is determined by each tribe. U.S. holds title to Indian land and Indian has right to use land. Ownership questions Indian sovereignty. This information along with that of Chapter 22 is the basis of Aaron's asymmetric designs indicating changing identities.

Chapter 27. George – Coastal Chilkut and Tlingit.

Chief George is famous for saying "Thank you for Making me a Human Being."

Chapter 29. Gus – Mixed Blood, Tongoss and Tlingit Bands, Skagway, Alaska.

Tlingit means "The People" Tongoss means "The People".

Chapter 33. Boeblingen, Germany – February.

Bruhns, L. *Tilman Riemenschneider.* Die Blauen Bücher.

Kutter, W. *Schwäbisch alemannische Fasnacht.* J. Fink, Ostfildern bei Stuttgart.

There are many additional similarities between *Fasnacht* and Indian Winter Ceremonies. In addition to fools who make fun of higher ranking citizens, there is the wolf ritual were novices are kidnapped by supernatural wolves.

Chapter 34. Spring Quarter – Friday Harbor.

Daniel may have asked "Why 10 Indians in the *Ten Little Injuns*? And why 10 Indians in Quanah's Whaling canoe?" Quanah may have asked "Why does the Jewish Minyeh require 10 for prayer?" Politically incorrect: 'Redskin' and 'Redman' are equivalent to 'white trailer trash.' The Friday Harbor Laboratory boat is the Centennial.

Bartsch, P. *Pirates of the Deep – Stories of the Squid and Octopus.* Smithsonian Treasury of Science.

Chapter 35. Spring – Underworld –Ebb tide at Friday Harbor.

Kozloff, E. N. *Seashore Life of Puget sound, the Strait of Georgia, and the San Juan Archipelago.* University of Washington Press.

Ricketts, E. F. & Calvin, J. *Between Pacific Tides.* Foreword by John Steinbeck. Stanford University Press.

Chapter 38. Seattle – Incident at Ballard Locks.

When Whites lowered Lake Washington by 14 ft, the Indians lost the salmon run in Green River which drained the lake. Thus, the federal government gave fishing rights in the man made Ballard Locks to Native Americans.

Chapter 40. Interview with Robert Zachary Gould, Neuroscientist.

Chen, I. The Social Brain. Smithsonian, June 2009.

Freud, S. (1878). Über Spinalganglien und Rückenmark des Petromyozon. [On the Spinal Ganglia and Spinal Cord of Petromyzon (hagfish). S. B. Aked. Wiss. Wien. (Math.-Naturwiss. Kl.) III abt. 78, 81

Freud, S. (1882). Über den Bau der Nerven fasern und Nerven zellen beim Flusskrebs. S. B. Akad. Wiss. Wien. (Math.-Naturwiss. Kl.) III Abt. 85, 9.<u>3</u>:230.

Freud, S. (1886) Über den Ursprung des Nervous acustics. Mschr. Ohrenheilk. N. Folge 20, Nr. 8, 245.

Chapter 41. Interview with Carmen Lorenzo, Behaviorist.

Ewert, J-P. *Neuro-ethology. An Introduction to the Neurophysiological Fundamentals of Behavior.* Springer-Verlag

Foer, J. *Thinking Like a Dolphin.* National Geographic, May 2015.

Gould, J. L. & Gould, C. G. *The Animal Mind.* Scientific American Library.

Lilly, J. C. M.D. *Communication Between Man & Dolphin.* Crown

Morell, V. *Big Love.* Smithsonian, Feb. 2008.

Moss, C. *Elephant Memories.* Fawcett Columbine

Chapter 42. Solved cold case; How Robin Morton was killed.

Morton, A. *Listening to Whales*. Ballantine Books.

Chapter 45. Camping at Principe Channel.

Campbell, K. M. *Cannery Village: Company Town. A History of British Columbia's outlying Salmon Canneries.* Trafford Publishing

Rearden, J. Ed. *Alaska's Salmon Fisheries*. The Alaska Geographic Society, Alaska Northwest Publishing Company.

Chapter 46. September, Friday Harbor.

Bevington, D. *The Necessary Shakespeare.* Second Edition. Pearson Longman.

Hodges, Glenn. The first face of the first Americans belongs to an unlucky teenage girl who fell. National Geographic. Jan. 2015.

ACKNOWLEDGEMENTS

Without the help of many friends, old and new, I could not have written about many of the complex issues in this novel. Virginia Walters, Oliver Brown, Sam Pambrun and James Graves read the entire novel at various stages. Mary Ellen Trimble read almost all the revisions and made critical suggests to the story line as well as close editing. I'm especially grateful to James Graves for the limerick; to Sierra Nelson for introducing me to the power of poetry and to Gil Seeley for editing poems and vocals. Oliver Brown helped with dialogue of 'expert witnesses'. The late Gus Morley, a pilot, simulated the plane crash into the ocean. I am grateful to Captain Ben Maxson and deck hand Zak Greene of the Windsong Charter Company for an experience in rough seas around Cape Flattery. Bill Peal made sure that I have logging skills and jargon correctly discussed. Linguist Dr. David Robertson explained syntax in understanding the language of Chinook Jargon. The late Gary Brunner, a retired coast guard sailor, taught me some fundamentals of seamanship. Neurosurgeon Dr. James Holsapple checked ambulance and ER dialogue. Input by Sam Pambrunn and Greg Red Elk was important in understanding the 'Indian Condition.' Ron Dearlove and Bruce Keller made suggestions concerning physics and engineering. I had long discussions with Dr. Scott Tyler concerning the Makah Tribe. Scott has provided photos of his g-grandfather as a young man and his grandmother as a young girl. Both are beautiful and powerful. Scott has also provided history as well as information about the Makah and has graciously looked over the manuscript. My wife Monika provided support through the entire process, listening at three in the morning and correcting German passages; and of course, editing many versions. I thank my three granddaughters, Amrita, Kati and Carmen who helped me understand my female protagonist. My daughter, Julie, redlined the first four chapters which guided me in rewriting dialogue for the remaining chapters. My son Kurt helped edit an early version. I am especially grateful to Warren Seyler, Frank SiJohn, the late Cliff SiJohn and Martin Whelshula for introducing me to Indian humor and helping me understand what it means to be Indian. Amrita Stützle painted the cover and worked on several old images. Dennis Willows invited me on the Friday Harbor collecting boat for several outings. Bruce Willet drew the two maps. I had many conversations, sometimes short, other times lasting days with many additional friends and acquaintances: Merle SiJohn, Geoff Fox, Buddy and Charlotte Mullis, Mark Hellinger, Mary Jane Engh, Jimbo Seyler, Jane Kepner, Kennedy Seyler, Laura Stensgar, David Blank, Greg Urhquat, Father Connolly, Lilly Salvador, Les Porter, and Quanah Matheson.

I had the good fortune to present lectures in adult educational programs with Frank SiJohn, a Coeur d'Alene Indian, on the Indian Plateau Battles of 1858. With Frank's fierce nature I learned differences in our two cultures. Native Americans know white culture out of necessity but white people know little about Indians living on their sovereign lands that whites call reservations. Nevertheless, I discovered that many whites want to learn about Indian culture and history. Consequently, I have deviated from the standard novel format by incorporating historical images as well as a few images portraying the modern Indian. Adding photos was inspired by Eowyn Ivy in her novel *To the Bright Side of the World*. Irvin D. Yalom demonstrated that complex history can be presented in novel form with his book *The Spinoza Problem: A Novel*. Yalom said he was inspired by a saying "Good fiction is history that did not happen and history is fiction that did happen." I was lucky to have found Janet Hill, my editor, who has embraced my wish to include historical images as a visual foundation for the Native American story in this novel. Janet has made many passages readable and concepts understandable.

Special Thanks to:
Paul Owen Lewis for quote from his book *Storm boy*.

Helga Schmidt-Glassner of Langewiesche Nachfolger KG, Koenigstein/Taunus Germany for Riemenschneider photo.

Dover Book, F. Boas, *Primitive Art*, for Wasgo in Chapter 43 and trap for Wasgo in Chapter 45d.

Made in United States
Troutdale, OR
09/19/2023

13050517R00226